DAVID WILLIAM PEARCE

WHERE FOOLS
DARE TO TREAD

A MONK BUTTMAN MYSTERY

Black Rose Writing | Texas

ISBN: 978-1-68433-203-8
PUBLISHED BY BLACK ROSE WRITING
www.blackrosewriting.com

Printed in the United States of America
Suggested Retail Price (SRP) $20.95

Where Fools Dare to Tread is printed in Chaparral Pro

This book is dedicated to Nancy K
for her patience and support.

WHERE FOOLS
DARE TO TREAD

1

"Who are you?"

"Buttman, Monk Buttman."

"Buttman?"

"That's what I said, Buttman. I've been here before, you know."

"Are you expected, *Mr.* Buttman?"

"I am."

"Then have a seat."

The receptionist, a remarkably undesirable Desiree, pointed to a bank of nondescript chairs lining the back wall. I obliged the woman with the rose tattoo snaking up from under her collar and found my seat. It was a drab room. Here at the law offices of Aeschylus and Associates, I sat. No windows brought in the light of day, no Muzak wafted through the conditioned air, no pictures or artwork marred the bleak walls. I watched and waited as a series of couriers came and went. Most met the standard of overgrown skateboarders or aspiring actors, thin, tanned, and lackadaisical in the art of personal grooming. They were uniformly handsome in the way that young men in LA seemed to be. No women were among them. Their comings and goings were closely controlled by the put-upon Desiree Marshan, who channeled her contempt through monosyllabic commands:

"In the box."

"What?"

"No!"

Needless to say, there were no conversations to break up the monotony. Desiree was a hard miserable woman stuck in a back room with the rest of the riff-raff. That included yours truly.

It was not, as they say, a happening place.

Desiree wasn't particularly old, maybe in her early thirties. She had a flat face, a small nose, and cold eyes surrounded by black mascara. Her hair was shorn along the sides, though the left was covered by the brownish blond wave cascading down from the top of her head. It was held in place by a fair amount of lacquer. A small hoop pierced her right nostril, which matched the three attached to each ear, though they were larger. For the purposes of killing time, I decided to concoct a back-story for this woman, which would allow me to be more sympathetic to her unfriendly disposition.

I believe we all need a certain amount of empathy, however acquired.

It was readily apparent, given her disdain for every male she encountered, that her infatuation with the opposite sex had cooled. Desiree had paid the price for her poor choices; you could feel it radiating out in her contempt. All the bozos, who promised the moon and the stars, lived in the rest of us. We were all liars and thieves. I pictured the layabout waiting for his Desiree to bring home the loving, assuming he wasn't off with someone else, while she rotted away in this backwater of A and A. Home was a beer, a toke, a few beautiful words.

You know I love you, baby!

There were no pictures on her desk, a relic of metal and laminated pressboard. A phone, a box, and a laptop; they were her only companions. If she had kids, they weren't with her, in image, anyway. The illustrations tattooed upon her were out of sight, hidden behind the tan blouse; close around her neck and wrists. No wedding ring comingled with the others on her hands. She was definitely trapped. As the old man said, once in the machine, the only way out was with the trash. I thought that was a little severe, watching her from the wall, maybe not.

Our Desiree trapped in an ugly dead-end life.

My reverie was interrupted by the appearance of one Todd Boyer, a noxious up and coming little prick. He had entered from the office door; the one that led to the sunny side of Aeschylus and Associates. I, and my confederates, came in through the stairway door, back by the service elevator.

"Butt Monkman!" My handler had a fondness for rearranging the name I had taken.

"It's Buttman!" That was Desiree. I felt no need to correct him.

"Aren't we all, honey, aren't we all!" Boyer laughed. Todd's hard-on for Desiree was plastered all over his unctuous doughy face. Desiree, on the other hand, gave the distinct impression that what she most wanted to do was gut

Boyer like a fish. "Please come with me, Mr. Buttman."

I passed along as wan a smile as I could legitimately produce to the object of Boyer's desire. The delightful Desiree seethed.

Such is life.

Boyer led me through the door from which he came. Down the hall we lumbered, past the mailroom, and into a small room at the end. It contained two chairs. What it was before I couldn't say, maybe a storeroom. Boyer gestured to a chair and we sat down. He handed me a package and leaned back in his chair. He was a medium sized man with nothing physically to recommend him. Only the sharp edges of his eyes stood out. His face and body were of the same soft featureless consistency. I assumed he had a kinder look for those he worked for, the rest of us got the smirk. It was easy to see that our man Todd had plans. He let those of us that came into his orbit know that we were his functionaries and as such quite deserving of the smirk.

"We have a few stops we'd like you to make today..." Boyer liked to draw out our meetings.

"When and where?" I did not.

"Our Mr. Buttman, all business; what's the rush? You should have plenty of time." He was playing with his red silk tie.

"Of that I have no doubt. When and where?" Boyer sat there with his smirk. I wondered if Desiree had a stiletto. I could save her the trouble.

"Patience," he said at last. Out of his shirt pocket he removed two small pieces of paper and passed them to me, messages for John, out in the valley, and Martin up in the Hills. There was a package for Martin. As for the notes, each piece of paper contained a phrase, which I was to give to the aforementioned. I memorized the addresses and the phrases. I handed the notes back to Boyer. We spent a few minutes contemplating each other in silence. It didn't lead to any profound changes in our opinions of one another. I was a flunky and he was a conniving little prick. He spoke as I was getting out of my chair, "I don't get you, Buttman."

"Why would you need to get me, Boyer?"

"You don't fit the name, you don't fit the job. Something about you doesn't fit. That bothers me."

Funny, it didn't bother me at all. "Take it up with Durant. Anything else?" He tightened up at the name of his boss. That made me smile. "Give my best to Desiree."

"Don't concern yourself with her. She does what I tell her to."

"My concern is for you, smart guy." His eyes closed on me for a moment. Something was churning there behind them.

"I'll need those papers back today."

"Sure."

The smirk was back. It made leaving even better. I followed the mental breadcrumbs that would lead me back out into the sun. I stopped momentarily, for no good reason, by Desiree's desk. She did not look up. The door closed behind me.

There were places to go.

The first stop was out east at a strip mall along I-10, in West Covina. The fact that my second stop was five miles from Boyer and company, while the first was a ways out east; that I'd be going back and forth, did not particularly bother me. I knew it was part of the gig. It would have been more efficient to hit up Martin first, then John, but these little trips required a certain pathology that wasn't obvious to the casual observer. It's what they wanted, it's what they paid me to do. Maybe Boyer thought it would be cute to run me around town, but I wasn't going to get worked up about it.

The breeze carried me and traffic for this time of day wasn't bad. The mass of mechanized lemmings around me rumbled along to whatever cliffs they were destined for. Most were invisible behind the tinted glass wrapped tight on cars these days. I, on the other hand, was exposed to the world behind the wheel of a 1964 Ford Falcon convertible. I liked it that way. It went with the clothes, classic mid-century suits. A few, here and there, would look my way, but most did not. I was just another driver going God knows where.

The car, a light metallic blue, was a gift long ago from a friend of the old man. He didn't need it anymore and knew I wanted it. I had a jones for that period in time, even if I was too young to have been a part of it. Keeping the Falcon running was no problem, this being the land of the automobile. Bernie's shop took care of that. He and I had an arrangement, cash on the counter, easy money. It allowed me to move, in the style I desired, in whatever direction the day might take me.

That direction was to a place called JD Financial, to a man called John. There were no pictures to go by, Just a name. Then again, I had no reason to be concerned one way or another. If a ruse were being perpetrated, I wouldn't know. I was just a lackey, and that was fine by me. There were enough A-types to keep this grand farce going without my being one. I was content being a human message board.

The strip mall housing JD Financial was distinguished by its 70's despair. It lacked both the faux Spanish trapping of its younger neighbors and the mid-century charm of the older. Buttressed between a dry cleaner and a bar, the office consisted mainly of a door and a small window, upon which JD Financial was stenciled. The parking lot was worn and cracked, much like the faces of the bums living by the building. A couple of punks were holding the walls up outside the bar. Inside JD Financial, a woman named Agnes sat behind the desk in the room. There were two chairs by the window and a door behind her leading to parts unknown. It was another happening place.

"And what can I do for you?" Agnes was pleasant enough, easy smile, nice features. She appeared to be in her early forties with a tanned face. Her hair was pulled back and her blouse allowed an admirer a discreet view of her large breasts. Surprisingly, she had on very little makeup.

"I'm here to see John," I told her.

"John?" A wry look followed. "Have a seat. I'll let *John* know you're here, Mr...."

"Buttman, Monk Buttman." Her smile widened.

"Buttman, that's quite a name." She rose and disappeared through the door behind her desk. I sat down. Looking down at my hands, I noted that I needed to trim my fingernails. Agnes returned and came around to the front of her desk. She was wearing black form-fitting slacks that accentuated her curvy hips. The smile was still on her face. "John is next door in the back of the bar. He'll meet you there."

"Thanks."

As I stood up, Agnes moved to the side of her desk, watching as I opened the front door, smiling all the while.

"Goodbye, Mr. Buttman."

The punks greeted me as I headed into the bar. They were being mindful of all things happening here at the strip mall. Evidently, there wasn't much action on a Friday morning.

"Something we can help you with, dad?" the blond one asked.

"I doubt it. I'm here to see the man inside." Both were tall and beefy; it was unlikely I'd be strong-arming my way in. The blond seemed more interested in me than the Latino.

"That your car, man?" The Latino pointed to the Falcon.

"Yeah, '64."

The blond didn't care about the car. "What the fuck do you want in here, *dad*?" He moved closer.

"He wants to go inside, dumbass." Agnes had stepped outside. "Leave him alone. He has work to do." The blond, surprisingly quiescent, stepped back and opened the door. Apparently, Agnes wasn't to be trifled with.

"Go on in, dad." I didn't care for the reference. I didn't think I was that old.

"Thanks." I nodded to Agnes as I went in. I kept the image of her with her hands on her hips, smiling, in my head for some time.

Inside was a large room filled with booths, round tables and an assortment of chairs. I couldn't quite discern what covered the walls. The bar was off to the right flanked by what passed for a stage. A solitary mic stand stood next to an abused tweed covered amp. A string of colored lights hung above the stage to lend a measure of ambiance. The room was dark other than a light or two illuminating the bar. Fortunately, there were enough mirrors and shiny objects to keep the place from being completely enveloped in darkness. At the bar, a man stood watching a flat-screen TV with whatever passed for entertainment. I assumed John was somewhere in the back beyond the bar. As I approached, the bartender motioned for me to have a seat.

"It'll be a few minutes." He was short and old, at least eighty, with a head of thick white hair. He wore a white collared shirt with the sleeves rolled up to his elbows, "Name's Rey, with an e."

"Monk Buttman."

"What'll ya have, Monk?"

"Whiskey, with a little soda thrown in."

It was at this point that the murmur from the back office grew into distinguishable voices. Rey was unconcerned. He handed me a glass filled with my request and returned his attention to the silenced TV, where a group of half-naked men and women were running around the desert. The voices behind us were unhappy about the wait. They had things that needed to get done. The group on TV appeared to be looking for shelter from an impending storm. The voices were running out of time. The whiskey was smooth. Rey changed the channel, football from the Seventies. The voices lightened as the door to the back office opened.

"Patience, my friends, patience..." Four men emerged, three black, one white, all impeccably dressed. The three black men wore suits that shimmered in the diffused light of. Two had close-cropped hair, but the third had a glorious Afro that sent me back to my youth, back to the good old days.

"Our schedule is tight, Johnny D, we ain't got time for any last-minute changes. The word is out, and our word is on the line. We need the financing now. I don't like having to wait when we were told everything had been arranged." The one talking wore thick-framed glasses. He appeared slightly older than the other two.

"It will be ready as I told you. I need you to be patient, just a few more days. I guarantee it'll be worth it," the white guy, John, brought out his best smile as he ushered the three towards the front door. The man with the Afro noticed I was looking.

"What's with you, brother?" That too sent me back.

"Just admiring the fro." He stopped for a moment to make out my intent, but John kept them moving.

"I have other matters to contend with, gentlemen. Give my regards to Mr. Jones." With that they were back in the sunlight, beyond the blond and Latino gatekeepers. John headed my way. Rey handed him a drink.

"This is Mr. Buttman," Rey said with a snort as he resumed his place behind the bar.

"Mr. Buttman, our esteemed emissary. What greeting brings you to my door this fine day?" The thin dapper man put the drink to his lips. He was not what I expected, but then, what did I expect? I looked at Rey as a way to determine if I should spill my communiqué now or wait. John understood the cue. "This way, if you please, Mr. Buttman."

The door led into a well-worn office. John sat behind the desk as I took my place in one of the leatherettes facing it. The desk, other than a phone and a pen, had nothing on it. A standing lamp in the corner produced just enough light that we were able to see one another. I took a sip of whiskey. "You're something of an anomaly, Mr. Buttman," he said this while sipping his own drink.

"In what way?"

"I like to know who I'm dealing with no matter who or what they might be, so I always do a little digging. With you, there's little there. No history beyond a few years ago. I find that interesting, especially in this day and age. Maybe something's up, maybe not... we'll let that pass for now. You've been vouched for, so to speak." The man took another sip. "Yet I'm curious. You're no spring chicken; those years went somewhere. Most men your age have a trail a mile long. It's curious that you don't. I get why they use you, but now that I see you, I wonder..." The man had doubts, and it didn't matter what Boyer or Durant or whomever his contact said to assure him of my value, he had to see for himself. "The message?"

"The cart at the abattoir is blue. The pears arrive at two." Whatever that meant, it made the thin dapper man smile, then sit back.

"Mean anything to you?"

"No, I'm just here to spread the good word." I finished the last of the whiskey and soda. "Anything else I can do for you?" This was generally my way of saying I had nothing else to add. I wasn't here to chitchat.

"No, that's all." We stood and I made my way to the door. "Goodbye, Mr. Buttman." I nodded and closed the door behind me.

Agnes was at the bar. Rey's attention continued to be held by the glowering box. I took a step in her direction, to which she replied in kind. We walked together to the door. She took the glass from my hand. I watched as her eyes made one last pass up and down yours truly.

"Tell me, are you attached in any serious way, Monk Buttman?" Her hand found the sleeve of my jacket.

"Not in any serious way... why do you ask?" That smile was bright and alluring. It channeled an impulse I found hard to resist, to move closer.

"I was thinking, if it's not too far out of your way, how about a drink one of these nights? Might be interesting." It might be.

"How's tomorrow, eight or so?"

"I'll be here, at the end of the bar." Her large breasts brushed against me as I opened the door, "I'll see you then."

"I look forward to it." That smile wandered off, back towards the bar.

2

My next stop was worlds away from John's little hole in the wall. Up in Beverly Hills, above the city, well-appointed homes with tasteful walls and gardens adorned the gently curving streets. Martin lived here. The people here did not make do with what they had; theirs was that small enclave of the charmed, what they wanted they got. Living in the land of the rich and famous required a sense of style, and the money to make it happen. Nothing appeared out of place, wild or natural. Nothing like the world I grew up in. Martin's home was at the top of the curve, set back at the edge of the hill, surrounded by a stone and wrought iron fence. The driveway was blocked by an ornate gate. I pressed the button on the intercom and mentally restated the phrase Boyer gave me. This would let Martin know I wasn't an encyclopedia salesman or any other undesirable interloper. A woman's voice came over the intercom.

"Yes?" I was surprised by the sonic clarity. I don't know why.

"I'm from Aeschylus and Associates to speak with Martin."

"Then we certainly mustn't keep you waiting. Please come up." The gate opened with a quiet stately grace, ushering me onto the manicured grounds. The city below, and the ocean beyond, shone in the filtered sunlight. A woman was leaning against a pillar by the front door. I parked the Falcon, grabbed the package, and made like I had any business being here. The woman, slender, as all these women tended to be, took me in with a kind of offhand observation reserved for those with nothing better to do.

"You're not at all what I expected."

"No?" A slow grin came to me. I enjoyed being the unexpected.

"No." Bemused, she turned and we went into the house. The entry, complemented by small tables dressed with flowering vases, led into a great room with a broad panorama of our megalopolis. "Quite a view, isn't it?"

"It certainly is. I envy your good fortune. The view from my window, such as it is, is of a few lilac bushes and my neighbor's walls. It must be something to have this every day."

"I try not to complain. Please sit down."

The woman, Martin's wife I presumed, stood next to me as we admired the skyline. Like Agnes, she was not a young woman, but time had treated her with a kindness not afforded Agnes. If she was cosmetically enhanced, I didn't see it, but then I wasn't looking that hard. An attractive woman, no matter her age, is just that, and to my mind, to be admired. Her perfume was subtle and alluring. I wondered if she had time for a drink. I was in a bit of a dry spell as far as women were concerned, so my desires were interfering with the job at hand.

"I'll go find Martin," she said.

I found a chair and sat down. The room was sparsely decorated given its size. The windows were actually a series of sliding doors that allowed the room to be opened up to the outside. A pool, the type that seems to literally fall off the side of the hill, lay beyond the sliding doors. The place was far too quiet for my taste; too reverent. Quiet was meant for the woods, places like that. I needed some noise. Cities required noise, sound, reverberation. Fortunately, noise came in the form of Martin, grousing to the woman.

"What do they want now?"

"Given how little you discuss anything with me, how would I know?" The woman was almost playful in her response. I didn't sense a great deal of affection between them. Visually though, they made a striking pair. Martin was a tall angular man, lean and athletic. They had that beautiful people vibe despite the verbal jabs. The woman pointed to me.

"This is…" She didn't know who I was.

"My name is Buttman, Monk Buttman."

A wide smile found the woman of the house. "Mr. Monk Buttman."

The man of the house was not nearly as amused.

"What do you want, Buttman? Why are you here? You'll find I'm not as entertained by this as my wife." He was clearly unnerved to see me. I noticed his hands were shaking. I thought that an odd response to a glorified messenger boy.

"Lighten up, Martin, he's only doing his job. There are people in this world who still work for a living. You used to work once, remember? " The eyes above her smile narrowed.

"I'm not interested in your worthless banter today, Judith. Why don't you do us both a favor and run off and fuck the pool boy. It'll give you something to do." Judith leaned up against the wall near where I was still sitting. I felt obliged to stand up.

"Seriously, Martin, you know pool boys aren't my thing. I'm more of a..." She glanced in my direction. "...Courier kind of woman." Martin stepped towards us.

"I'm not here to aggravate any disagreements the two of you may have or add to your personal difficulties. I have a package for you that I'll need back, and a message for you alone." That stopped him. I handed him the package. He took it and sat down on the couch.

"Will you give us a minute, Judith? Please." The tone of his voice softened. She was no longer smiling. The regard she gave Martin reminded me of Desiree and Boyer.

"Of course, dear." She headed out towards the pool. On the way, her hand ran along the sleeve of my jacket. I was two for two. "Try not to keep Monk here too long, otherwise I won't be able to live up to your expectations."

I couldn't help noticing that she swung her hips with a little more accentuation as she left. A mischievous thought crossed my mind; maybe Martin would like to watch. He noticed my roving eye.

"Buttman!" I tried to clear my mind of the man's wife. "The message!"

"My apologies. Chickens and aprons, spoons and spores; late night is no good. Saturday is finished."

The color went out of his face even as he continued to look at me. His hands fiddled with the envelope. He sat back and pulled the papers out. Whatever they were, whatever they meant, Martin wasn't having any of it. With each page turned, he grew more agitated, finally throwing them all across the room.

"I'm not signing them! I'm not doing this! They can't force me to do this. I won't! I won't, you understand, I won't!" Judith was watching. Martin saw her and began to rise, as if he was about to rush his wife. Instead he turned to me, "Take these goddamned papers and get the hell out of my house! OUT!

NOW!" He bumped the corner of the couch as he got up. He screamed an obscenity and sent the couch tumbling across the polished wood floor.

"Martin!" Judith yelled after him as he left the room. I went around picking up the papers. After a moment Judith joined in. One of the papers caught her eye and she stopped to read it. A giggle came out of her just as she handed the paper to me. It wasn't a cute or funny giggle. A cloud had found her eyes as it had found Martin's. "Would you care for a drink, Mr. Buttman? I certainly need one. And maybe you could help me put the couch back."

"Sure." Together we righted the couch and put it back where it belonged.

"What do you drink, Mr. Buttman?"

I was having second thoughts about the drink. "Maybe a drink isn't the best idea right now."

She gave it a second.

"Sure it is. If it's Martin you're concerned with, don't be. He's not particularly interested in what I do to amuse myself, and who knows when he'll come out of his precious little room. I may not see him for a week. Besides, it's too nice a day to sit here by myself. Certainly, you have a few minutes you can spare? Now what can I get you?"

"Whiskey is fine." There are worse things to do than have a drink with an attractive woman on a beautiful day. Even the old man would give me that. I followed her to the bar where she poured my drink. She then made one for herself. We sat by the pool, mostly in silence. "Is this what you do, Monk? You don't mind if I use your first name, do you?"

"You can call me whatever you like. And yes, this is what I do." Judith's whiskey was better than Rey's.

"Seems like an odd profession for a man your age."

I was pretty sure she was simply making conversation.

"To some, sure, but I find it an interesting way to pass the time and make a little money. Plus it affords me the opportunity to do what I want. I'm not stuck to any timetable or schedule. I prefer it that way."

Judith turned to me, a glint of mischief in her expression.

"You mean you don't long for all this wealth and privilege? The prestige of telling everyone you meet what to do, to gloat that this is your home? You'd be amazed at what this view is worth. It's a statement of position, you know, of importance. People in this town believe that's what you're meant to strive for. Don't you?"

I stood and looked around.

"No. I won't deny the beauty of your home, or that you've got one of the finest views, but to me it's all too much; too much time, money, and effort to keep up; too many people wanting to take it from you, and for what? It can't be anything but the experience because at some point you give it away, sell it, or die and it becomes someone else's headache. I like things simple, easy going; a little here, a little there. There are so many beautiful things in this world to experience. Take this suit for instance. Well made, well-tailored, yet because it's second hand, I got it cheap. It's like the car out there, after time it becomes precious only in the sense that there are so few of them left, and, like the suit, cheap because someone decides it's too old, or not stylish enough, or has no redeeming value. Still, they have value to me, and they require so little, monetarily, to maintain. It makes life easy."

Judith's gaze drifted off. She'd finished her drink. She got up and stood next to me.

"I don't like to think about the nature of existence. It makes me uneasy. I've been here too long to think of it belonging to someone else, even though it was here when Martin and I were poor and living in a hovel down in the valley. It's mine now, and it's going to stay mine even if I have to throw that bastard Martin down the hill." That made her laugh. It made me think it was time to go. "Interested in another drink, Mr. Buttman?" Her hand had found its way, once again, to the sleeve of my coat.

"Yes and no. I'm not immune to temptation, and I can't think of anything better than being here with you on this very pleasant afternoon, but unfortunately I need to get these papers back." We stood close together. It was turning into an unusual day. All the women I'd encountered, other than the delightful Desiree, were far too inviting to someone like me. I was usually invisible to them. I wasn't sure how far to push it. The other jobs had been uneventful, in and out with little conversation. Women were rarely even present. As I said, I was riding out a dry spell. The water they sprinkled on me felt nice and I wanted more. If there was more, I wasn't going to dwell on it too deeply.

"Maybe you're right. One more drink and I might misbehave, and we wouldn't want that, would we?" She took my hand and placed it on her nice firm ass.

"Probably not." I had no interest in moving my hand. I liked where it was.

"Maybe another time?" I didn't believe it for a minute, but it didn't hurt to dream of the possibilities.

"I can't imagine saying no." Reluctantly, I pulled back and she walked me to the door. I put the envelope on the front seat as I slid into the car. Judith was once again leaning against the pillar, watching me.

"Goodbye, Mr. Buttman." Another smile to remember.

The drive back to A and A centered mostly on those two smiles, those two women. As traffic was slow and congested, I let my thoughts drift elsewhere, into the possibilities, fantastical or not. I found it interesting what they had in common and what they did not. Agnes did not disguise the wear and tear that living had done to her; it was part of her allure, just as Judith's was the way she seemed to defy the ravages of time. Both had fine figures; Judith being more refined, Agnes more voluptuous. I found this a rather delightful way to pass the time. I imagined the way they liked being made love to, what might be their secret desires. It kept me from fixating on the screeching, stinking, ramshackle of a truck in front of me. I was stuck behind it all the way to my exit. Sadly, as I entered the parking garage, I had to abandon my fantasies, it was time to get back to work.

I walked into the drab room.

Some things you never forget, much as you might try.

I expected to find Desiree at her desk; the same dour look on her face, the same dismissive attitude. Instead, I found her bent over the desk. Her blouse was pulled up over her breasts; her skirt up around her waist and her underwear pulled down. Boyer was behind her, his pants down around his knees, his hands pawing her breasts. Her eyes were closed; anguish and revulsion contorted her face. Boyer was in his own sick little world. I stood there like a chump. It all felt like some slow motion sex film and I could do nothing but stare. I started backing towards the door. Boyer noticed me with that fucking smirk of his.

"Give me a few more minutes, Monk-man..." He was slamming Desiree into the desk. "If you'd like, you can have some sloppy seconds when I'm done." Desiree was fighting back the tears, the anger. "You'd like that wouldn't you, you stupid bitch. I told you she'd do what I..."

Turns out there was a knife, a switchblade; she had it in the top drawer.

It was in her hand while he was mouthing off. Then it was in his groin. She forced him back against the wall as he was regaling me of his complete control over this angry woman. She'd had enough. The blade stayed in him till it reached his navel. As he began to realize what was happening, his mouth opened just as she drove the blade into his neck. A mangled gurgle accompanied the gush of blood spilling out over the front of the exposed Desiree. Boyer slumped down, his hands grasping what was left of his penis. His uncomprehending eyes fixed on us. We watched as the little prick bled to death.

Desiree turned to me with the knife still in her hand. The blood rolled off her cheek and breasts and on to her belly and thighs. It followed the trellised rose tattoo, stretching from that same thigh up to her neck. We stood there. Slowly she rearranged her clothes, pulling up her underwear, covering herself up. She never took her eyes off me.

"I'm taking the money," she whispered.

"What money?"

"In the bag; I want the envelope too." She gestured to a bag by the chair next to me, and to what I held in my hands.

"Why?"

She wiped away the blood on her face while trying to compose herself.

"So they don't kill me, that's why." Over Boyer? Why bother?

"Take the money." I picked up the bag and tossed it to her. "But the envelope stays here." She reached for the bag and clutched it to her chest. Fear crept into her eyes. She knew she couldn't stay much longer, not in the condition she was in, not with Boyer lying next to her in a pool of his own congealing blood. "If you're going, now's the time. Otherwise, we can wait for security or the cops, your choice."

"I want the envelope." She was shaking, the knife barely in her hand.

"No." I wondered if she knew how badly I was shaking.

"I need that fucking envelope!" She was moving towards the door.

"Why?"

"What the fuck do you care. Give it to me." The knife in her shaking hand, shifted as she moved and clanked as it fell to the floor. I kicked it to the corner. Desiree thought about going after it, but the terror of the moment was overwhelming her, whatever bravado she had died with Boyer. Now she was simply terrified. "Goddammit, look what you've done! I was just going to steal them. Stupid fucking bastard! Why couldn't you leave me alone? Why can't you miserable bastards just leave me alone?" The tears, black with mascara, were streaming down her face, mingling with the blood. She stood there shaking and crying.

"I'll give you a little time to get out of here." I don't think she had a plan for what she was going to do next. "You might want to get going before you really shit yourself."

Her face, wet and ugly, burned with hatred and loathing. She spit at me, but most of it drooled onto her blood-soaked blouse. With that, she was out the door.

I moved closer to Boyer.

So much for that good vibe I was having. I took a seat in one of the chairs against the wall. I was still shaking when I opened the envelope.

3

Hanson Bartholome did not like this one bit, not one bit. As we waited for Durant, the head of security bemoaned being dragged back into the kinds of things he'd left the police force to get away from. It had been a struggle enough for me to get him down here. For a moment, I seriously considered calling 911, but I knew people like Durant did not want surprises right under their nose, right in their house, being broadcast to the outside world without their consent.

Bartholome resisted my entreaties to get his ass down here.

"Down where? Who is this? Why can't you tell me over the phone?" he demanded.

Phones can be tapped, recorded. I'm an off the record guy.

His reaction to finding me sitting in a chair against one wall and Boyer decaying against the other; carved, bloody, and beginning to stink was quite amusing. Apparently, dealing with the newly dead wasn't something he regularly did in his policing days. I watched as he lost the color in his face as well as his lunch into the wastebasket.

So much for a pristine crime scene.

"What the fuck am I supposed to do with this?" he muttered.

"I'd recommend calling Durant."

"That's Mr. Durant, Buttman." Ah, another suck-up.

"My apologies; Mr. Durant."

Bartholome inched closer to the remains. It wasn't pretty. Some of Boyer's intestines had leaked out. His eyes, with a hint of wonder, gazed out into nothingness. It reminded me of the hogs we slaughtered in a previous life. It took some getting used to. It was one of the reasons I left, I was getting used to it.

"Seems like a terrible way to die."

"It was actually pretty quick, a couple of minutes or so."

Bartholome's eyed widened, his expression a cross between disgust and alarm. "What are you saying here, Buttman? Do you know what happened?"

"Let's just say that sometimes it's a bad idea to sodomize those working for you." I applied the requisite smile as a means of emphasis. "Besides, it's fairly obvious, with his pants down something less than platonic was going on, wouldn't you say?"

"Even so." His voice trailed off as the door opened.

Having taken his private elevator down, in strode the managing partner, Mr. Marsyas Durant, a member of that class of smart beautiful people littering our fine metropolis. He was one of the drivers of the machine my father so loathed; one of the many characters this job gave me access to. Like Martin, he was tall and angular, almost as if from the same mold. Durant, unlike Martin, was very bright, and very clever, and not someone to trifle with. Durant noticed me first, then Bartholome. He, like Bartholome, was stopped, momentarily, by the carnage he did not expect.

"What in God's name happened here?" I thought the comment rhetorical.

"Mr. Boyer's been murdered, sir." Bartholome did not.

"Jesus Christ, Hanson, I can see that!" Durant cautiously made his way around the room, careful not to touch anything or step in any blood. He took in what was left of the up and comer, noting the fact that his pants were at his ankles and what little was left of his genitals. He turned to me. "Are you the one who called Hanson about this, Mr. Buttman?"

"Unfortunately, I am."

I expected more questions, but instead he turned to Bartholome.

"Hanson, call Captain Goncalves, and ask him to please come down here with his people and assist us with this unfortunate situation." He looked at me as he uttered the word, unfortunate. "In the meantime, I don't want word of this getting out even among the people here in the building. Keep the door closed till the captain and his people arrive, and even then I don't want anyone not authorized to be let in here, no one!"

"Yes sir." Bartholome reached in his pocket, retrieving his phone.

"Let me know when he gets here. Mr. Buttman, please come with me."

Bartholome kept a close eye on me as I followed Durant out the door.

Together, we entered his private elevator and rose to his office high atop this architectural marvel. The office, as one might expect, was as distinguished as its occupant. I assumed the furniture to be handmade of only the finest materials, the photos and testimonials to be genuine, and the view, a good 270 degrees around, to be quite spectacular. I was not disappointed. Durant motioned me to a couch by one of the windows as he sat on the edge of his desk.

"What do we have going on here, Mr. Buttman?"

"To the what, I can't say. All I know is that Mr. Boyer had me run a couple of messages today, one of which included this package. I came back to return it, as he requested, and that's when the shit hit the fan."

I handed the package to Durant. He removed the papers and began examining them. On and off he would look over at me as he paged through them. He began re-organizing the papers, I assumed, to their proper order.

"Are these all the pages? There are no others?"

"As far as I know. Martin, I apologize, but I don't know his last name, grew very angry while he was reading the papers and threw them across the room. His wife and I gathered them up."

"Judith was there, was she?" That drew a thin smile. "Did you notice her reading any of the documents the two of you were picking up?"

"Yes, she did. It made her laugh."

"I imagine it did." The smile grew. He collected the papers and set them on his desk. "Who else did Mr. Boyer send you out to see today, and the messages?" I told him of my day, the trip east to John's hole in the wall, and back west to Martin. I relayed the same messages I had given John and Martin. He kept his eyes on me for an almost uncomfortable period of time. "How would you say the recipients acknowledged their messages; one more time, if you don't mind."

"John took his in stride, although I would say it gave him pause. Martin seemed shocked by his, and became more agitated as he looked over the papers. He said he would not sign them, that he couldn't be made to."

Durant sat quietly as I spoke. I tried to stay serene, unattached. It would help with the shakes. Though Boyer wasn't the first man I saw killed with a knife, it still freaked me out; something about the sensation of a sharp blade easily breaking the skin and penetrating the organs gave me the willies, too many bad memories.

Durant wandered over to the window next to the couch.

"I think it best if these conversations were not shared with Goncalves' people. You and I may need to review them at a later time, so I would ask that you keep this to yourself for now."

"Sure."

"Is there anything you think I need to know concerning the death of Mr. Boyer?"

"That I can't speak to, either. I can answer any questions you might have, but you'll have to elaborate on any specific aspect of the event." I found this kind of tiptoeing oddly fascinating. He continued to gaze out at the world beyond.

"Will they be looking for the woman?" I assumed he meant Desiree. I gave it a few moments.

"I would think so, yes."

"That's disappointing." The phone on his desk began filling the room with its elegant chime. Durant walked to his desk and picked up the phone. "Yes? Thank you, Hanson." He ushered me towards the elevator door. The police were here.

The captain met us by the door. He was the epitome of everything I was taught to believe about the cops, the fuzz, or the old man's favorite, pigs: big, stern, and not to be fucked with. He and Durant huddled while I watched the investigators and techs come and go. It seemed obvious to me that the two of them, Durant and Goncalves, had developed a relationship such that it was mutually beneficial. No doubt someone like Durant was important to cultivate if you had ambitions. Durant did most of the talking with the captain nodding in a serious upright manner.

The captain called one of his people over and pointed at me. It was my turn. The officer ushered me to a corner away from the hurly-burly all around us. Durant had opined as we rode down in the elevator that, for now, it would be best if I did not implicate the woman, as he called Desiree, in my statements to the police. I thought it interesting that he would protect the killer of one of his own. I didn't ask why. I figured if I were meant to know it would come up later.

The officer started the questioning. Was I the one who discovered the body, I was; about what time, roughly five-thirty; did I see anyone, not that I recall; did I touch or disturb anything in the room, only the doorknob and phone; why were you here, finishing up my errands, it's where I checked in; How can we reach you if we have further questions, I gave him my address. No phone? No Phone. That was the only time I got a rise out of him. I could see the semi-scorn on his face. Who doesn't have a phone in this day and age? That would be me. He asked me to wait, so I did. After an hour or so of doing nothing and my legs beginning to ache from standing so long, I was released. Durant motioned me over just as I was ready to bolt down the back stairs.

"I may need to see you later, Mr. Buttman. I assume that can be arranged in the usual manner?"

"I don't know why not, it's not like I have a lot on my calendar." He raised his eyebrows at that.

"Excellent. As always, I appreciate your cooperation and discretion in this matter." I'm sure he did. "Good evening, Mr. Buttman."

"Mr. Durant." We went our separate ways. As I walked to the car I made it a point to look for cameras. The only one I found was at the entrance/exit of the parking garage.

The evening was warm. The sunlight cut in and out as I moved between the buildings. I saw no reason to take the interstate; it was like walking in sand. The pace along the boulevard was uneven, but I wasn't in any particular hurry. I stopped at the market down the street from my place and grabbed some chicken and salad. I had to eat something. I couldn't remember eating anything today, but that can't be right? I must have had something this morning? Now there was this murder, it made my head hurt.

My place was in an old part of LA. It was one of those bungalow types that used to pepper what was once the outskirts of town. There were ten bungalows in our little enclave, the Moonlight Arms, rented to a mostly geriatric crowd. Other than Joanie, me, and the hipster couple two doors down, everyone was a senior citizen. Though I knew most of the tenants by sight, and a few by name, Joanie was the only one I had any communication with or interest in.

It was nice and quiet. I put the food on the table in the small kitchen and sat down. I had no interest in the food and was not hungry. Much as I tried, I could not get the images from the afternoon out of my head. Desiree, standing there with that crazed expression as the blood dripped down the front of her, and Boyer, with his look of disbelief, that this would be the way his life came to an end.

I choked down a few bites. I should be hungry; I hadn't been eating much lately. That didn't hurt my manly figure, but my energy level was down and I was tiring too quickly. I put the leftovers in the fridge, promising that I would eat them this time unlike all the other times I let the food go to waste. We can't let food go to waste the old man told me repeatedly; people were starving, out there, somewhere.

I needed a drink. The glass was where I left it, where it always ended up, in the freezer. A few chunks of ice were left in the bag next to it. I combined the two with a splash of Jack and wandered to my only piece of outdoor furniture: a green and white folding chair I bought for a buck at a yard sale down the street. The sun was past the point where it could do me any harm. I closed my eyes and let the breeze take me away. Maybe it was time to go back to the farm. I'd been gone for years, a part of me missed it; missed the land and the lack of faces, unlike here with the millions of them bouncing back and forth off one another. I had planned to see the old man but with no real timetable. That was months ago.

I always made plans.

Today felt like a spur to get me moving. Maybe tomorrow, no, tomorrow I was having a drink with Agnes. The sound from the TVs was beginning to pick up. Staccato noises and laugh tracks insinuated themselves within the soft whistles of the breeze. A couple of kids were hollering at each other.

A whiff of perfume joined in.

I had company.

4

"It continues to amaze me that you only bought one of these chairs. A gentleman should be able to offer a lady a chair rather than have her just stand around." I opened one eye. Joanie stood there, beautiful as always, with her hair flowing down along her shoulders, caressing the straps of her dress, a flowing chiffon kind of thing that stopped just above her knees.

"They only had one! If they had had two I would have ponied up the other buck." It was our standard greeting. That I'd had the chair now for four years didn't particularly matter, nor did the fact that her own folding chair rested in the hand not on her hip. It was how we started our conversations. "Besides, I see you brought your own seating arrangements." She unfolded her chair and sat next to me.

Joanie was a small woman whose green eyes were slowly washing out. In the late eighties, as a teenager, she had come here intent on joining the girl band craze. When that fizzled out it was the Riot Grrrl thing that kept her going. When *that* faded and she had nothing else to do, one of her many boyfriends talked her into doing a lounge act with him as a kind of ironic metaphor, but with her beautiful raspy voice, and the not so insignificant fact that she could actually sing, she found herself with a fan base and a series of rotating gigs that kept her afloat while she worked her way through any number of potentially suitable mates which, for a brief glorious moment, included me.

I was, it must be said, something of a fling, and during those times, when neither of us had any pressing relationships to nurture, we found a modicum of comfort in each other's arms. Sadly, at least from my perspective, this didn't happen often enough. For the last four or five months I'd seen little of her and our talks, such as they were, were few and far between.

"Can I get you something to drink?" I offered.

"Only if you have something other than that awful whiskey." Her nose crinkled at the thought.

"There's wine, Kahlua, maybe a soda. Water?"

"Any ice left?" Some things you never live down, like being out of ice at the most inopportune times.

"A couple of cubes, help yourself." I closed my eyes as I listened to her fetching her drink. We sat and watched as the old couple next-door left for their evening walk. Joanie thoughtfully reminded me that they were the Madison's. They had to be in their late eighties. He held her arm as they slowly shuffled by. Both waved as they passed us. We waved back.

"I wonder what it's like to be with someone for that long. Ardis told me they've been married for almost seventy years."

"Who's Ardis?" That brought a smack to the back of my head.

"Mrs. Madison. I told you that. Many times! They came out here because of the war. He was in the Navy. When he got out, they stayed here and worked in the film industry. He was a set designer, she did costumes. They used to own this place. That's why they have the biggest bungalow. The person they sold it to said they could stay as long as they wanted." Joanie had a fascination with the old couples that lived here. She knew them all quite well. Joanie and I were the only ones not married. Amazingly, given their ages, all the couples were still together, still relatively mobile and alert; none yet widows or widowers. All had persevered through the good and the bad. The only time I thought about it was when she brought it up, and she brought it up whenever we sat outside on these quiet languid evenings. The hipster couple had the jazz playing; soft mournful stuff, not the raucous bebop sound most people associate with jazz.

"Shouldn't you be at a gig tonight?"

"Yeah, usually tonight is request night at Ballinger's, but I took it off because Mikal said he'd be back today, but it turns out that he'll be gone for some time."

Mikal was the new guy, and given how much time she'd spent with him, I had reluctantly accepted that he was the one she'd been looking for all these years. Like most of her boyfriends he was a musician, a keyboard player and arranger. Supposedly, he heard her one night, based on a friend's recommendation, told her how much he liked her, and they've been an item ever since. He was going to get her recorded; get her moved up to a better circuit of gigs. Joanie assured me he was well known around town.

Lately though, he and his *combo*, as she liked to put it, were on the road opening for some big named act. I watched as she absentmindedly swirled her drink.

"He called and asked me to take my key back to the manager of his place since, apparently, the tour's been extended to Europe and then Asia, and he was going to have his stuff put into storage rather than pay to keep the place. I got the impression there was something else going on, but he told me the move was no big deal, besides the tour was a great opportunity for them to pick up some more positive exposure and fans. So I took the key over to the manager, a guy I call Skeevy Rob, and asked where Mikal's stuff was going. He said he couldn't tell me; that's confidential you know, but if I gave him a blowjob he might be more forthcoming. Like that was something I'd have any interest in, but it made me wonder, so I called Mikal's brother and he hemmed and hawed and yammered that he didn't really know, that I should wait till Mikal gets back and so forth." That explained the long look after the Madison's.

"Well, he didn't actually blow you off, so it's possible it's not a big deal other than he'll be gone longer than he thought."

She sighed which was followed by a half-smile. "You may be right. It's just that I was anxious to see him and missed him and given my history worried that our time was winding down."

"No to worry, if you get desperate, there's always me." This elicited a laugh. Charm is a man's best friend.

"So, you still want to marry me?"

"Sure, what the hell." More laughter. I wasn't technically joking but I'd already made my feelings known so why open that up.

"So, how is your love life? Still slaying the babes?"

"Not lately, although I did get invited to have drinks with a woman I met today."

"Really, well that's something isn't it?"

"I suppose it is."

She asked about my day. I gave her the nuts and bolts of my trips and the sordid business with Desiree and Boyer. An odd look crossed her face as she regarded me with this last bit of news.

"I'm surprised *you* didn't throw up. I'm pretty sure I would have. Sounds like a terrible thing to witness."

"I guess it was. I wish I could say I'd never seen anything like it before, but sadly, I can't." That got her looking even harder. She turned directly towards me.

"Should I ask?"

"No. It was years ago, bad timing, bad mojo. Let's just say it made me take a very hard look at what I was doing, and it had a lot to do with why I moved down here." Now along with Desiree and Boyer, I was seeing James again, lying there, bleeding to death, his body, tied to the back of a truck, being dragged away. Had it been more than twenty years? I looked at Joanie; she was still staring back at me. "I don't suppose I could talk you into some meaningless sex tonight?"

"I don't know... It's tempting, but I don't think I'm ready to let go of Mikal yet, and I wouldn't feel right if we did, besides it might mess up your date with..."

"Agnes."

"Right, Agnes."

"It's just drinks." More laughter. "What?"

"How long *has* it been, Buttman?"

"Too long," I tried to look pathetic, in need. "Can't you throw a lonely man a bone?"

"I could, but then you might expect it every time your prospects got thin, and I don't think I can make that kind of long-term commitment. Sorry." This was accompanied by her best puppy dog frown. "Besides, you might get lucky tomorrow. You never know?"

"You never know." I leaned over and gave her a kiss, which, thankfully, she returned. "So, what are you going to do about Mikal? Stick it out till he comes back? Do you know when he'll be back? Did he say? Too many questions, what?"

"Too many questions. I don't know what I can do till he returns, other than wait." She reached out and grabbed my hand. "You know how much I like the guy, right?"

"I know." I squeezed her hand. The worry was back on her face. The man she loved wasn't where he was supposed to be. There was only me.

The rest of the evening was fairly quiet, some small talk about bands and gigs and people with too much money. We were too jaded to wallow in dreams, better to focus on what we could do, whatever that was. Another drink and I was ready to ask her the question I really wanted to ask.

"How would you like to go up to the farm with me this weekend; sometime, soon?"

"The farm?"

"The farm."

"Why don't you go by yourself? You don't need me to go." She was well aware of my unwillingness to go alone.

"You know why, and I do need you. What do you say? It's that or the sex."

"So this was just a set up to get me to go back home with you? Maybe I should rethink the sex?" She laughed at that too.

"Maybe." The light was gone from the sky and we were both tired. I was ready to crash, sex or no sex. Joanie stood up and folded her chair. She leaned over and gave me a big wet sloppy kiss.

"That ought to hold you for a day. I'll let you know about the farm. Try to get some sleep, huh, you look tired." She left me for the relative safety of her own bungalow. I folded my chair, set it inside the door, and made my way to the bedroom where I attempted to sleep without dreaming of knives and the damage they do.

The night passed without too much turmoil.

With the morning light driving me out of bed, I prepared for the day ahead.

On the off chance the day might take its own turn and leave me high and dry with regards to nourishment, I made myself an egg sandwich and a cup of tea. You never know. The birds were chirping and flitting about as I waited. The thump, thump, thump on the door aroused me from my stupor. Two uniformed cops stood in the doorway. The one to the left had his hand on the holster of his pistol. Neither felt the need to smile.

"Monk Buttman?" The lead cop spoke.

"Yes?"

"We're here to escort you downtown for the purpose of questioning in the death of Todd Boyer."

"And if I refuse?" It can't hurt to ask.

"Then we will arrest you as a material witness. What'll it be, Mr. Buttman?" I weighed the options.

"Let me get my jacket." They watched as I retrieved the aforementioned jacket and locked the door.

The drive, other than being detained in the back of a car designed for the class of society, was quite pleasant. At one point I fell asleep. This must have irked the two up front, with one pounding on the steel mesh dividing us. Once we reached headquarters, I was escorted past the usual cast of characters and ushered into a fairly plain interview room. I was asked if I wanted a cup of coffee, I said no. I asked for water and with cup in hand waited to be interviewed. After a half hour of daydreaming about Agnes, Joanie, Judith, or any woman I could think of, two detectives, calling themselves Mallory and Descartes, entered the room.

They were both wearing white shirts with dark trousers. Mallory's tie was brown, Descartes' blue. Both men were of an average build with Descartes being a little taller. He was also better looking with a full head of thick black hair while Mallory's head did what it could with the last strands of blond hair combed straight back. To me, they appeared to be about the same age. Mallory was all business, with no discernible facial expression, while Descartes had an open face with a snarky grin. They sat down across from me with Mallory thumbing through what I presumed was the file on Boyer's demise. Mallory spoke first.

"You found the body of the deceased, Mr. Todd Boyer, at approximately five-thirty yesterday afternoon, is that correct?" I assured him it was. I also reiterated the other points of my statement. "So you did not see the woman who was working there in the morning when you first went to the building, Ms. Desiree Marshan?"

"Not that I remember."

"Not that you remember?"

"Not that I remember," I repeated.

"Interesting, meaning you may remember at some point in the future when allowed to by Marsyas Durant?" Descartes chimed in. It was a curious statement. Hadn't the captain, taken into confidence by Durant, greased these wheels?

"I can't speak to what Mr. Durant may or may not allow. You'll have to ask him."

"We'll find out, Buttman, no matter who we have to ask, you can be guaranteed of that."

"If you say so."

Mallory continued to page through the report. It dawned on me that they were probably more interested in the goings on at Aeschylus and Associates than just in the slaying of Todd Boyer. It should have occurred to me earlier when Durant counseled discretion. I can be slow that way. I'd heard stories of A and A that were not particularly flattering. There had been some characters through the years that had brought unwanted attention to the firm, mostly politicians, but also lawyers skirting the law. There was always talk that they had their fingers in any number of possibly illegal pies, but that Durant was too clever to ever get caught or be taken down. Perhaps I was seen as a way in, a chump or fall guy; somebody who might know something, who might squeal if pushed hard enough.

"What's on your minds, officers?"

"We're detectives, Buttman." Descartes acted indignant.

"That's Mr. Buttman, detective." Oddly, he did not find *my* correction humorous. Such is life, next question.

"How well did you know Boyer?"

"I didn't know him at all. Nor, just in case you were interested, was I privy to anything he may have been involved with at Aeschylus and Associates. I'm nothing more than an independent contractor who does some detail work for them." So far, so good, and it made me sound more important than I was.

"I heard you were a glorified errand boy." I don't think Descartes liked me. From my end I hadn't decided whether I had any regard for the two detectives.

"Call it what you like."

"I did some checking on you, Buttman, and there's not much there."

"What's your point?"

"It tells me you're not who you say you are; that somewhere along the line you changed identities, and who does that?"

"You tell me, detective?"

"You're hiding something, Buttman, that's what!" Descartes leaned in.

"Think what you like." I leaned in.

"Did you see any kind of conflict or trouble between Ms. Marshan and Mr. Boyer?" Mallory looked up at me as he asked this.

"I can't say for certain. I was only there for a moment or two, but my impression was that Boyer had an attitude towards Ms. Marshan that she didn't care for. Beyond that I couldn't say." Mallory leaned forward.

"What attitude would that be, *Mr.* Buttman?" I didn't care for the spite on the honorific. Odd the things you focus on.

"That he had a thing for her and that she should abide."

"So you think she killed him?" Descartes decided to stretch his legs.

"I couldn't say." He stood next to me, hands in his pockets.

"Maybe he can't say because maybe he killed Boyer?" Apparently, it was for my tearful confession.

"Like he had a thing for me, detective?"

He was smiling. "Like it doesn't happen between men. You were there, Mr. Buttman; you've even got the right name, don't you think?" He was pacing now. "Something went wrong, maybe you planned it, maybe not, but you were there. People do all kinds of things to one another, including murder."

"I think you're killing time, my time." Mallory kept watching for my facial tics. It was probable that I had a few.

"It's ok with me, I can take all the time I want! They pay me to do it." Descartes sat back down next to Mallory. "You know more than you're telling us, *Mr.* Buttman, and I'm curious as to why. Maybe Durant is pressuring you, maybe you and Boyer were butt buddies, something, but I think you're holding out on us, *Mr.* Buttman, and I want to know why. I've got all day."

"You know as much as I do, gentlemen. There's nothing more to tell, disappointing as that may be."

It was at this point that a young uniformed officer knocked and came in. The two detectives turned to him as he whispered in their ears. Whatever he said caused them to look at me in less than loving terms.

"Your attorney is here, Buttman."

"*My* attorney?" Mallory didn't care for my sarcasm.

"You heard me."

"That's true, I'm here to represent you." Walking in, she gave me a faint smile then turned to the three cops. "Gentlemen, I think you've learned all you can from my client. He came here of his own free will. I've talked with Captain Goncalves and there's no reason for this continued interrogation. There's nothing to indicate Mr. Buttman knows anything more, nor is he, given the evidence collected, a viable suspect. Is there anything else, gentlemen?"

"We'd like a set of fingerprints, if you don't mind." Mallory was at this point glowering at me.

"Unless you plan to book my client, I do mind; at the proper time, gentlemen, along with proper recourse." She gave them a rather unctuous smile. The detectives didn't care for that either.

"We'll be talking again, Mr. Buttman." Detective Descartes had risen from his chair.

"That may be, but before you do, I want to know about it." My attorney turned towards the door. "Please come with me, Mr. Buttman." I stood up and followed her, the three cops watching.

"See you later dudes." I couldn't help myself.

5

"My name is Taylor Lagenfelder, Mr. Buttman."

Taylor was the female version of the modern company man: young, smart, well dressed, and motivated. Other than being reasonably well dressed, I was none of those things. When I was young, it would periodically occur to me that I should be doing more with my life. Fortunately, I had a knack for dismissing such existential quandaries, but people like Taylor fascinated me; such dedication to the idea that they intrinsically mattered to the fate of their times and by extension to the world and the universe beyond it.

"Mr. Durant would like to talk to you."

"Sure." She didn't ask if I wanted to, or had other plans. In her world Durant came first, and as he had sent her to my supposed rescue, I was willing to go along for the ride. "How long have you been lawyering, Ms. Lagenfelder?"

"Four years," she replied, no doubt the product of a good family, good schools, all of that. No farm populated by freaks and peaceniks, no longing for a return to a bucolic agrarian American that never really existed, no flight from the military industrial complex that turned us all into sheep for her.

"School?"

"Harvard law." This she stated with evident pride.

"Then I'm in good hands."

"You are a fortunate man, Mr. Buttman."

"Yes, it's looking that way."

Having answered my questions, the remainder of the drive was of silent observation. I was always watching, wondering. For no good reason it made me consider how a deity, any deity, could keep up with everything all these people were up to, good and bad. I looked at my attorney wondering if she believed in any faith.

The old man grew up in the church and was a true believer until his brother died. No one could explain to his satisfaction why God let Elijah die so young, so he started to dig into the liturgy and history and was disillusioned by what he found, was deeply disappointed that humanity wasn't living up to his expectations. He never said much about Elijah. Elijah was nothing more than a few faded Kodachrome snapshots set in a frame on a dresser. When and if I get up the nerve to go back, maybe I'll ask. Moses did, in his own way, make peace with God. Maybe age does that to you as you draw closer to the end.

Maybe.

The efficient Ms. Lagenfelder called to say we were close. We entered the garage, parked, and proceeded to the elevator that led to Durant's office. She keyed in the proper code and the elevator came to retrieve us. Durant was waiting.

"Thank you, Taylor. I appreciate your taking time to assist Mr. Buttman." He then turned to me, "Mr. Buttman, please contact Ms. Lagenfelder should the police again request any of your time." She handed me her card.

"I will." Taylor excused herself. Durant and I sat down, he behind his desk, and me in the chair facing it. I sat there as he kept his gaze on me. A sly grin slowly made its way across his face.

"Mind if I ask you a few personal questions?" He sat back.

"If you feel the need." I did the same.

"Where are you from, Mr. Buttman?"

"Why do you ask?" I am known for disliking questions about my past, who I am, where I'm from, stuff like that.

"Because you remind me of a man I knew years ago, a man named Moses Bohrman. He and a few of his fellow travelers had a commune up north, near Ukiah. Ever been there?"

"I've been there."

"And Moses?"

"I know him." It began to dawn on me that I knew Durant, if only vaguely. He was that passing face, somebody to see the old man or one of his fellow travelers, an outsider, a man from the machine, a conduit to another world.

"I thought so. Many years ago, just as I was starting in this business, I was sent up north to run a few errands, and I had some dealings with Moses, a bit of a character as I remember. You're his son, correct? I remember you with the other kids working the animals, all that fun farm stuff."

Damn.

"It was what it was. I haven't seen the old man in some time, but I doubt he's changed any." I hadn't anticipated talking about my past. I thought this would be about Desiree and the cops. A dull ache was creeping up the back of my neck. The word setup accompanied the ache. "Not that I don't want to talk about the long-lost past, but what's the connection here, Mr. Durant? I thought we'd be discussing something other than my unconventional childhood." He had a pencil in his hand and was taping it on the edge of his big expensive desk.

"So did I, and we will get to the matter at hand, but there was something about our first meeting that stuck, and for whatever reason today, probably because of this sordid business, a light went off as to why, and it was that you reminded me of someone, and that someone was Moses. It's just something that popped into my head. It's not my intention to make you uncomfortable." I could see that was untrue.

I had first met Durant in the middle of nowhere, north of the city, on the secondary roads that lead to the palaces of the rich overlooking the ocean. It was a beautiful day and I had no interest in working, so I went for a drive. He was to the side of the road standing by his car. The front passenger wheel had collapsed on itself and he flagged me down. It was a classic Mercedes convertible, silver with a white interior. It looked well cared for so I was a little surprised that the bearing had failed. Durant seemed more perturbed that his phone didn't work than what had happened to his car. It turned out he had forgotten to charge it. He asked to use mine and was perplexed that I didn't have a phone to call for help.

"Who doesn't have a phone these days?"

"I might be it." I gave him a lift and that led to talk of old cars, clothes, and my contract work at A and A. As they say, it's who you know. I considered it happenstance, but now I wondered.

"How did your talk with the police go?"

"Oh, pretty much as I expected. They asked about my statement, what I saw, what about Desiree and Boyer, and what were you and your associates really up to and why was I covering for you; maybe I killed Boyer in a jealous rage. It was what I assume to be the usual."

Durant smiled at that.

"They like to believe that Aeschylus and Associates is always up to something. You were circumspect in your responses concerning Ms. Marshan?"

"I played dumb, and in truth, other than what I saw, I really don't know much. I have my suspicions, but nothing I could swear to." He sat back, looking off towards the ocean. For a moment he seemed someplace else. I waited for him to come back. "Should I ask why I'm not telling them everything? I would think that if a low-level employee killed one of your up and coming young lawyers, that you'd be quick to turn her over, even if you were looking to do it as quietly as possible?"

He turned his attention back to me.

"Monk," he put the pencil down and leaned forward, "ordinarily, you and I would not be discussing this, one of our, as you say, up and comers would be handling whatever work we were asking you to do. I'd hear of it if they thought it important enough. Obviously, we don't expect our employees, whatever their position, to be killing one another. It doesn't make for a harmonious work environment, nor does it speak well of those we choose to hire. Even in this case, normally, I would have had Ms. Lagenfelder, or another of our associates, interview you, communicate our wishes and so on. But this is, unfortunately, more problematic, and I'm concerned enough that I've decided to permit you to be more informed in this matter. Some of this has to do with my questions about your history. I don't consider you to be the usual type of courier or messenger that we routinely employ. I assumed you gathered that given the kinds of messages we give you as well as the responses they sometimes elicit. Some things we like to keep quiet until we feel we have enough information or control over the situation. You don't attract a lot of attention, Monk." That was twice now that he used my first name. "I believe I can bring you into my confidence and that you will be discrete with what we discuss."

He stood up and walked over to the window. I didn't know whether I should say anything or not. "I'll do what I can, Mr. Durant."

He stood there and I felt an impulse to run for the door. Lately, my one goal in life has been to avoid as many entanglements as possible. Over the years I'd found that people will get themselves mixed and twisted up to the point where there's no unraveling them. It's like standing, mesmerized, on the precipice of a deep dark hole from which, if they took that step, they would never return. I was feeling that tug, that tangling, and I didn't like it; too much like James and what killed him.

"I need to talk to Ms. Marshan. I need to know what she was doing with Mr. Boyer. Beyond their sexual encounters, which I believe were predatory, it appears they were engaged in a plan they meant to keep from the rest of the firm. It involves the individuals you met yesterday, John and Martin, and I believe it was meant to finance illegal activities. For now, the police think this was just a sexual tryst gone bad. I think it best they continue to approach it that way. They are unaware of the money Ms. Marshan took with her." He turned to me and leaned against the glass. "Were you aware that she left with a satchel of money?"

"Yes, she said she was taking the money. She wanted the documents too, but I refused. I asked her why she wanted them, but she wouldn't say. At the time she was, understandably, freaked out. I don't know that she meant to kill Boyer or if they were partners in anything. I think he went too far and she lost control."

"That's why we need to find her. And that's where I want you to come in. As you noted, the police will be more attentive to the activities of this firm as concerns Mr. Boyer. They may or may not be watching you. I have some contacts in the police department that will advise me of their suspicions. We can use that to our advantage. The money was to go to John. I expect he'll want answers, and he has people who are good at finding people. I want you to tag along."

Tag along doing what?

"I'm not a detective, Mr. Durant." I'm a nobody remember?

"I'm aware of that. I've had a chat with John, or as he's better known, Mr. Dulcimer, or Johnny D, and made it clear that it benefits both of us to find and interview Ms. Marshan. He has a man who is experienced in finding people, and I explained that it's important for you to be a part of this."

"Can I ask what this is all about? Am I going to be involved in something violent or illegal, because if it's that, then I'm out? They're not going to find bits and pieces of me along the highway."

That made him smile in a way that suggested he'd heard about James. He moved to the cabinet discreetly hiding the bar. "So you know that story? I thought you might. I'm probably more aware of your past than you'd like. You've gone to great lengths to distance yourself from it and I admire that. Many of your friends did not end up as they thought they would. Would you like a drink, Monk?"

"Whiskey is fine." He brought out two glasses from the bar and a bottle. After filling the glasses, he handed me one before sitting on the couch by the window.

"To answer your question, it appears Mr. Boyer was looking to transfer certain overseas funds back to the states. The question is why? Mr. Dulcimer is in the business of financing activities that can sometimes border the letter of the law. However, in my talk with Mr. Dulcimer yesterday, he was unaware that Mr. Boyer had plans to utilize his services. He was expecting the money Ms. Marshan took and was none too pleased that she had run off with it."

"And Martin?"

"That I don't know. I have certain suspicions, but until I have more information I don't have an answer to that or that Martin Delashay is in any way involved."

"Can I ask what Martin Delashay does?"

"You don't know?" Durant took a drink, probably to hide the grin on his face. Fortunately, or unfortunately, I was not a connoisseur of people and what makes them well known. "Mr. Delashay is prominent in the computer software industry. Anyone with a computer or smartphone is aware of his company's contribution to our modern marvels. But as the last man on earth, or in this country, without a phone, I guess your ignorance is understandable." Apparently he was still amused by that.

"So how will I get in touch with John's man?"

"He'll be in touch with you, if not today, then soon." He finished the whiskey in his glass and stood up. I took this to mean we were winding things down. "I expect that you'll keep me informed concerning the search for Ms.

Marshan. I would also advise that you keep your eyes and ears open just in case."

"Just in case of what?"

"I believe you'll know when it presents itself to you." Let's hope so. He went to his desk and made arrangements for my safe return home. The elevator delivered me to the parking garage, which delivered me to the cab. I spent the ride home contemplating my options.

I forgot to ask about compensation.

6

Mr. Jones was at the front of my door. He was at least six foot four and looked to be as solid as a rock. He was a dark-hued black man with a shaved head, thick sunglasses, and a black suit. He looked like everything white boys were scared of in a black man. A sheen of sweat covered the top of his head. It amazed me that anyone would wear a black suit this time of year. I approached him with some trepidation.

"Can I help you?"

"You Monk Buttman?"

"Yeah, you Dulcimer's man?" His eyebrows rose at that.

"I'm my own man, Buttman. As I understand it, you and I have business to attend to."

"Yeah, I heard that too." We stood there eyeing one another for no particular reason. "Would you like to come in?" He said nothing but motioned towards the door. "Can I get you anything to drink, Mr...?"

"Jones, and I'm not here to socialize."

"Not even water?"

"Not even water." He stood and watched as I retrieved a bottle from the fridge. I felt oddly self-conscious drinking water in my own place.

"So what's the plan, Mr. Jones? Or, more precisely, what can I do to assist you in finding Desiree Marshan?"

"I don't think you can do a damn thing to help me, Buttman, but I need to find that woman and my money, and Dulcimer tells me you have to tag along. I don't like that, but sometimes life makes you walk a crooked mile."

"I see. Are we heading out now...later?"

"Don't worry, you won't miss your date with Agnes. Besides, I'm waiting to hear from a man I know about where this Desiree likes to run off to." He faintly smiled at the mention of my date. "I'll be here tomorrow, bright and early. If you're not going to be here then you can call me at this number." A small card materialized from the breast pocket of his suit. "What's your number, Buttman, in case I need to call?" He handed me the card.

"I don't carry a phone, Mr. Jones."

"What?" A moment of silence fell between us. I could hear the birds chirping outside. "What kind of motherfucker doesn't have a goddamned phone?"

"Motherfuckers like me."

"Well, motherfucker," he said with a smile that completely changed his demeanor from that of hard-determined man, "let me give you some advice."

"Yeah?"

"Yeah, get one."

"I don't like phones."

"I don't care about your personal bullshit, Buttman. Get a phone. We got work to do!" He opened the door letting in the light, "Bright and early, Buttman; bright and early."

The birds continued singing as the large black man took his leave. I was curious how he knew I was to see Agnes tonight, but as he had to have seen Dulcimer, and Agnes worked there; it might have come up. The sunlight was streaming through the window above the shade. I had a few hours to kill before my rendezvous with what I hoped was at least a pleasant woman, and decided a nap would work out well. I locked the door and fell asleep on the couch.

The light, which had been so warm and inviting before, had thinned, waking me. If I was going to make it out to meet Agnes, it was time to go. I got off the couch and took stock of myself, I'd looked worse. Other than too many people on the road, the trip to the bar and Agnes was uneventful. There was plenty of parking in the deteriorating lot, and the joint was ambling along, filled with what I assumed were its regulars. Agnes, as she had said, was situated at the end of the bar. Rey tended to the others while keeping an eye on the ballgame illuminating the rather dank establishment. I raised my hand as she saw me and we met about halfway across the room.

"I'm glad you made good on your promise to have a drink with me." Her hair was down, caressing her shoulders. The smile I remembered was there as she looked up at me. An incredible feeling of desire drew me in. Agnes's visual charms were self-evident. It didn't hurt that the blouse and slacks she was wearing accentuated her fine curves, or that one more button on her blouse was undone, allowing an even better appreciation of her wonderful breasts.

"I'd be a fool not to accept such an offer."

"Yes, you would." Her hand took hold of my arm. "What would you like to drink? Are you hungry? I could have Mel make you a little something if you'd like?"

"A drink would be nice, soda and whiskey, and since you mentioned it, I am a little hungry. What's good here?" I wanted to say besides you, but I knew better; one step at a time.

"The steak sandwich is good. Care to share one? Mel doesn't scrimp when I order."

"Sounds good."

She led me to a circular booth off in the corner. "Have a seat. I'll be right back." The booth offered a strategic viewpoint from which to observe the comings and goings of the joint. I watched Agnes' hips sway as she approached the bar to put in our order and retrieve our drinks. It was easy to imagine how delightful she might be, warm and naked, lying beside me. She was speaking to who I assumed was Mel. There were maybe twenty people in the bar. Dulcimer came out from the back with a tall slender man. Both were overdressed given the location. I was the only other man wearing a suit, tee shirts and jeans being the couture of the place. The man with Dulcimer looked familiar, but I couldn't make out his face. Agnes returned with our drinks, sliding up next to me, her perfume filling my senses.

"Here you go."

I took the drink from her hand.

"You look good with your hair down, it accentuates your smile."

"Thanks. It's always nice to hear a compliment." She was wearing more makeup than she had the day before, highlighting her eyes and mouth. "You'd be surprised how little that happens anymore. You look good in that suit, it goes with your eyes." Her hand was caressing the sleeve of my jacket. "I like a man who dresses for the occasion."

I got the impression that if I leaned in for a kiss, I would not be rebuffed.

Her breath carried the scent of gin. I could tell this wasn't her first drink. That made me both apprehensive and excited. She must have noticed something in my eyes, or was adept at reading my mind, for the next thing I knew she was pulling me close and putting her lips to mine. It was a wet, sloppy kiss. Agnes used her whole mouth. I saw no reason not to reciprocate so ten minutes into our drink together we were necking in the corner booth. After a minute or two we sat back.

"I like a man who knows how to kiss a woman." I was now wondering how many drinks she'd had. Maybe my eyes had nothing to do with it.

"I try not to disappoint."

Rey approached with our meal. A large steak sandwich cut in two with a generous side of fries and a bottle of ketchup.

"Here's your food, folks." He put the plate between us. "I don't mean to interrupt, but Johnny would like a word with Mr. Buttman." Agnes frowned at this. I looked over at the bar and could see Dulcimer leaning against the bar. He made a quick gesture to me.

"Sure." Turning to Agnes, "I'll be right back." She took a fry and placed it in her mouth, none too thrilled. Rey and I went to the bar.

"I apologize for calling you over, Mr. Buttman; I can see that Agnes is unhappy with me. I just need a minute of your time."

"Not a problem."

"Good. You and Mr. Jones will be looking for Ms. Marshan, and that inquiry may bring you into my business concerns. I expect the same level of confidence you provide to Mr. Durant and his associates. Any information concerning me and my affairs I expect to be informed of. I'm a generous man to those who appreciate and contribute to my endeavors, but not so much to those who do not. Do we have an understanding, Mr. Buttman?"

"We do."

"Excellent." He turned towards Agnes. "I expect that you'll take care of and show a measure of kindness towards Agnes. I'm very fond of her and do not want her to be hurt."

"It's not my desire to hurt her." He smiled and raised his hand towards Agnes.

"Then please enjoy your evening." It was then that I noticed the two goons waiting at the door. Agnes was also waiting.

"Your sandwich is getting cold."

I slid in next to her and took my half. Fortunately, her admonition wasn't true. The steak was tender with just the right amount of seasoning. Once again I realized I had eaten very little and was far hungrier than I thought. We quietly finished our meal leaving nothing other than a small patch of ketchup on the plate.

"The sandwich was a good choice. I feel better now."

"It's not healthy to skip meals, Monk. You might need your energy later."

"I might." Her smile returned now that there was no boss to interrupt us. "So, can I ask what prompted you to ask me for a drink?"

"Cause I liked the way you looked. Not many men come here wearing a suit, and, I don't know, there was something about you that appealed to me, so I thought what the hell. Why'd you say yes?"

"May I be honest?"

"Please." I leaned in.

"Because you have an engaging smile, because I was curious, because it's been a while and you have great boobs."

She laughed. "They are nice, aren't they? Men have been admiring them for years. It's been a while for me too. Maybe we're just two lonely people looking for a little company."

"I would think an attractive woman like you would have all the company she desired."

"You would think, but I foolishly spent most of those years trying to hold on to the wrong man. After that I floundered for a while, so I took a break. Only it lasted longer than I thought it would."

"I know how that goes."

"So you're all mine for now."

"I'm all yours."

"Good." She raised her glass. "A toast, to the two of us, and a glorious evening together."

"To a glorious evening." Rey strolled over to pick up our plate and refill our glasses.

Agnes pulled herself even closer to me. "Do you like to dance, Monk?"

"I know enough to be dangerous."

"Then let's dance. Rey, would you be a sweetheart and put on my dance music?"

"Coming up." Rey obliged, turning up the sound in the bar.

Agnes loved to dance. There was a little of everything, but I liked the slow stuff. She held me close and pressed those delightful breasts to me as often as possible. A break here and there for a drink, then it was back out for more. The air around us was filled with perfume, musk, and perspiration. Towards the end she would kiss me more and more.

"Monk…"

"Agnes…"

"Would you like to come home with me?"

The answer was self-evident as she pressed against me, but there's nothing wrong with saying it out loud. "Yes, I would."

In a fluidity remarkable given the drinks we'd consumed, we gathered our belongings, bade farewell to Rey; who barely acknowledged us, made our way to my car; apparently, I was driving, made it to her place just down the road, and fell into bed wrapped around one another.

It was, indeed, a glorious evening.

7

It's amazing how good it can feel to be with a woman. I drifted into a deep sleep until the sun woke me. Agnes was still asleep, pressed next to me. I ran my finger along her shoulder. I thought about morning sex, but my bladder couldn't wait. By the time I was done I'd found the clock and knew I didn't have as much time as I thought. Her phone was by the door. I fished Jones' number out of my pants pocket and called the number.

"Jones?"

"Yeah?"

"It's Buttman. I'm over by Dulcimer's joint. Where do you want to meet?"

"I'll meet you there. There's a guy up north that knows this Desiree. How much time do you need?"

"Maybe an hour."

"I'll be there in an hour. What are you driving?"

"64 Falcon convertible." I noted the sigh on his end.

"That figures. Be there, Buttman."

"Goodbye, Mr. Jones."

Agnes was still in bed, and while it was tempting to jump back in with her, I hit the shower instead. The next stop was the kitchen. I was hungry and needed to eat before my time with Mr. Jones. He didn't strike me as someone who spent a lot of time thinking about food. Fortunately, Agnes had a little something in the kitchen. I got the coffee started and heard her coughing. I filled a glass with water and grabbed the Tylenol out of the bathroom. She was sitting up, the sheets around her waist. When I came in she crossed her arms out of a sense of modesty, which made me smile. After all the time I spent indulging myself with her fine breasts and now she was self-conscious.

"Good morning." Her hair, makeup, and demeanor were what you'd expect after a night of drinking, dancing, and sex.

"Morning." She half-heartedly brushed the hair out of her face. "I thought you were gone already..."

"No, not yet, I have to meet Jones in a little while. Here..." I offered her the water and Tylenol. "In case you might have a headache."

"Thanks." She carefully opened the bottle, taking a number of tablets, and slowly washed them down with the water.

"Hungry? I need to eat before I go. I noticed you have some stuff for breakfast, would you like some?"

"That would be nice."

I started breakfast while I assumed she was doing whatever she does in the morning. I found some plates and silverware and placed them on the small table adjacent to the kitchen. I poured two cups of coffee, toasted the muffins, and filled the plates with eggs and sausage. She wandered in and sat down. Her hair was pulled back and she had removed the previous evening's makeup. There was a glow to her skin after our night of debauchery.

"I can't remember the last time anyone made me breakfast."

"It's nothing special, eat up."

We quietly ate our food as the morning light filled the room. It was the kind of domesticity I occasionally longed for. Agnes would periodically peer over at me as I finished the meal. I couldn't tell if she meant to say something or not.

"I assume I need to drop you off at work?" I asked.

"That would be nice. My legs are a bit wobbly from last night. I can't remember the last time I danced that much!" She smiled at repeating herself. "I'd prefer not to have to walk today."

"Sure, but I have to get going soon..."

"I'll hurry." She finished the last few bites and headed back to her room. I cleaned off the dishes and put them in the dishwasher. She was quiet on the short ride back to her office. I parked the car, surveying the lot for Mr. Jones.

"I had a good time last night, Monk."

"So did I."

"I wouldn't mind doing it again sometime, if you'd like?"

"I would like. I had a wonderful time, you're a beautiful woman." She smiled at me sadly. She reached in my coat pocket and retrieved Mr. Jones' card.

"Here's my number." She wrote it on the back of the card. A long sweet kiss followed. "Bye."

"Goodbye," I watched as she made her way across the lot, disappearing behind the door of her office.

I did not notice Mr. Jones.

"You ready, Buttman?" he semi-shouted, causing me to jump like a fool.

"Yeah!"

"About fucking time. Head over to I-5, we're going north."

Mr. Jones ran his hand along the edge of the dashboard. There wasn't much else to do as we drove past the endless subdivisions, malls, and indistinct buildings that made up this never-ending town. The weather was, as it generally is, sunny and warm. I pulled the top down before we took off. I liked it that way. Jones seemed to enjoy the air cascading across his domed head.

"You got a nice ride, Buttman. When you first told me what you were driving I pictured something a little different, but I can see you keep this baby up. I like that."

"Thanks. I've had it for more than twenty years. A guy not far from here takes care of it for me."

"I knew a guy years ago had a car like this. Not a bad way to go."

"Speaking of which, where are we going?"

"We're going to see a man named Frankensense. Apparently he knew Desiree when she worked in the porn industry. Might know who she's shacking up with. The cops checked her home address, but there was no one there. Whatever she's up to, leaving was a part of it."

"Are you a PI?"

He seemed dismayed by the term.

"No. I do security; have for years after I got out of the army. I know a lot of people in the PD, and over at county, so I know people who can help with information, but I don't do that too much anymore. My thing now is production, music acts and entertainment, that sort of thing. I'm not happy that I've got to waste my time chasing after some damn woman. But, she's got my money, twenty-five G's worth; money that I need to get my acts through to the next level, so here we are."

"That's a lot of cash to have on hand."

"It is, but in this business, cash still speaks loudest, and very few people will take checks or swipe your debit card. It's money under the table; it's money that gets your people seen. Shows, websites, tweets, all of it, exposure is everything, Buttman. If they don't see you, they don't know you."

"I see." Other than Joanie's occasional comments on the state of local entertainment, I knew very little of how it all worked. Jones could be blowing smoke. The traffic thinned as we rode north. Not every hill had houses on it. More and more there were industrial parks dotted on either side of the interstate.

"Get off at the next exit. Go right," he directed.

This led us to a nondescript warren of single-story buildings, one of which was a small office complex. I parked the car and we went into suite 106B. A woman with long hair and a bright smile greeted us. It was hard not to stare at her rather prominent and well-displayed breasts.

Jones ogled behind his sunglasses. "We're here to see Frankensense. Jones and Buttman. We're expected."

"I'll let him know you're here." She hit the buzzer and out came her employer. Frankensense was a middle-aged guy with graying hair and a paunch. Not at all what I expected. We could be at Walmart and he'd fit right in.

"Gentlemen." We followed him into his office. There was little to indicate that pornography was his business. A few pictures of clothed adult films stars, a calendar and a landscape of the cliffs off the ocean adorned the walls. His desk was a lot like Desiree's, only more papers and files littered the top. There was a couch and three chairs. Frankensense motioned that we sit.

Jones spoke first. "We here to get some information on Desiree Marshan. It's my understanding that you know this woman."

"I do indeed, Mr. Jones. I also understand that she's gotten herself into a bind."

"Apparently. I'd appreciate hearing what you know about her and where she might be or who she might know. "

"Word got to me that this is through Johnny D. Are you here on his behalf?" I noted the slight change in Frankensenses's voice.

"Buttman might be, but she has something that belongs to me; that's my interest."

"Good enough." Frankensense opened up his laptop and tapped on the keys. He smiled in a way that suggested he'd done this before and then looked at us. "Desiree came into this business about seven, maybe eight years ago. Most of the time the people I see are looking for opportunities for any number of reasons; they need money, want exposure, want to be famous, think this is a good way to get some pussy, and so on. I don't normally deal in coercion; I don't like it. I can find plenty of talent through normal channels. Desiree, whose working name was Rosarita, was a little different. When she was first brought to me it was made clear that I would find work for her in specific genres, and she was to work until she had paid off her commitment. The individuals making this request were not the kind you say no to and I like being known as a cooperative guy."

"Which individuals were these?" I asked.

"I'm not going to name names. Let's just say that the story going around was that Desiree got mixed up with a man who thought he could steal from the wrong people, and they believed she knew about it. They gave her a choice, pay us what you owe us, or find yourself in a bad way, if you know what I mean. Adult films were an option for paying them back, and they wanted a dose of humiliation thrown in, so she became the girl doing anal in our interracial films." Frankensense gave Jones a sidelong glance at this last comment, maybe to see if that was his thing, or if he was offended.

"How long did that last?" was Jones' response.

"About three years. And they worked that girl hard, no pun intended, even though she rarely smiled and looked bored most of the time, but then I don't think many people were looking at her face." Frankensense cracked a smile at that. "Amazingly, a kind of cult evolved around her; chat rooms, file sharing groups, stuff like that. She sold well. I even heard there was a small club called Rosarita's Riders devoted to her; men who would pay, and pay well, to enjoy Desiree's ample ass."

"And then?" I asked.

"She split. I heard she hooked up with a tranny called Derek/Dahlia. The two of them made movies together or with another guy, something like that. Anyway, that lasted about a year. From what I heard Dahlia left to be a counselor in the tranny community. As for Desiree, I was told she found a guy who got her a job with some lawyers, but I assume you knew that."

"What's this Desiree look like, any distinguishing marks?" Jones sounded bored.

"She has a long rose tattoo." Both Jones and Frankensense turned to me. Frankensense had a sly grin on his face.

"That's true. So you know Desiree, Mr...."

"Buttman, Monk Buttman. I know her from the law office. Her tattoo peeked out from beneath her blouse at the neck and wrist."

"More than that, Mr. Buttman. See here..." He turned his laptop our way. There in all her pixilated glory was Desiree Marshan glaring at the camera without a stitch of clothing. Frankensense toggled between pictures showing her front to back. "As you can see it's quite a tattoo. It starts at the small of her back, winds down her left cheek, between her legs, with a rose around her asshole, then it comes out the other side, along her thigh, up around her tits to her neck, and then down her arm. "

"Yes, it's something else," said Jones in a flat voice. "Do you have a headshot of her, and do you think this Dahlia can help us?"

"I'll see what I have. As for Dahlia, I couldn't say. I didn't know her and Desiree never brought her around."

We got up as Frankensense printed a picture of Desiree for Jones. For some reason, he gave me his card. We thanked him and returned to the car. Jones sat there lost in thought.

"I'm hungry, Buttman, and we need to talk. There was a Denny's just off the freeway. Let's go."

8

The man in black was not a happy camper. As we waited for my club sandwich and his chicken salad, he worked the phone while growing increasingly agitated. From what I could tell, he was being threatened with the loss of whomever he was representing if he couldn't get the ball moving on whatever was coming up. Between calls to people unknown he would glance towards me with a look of either exasperation or what have you gotten me into. More and more the tone grew tense until he slammed the phone onto the table. The waitress cautiously approached with our food.

"Is everything alright?" She set down the plates with a delicacy usually reserved for nitro.

"It's alright. Just business," I replied. Jones glowered, but said nothing. "Thanks for your concern. The food looks good."

"Enjoy your lunch, gentlemen." She eased off towards the kitchen. Jones picked at his salad, his shoulders hunched forward, his eyes canvassing the contents of his meal. I didn't believe his heart was in it. My sandwich, on the other hand, was quite good. I was proud of myself; I'd had both breakfast and lunch at the socially accepted times in God knows how long. Jones must have noticed my reverie.

"What are we doing here, Buttman?"

"Having lunch?"

"I'm serious, man. What the fuck are we doing here?"

"We're looking for Desiree Marshan."

"Why?"

I understood the point, but wondered whether it was wise to play too many cards with essentially a stranger. I didn't feel uncomfortable around Jones, but I had no idea as to his motives beyond a claimed desire to recover stolen money.

"I don't really know."

"Then why are *you* here, Buttman? What the fuck good are you if you don't know why you're here?"

"Why do you think I'm here, Mr. Jones?" He sat up and put his fork on the plate.

"Cause maybe, motherfucker, you took the money and this ruse about Desiree Marshan is just a runaround. Maybe the expectation is that sooner or later I'm goin' hafta beat it out of you? How 'bout that?"

"Why do you think I have the money?"

"Maybe, because you were there, and the only reason we think this woman has it is because you said so." Jones subtly moved towards me.

"Maybe. But if I did take the money, I must have hidden it at Aeschylus and Associates because I didn't leave prior to the police arriving. So in that case, then yes, this is a contrived waste of time on our part. It also means the money is still there, and if that's true, then Durant must suspect it and therefore wants me out of the way in order to have his people search for it."

"Maybe, Buttman, maybe!"

I considered that for a moment. There was no proof I didn't have the money. The only witness was the missing woman. A part of me thought about opening up to Jones just because, to see what his reaction would be. "Do you believe that? If you think I have the money why not beat it out of me now rather than waste your time running around?"

He considered it.

"Because it's a little too convenient. If that's what they thought, they have people whose job it is to beat the shit out of people like you. It ain't my job, never was. I think this is Dulcimer's way of beating me down over control of my clients. Twenty-five grand can't be shit to him, or Durant for that matter; the two of them probably make that in a day, but to me it makes a big difference. I don't know what the fuck you do or why you're here other than you know that Marshan took the money, and even that's in question. Who the fuck are you, Buttman?"

"I'm nobody," I assured him.

"Nobody?"

"Nobody."

He snorted and then returned to his salad. We finished lunch to the sounds of the other patrons delving into their particular problems with kids, bosses, spouses, and one another. I kind of missed that. I decided I didn't need a whole plate of rapidly cooling fries and pushed the plate away. Jones picked at his salad. His phone went off.

"Jones." He looked at me. "Yeah, I'll ask." Setting the phone aside he said, "Agnes wants to know if you're free tomorrow night?"

"I don't have any plans."

"You're living quite the life, Buttman." He returned to his phone. "He can be there. What time?" He was rolling his eyes. "Fine. Goodbye, Agnes." I waited for the word. "Be at her house tomorrow at six or so."

"Thanks."

"Get a fucking phone. It's not my job to be you answering service."

"I didn't tell her to call me here."

"Ha, ha, Buttman." The waitress came and picked up our plates and left the check. "You get that, I'm going to call down to the tranny center..." Jones' discomfort was evident. "They wouldn't call it that, would they?"

"LGBT," I offered.

"Uh-huh." Once found on the all-knowing phone, the call was quick and to our misfortune Dahlia couldn't see us till the next day. We shuffled out into the sunshine and headed back to town.

The breeze felt good as it streamed across the tops of our heads. Jones continued to work the phone as I drove. It would be ok, he just needed a little more time, he was good for it, have a little faith. I wondered why Dulcimer didn't just front him the money? Maybe he was fucking with Jones, making him sweat. When he wasn't talking, Jones spent the drive looking off into space. My company wasn't doing it for him. I tried not to take it personally. His phone rang again.

"Jones." He gave the phone to me. "It's for you. Some lawyer."

I took the phone. "Monk Buttman."

"Mr. Buttman, this is Taylor Lagenfelder. The police are requesting an interview with you. It concerns Martin Delashay. Apparently he's disappeared, and as one of the last people to see him, they'd like to talk to you."

"Didn't they talk to his wife? She saw him after I did?"

"I'm sure they did, but when they heard you were there just before that, it's safe to say it piqued their curiosity. Are you available this afternoon?"

"Yeah. Do I have to go down to headquarters?"

"No, it'll be conducted here at the office. Ask for me at the desk. About how long until you get here?"

"About an hour; maybe a little less."

"Excellent, I'll let the police know. Goodbye, Mr. Buttman."

I handed the phone back to Jones. "I know, I know; I need to get a fucking phone."

Jones didn't seem particularly interested in Delashay or my impending dance with the fuzz. As they say, he had his own problems. I dropped him off in the near-empty parking lot, gave an idle thought to barging in on Agnes, thought better of it; I would be seeing her the next day, and reluctantly returned to the rat's nest with the rest of the vermin.

Ever since that day out by the Gentry's cornfield, I struggled with the contrast between the glorious weather and the less than glorious activities committed in its light. Not only was I going back to A and A, but also to session two with the fuzz over things I knew nothing about. Maybe having Ms. Lagenfelder there would help. Gloom mingled with the light as I inched my way there.

The lobby was, as I hadn't actually come in through the front door on my previous visits, rather inviting. It wore its appointments well, there was nothing garish or out of place. A young man at the desk called Ms. Lagenfelder and no sooner had I sat down, I found myself right behind her, back on my feet. Inside her office, she asked if I needed anything before we summoned the police who were here interviewing the staff about Boyer and Desiree.

"Do you know what Martin Delashay's wife told the police about his disappearance?"

"I don't know any specifics. Mr. Durant told me to ask you to not divulge anything you may have noted about the correspondence you took to his house, but other than that, there is no reason not to answer their questions. Does that help?"

"It's good enough."

"They're in the conference room; shall we?" She smiled as we approached the door. "I'm sure it will be fairly uneventful, Mr. Buttman."

"I'm sure it will be."

Descartes and Mallory were conferring as we entered. The shades were drawn just enough to let in the light but not overpower the room. I found a chair across from them. Ms. Lagenfelder sat next to me. Neither detective seemed delighted to see me and here I thought we'd made some kind of connection.

Mallory spoke first as he had just the day before. "It's our understanding that you visited Martin Delashay the day Mr. Boyer was killed. You didn't mention that when we talked yesterday?"

"You didn't ask about my day beyond how it involved the death of Todd Boyer."

"We're not here to play games with you, Mr. Buttman. A few straight answers are what we're looking for. You think you can do that?" Descartes was already bristling. There had to be more going on than my supposed lack of appropriate supplication.

"There's no need for that tone, detective. Mr. Buttman is here to answer your questions." Ms. Lagenfelder to the rescue.

"I did see Mr. Delashay on the day Boyer was killed. I had some papers for him to sign."

"What kind of papers?"

"I couldn't say. I was only there to deliver them."

"Did you notice anything in his attitude or demeanor that struck you as unusual?"

"I know he didn't care for what I gave him. He refused to sign the papers and then threw them at me. His wife and I collected them and I returned here." Mallory noted my comments in a small notebook.

"And his wife, how did she react to his throwing the papers at you?"

"I think she was as surprised as I was. Mr. Delashay left us and I didn't see him again."

"Did his wife say anything to you that you remember? Anything that might help us in his sudden disappearance?"

"Not that I can think of. We only spoke a few words before I left. That's all I know." The two detectives, devotees of the need for answers, did not appear satisfied.

"Is there anything about Mr. Boyer's death that you forgot to note in our talk yesterday, but remember now?" Mallory added.

"I'm afraid not."

"If you think of anything, you'll let us know, Mr. Buttman."

"I'll let you know."

Whatever their feelings as to the veracity of my comments, they kept to themselves. They may have wanted more, but it would have to wait for another time. I said farewell, and Ms. Lagenfelder and I left the conference room. She showed me to the lobby.

"Do you think the detectives will have me followed?"

"It's possible, but I wouldn't be too concerned. If you need any assistance, don't hesitate to call." She gave me her most reassuring smile. It was good enough.

On my way out, I paused to take in the beauty of the lobby one last time. I wanted to go home. My head hurt and I was tired. I took my time, taking side roads, just driving around. Desiree was out there somewhere. Now Martin Delashay had gone missing. Coincidence? Was there something connecting them? Maybe Boyer? Boyer was dead. Who knows what he was up to? Desiree? Martin? The thought crossed my mind to pack up my few belongings and head back to the east coast. See my mother. Find out what Astral was doing, see how my daughter had changed, matured. I hadn't seen her in nearly a year. She was talking about having a baby. I didn't want to continue looking for Desiree Marshan. After our visit to Frankensense, it was all I could do to not picture the woman naked, the tattoo working its way around her pale body. God only knows what was in the films she was forced to make.

The sun was fading as I opened the door to my bungalow. The light was on and a well-dressed man was sitting in my chair.

He hadn't changed in more than twenty years.

9

"Benitez?"

"Amigo!"

"What brings you to my little hole in the wall?" Here he was, the last man I ever expected to see. A spectre from a long-suppressed past. We'd grown up together, been pals even though he was a few years older. He and James worked with me on the farm and then, when we were older, the three of us had a side gig supplying weed to the locals to make a little money, just for fun. Benitez was there when James was killed.

"Business."

"Business? Really? I haven't seen you since our encounter with Frankie and Gene?" He smiled at the names; they were the reason for our forced separation. "How are they?"

"Those two are long gone. Like our friend, they thought they could game the system, do anything they wanted." The smile fell from his face and the cold returned, the cold I remembered so vividly as they dragged James away. "It never changes." He stood up. For a minute I thought this was it! He'd finally come for me. "I'm hungry. Why don't we try that Mexican place down the street?" The smile was back. "Is it any good?" Come for what, food?

"It's not bad. The tamales are my favorite," I said.

"Then we should go." I opened the door. There was nothing to do but go. Perhaps foolishly, I assumed I'd never see Benitez again. I was out of that world.

I left because I had to for the safety of Astral and Rebekah, and for my own sorry neck. If he was here to settle old scores, real or imagined, I wasn't going to get away. Like all good killers, Benitez was prepared for any stunt I might pull. He was smart to wait; I had no passion for running or fighting at this age.

"Why not. I hear last meals are customary," I mumbled.

"Still the same, amigo?" Benitez shook his head. "All that is forgotten. This is about today and tomorrow."

It was a short walk, only two blocks. Las Cerritos was a small family run place with plain tables and little in the way of ambiance. Florescent fixtures and faded pictures of the Mexican coast shared the room as we sat near a window. One of the daughters brought chips and salsa. Benitez ordered a plate of beef and rice with tortillas on the side, I asked for the tamales. Two beers, two limes, and two napkins set the table. It was time to talk.

"So what's on your mind?"

"Do you think I'm here to kill you?" he asked this while dipping a chip into the homemade salsa.

"I would like to think you're not, but truth be told, your reputation precedes you." I'd heard rumors after I'd left that Benitez had become a hired gun, working for his cousins.

"I suppose it does. You know, we take roads so thoughtlessly when we're young, never considering how it will affect us, as we grow older. After James... after what happened, I put away that anger because it made the job easier and anger in this business will get you killed faster than fear."

It was oddly remarkable that half an hour into seeing one another, after so long, we were casually talking of the murder that had so damaged and changed us; Benitez, the knife, James stabbed and dying, and me, standing there.

He kept talking, "That look is still in your eyes, amigo..." Fear.

"Is it?"

"It's not something you forget," he said before taking a drink.

"No... Do you think about it much?"

His eyes stayed on me. "I did once, but I haven't in some time. Besides, it's like a lot of life, a dead end. As for James, you know I told him he was making a big mistake. I told him we shouldn't go to that meeting. I warned him he needed to forget the money, but he didn't listen. It never occurred to him that they might kill us. As for the rest, we did what we had to do because they would have killed us if we hadn't. It's the code, my friend. Once we got into that business, and the Prontos moved in, we had to make a choice; you know that as well as I."

"I know that, and, for what it's worth, I've come to terms with it. You chose to stay, and I chose to run. We're both here now, so in a way, I guess it worked out." The food arrived. As usual there was too much. "So what business would you have with me if it's not about the money or the past?"

"Nobody cares about the money, that died with the brothers. No, I'm here because of Desiree Marshan." Miguel Benitez sat back, a cat's grin on his face.

"Desiree? You know about that?"

"Whispers, my friend, have been carrying her name," he continued smiling as he said it. He'd been playing with me, or my irrational fears. James was my ghost, not his. I felt like an idiot.

"That doesn't answer the question."

He took a bite while pondering the answer. "No? How's this, change is coming in this business and the smart money is lining up to take advantage of that. More than a few people want to bring the business into the light. They're tired of the violence and the insecurity. They want to focus on product and distribution, profit margins, things like that, not whether the people you're doing business with will send over a shooter or kidnap your children if they think you're trying to move them out or screw them over. That's why I moved on, sooner or later I'd end up marked and that would be that."

"And Desiree?"

"She's an unknown. An investor in these ventures was brought to us, and it was whispered that he, and another man, were involved with Desiree Marshan. She wanted to be their liaison to our group. Why, nobody knew. All we could find out about her was a story that she and a former boyfriend had a run-in with the locals. After the incident the other day, the people I work for are concerned with what she might know and who she may be working with."

"And these people are?"

"Very important!" He took a sip of beer, smiled, and leaned towards me, gesturing that I do the same, "This involves a great deal of money, my friend, and they don't like it when outsiders try to push in uninvited."

"Ok, so they think Desiree's trying to push them, how does this involve me?"

"You're looking for her, right?"

"Maybe." He smiled at me like he knew better. I didn't like where this was going.

"When you find her, assuming we don't hear from her first, you let me know." He pulled a small case from the inside of his jacket, took out a card, and handed it to me. I almost hesitated to take it. "Here's my personal number."

"So, you'll let me know if she contacts your people."

"I can, what's your number?" He had his phone out ready to enter my information.

"I don't have a phone."

"You don't have a phone?" His look was much like Jones'. "Who does business without a phone? How are you going to call me?"

"I know a guy?"

"Very funny." He wasn't laughing. "Get a phone, amigo."

"I don't like them, I don't want them tracking me." For some reason I thought this would appeal to his sense of being apart, from the need to be unseen during his years as a paid killer.

"Shit, if you're worried, have it disabled, but you need a phone these days, so I recommend you get one."

"Sure."

We finished the meal and paid the daughter. Benitez walked beside me looking around at the neighborhood, taking in the houses, the street, and the trees that lined it.

"Moses was asking about you."

"Yeah, I need to go see him one of these days. How's he look?"

"Like he'll live forever. Maybe we should have stayed on the farm?"

"Maybe."

"And your family? How are they?" I was surprised by the interest.

"They live back east, in Virginia. They're all fine, all married to good Christian men."

"You see, it all works out."

Yeah, it all works out. We'd reached his car.

Benitez turned his attention to the car's door handle, once more lost in thought. I could feel his discomfort, his unease. Strange, the two of us had been as close as people could be; even now it was easy to talk to him, to see him as the boy he once was, the friend for life he told me he would always be before he put the blade... I knew he was right about James and what happened, but it blew the two of us apart. Odd how the years didn't take away the ache or dulled the memory of that day? I had put faith in the idea that it would.

"There's no need to stay away, or to be careful. He misses you."

"I know."

He found his keys and unlocked the car. "We shouldn't be strangers."

"We shouldn't be." He looked me in the eye and smiled.

"Take care, Sunshine. Hopefully, we'll talk again soon."

"Take care, Miguel."

The car started, and just as he had popped in, seemingly out of nowhere, he popped out in much the same fashion. Out of sight, but not out of mind. I made a mental note that I'd probably see him before another twenty years came and went. I returned to my bungalow. On the table, next to the chair, was a small lamp with just enough light to keep me from tripping over what little furniture I had. It was quiet. I had time to try and make sense of the last three days.

Instead, I fell asleep.

The next day began with a bang on the door. Sometime during the night I had slinked off to bed. The pounding was insistent enough to wake me. I put my pants on and made it to the door. I had no idea what time it was. Jones was standing there in full regalia, black everything from shades to shoes. A cool breeze worked its way around him.

"Time to get active, Buttman. I ain't got all day to play. This Dahlia woman is expecting us in thirty minutes, so let's go. I got the impression she ain't too happy to have to talk about our little tattooed thief. So we need to get there before she changes her mind."

"I can't imagine why she wouldn't want to talk to two delightful characters such as ourselves." His expression didn't change. "Alright, just give me a minute." A quick rummage through the closet and I was set other than rinsing out my mouth and voiding my bladder.

"Let's go, Buttman; you drive."

"Where are we going?"

"Hollywood." Great, the one place in this town I had no interest in.

The LGBT outreach center was a storefront in West Hollywood. Other than a small sign and a number of posters, there was nothing to distinguish it from the other tract buildings lining the street. The woman at the front desk took our names and asked us to sit. Here in a land neither of us knew anything about or understood, we sat waiting to talk to the transgendered Dahlia about the glum Desiree. Even on the farm, where everyone was free to be whatever they wanted, provided they pulled their weight, the sexes and their roles were well defined. We had no individuals with gender issues, at least none that I knew of. Jones was stone-faced as we waited. He uttered not a word. Three women came in and talked quietly to one another. They looked over at the two of us, whispered to the person at the desk, and then sat in the chairs across from us. Nobody made a sound. I tried to find something to look at. There were a few fliers on the counter. Dahlia arrived just as I was getting up to read one.

"I'm Dahlia. You wanted to talk to me about Desiree?"

Jones and I rose. "Yes, we did," I said.

Dahlia was a tall slender woman with soft blond hair pulled back in a ponytail. She wore a flowery summer dress. She didn't smile and it was easy to tell she wasn't thrilled to see the two of us.

"I'm pretty busy today, so I don't know that I can give you much time..."

"We appreciate whatever time you can spare."

"Fine." She turned to the person at the desk. "Marlee, I'll be back in a few minutes. Gentlemen, there's a coffee shop two doors down, we can talk there."

We followed Dahlia to the coffee shop. We stood in line saying nothing till it was our turn to order and then found a small table in the corner next to a guy on his computer, and two women talking about another woman, someone named Jackie. We sat there staring at our caffeinated confections, waiting for them to cool, when Dahlia became a different person.

"So who the fuck are you two? You're not the cops; they came by yesterday?" Her earlier quiet careful demeanor was gone and I could swear her voice changed.

"Mallory and Descartes?"

A smirk came to Dahlia. "You know those two? Seems they're looking for

Desiree too. Again, who are you, and why should I say two fucking words to you, and you better not be one of those creepy rider freaks?"

"I'm Monk Buttman, and this is Mr. Jones."

Dahlia burst out laughing.

"Those are your names? Really? What are you, a former porn star and a Superfly?" The two women at the table next to us took a moment to glance our way.

"No," Jones stated matter-of-factly, "I'm a music promoter and Buttman's a nobody."

"A nobody?"

"Yeah, before that I was a farmer," I added.

"A Farmer?" She slid back in her chair. "So what do you want with Desiree and what makes you think I'm going to help you?"

"She took my money, and I want it back. I don't particularly care whether or not she killed that dude. I'm just looking for some helpful information." Jones took a turn.

"And you, Mr. *Buttman,* what's a nobody want with her?"

"There are people who want to talk to her and they gave me the task of finding her."

Dahlia was more intrigued by my answer than Jones'.

"And you think I know where she is?"

"You lived with her, didn't you? I know she's frightened, and we think maybe you might know where she'd lay low while the heat's on?"

Dahlia continued laughing at my feeble attempt at sleuthing. "Maybe. Let me ask you something? Have you ever done this before?"

"Done what?"

"Track people down."

"No, I'm new to the game."

"Really? How shocking. I was sure you were one hard-boiled private dick." She let that last phrase linger in the air, allowing it to filter across the room. "Listen to me, cause I'm only going to say this once, I don't know where she is, and I don't care to. If you've met her then you know what she's like. Throw in the fact that she's a liar and thief, and I don't care if she ends up dead in the street. Last time I saw her she was running off with some guy she said was going to finally treat her right. I don't know who he is, what he does, or where he lives. Now I've got a job to do, and that doesn't include you two."

She got up and took one last sip of her latte. Jones and I stood. He extended his hand and a card. "Here's my number. If you change your mind or you hear something, let me know."

"Why, so you can turn her over to the police or rough her up?"

"I thought you didn't care what happened to Desiree?"

She took the card from Jones' hand. "I don't. Goodbye, gentlemen; thanks for the coffee." The woman who was once a man, or maybe still was, or wasn't turned and left us. We sat back down to consider our options. The two women next to us were still complaining about Jackie.

10

"It's a different world now, Buttman," Jones removed his sunglasses and placed them in his pocket.

"In what way?"

"As with our *friend*, Dahlia. When I was a kid, men were men and women were women. That's the way it is, or was, but it's not that way anymore. I see it all the time in the entertainment business, but I don't understand it. I don't remember it being like that. I don't want to be judgmental, but it don't seem right. I guess you got to be who or what you are, but I don't get it. Do you, Buttman?"

"I don't know. I think maybe it's always been like this, we just didn't see it. People held back to stay out of trouble. Maybe now they feel more secure, at least enough to be more open about it. I've found over the years that people are into a lot of different things and always have been. We just didn't know about it because it was safer to keep it hidden. Sometimes it surprises me, but I've become more live and let live over the years. Besides, they're not going to change one way or another on my account."

"Maybe so."

We sat there enveloped by the cacophony of coffeemakers, yakkers, and people hunched over computers. Like a flock of birds together, but in their separate cages, an aural and visual testament to the private/public miasma of the western materialist zeitgeist. I didn't care for it and wanted to leave. Jones, unlike the day before, appeared to be in no great hurry regarding Ms. Marshan. He had found his phone and was enmeshed in its many timely messages.

"So what's our next move, Superfly?"

At last, a smile. "I'm more a Shaft than a Superfly."

"Alright, I'll give you that, and I'll play along, so what do we do now, Mr. Jones?"

"Maybe we shadow this Dahlia woman, see if she's on the up and up."

"I don't know." I didn't find the idea of waiting around and spying on Dahlia appealing. There had to be something else. "If as you say, you know people in the police department, maybe you should ask what they think is going on here."

He returned the phone to his pocket. "What do you mean?"

"Come on, don't you think this whole thing is a little off? Why are the two of us doing this? Neither of us has any compelling background in finding people. A guy is brutally murdered and you and I are after the killer for a measly twenty-five grand?"

"Yeah, so?"

"Yeah, so maybe there's something else going on. Yesterday, you were all worked up about how this is fucking up your business model, that maybe Dulcimer was poaching your talent. Yet today you seem not to care. Makes me think that after I dropped you off, you had a little heart to heart with Dulcimer. If you did and you got your money, what's your interest now? Keeping an eye on me, a nobody? Or maybe you've realized a lot of people are looking for this woman and there might be some real money to be had in finding her."

"Yeah, maybe..."

"So maybe the cops have some ideas that can help us."

"In what way?"

"Like in whether we should get the hell out of it."

Jones let the wheels spin. At some point this silly little enterprise would either get serious or burn out and that depended on our willingness to play our cards. Mine made no sense, and I had the sinking suspicion I was a patsy doing nothing more than busy work until my usefulness as a patsy ended at which time I might be squished like a bug. Jones was tighter with his motives, which considering how little we knew each other made more sense to me even if it didn't help.

"I know a few people downtown who hear a lot of things. I can ask around. And you, what are you going to bring, Monk Buttman, private dick?" He said this as condescendingly as he could. I couldn't blame him for seeing me as an unhelpful appendage.

"I have some ideas. I'll start with Agnes. She might know why Dulcimer would care about this former porn queen."

"That's some idea, but I guess it'll have to do." He pulled the sunglasses from his coat. "Might as well get to it." We left the bustling hive of the caffeinated. I glanced over at the LGBT outreach center. Dahlia watched as we were leaving. I considered waving, but thought it too soon. We weren't that close.

I moved here for the anonymity, to get away from the stultifying conservatism my mother and former wife had fallen into. I didn't mind the church stuff so much as the demands that I join them in this new calling; one I didn't find all that different from the old calling, other than what you were now for or against. From freak to fascist as the old man would say. I didn't care for his rigidity in fighting the Man any more than my mother's rigidity in embracing her particular brand of religious conservatism. I was tired of them, ruralism, and wanted to live in the city where no one knew your name. My idealized vision did not include traffic and every moment out on the freeway reminded me of this. Jones, laconic and dismissive, had fallen into a kind of vehicular narcoleptic state leaving me to the least attractive feature of urban living. Mercifully, his phone went off.

"Yeah, this is Jones." He turned to me with what I perceived to be a withering expression mostly hidden behind the shades. "It's for you, Buttman!"

I took the phone. "Monk Buttman."

"Mr. Buttman, this is Taylor Lagenfelder."

"Yes, Ms. Lagenfelder, what can I do for you?"

"We'd like you to go to the Delashay house and pick up some documents for us. Apparently, she'd rather not come down to our offices, and if I may anticipate your next question, Mrs. Delashay, and I quote, specifically asked if that nice Mr. Buttman could come up."

The patsy party was gathering company.

"Really?"

"We'd appreciate your taking care of this, Mr. Buttman. You can drop off the documents at the front desk."

"No back door drop offs anymore?" I was sorry I couldn't see her face as she responded to my question.

"No, for now that position is vacant. If you have any questions, please give me a call."

"I'll do that." I returned the phone to Jones. He was still giving me the look. "It's on the list, I promise."

"Yeah, no doubt." I had reached our exit, coasting easily to the curb. I let Jones out and watched as he walked away shaking his head.

Good times.

Judith was waiting at the door. An attractive young Hispanic woman stood by her side. Her name was Theresa and she was on her way out.

"Goodbye, Mrs. Delashay, I'll be back on Tuesday."

"We'll see you then." The young woman had a beautiful smile. I watched as she walked along the curved driveway paved with stone. Judith slipped her arm around mine and pulled me close to her as Theresa disappeared behind the Bougainvillea, "Come have a drink with me, Monk, it's another glorious day and I could use the company."

We went into the house, round the kitchen, and out to the pool. It was indeed a glorious day. Judith wore a white dress that fit her lithe figure as you would expect of an expensive piece of clothing, neither too tight nor too loose. The material had an almost hypnotic quality as she brushed against me. It was soft and cool and seemed to demand that it be caressed. Her fingers ran along the cut of my jacket sleeve as she led me to the bar in the cabana by the pool. The pool itself sparkled in the sunlight as a light breeze kissed the trees that bordered the north end of the yard. I took off my jacket and placed it on the back of a recliner. I had time before my other pressing engagement.

"I hope you're not in any particular rush," she said as she handed me my drink.

"I have an appointment later this evening, but my afternoon is open."

"I'll try not to spoil it then."

There was a divan along the north side of the pool just off the wind kissed trees. Having collected our drinks, we sat down to enjoy the weather, the surroundings, and each other.

"Ms. Lagenfelder told me you had some documents for me to pick up."

Judith lay back on the divan. A playful smile curled her lips as she spoke.

"I do, but mostly I had a desire to see you again. Our talk the other day got me thinking, and with Martin having run off, it occurred to me that we might have an opportunity to continue where we left off. I hope you don't mind the pretext."

"A beautiful day with a beautiful woman, I can't imagine a better way to spend the afternoon. I might be a little surprised that you'd think of me, but I'm not going to think too hard about it." She moved next to me, our shoulders together. Her hand found the edge of my slacks with her fingers moving in a slow circle.

"I don't judge men solely by their material status if that's your concern. I like men who appeal to me intellectually and physically regardless of whether they can, quote, afford me as my delinquent husband might say. For me, it's enough that I find you attractive, like what you have to say, and we'll let the afternoon take us where it will."

I leaned in. Her lips were soft as she pressed them to mine. A long kiss and the scent of her perfume and I couldn't help but put my arms around her.

"It's good to see that you share my enthusiasm for the sensual pleasures," she said as her hand caressed the edge of my erection.

"I'd be a fool not to. Should we move inside?"

"No, I like it out here. It's quiet and secluded. If someone wants to watch us that badly, I say let them."

Whether a smart move or not, and at this point who was I to judge, we undressed each other and pursued our sensual passions. Judith was a woman who knew what she liked and knew what men liked. I caught on quick that it had been a while since she'd been with a man. Evidently, life with Martin was a sexual dead-end, but given his outburst the other day, that didn't surprise me. Just because they looked good together didn't mean they were good together. The sex had an easy flow to it with an undercurrent of need. I liked that she wasn't shy about what she wanted me to do. I preferred not to guess, but it's not like I didn't know what I was doing. I felt a little self-conscious with my naked butt for all to see. Out in the great wide open wasn't where I normally enjoyed sexual activity. Judith enjoyed it, liked being naked. When we were finished she stood before me in all her glory.

"How about a swim?"

"Straight up?"

She laughed. "I never wear a suit in my own pool. Jump in." In she went, and in I followed. The water was warm and inviting. I floated along the edge as Judith swam slowly, back and forth, up and under. After a few minutes she drifted over, sliding up next to me. I closed my eyes as she ran her hand across my chest and stomach.

"How did you like your rich piece of ass?"

"I liked it very much. And you how did you like your poor piece of ass?"

"It hit the spot." I felt her hand land on my cock. "Any interest in another turn of the wheel?"

"Only if we can eat something when we're done, I haven't had any food today."

"I'm sure there's something in the kitchen. Now, up on the ledge..."

I did what I was told.

I try not to think too much about where I find myself, preferring to let life roll along. Still, the last few days had a certain unreal quality about them. Today was no different. After spending the morning with a black man I didn't know trying to ply information out of a suspicious transgendered woman I didn't know, I was watching a beautiful wealthy woman make me a sandwich buck-naked after sex outside by the pool. As I said, she liked being naked. This, she said, was her preferred state, something that Martin detested. I got the distinct impression she wouldn't miss him should he never return. I couldn't complain too much, all I had on was my underwear.

"Here you go. I hope you like it." She placed the two sandwiches on the table and sat down beside me.

"I'm sure I will." It was a turkey sandwich with lettuce and cranberries, and it was very good.

"Have you ever had lunch with a naked woman before?"

"Not that I can remember. Most of the women I've known had body image issues. So wandering around without clothes other than for sex wasn't their thing."

"If it bothers you, I can put on a pair of panties." I looked her up and down. She simply smiled.

"It's alright by me." The sandwich was now a memory. "I get the feeling you don't expect Martin to come waltzing through the door."

"Why do you say that?"

"He might not like to see you naked with the courier."

"I could care less what Martin likes. Would you like another sandwich?"

"No, that was plenty. Thank you very much."

"You're welcome. I'm glad you liked it."

I got up and collected the plates and glasses. I assumed our day was done. "It was very good."

She stood by the table staring out towards the pool and the city beyond. "Do you have to leave?"

"No, I don't have to. I have a couple of hours before I have to get ready." I felt her move next to me.

"Why don't you stay a little longer? Our little swim wore me out and a nap sounds nice. What do you say? You can clean up here before you go."

"It's very tempting and I'm having a hard time saying no. Why don't I follow you?" She took my hand and we returned to the cabana. A chaise lounge big enough for two under cover of an awning beckoned.

"We don't want to get sunburned, now do we?" This from a woman with no tan lines.

"No, we wouldn't want that."

We settled in as best we could, being relative strangers. As she nestled beside me, I watched the clouds take their time traversing the sky, listened to the trees shimmy in the breeze, and wondered what the hell I was doing. So far being a patsy had its upside. The barren wastelands of loneliness had opened onto a sea of delightful creatures and sensual pleasures. If this was the end of the line, I saw no reason to complain. Whether this was the penultimate moment all the diffused directionless roaming of the last few years led to, I didn't know. Maybe Judith had ulterior motives, maybe not. I wasn't going to press the issue. It was easy, simply to be a convenient passerby in a nice suit with a willingness to say yes. Like I said no reason to complain.

"You're not much of a talker, Monk."

"I thought you wanted to nap?"

"Rest, I'm not necessarily sleepy."

"I see. Then what would you like to talk about?"

"Anything other than business or money, that's all that Martin cared about."

"It got you all of this, didn't it? So, materially, it has its benefits."

"Yes it does."

Talk of money and Martin made Judith pull in closer, if that was possible. I continued to be conscious of her breasts pressing against my chest and my wandering hand on her naked hip. I tried to think of something else.

"The fuzz questioned me..."

"The fuzz?"

"Sorry, bad habit. The police questioned me about Martin."

"Did they? What did you say?"

"I was advised to be honest, so I told them what I know. Do you think he's disappeared?"

"Would you be shocked if I hope he has?"

"Not particularly, but wouldn't you be concerned that he'd take the money and run?"

"No. He might be able to take some of it, but the rest requires my acquiescence, and he's not getting that. I don't know why Marsyas felt the need to alert the police. Martin has taken off before and he's always come back."

"Maybe whatever he saw the other day spooked him?"

"Maybe, Martin certainly has his tics, but I don't want to talk about Martin, if he's gone, good riddance. More than likely he's run off to one of his little whores. They can have him. I want to talk about you, Monk Buttman."

"What about me?" Once again her hand was caressing my leg.

"What kind of name is Monk Buttman? It's not particularly common or complimentary."

"It's just a name."

"Really, what was your father's name?"

"The old man's name is Moses."

"No last name?"

"Bohrman."

My naked companion lay back on the lounge. Life had been good to Judith Delashay, if I held up as well as she had, I'd run around naked too.

"I see. So tell me something about yourself, Monk Buttman. You weren't always a courier, or whatever your role at A and A is. Have you always been this amicable? Any overt ambitions thwarted? Children? Wives? Girlfriends?

Deep dark secrets you've hidden in the recesses of your heart?" Her hand took mine and was using the fingers to fondle her breast.

"Why the interest?"

"I'm nosy. Now own up." She next put my fingers, one by one, in her mouth, slowly sucking on them. It was a little distracting.

"Well, if you must know..."

"I must!" She snickered between fingers.

"...I've never been terribly ambitious. Some of that comes from my upbringing on a collective. Ambition was for dictators and slaves of the state in order to propagate and perpetuate the capitalist materialist machine. I promised I would never be a part of that. I have one child, a daughter named Rebekah, named after my mother. She lives back east with her husband, a man named Farrell. I've never been legally married, but I was with Rebekah's mother, Astral, for more than twenty years till we had a falling out over my lack of righteousness before the Lord. I left so she could marry her conservative boyfriend, Judah.

"There was a time when I was very angry but life kind of burned that out of me. As for the name, it came to me when I was a teenager, as sort of a joke, but I kept it for reasons I can't adequately explain. It is what it is, I suppose. I grew up farming, and that's what I did for years because it was good honest labor and something a man could be proud of, the words of Moses verbatim. I came back to California because I wanted to get away from the past, to be anonymous, to be forgotten. I'm not leading man material. I think that sums things up nicely. And you, what about Judith Delashay?"

Judith Delashay rolled onto her side, back up against me.

"Where to begin. I grew up in Ann Arbor, Michigan, came out here for school. That's where I met Martin. He and his roommate, a man named Jeremy, had a software business and they came up with this security program that they sold for a lot of money. We got married. I was a party girl for a while when I was young and stupid, probably as a reaction to Martin's not wanting children and his increasingly odd behavior. Then I became a respectable patron of the arts, which gives me something to do. And for the record, I don't commonly have sex with any man in a nice suit and an easy smile."

"If you don't care for Martin, why not leave or get a divorce?"

The question took away the light in her eyes.

"I don't have a good or easy answer for that. I should, and at some point I probably will, but for now it's too complicated and I don't have the desire to fight with him over it; maybe someday." Her head found my shoulder and we lay there quietly, her need for answers sated.

I closed my eyes expecting to wake up somewhere else. Didn't happen.

"You can use Martin's bathroom to clean up. It would piss him off to find out you used it without his permission." Judith directed me to the door on the other side of the pool.

Martin's bathroom was large with a tiled shower, mahogany cabinets, and marble sink. No tub. The towels, Judith informed me, were in the closet. It was there I found it. A computer tablet was partially hidden behind the towels. On it I found pictures, lots of pictures, but, surprisingly, not an access code or password required. I only had to scan a few to get what Martin was into. I put the tablet back.

The shower blasted me from all angles as I tried to figure out the controls. If nothing else, I came out completely clean, no crevice untouched. From his vast collection, I bummed some aftershave and cologne. I was ready for date number two after a quick stop at A and A. Judith met me at the door and escorted me to the front of the house. A long kiss goodbye from the still naked woman, a handful of papers, and I was on my way.

11

I rolled in front of Agnes's house a little after six.

I worried I might be late as it occurred to me I should bring something. Wine, I can do wine. Then it was time to drop off Judith's correspondence. The young man at A and A had taken the papers with little more than a grunt and a certain amount of churlishness, as the papers were not contained in the proper envelope. I wondered if the papers were of any importance. It didn't matter, and it didn't keep me from whatever was awaiting me inside the comfortable little house Agnes called home. The curt young man had an envelope and I was on my way.

Agnes opened the door and smiled. It clashed with the evident anxiety on the rest of her face. "You look quite handsome, Monk, come in." It was apparent that she had been cleaning, the house looked immaculate. It made me feel rather important. I handed her the wine.

"And you look very beautiful tonight, Agnes. I like what you've done with your hair." She had pinned her hair back at the sides so it still fell on her shoulders, but was out of her face. I was certain she had trimmed her bangs: they danced just above her eyebrows. The compliment was more than fine words; she did look beautiful. A sparkly white top and lavender skirt accentuated those wonderful curves.

"Thank you, I worked on it all day, just for you." It was good to see the anxiety fade a little.

"Then I'll be on my best behavior."

"Well, let's not get carried away." I felt her hand take mine as she drew in close to me. "You smell wonderful, Mr. Buttman." I leaned in and kissed her. Those lips still tasted good.

"It's just something I thought I'd try. I'm glad you like it." I had no idea what it was. It smelled nice, so I put some on. I probably shouldn't say where. "What would you like to do tonight?"

"I'm making dinner. Then we can talk about where our relationship is going. No pressure."

"Yeah, sooner or later these things come up, best not to wait. Whatever you're cooking, it smells good."

"It's my friend's recipe. Not to alarm you, but cooking isn't one of my strong suits. I was assured I could not screw it up. I have my fingers crossed. Would you like some wine?"

"I would. The guy at the store told me it was good stuff. His words. I can't think of a better endorsement from a liquor store sommelier than good stuff."

Agnes laughed. "Have a seat. I'll get some glasses and the wine opener. I'm not very good with those either. Just so you know."

The house was a small craftsman built in the early part of the last century. It was the house version of my bungalow, small and efficient. The entry opened to the living room with the dining room off to the right. Behind a wall was the kitchen, which had been remodeled, but not enlarged. Three bedrooms and two baths were down the hall, none of them very spacious. Agnes had more furniture than I did, most of it Mission style. A sofa, loveseat, and chair surrounded a coffee table. Two companion tables adorned the sofa and loveseat, both with a small glass lamp. Agnes, as promised, returned with two wine glasses, an opener, and a smile. She handed them to me.

"If you don't mind, that way we don't end up drinking bits of cork."

"No, we wouldn't want that."

She sat beside me on the loveseat and watched as I liberated the cork from the bottle. It was plastic. "Interesting, isn't it. It's actually better than cork. Plus, it doesn't crumble. Have no fear."

"Maybe, but I still prefer to have someone else do it." We both took a drink and wondered what we should do next. The dude was right, it was pretty good stuff. A soft kind of quiet pervaded the room as we listened to each other breath.

Agnes cracked first.

"Dinner's ready if you're ready. It's just a crock-pot meal. I hope that's ok, nothing special. It's meat and vegetables and MaryAnn's ingredients. She said just throw it in and let the cooker do its magic. There's also salad and rolls, if you like." Her nervousness was back. The confident Agnes from the office seemed to slip in and out of the room. This was the Agnes from the other morning, self-conscious and unsure.

"Then we should eat."

We took our glasses and discomfort to the dining room. Two places were set with plates, napkins, and silverware. There were candles and a small centerpiece of flowers to compliment the settings. Agnes took the salad out of the fridge and set it on the counter with the dressing, a type of vinaigrette. There were rolls in a basket. With plate in hand I helped myself to the stew in the crock-pot, the salad and the rolls. I could feel her watching as I navigated through the kitchen and our second get together. It was our first real date minus the drunken dancing sex of the other night. There was still time for more of that. I pushed the memory of Judith to the back of wherever my brain stores such things, one step at a time.

We sat down. She watched as I took a bite of the crock-pot stew. MaryAnn knew her stuff. It was good.

"How is it?" Hope springs eternal.

I smiled at Agnes. "It's very tasty."

The nervousness lessoned as she took a bite. "It is good. God bless, MaryAnn."

"You were worried?"

"A little, I've never really had to cook. Simon did the cooking. He's a chef. He and his partner have a restaurant in San Francisco."

"Simon was your husband?" Agnes' eyes darkened. I had the feeling Simon would come up often.

"He was the proverbial love of my life. I shouldn't talk about Simon. MaryAnn told me to avoid bringing him up. Talking about your exes isn't good when you meet someone new."

"That depends on whether you see me as a substitute or a fresh start. Joanie told me that. She's well versed in how to screw up a new relationship by living in the past."

"Is Joanie one of your exes?"

A kind of nervous laugh came out of me, causing me to choke on the bit of salad I had in my mouth. "No, I was more of a summer fling. We weren't together long enough for her to be a proper ex. We're friends. Joanie's never been married or had a true longtime relationship. She's one of those women who's in a perpetual search for her perfect man. She's been with Mikal now for about a year, which is eons for her, so she's starting to get nervous because he might actually be the one. Anyway, we talk a lot about love and sex and death, but there's nothing between us anymore." I was rambling. The look on her face made me wish I hadn't brought Joanie into the conversation.

"How'd you meet her?"

"We're neighbors." That should help. "My point is you shouldn't feel you can't talk about Simon, or anyone else. I'm not that judgmental or skittish. Besides, these things are bound to come up, and it's good to know how you feel and where you're coming from."

"Yeah, I guess that's true."

We finished dinner in relative silence.

I watched as she cleared the table, and cleaned the plates. I poured the two of us another glass of wine. As a rule I try not to let too many idle thoughts crawl through my head. It serves no purpose other than to complicate matters. It was obvious Agnes liked me; just as it was obvious she was struggling not to come off as rushing things, or asking too many personal questions. It was probably best not to push the Simon issue. If she wanted to talk about it fine, if not, then I wouldn't bring it up. Still, I have a natural interest in people's lives. Makes figuring them out easier, and Simon might explain a lot about Agnes.

I made sure the wine followed us back to the living room. This time we settled onto the sofa. Agnes turned to me.

"So how was your day?"

Hmmm, what to say?

"My day. Well, I met the always-loquacious Mr. Jones. We went to Hollywood to talk to a distrustful transgendered woman about a missing ex-porn star. Then I ran an errand to pick up some papers from a rich woman whose husband has, apparently, gone missing. Kind of a quiet day, all things considered. You?"

"I spent the day cleaning and not over thinking things."

"Over thinking what?"

"Things. Your day sounds more interesting."

"Maybe if I'd actually learned something. I'm thinking detective work isn't my calling."

"At least you're willing to try. Mr. Jones isn't bad once you get to know him. In fact, he's really a big teddy bear. He just does the badass thing to help business. We should go hear his guys play; they're very good, very soulful." I was trying to imagine Jones as a teddy bear. "If you don't mind my asking, how did the woman look? Was she passable? I've always been curious. Simon knew a number of transvestites, performers, some of whom looked just like a woman. Did she have big tits?" She wiggled hers as she said this. The wine was getting to me. All I could think of were her beautiful breasts.

"Um… I didn't look that close, but she looked like a woman to me. She was tall and thin with blond hair and small breasts."

"That's probably good. These things tend to draw the wrong crowd." She shook them again for effect or to see if I was paying attention. I was.

"I'll try to behave, but they are quite lovely." Every woman loves to hear that.

"And the rich woman, did she have big tits?" Agnes seemed to have a thing for big tits.

"Well, I wasn't there to socialize or to ogle, but no, she didn't have big tits either. I'm afraid you're it." She was loosening up; I got a laugh out of that.

"It's nice to stand out in a crowd."

"I'm not going to complain." I took a drink of wine. "Now that we're relaxed, why don't you tell me something about yourself?"

"Like what?" She was still smiling, so I assume we were good.

"Oh, like how long have you worked for Dulcimer? What were you like as a child? Did your ex spend a lot of time with transvestites? Why were you nervous when I came over, stuff like that. No pressure." Now I was smiling.

"Tell you what, why don't you go first. That way I'll know what to own up to and what to omit, just in case there's a get together after this."

I took a deep breath and started babbling.

"If you must know, I'm a self-professed nobody. Before that I was a co-op farmer, supplying fresh produce to high-end restaurants and stores. Before that, I was born and grew up on a farm run by a group of freaks led by my father. My parents were both from deeply conservative Christian families and both rebelled in their teens. My mother left when I was ten after my father started sleeping with another woman. I fell in love with a girl named Astral when I was seventeen; we had a daughter, and then fled to the east coast after I had a fateful encounter with the local pushers. After my relationship with Astral fell apart, I decided to make a fresh start as no one in particular and ended up out here. Your turn."

"Wait. I have a few questions."

"You only get two."

"Two? I don't think that's fair, but all right. What happened with Astral, and why would you want to be a nobody?"

"Good questions." As a theatrical move, I rubbed my chin for effect. "The Astral question is the easiest, and perhaps the more painful. My mother, after having rebelled, decided that she missed God and went back to the church. Astral and I needed someplace safe to raise Rebekah, that's my daughter; she was named after my mother against my wishes. So we moved to Virginia. My mother agreed to take us in with a few provisos. One, we had to go to church, and two, we had to get married. We did the first thing, which ultimately split us apart because Astral took to it far more than I did. We never officially got married, but made vows to each other in the church. For a while, that was good enough. We were together for almost twenty years. But like a lot of people who get together young, we grew apart. She wanted me to be more devout and I wanted to be left alone. She met a man at church that she wanted to be with, and long story short, now she is."

"And the nobody part?"

"That's just code for my personal philosophy. I don't feel the need to be anybody anymore. I'm perfectly happy being a nobody. I'm not interested in being rich or famous or even remembered. I'm comfortable living day-to-day, enjoying life for what it is, not what society thinks it ought to be. I have enough money to do what I want, and I live a frugal enough existence so that if I want to spend the week at the beach or reading or roaming the land, I have the freedom to do that. It's cost me some relationships because women are suspicious of what that means or want a man who is more ambitious. That's ok. There are plenty of guys like that out there. I'm just not that guy. I hope you don't find that too disappointing."

Agnes rubbed her chin to mock me.

"I know you said I only get two questions, but I have another, how about a gimme?"

"Alright, but only one. I think you're avoiding your turn."

"Oh, I would never do that, and I'm serious here; are you comfortable with your sexuality, and are you a player? I have good reasons to ask, but I need to know before we go any further." That anxious look had returned.

"Interesting. The answer is yes, and no. Now you have to explain your question."

Agnes's eyes glistened and the light in them danced as she began to speak. "Where to start. I had a speech all ready, but I'm not very good at talking about myself, mainly because it's embarrassing." She tried to laugh, but it didn't come out right. "Sorry."

"Don't be. If you don't want to talk about it that's ok."

"No, I shouldn't be afraid to bring it up. It is what it is. I want this to be a fun evening, but I get nervous sometimes." At least she was smiling.

"There's no reason to be nervous around me. I'm a nobody remember."

"I remember, but you seem like a really nice nobody. I had a wonderful time the other night and I wanted to find out if it was real or if I was hallucinating. And you didn't answer the phone when I called about you coming over, so I didn't know if you really wanted to or if it was just a sex thing. I don't know. Anyway, I had a perfectly normal childhood; at least that's how I prefer to remember it. I met Simon in school. He was very attractive, smart, athletic, funny. We got married right out of high school and I thought we were living a perfectly normal life. I mean I didn't have any complaints. I would have liked a little more sex but I didn't know any better. We had two kids, a boy and a girl, Barron and Anna. Simon was busy; he worked a lot of nights being in the restaurant business and I assumed he was tired, but it turned out he was seeing someone else."

She paused, looking out towards the living room window.

"He told me he was confused and needed time to work things out. I was confused as well. He was involved with a cabaret performer, a man named Eric, whose stage name was Penelope. Apparently, he'd always been attracted to men, but he told me he liked women too. I was stunned. It was like the world stopped turning. I didn't know what to do. We tried to keep things going, but his heart wasn't in it. About that time I met MaryAnn at a counseling session. Her son is gay. She took me to Johnny's for a drink, and that where I met him. We'd meet for drinks to commiserate about our disappointments. After Simon left, I needed a job, and Johnny said I could work for him. He also helped me get this house. He's been a godsend."

"That's nothing to be embarrassed about."

She genuinely laughed at that.

"Oh, there's more. After being dumped by my gay ex-husband, I made things worse by dating a guy fifteen years younger than me, Jordan. He was cute and he did like sex with women, but he also liked sleeping around. Nobody liked him. Not my kids, not MaryAnn; even Johnny expressed concern, but I wouldn't listen. I needed to be loved and desired and so what if he was a little unfaithful and a liar. It wasn't 'til he tried to sleep with my daughter that it all came crashing down. She left to live with Simon. My son left for the Army. Even MaryAnn was mad at me for a while. Johnny said he knew what people were like and I should listen to him." Agnes put her hand on my face. "I asked him about you, you know."

"Me?"

"Yes, you! Anyway, for a long time I hid out in the bar, staying safe with Rey and MaryAnn, but I was lonely. I haven't had a steady date in more than two years. I thought you were interesting, so I asked Johnny what he thought. He said I could do worse. I have done worse. That makes me nervous." She took my hand and held it in hers. "I'm anxious because I like you, because I'm lonely, because you like to dance, because you're fun to talk to, because you made me breakfast. But I don't want to scare you away or weird you out or seem like I'm totally desperate. How's that."

"It's enough." She was sweet and yeah, she was a little desperate, but I didn't mind. I needed a steady date too. I leaned in and kissed her, and when she kissed back, we slid onto the sofa in our mad embrace.

"Will you make me breakfast in the morning?"

"Only if you let me stay the night."

"It's a date."

We rolled off the sofa and made our way to the bedroom.

12

Our second time around was more intimate and personal. Agnes slept right next to me and was relaxed and playful when she woke up.

"Got any plans today?"

"Yeah, I'm going to take a shower."

"Sounds exciting."

"That's the way I like it, baby."

"I can see that. Would you like some company? To save water, we're in a drought, you know."

"I've heard that. If you'd like to join me, I won't say no."

The shower wasn't built for two, but we didn't care. We were both joyfully jumping into the deep end with one another. Why not, age and loneliness will do that to you. There's nothing like a soft warm woman longing to hold you tight. Two in twenty-four hours was new for me. I didn't quite know what to do other than go with it. Somewhere in my febrile little mind I knew it was the road to ruin, but I'd save that for another day. I was floating between the two of them. Judith was fun, but I didn't see that going anywhere; there was no guarantee I'd even see her again. Agnes was different, more my speed.

I watched as she devoured her breakfast. There was plenty to prepare in the fridge unlike the last time I cooked for her.

"You know, cooking's not that difficult. I'm sure you could master it with a little practice." She was dressed in a bathrobe, underwear, and a towel around her wet hair.

"I know, but I have an irrational fear about it."

"I'm listening..."

"My fear is if I learn to cook, I'll be condemned to a life of loneliness."

"Really, interesting..."

"I did use the word irrational!"

"Yes, you did use that word. Can I ask why?"

She thought about it for a moment, playing with the hem of her bathrobe as she slouched in her chair. "I don't know, I guess it's like a lifeline or maybe a pacifier; something to count on or save me from something I couldn't or wouldn't say out loud. I like to believe there's someone out there for me willing to do the small things that I'm not good at. If I can do all the things I need, then what do I need someone else for? I can do by myself..." Her eyes were intent as she looked at me. "But I don't want that. I don't want to be self-contained and independent. I want to be part of something, even if I have to wait or search for it. I spent years with Simon certain that with enough time and patience what I wanted would finally happen, that it would work out. How could he leave me if I couldn't feed myself? And yes, I know how pathetic that sounds, but even these years alone haven't changed my mind."

"So you'll never learn to cook?"

"I'm a stubborn woman, Monk Buttman."

"I'll be mindful of that. Can I get you anything else while I'm up?" I was rising to collect the last of the eggs and sausage for my empty plate.

"A little more coffee would be nice."

"Coffee it is."

The phone began to ring as I poured the coffee. Like all-important electronic essentials, it was by her side.

"Yes?" A soft smile found her lips. "Yes, Mr. Jones, the delightful Mr. Buttman is here." The smile widened as she held the phone to her ear. "Yes, I think he should too. Would you like to talk to him?"

She stood and handed me the phone.

"For me?"

She acted shocked.

"Mr. Jones is married, we only talk at work." I took the phone, watching as she sat back down. Her bathrobe had loosened and her delightful breasts were calling to me.

"Yeah?"

"It's a good thing I know a little about human nature, because I sure as shit don't enjoy tracking you down Buttman."

The warmth radiated through the phone.

"What can I do for you, Mr. Jones?"

"I got a call from that Dahlia woman, apparently she has more to say and wants to talk."

"So talk to her."

For an inanimate object, the phone was good at transmitting Jones' irritation.

"It's Sunday, Buttman, and I got church, and I damn sure ain't bringing some transgendered woman into my church. Besides, she wants to talk to you, so I gave her your address. She'll meet you there in an hour."

"And if I have something better to do, like church?"

"Then go to the afternoon service. One hour, Buttman; I'll be by later today so you can fill me in."

"It can't wait till tomorrow?"

"No."

The call was over. Sadly, these smartphones don't have that abrupt audible click at the end. I sat down to finish my meal.

"Bad news?" Agnes had finished her breakfast and was running her hands along the edges of the towel covering her head. This movement caused her bathrobe to continue its parting of the ways, exposing more of her breasts. The smile was still on her face. The towel came down along with the cascade of hair beneath it. She brushed it out with her fingers.

"Turns out I have a meeting with Dahlia in an hour. She has things to say, apparently just for me. So, I'll have to leave you here to fend for yourself."

Her smile turned to a pout. "I thought you might spend the day with me? Now you're going to run off to meet some strange woman."

"I have a thing for strange women. As for today, I thought so too, but sadly it's not to be. And looking at you now, I can't express how sorry that makes me."

"We're going to miss you." She stood. Her breasts were swaying gently from side to side.

"That doesn't help."

"I'm not here to help. I'm here to drive you wild." She shook her head to spread the hair about. Her breasts were now in full view.

"I appreciate that. I really do." Somehow the leftover food didn't seem very important. I pulled her to my side and kissed her while my hand found her breast.

"You can always come back later, if you like."

"I like." A tremendous dislike of Mr. Jones came over me as I fondled Agnes' wonderful breast. I did not want to go. I liked kissing this woman and wanted to continue. She did too. I could feel her hand fondling the zipper on my pants. "I'll try to make it a quick talk."

"I'll be here."

I reluctantly released her and headed for the door. She dropped her bathrobe as I looked back. I was finding it hard to walk. All I could see on the drive back was Agnes wearing nothing but a smile and a pair of white panties.

It was the high point of the day.

The door to my bungalow was open...

So I went in....

The first blow was a fist to the ribs, robbing me of my breath. That was followed by something crashing into the back of my head, sending me to the floor. I knew this was bad. Once on the floor there was little I could do to stop it. The next blow was a foot, boot, something hard and swift, to the face. My head recoiled, aching. I covered my face, obviously too late; curled up as best I could to ward off the kicks and stomps that were raining down upon me. There were two of them, swinging their legs at my head and torso. A few struck my legs. I heard voices and screaming along with the concussive reverberations of the air leaving my lungs as I was being beaten. There was blood in my mouth and I began to vomit. Something was being said, shouted, but I couldn't make it out. I thought I heard Joanie's voice. One word rang out amongst all the noise: Rosarita.

The attackers took off.

"MONK!"

It was Joanie, but I couldn't see her. My left eye was swelling shut and the right eye was covered in blood. I couldn't breathe. The vomit was collecting in my mouth, and I gagged as she tried to roll me over. It was then that I realized I couldn't breathe through my nose; it was bloody too. I tried to blow the crap out of my mouth so I wouldn't suffocate.

"They're coming, they're coming; hold on!"

"Who's coming?" I whispered. The pain was intensifying now that the beating was over. Any movement made it worse.

"The medics."

"I'm not going to the fucking hospital!" I spit this out along with more blood and vomit.

"I don't care if you don't want to go to the fucking hospital, you're going to the fucking hospital!"

Joanie was holding my hand. I was passing in and out of any coherent consciousness. I heard a siren in the distance, then people talking to me. I didn't know who they were, Medics? Something was put in my mouth and I could breathe again. The pain was exquisite as they put me on the gurney and then in the ambulance. I don't remember much else. There was a blur of activity once we arrived at the ER. The thing I remember most, other than wanting to die, was the euphoria as the morphine did its magic. After that I fell into a beautiful stupor. I knew I was fucked up but didn't care. The pain had receded. I was wheeled to several different places, and I think I remember being in a tube. I didn't care. It didn't matter; I was completely disconnected from reality. The pain, writhing in the background, was far enough away that I could stand it. At some point I fell asleep or passed out.

Joanie and a black man in a white coat were staring at me when I came back to earth.

"Mr. Buttman, how do you feel?" The doctor had the quiet demeanor and grace of a man not beaten to a pulp.

"I don't know how to answer that in a way that won't sound peevish or sarcastic. I'm numb and sore, it hurts to talk, and I feel like shit. But other than that, I feel like shit."

The man with the quiet demeanor smiled. "It's a good sign that you haven't lost your sense of humor. My name is Doctor DeMarius."

"When can I leave?" My voice was nothing more than a croaking whisper. I could barely make out the doctor's features. He was tall with what I assumed was a West African heritage. He reminded me of James. For a brief moment I thought to ask, but held back. He came closer and sat by the bed. Joanie hovered behind him. She looked both beautiful and sad which frightened me.

"Not for a while. On the positive side, given how badly you were hurt, we found no significant fractures or internal damage. However, you do have a concussion, lacerations, and a broken nose. We'll need to keep you here for at least another day or so."

"I see." I didn't want to be here, but I was stuck. Joanie would stand between me and the door. There was also the not so insignificant problem of how I was even going to get out of the bed. "So, I'm not going to make the orgy tonight?"

"No, I'm afraid you'll have to hold off on any sexual activity for a while."

"You're a killjoy, doc, a killjoy." He laughed at that.

"Sometimes it's a difficult job, Mr. Buttman. In any event, Marta is here to keep you on the straight and narrow till you're well enough to go home. I'll check in on you tomorrow."

The doctor with the quiet demeanor left. Joanie was next.

"I have to go too, sorry. I have a show, but I promise I'll be back later to make sure you're ok. You scared the shit out of me, Buttman. You look really bad, but I'm glad it's not worse. Get some sleep, I'll be back."

The woman I once wanted to marry left. Marta approached. She had the sincere face of a woman who'd been doing this for a long time. Having ensured the wires and tubes attached to me were as they should be, she put her hand gently on my shoulder.

"If you need me push this button." She put the nurse call box in my hand.

"Thanks."

She smiled and left me to my idiotic thoughts and beat-up body. I gave a moment of thanks that this didn't happen yesterday. If nothing else I had the memories of Judith and Agnes to get me through the next few days.

I lay there...

I hate hospital beds, you can't move! I'm a compulsive roller in bed. The fact that everything on my left side was battered made the night one long torture session. I couldn't sleep. The drugs kept me on just this side of consciousness. I concentrated on the sounds in the room; the air coming out of the diffuser, the clicks from the monitors; the muffled discussions I couldn't make out from the staff on the other side of the glass wall. Joanie did not come back, but I didn't expect her to. It was late and she would be tired after singing and having to put up with me. My thoughts drifted from place to place and person to person. Moses. Rebekah. Astral. Joanie. Judith. Agnes. Even the farm and Virginia came along for the ride.

James and Miguel. I pushed the button.

Marta came in, patiently listened to my whine about sleep, gave me a little something, and advised that I rest. Whatever she gave me did the trick. I awoke to find Joanie, Jones, and Mallory looking down upon me.

13

"I didn't do it." Nobody laughed. I was losing my touch.

"How are you feeling?" Joanie was the first to pipe up. Jones and Mallory stood back, both stone-faced. Marta was monitoring the bulk of company from just outside the door.

"Couldn't be better, but that might be the drugs talking. You?"

"You know, it's ok to say you don't feel good, Monk."

"I thought the fact that I'm black and blue and stuck in the ICU would pretty much confirm that, but if it makes you feel more sympathetic to my plight, then yes, I don't feel very good."

That got a smile from Jones. "You're being a dick, Buttman."

"I do what I can. And the rest of you, are you as concerned for my well-being?"

"I'm here to find out what happened. I expect the detective is too." Jones had his sunglasses on. That made me smile. It hurt to do so.

"I just have a few questions, Mr. Buttman. I'll talk to you later once you're more lucid." Mallory's voice hinted at a certain glee in seeing me in my present state.

"I'm lucid enough, fire away." I thoroughly wanted Jones and Mallory gone. If I had to be tied to this bed, better to have Joanie than the other two.

"Do you know who attacked you? Can you describe them? Any idea why they attacked you?" Fire away he did.

"Unfortunately, the answer to your questions is no. All I remember is that the door was open and when I went in the beating started. I don't know who they were. I didn't get a good or even a crappy look at them. I know they were wearing jeans because of how the kicks felt on my arms. They were screaming something about staying away, but I don't remember if they said from whom.

That's all I know, sorry."

"It'll do for now. Good day, Mr. Buttman." A quick nod and Detective Jackson Mallory departed. Jones, he of the monotonic expression, watched the detective make his exit before moving in my direction.

"Is what you told Mallory for real, or do you know more than you're telling?"

"And what did you tell Mallory, Shaft?"

"He didn't ask and I didn't tell," he said this with some exasperation.

"Then, with one exception, what I told Mallory was true. I don't know who they were or why they were there to kick the shit out of me."

"And the exception?" His veneer of cool was back.

"Are you worried? Maybe you're next."

He shook his head. "I'm not a babe in this business like you, Buttman. I know how to handle myself and know better than to enter a room if things don't look right. Are you goin' to tell me or not?"

For some reason I thought to shift my weight; it was a stupid thing to do. A sharp pain shot through the left side of my body and I visibly jerked. "Goddammit!" I cried, trying to catch my breath. Joanie came over and took my hand.

"Are you alright? Do I need to call the nurse?"

"No, I don't need the fucking nurse!" A wounded look crossed her face and a pang of regret joined the pain in my side. "I'm sorry, I don't mean to yell at you. I'll be alright. I just need to remember to ease into any new movement or change of position. It hurts, a lot."

Jones was unmoved. "Well?"

Joanie frowned at him but he didn't seem to care. He didn't want to be here any more than I did.

"Fine. I won't swear to it, but I'm almost certain I heard the name Rosarita while they were kicking the shit out of me."

He rubbed his chinny-chin-chin. "Do you think the Dahlia woman had anything to do with this?"

"I don't know, I never saw her. I guess it's possible."

"I'll find out." He turned towards the door. "I'll let you know when I know."

"You know where to find me?" He wasn't biting.

Joanie started to say something as Jones was walking away, but no sound came out. After he left she turned to me. "Who is that guy?"

"Mr. Jones. He and I are Jones and Buttman, hard-boiled private dicks."

"Really? I don't think you should hard-boil your dicks, but what do I know."

"Very funny."

"I thought so." She released my hand. "Now that I know the score, what are you two dicks up to?"

"Is that all you've got, dick jokes? Sad. I thought you'd have better material." I laid back on the bed and moaned. "But if you must know, we were thrown together as patsies in order to find a woman who took some money and to whom a number of rather powerful and connected men would like to talk."

"She's the one that killed that guy?"

"That's her."

"Is she this Rosarita?"

"Probably."

Joanie moved her chair closer to the bed so she could see the TV, which she promptly turned on. She liked the news. I detested it, corporate pablum for the masses hyping non-issues while ignoring the real problems percolating throughout this big country.

"You're a lot more interesting now that you're a hard-boiled private dick. Before you didn't have much in the way of stories. I guess that's pretty common for a nobody, huh?"

"I guess."

She turned towards the TV just as the good doctor arrived. He stood by the bed in all his serenity.

"Good news, Mr. Buttman, you no longer have to stay here in the intensive care unit. I'm having you moved to a regular patient room and if all goes well, and it should, you'll be able to go home soon, maybe as early as tomorrow."

"I'm thrilled, doctor."

"As you should be, Mr. Buttman. Marta tells me you got through the night without any additional pain medication. That's a good sign. Anything odd or different you've noticed since we talked yesterday?"

"No, the misery has been fairly consistent."

The good doctor smiled. "Excellent. I'll see you tomorrow."

I watched the doctor leave as Joanie watched explosions someplace in the Middle East. Death and destruction, the boilerplate of humanity was never stopping, never ceasing; a firmament on which we endlessly trod. Maybe it was the meds, the pain, or the never-ending cycle of war for the sole purpose of inflicting one group's insecurities on another that was getting to me. Whatever it was, I found it depressing.

"Isn't there anything else to watch, like a monster movie or a good old-fashioned white bread comedy?"

"No! Besides it's important to stay informed," she huffed.

"Informed of what? Who's popular, and who's killing who?"

"Exactly! Now be a good boy and shut up for a few minutes while I catch up on the latest, as you would say, trends, fashions, and fabrications of the ruling class."

This wasn't the first time we'd clashed on the topic, so the pickings for argument were lean. "And if I refuse?"

"I'll smack you where it hurts."

"That's a terrible thing to say to a man in my condition."

"It sure is. Now be quiet."

It was during these exchanges that I found her achingly beautiful. I thought about that; it hurt more than I thought it would. The next excruciating hour was filled with the usual dross of local and national bed-wetting, bad weather, sports, and a story of a valiant young man helping the poor by collecting teddy bears. I hate the news. This was followed by a syndicated comedy from the Nineties about nothing in particular.

I wanted a drink, whiskey in a tall glass. What I got was a slow drip through the tube in my arm. I was assured I should be able to have real food soon. I didn't care that my jaw was bruised and sore, I didn't care that some of my teeth were loose; I wanted something to eat! Joanie had a sandwich, chips, and a bottle of water. Envy crept into my heart.

She got up. "I have to go, Mr. Buttman, some of us have to work for a living." She graced me with that beautiful smile. Maybe it was the drip.

"Parting is such sweet sorrow, my love. It is with a heavy heart that I watch you depart from me this fine day."

She held my hand and softly kissed the cheek that wasn't purple and puffy.

"You're full of shit, Monk, but thanks anyway."

"I do what I can. See you tomorrow?"

"I suppose. How the hell else are you getting home?"

"Such sweet music do I hear; till then, my love, till then."

"Uh-huh. Get some sleep and easy on the meds." She let go of my hand and left me to my internal soliloquy. At the desk Joanie stopped to talk to Marta for a moment. Two young dudes in scrubs pushing a stretcher came to the room. Joanie disappeared in the distance.

"It's time to move you on out of here, Mr. Buttman. These fine gentlemen will do the driving." Marta disconnected me from the forest of monitors festooned around the room. "Is everything all right?"

"As long as I don't move, I don't feel too bad."

"Then you've discovered the keys to a good life. Take care, and don't let me see you in here again."

"Yes, ma'am."

The dudes carefully slid me from bed to stretcher, eased me out of the room, and delivered me to another part of the hospital.

It was a room for two.

Behind the curtain that separated us, I could hear the loud guttural snore that would keep me up all night. I tried earplugs to no avail. The only time the snoring ceased was when he coughed and gagged in hideous syncopation. Daylight brought no relief and death did not save me. The sunlight, filtered through the curtain, sprinkled the bed with the grim news that I did not get any sleep. Finally, in mid-morning, reprieve came in the person of the snorer's wife, who awoke him. She spoke softly, and it was then, mercifully, I fell asleep.

The bad motherfucker was standing by the bed, shades on, dome glistening in the fluorescent light. The nurse, needing my vitals, disturbed my restful bliss. My head ached with a feverish vengeance. As a remedy, a tablet and water was carefully ingested. Codeine and Tylenol began the work of soothing the pain radiating about my head like a crown of thorns. I wondered what my mother would think of such an analogy, blasphemy no doubt. It occurred to me that I hadn't talked to her in some time. Maybe I should. Kind of like the old man, out of sight, out of mind. Mr. Jones waited patiently for the nurse to finish before sitting down in a folding chair. We both noted the resumption of the sonorous deviltry from the man behind the curtain.

"That's some powerful noise! I don't know if I could deal with that for long," he said with some alarm.

"Yeah, it makes sleeping impossible." We took a couple minutes to truly appreciate the racket emanating from the other side of the room. It was an angry grate like metal on bone. "What's up? Did you find that woman Dahlia?"

Mr. Jones grinned at his favorite reference. "I did. Someone gave her a beating too, though not so bad. A couple of guys she said. Other than that she didn't say much. Or, I should say to me. She still wants to talk to you. Any idea why, Buttman?"

"I do have a few ideas, but you and I have to come to an understanding," I said as I twisted myself so that I could sit up in the bed. I uttered a few well-placed groans for effect. Jones made a half-hearted attempt to steady me, but I waved him away.

"You sure you should be doing that?" he asked.

I focused on him with my one non-swollen eye, "Probably not, but I'll survive. Since I'm expecting to be released today, I'm going to have to get moving whether I want to or not." The gown I was wearing came undone. Primly, I covered up my legs so as not to embarrass Jones assuming such things embarrassed him.

"And our understanding?" It was back to business.

I gave myself a moment to craft my response.

"I don't like getting the shit kicked out of me! I don't like it when I can barely see. I don't like it when every breath hurts or when sitting up is a fucking exercise in existential pain. It's one thing when we're flopping around like Abbott and Costello, but it's another when I come a few kicks from being a brain dead invalid. So you and I are going to come to terms over this little adventure of ours or I'm out, understand?"

"Yeah, I get it, no one likes to get the shit kicked out of them..." He leaned back in his chair.

"And?" I was getting impatient!

"And our friend, Detective Mallory is waiting. You're a popular nobody, Buttman. Tell you what; it's *my* understanding, having talked with the doctor, that they're letting you out at four. There's some concern about who's going to watch out for you..."

"Joanie will take care of me..."

"Yeah, except I spoke to her and she's got a gig in San Fran. So till she gets back, you need a sitter. You can stay with me for a few days. I talked to the wife, and she's ok with that so long as you don't have a problem being in a black neighborhood."

"Why would I have a problem with that?"

"Because people do, Buttman." Jones stood up and acknowledged the detective hovering outside the door. "We'll talk about our little adventure later." He passed Mallory with a nod. He had one more comment before he headed out.

"Agnes called."

14

Mallory watched Jones glide down the hall past the nurse's desk. I slid back on the bed, raising its head to better chat with my inquisitor. Mallory took the chair previously occupied by the bad motherfucker.

"Interested in talking with me for a few minutes, Mr. Buttman?"

"That depends on what you want, Detective Mallory."

He was much more casual this time. Unlike our previous meetings there was no threat in his voice or edge to his words.

"You don't care for the police do you?"

"I have a deep, yet personally unsubstantiated, antipathy as concerns the police, yes."

"And why is that?"

"Because the cops, the fuzz, the pigs are the head busting, jack-booted thugs that allow the white power structure to continue to oppress the people. They abuse their social contract, hide their miscreants from proper adjudication and reinforce all the ugly stereotypes permeating American society. They are the bugaboos of an American life where we want to be protected from the other guy, but not hassled about all the silly shit we do because everybody else does it too. I think, in short, that about covers it. Naturally, that flies in the face of the good cops I've gotten to know, but there are exceptions to every rule."

Mallory laughed as I finished.

"Excellent. However, you're a little young to be a sixties radical, so where did all this antagonism come from?"

"I got it from my old man, a true radical. He was a part of that time and did not hesitate to indoctrinate me in the way the world really works. And given all the stories I've heard about the police, it's fair to say it's not completely off the mark."

"Perhaps, or it's the long-haired pinko freaks, with no respect for the law, talking trash, throwing bombs, assassinating cops, and trying to overthrow the greatest country in the world who are the real pigs. Ever heard that side of the story?"

"I have. Son of a cop?" It was my turn to smile, or try to.

"Lifelong patrolman. I got to hear all about it growing up, through the academy and on the beat. Just like you, but in reverse. We're two sides of the same distrustful coin, Buttman."

"So we are."

We let that thought marinate as we sat there. I wasn't exactly sure what the good detective wanted. They didn't need me to find Desiree, Martin, or the missing money. Nor did it seem reasonable for a police detective, one assigned to the homicide squad, to wander down and inquire into the beating of a nobody. Mallory had other ideas, just as I did, our true coin of the realm.

"Have you found Desiree Marshan yet?" I was curious.

"Yet?" Ah, the smiling detective. "We've already talked to Ms. Marshan. As far as the department and the DA are concerned, the matter is closed."

"Didn't she kill Boyer?"

"She did," he said as if it were no big deal.

"And?"

"And what?" His instincts were showing and I had unwittingly owned up that maybe I knew more, but in truth, we both knew that.

"Is she in jail?"

"No, Ms. Marshan is not."

"So what happened?"

Mallory looked me in the one good eye, "You should know, you were there."

"Says who?"

"Come on, Buttman, this isn't my first rodeo. I know you know more than you've admitted."

"Maybe. Tell me what happened on your end, then we'll see if I have anything to add."

"If that opens your mouth..." He leaned back and crossed his legs. "Ms. Marshan, in a statement, told us that she killed Boyer because he was sexually assaulting her at knifepoint. She was found to have cuts on her neck and hands, and, during a medical exam, showed evidence of injuries consistent with sexual assault. In examining Boyer's body, we found physical evidence consistent with her statement."

"And Boyer?"

"She claimed he was harassing her at work and that the harassment increased after he found out about her previous employment in the adult film industry. She said he was threatening to have her fired if she didn't do what he wanted and that she feared for her life. This culminated in the attack in which she killed him. Apparently, he dropped the knife in the throes of orgasm, or something to that effect, and she picked it up and stabbed him to death. After she left, she turned herself in and provided her statement."

"I assumed you went through Boyer's effects to corroborate her allegations?"

"Nope, never occurred to us, Buttman." He shook his head. "We did, however, find a large number of files on Boyer's computer containing images and videos of Ms. Marshan. And staff members at Aeschylus and Associates reported that they heard Boyer making improper comments to Ms. Marshan."

"There wasn't any pushback from A and A, or Boyer's family?"

"No." Mallory raised his eyebrows for effect. "There was no interest in pursuing any other possible motives for what happened; not from the department, not from Durant. We've had no contact from the family. Everyone wanted it swept under the rug and forgotten."

"Don't you find that a little odd?"

"Why would I? There was nothing to indicate she was lying. You said you didn't know anything. The evidence collected corroborated her statement. Do you know something that would challenge that?"

"And if I did, would there be any support, from the department, the DA, Durant, or the Boyer family to pursue it?"

"Probably not, but that doesn't mean that I no longer care about what you have to say."

"I'm touched." I tried to smile; it hurt.

"You should be." His smile seemed oddly genuine.

So now what?

"I don't get it? If you have no loose ends, other than whatever I may or may not know concerning Boyer's death, why you're even here? It can't be the beating, I'm not important enough. I don't know anything relevant about Martin Delashay's disappearance, and I doubt it's my sterling personality or staunch support of the police."

"Let's just say it's for my own personal edification. There may be little I can do to reopen a case no one is interested in, but certain things don't add up. Unfortunately, they're tangential to the death of Boyer and with Durant pushing Goncalves I'm as much an outsider as you are. As for Martin Delashay, his wife assured us he's prone to disappearances and that we shouldn't be concerned. Apparently, he always returns. How's that?" Mallory leaned in. "Work with me on this. It's not a bad thing to know someone in the police department. I'm not a bad guy, Buttman."

I wonder how Moses would answer that?

"Yeah, I've known monsters who told me the same thing, but I'll be nice and won't lump you in with them, at least not yet. It's tempting, detective, very tempting. I still don't know why you think I know more than I say, but right now I can blame the drugs and if need be I can blame them later. Some things, for now, I'll keep to myself, mostly so if I'm full of shit I won't come across as a complete bozo, but I'll play." I slowly turned and sat up. This time the robe stayed put. "What do you want to know?"

"Is what you told me about Boyer's death complete?"

"Complete? Very diplomatic..."

"So why not tell what you do know, all of it?"

"Because influential individuals asked that I be discreet, I have to honor that. I'm small potatoes; I know my place, but you know that already. As for what I did not pass on initially, well that seems to be so everyone could get their story straight."

"And your story..."

"My story... I was returning the documents from Delashay when I walked in on them. I can't say, for sure, that it wasn't a sexual assault, but there were no cuts on Desiree Marshan, and I don't think this was the first time they'd engaged in what they were doing. The knife was in the desk drawer. She got mad when Boyer got cute about letting me watch and my taking a turn if I wanted. I don't think her killing him was premeditated, but I don't know for sure. Desiree was never a delightful character as far as I was concerned. I found her moody and petulant, but again that might just be me. After she killed him, she demanded a satchel that contained money and the documents I had. I gave her the money. I didn't care about that, but refused to turn over the documents. I don't think she knew what to do at that point, so she took off. I gave her five minutes and called security. That's my story."

Mallory mulled this over. "Why would she want Delashay's documents?"

"She wouldn't say, but she was pretty pissed off when I refused to turn them over."

"Weren't you afraid she might kill you too?"

"No. She was already freaked out after killing Boyer. The knife was on the floor, so I kicked it away. I didn't think she had the nerve to find the knife and kill me before I could stop her, all while half-naked and bloody."

"Do you know what was in the documents?"

"Not really."

"What does that mean?"

"It means I don't know."

"And the money, do you know how much was in the satchel?"

"Twenty-five grand."

"Know anything about that?"

"No."

"Seems like a lot of money to have in cash at a back office, don't you think?"

"I do, but I don't know what it was for. Maybe it was her payoff for grabbing the documents."

I was about to lie back down when a small intense looking woman in a doctor's coat came into the room. Mallory stood up and moved the chair back to the wall.

"Thanks for the opportunity, Mr. Buttman. You have my number, keep in touch."

Mallory left me to the care of the doctor. She asked how I was feeling. I replied that I was in pain, but felt better for the most part, all things considered.

I was almost ready to be introduced back into society.

In a matter-of-fact drone, she slowly went over my condition, the medications I would be given and the best way not to abuse them. She recommended a follow-up be scheduled and that physical therapy might not be a bad thing once I recovered enough for physical horseplay. I thanked her for her cogent application of medical professionalism. The nurse came in moments later to repeat everything the doctor had just said. She asked if anyone was picking me up and I replied that a big black man was coming to take me away. She smiled in a thoroughly condescending manner and promised to return later with everything I would need to get the hell out of here. I laid back on the bed and promptly fell into a dreamless sleep.

When I opened my eyes, Mr. Jones was waiting.

15

I don't know exactly what I was expecting as the always somber Mr. Jones drove me to his house. Having never spent any time in the black part of town, most of my expectations were of rundown buildings and homes with people hanging out on the street, as if I were in some movie from the Seventies. I felt completely out of place not only because of where we were, but with what I was wearing. My clothes had been removed and were unfit to wear anyway from the blood, sweat, and vomit covering them. Jones thoughtfully brought me a pair of baggy sweatpants and a tee shirt emblazoned with the words, Big Daddy. A wide grin covered his face as I gingerly put them on. They wheeled me out after I signed the required paperwork and carefully put me into Jones' minivan. To my rather chagrined surprise, his neighborhood wasn't any different than mine. His house was a ranch with a pleasant front yard. Mr. Jones' wife, son, and daughter were waiting for us as he pulled into the driveway.

His family was courteous and solicitous, helping me out of the car and into the house. I sat on the couch as they took their places around me, ready to inquire about the sad-assed white dude invading their personal space. The kids, both in their teens, quickly lost interest in my problems and disappeared; off, I assumed, to their own rooms. Mrs. Jones sat across from me.

"I don't know what exactly Orville has told you, but my name is Coretta." Orville?

"Like Coretta Scott King?" I asked.

"Yes, I was named after Dr. King's wife. My parents were deeply involved in the civil rights movement and wanted me to remember their struggle. I want you to know that you're welcome in our house."

"I appreciate your letting me into your home, Coretta. I promise not to overstay my welcome." Coretta smiled and took my hand. She was a statuesque woman with thick black hair and eyes that sparkled. Jones squirmed next to her. She didn't strike me as the kind of woman a bad motherfucker would marry, but then I didn't expect him to live in the burbs with a wife and two teenaged kids.

"I do have one rule, Monk..."

"Yes?"

"This is a Christian home, so I won't tolerate any foul or offensive language."

"Not to worry, I'll be mindful of what I say."

"I appreciate that. Orville, please show Monk his room."

Orville and I watched as Coretta left, moving towards the kitchen. Clearly Orville was a different person at home. I thought something was up when he arrived at the hospital. The clothes he wore were not black, but rather colorful and the glasses he wore were not evocative of a mid-Seventies black badass. He held out his hand.

"This way."

It was a tidy room with a twin bed covered by a flowery comforter that matched the curtains. A small table with a lamp and a bureau complemented the bed. The light from the window filled the room with a warm glow that made me want to rest my weary soul. As I had no baggage, of the material kind, there was nothing to find a home or place for. Mr. Jones eyed me as I gently lowered myself on to the bed.

"What time is it?" I asked. I had no idea and for some reason thought it important.

"It's a little after five. I expect we'll have dinner in a half hour or so."

"I'm not very hungry."

"Don't care, you need to eat." It was good to hear his patronizing tone, something familiar to hold on to. He handed me a small bag. "This is for you, toothbrush, toothpaste, some floss, deodorant, and a comb. There are towels in the bathroom for you, they're the white ones." He almost smiled at that. "Oh, and one more thing..."

He reached into his pocket.

"This is for you. I took up a collection."

It was a small phone.

"Now you don't need to use mine. Agnes already has your number. Hers is in there. For some reason she's worried about you. You don't have to call, but you know."

"Thanks. I appreciate this."

A look of disapproval came over him.

"Don't thank me, thank Coretta. I foolishly mentioned your situation to her. I'll let you know when dinner is ready."

He left me to my discomfort and I to his. I figured we could talk about Orville another time. I briefly flirted with the idea of calling Agnes, but changed my mind, maybe after dinner. I put the phone on the table, carefully laid down, and closed my eyes. I put my hands to my head and felt about the bandages. There was less swelling, and so long as I didn't press too hard there was little pain. My eye and nose were a different matter. The eye was still swollen to the point where I couldn't see out of it, and my nose was plugged with gauze that I gingerly pulled out. I was tired of breathing out of my mouth. A small amount of air passed through my nostrils. It was a start.

The rest of my left side was stiff and sore, but otherwise in one piece. My ribs ached, but not like they had when the tractor fell on me, breaking four and nearly killing me. This wasn't so bad. Same with my leg, there were nasty bruises, but nothing that wouldn't heal. All in all, I had survived the beating intact. It could have been much worse. The question now was what to do? It was one thing to mount a half-assed inquiry into a missing woman, who wasn't actually missing. It was another to get the shit kicked out of you and not reflect on your motives and of those who administered the beating.

It was time for answers.

The first would have to come from the man of the house. Whether from Orville, or the chill Mr. Jones, it didn't matter. His motives I needed to know. Otherwise it was time to split. I drifted in and out of consciousness. The sunlight was fading, and with it the warmth I first experienced here in my little room. There was a noise I didn't recognize coming from the table. The phone was making itself known, squawking, demanding attention. I picked it up and pushed the talk button.

"Yes?"

"Monk?" It was Agnes.

"Yes…"

"I see you got the phone. How are you?" I could hear the worry. For some reason it sounded strange to me. I was starting to wonder if I should be worrying too, but for another reason. I liked Agnes. I was fine with that. Was Agnes? What did she really want? My earlier fantasies felt as beaten as my face. It was Virginia all over again.

"I've been better. How are you?"

"I'm ok. I just wanted to hear how you were doing. Mr. Jones said you'd been hurt. I was…concerned." Thank you, Mr. Jones.

"I'll be fine. I need a little time to recover, that's all. When did you speak to Mr. Jones?"

"Yesterday, he came by to talk to Johnny… and he told me you were in the hospital after some guys beat you up. It was kind of shocking and I was worried. I didn't know how to reach you, so we decided to get you an inexpensive phone just in case you might need it, in case you wondered. I hope that's ok. Are you out of the hospital now?"

"Yeah, I'm at Mr. Jones' house. The doctors wanted someone to keep an eye on me, so I ended up here."

There was a brief moment of silence that left me feeling oddly uncomfortable.

"Well, if you want, you could stay here. I mean, if you'd like, or if it's inconvenient there, or, I don't know. I guess I'm babbling. It's an option to think about."

"I'll do that. I don't want you to worry, Agnes, I'll be ok."

Like the worry, I could sense her disappointment. I felt both bad and indifferent about it, if that's possible. It was probably the drugs. Yeah, that was it; it was the drugs.

Or it was anger.

"Ok. I hope you feel better soon. Let me know if there's anything I can do."

"I will. I'll talk to you later, goodbye."

"Bye."

The phone went dead. Apt. A woman, not my mother, or my ex-wife, or the one in San Francisco on whom I had a foolish crush, cared for me. It was a woman I met in passing, in a bar associated with a financier who had known ties to various and sundry characters. I knew Joanie cared, but she had a life independent from mine. Agnes, it was possible, did not. After Astral, I didn't think much about a life with another woman. Sex, yes, but another round of commitment? No.

I liked Agnes. I did. I think.

Jones interrupted my mental wandering to let me know it was time for dinner. I got up slowly and followed him to the dining room. The food smelled wonderful, the aroma filled the air and with my nose unplugged it spread about my senses in glorious waves. Coretta and the kids, sitting at the table, were waiting on me. My head began to throb. Maybe it was time for another dose of pain relief. I took my place and prayed that I didn't do or say anything stupid. There was roast, potatoes, Brussels sprouts, and bread. I took a little of each and waited for everyone else to be served. Orville said grace, and we ate in subdued silence, broken only by futile attempts to engage the kids on their school day.

Both were tall and lanky with their mother's beautiful eyes. Marcus spoke of practice, and Ella had to go to her friend's house. It reminded me of when Rebekah was that age; she too had little use for me and my questions. A connection of sorts and the tasty food allowed me to relax a little. I was keenly aware of everyone there. I watched as they interacted, even in silence; noted the physical responses to the questions and to each other. An incredible sense of loneliness took hold of me, like a song, sweet and sad, singing of a lost life of family and love. The thought of Rebekah nearly brought me to tears. I missed her terribly. Somewhere in my head was her number. I should call.

"Are you alright, Monk?" Coretta and the kids were looking at me.

"I think so, why?"

"You're crying!" She was right. I felt tears running down my face on the right, and pooling around the swollen left.

"I'm sorry, seeing you here with your family made me think of my daughter. I didn't realize I was getting so emotional."

"It's ok to be emotional. You've been through quite an experience. I still remember how frightened I was the night Orville was nearly killed. It was a terrible thing."

I looked over at Orville. His expression didn't change.

"When was this?" I asked.

"Long time ago," he said, "during the conflict between the east and west coast rappers. I was running security for a group, and some guys started shooting. Fortunately, they were lousy shots."

Coretta was dismayed at Orville's nonchalance. "He was hit twice in the leg!"

"Like I said, they were lousy shots." Marcus and Ella watched intently as their mother glared at their father. I decided, for some unknown reason, to add my two cents.

"Security can be a dangerous business..."

The family turned in my direction, all with the same expression. The tiny voice in the recesses of my addled brain whispered that they were well aware of that.

"Sorry. I'll keep quiet."

It must be the drugs. It was all I had for an excuse.

The rest of the dinner was without comment. The kids excused themselves, and I sat there like a flunky as Coretta cleared the table. Jones was lost in thought.

"Why don't you two go watch the game or something, I need the table."

Jones snapped out of his solitude. "Sure. You like basketball, Buttman?"

"Depends on who's playing."

"This is a Clipper house, Buttman."

"I'll keep that in mind. Lead on, Orville."

Orville smiled. We got up and headed to the back of the house. There, along with a big couch and rather large television, were the talismans of his sports faith: posters of players past and present, team banners and a signed jersey in a frame. The Clippers were hosting Indiana. I found a spot on the couch and did my best to keep up as Orville provided a counter analysis to that of the broadcasters on the boobtube. I didn't make it through the first quarter.

It must be the drugs.

16

At some point they put me to bed, probably for the best. It was likely I was snoring loudly through my damaged nose and disturbing the flow of the game. During the night the pain welled up, and unable to stand it anymore, I took another of those goddamned pills. Coretta had thoughtfully placed a bottle of water on the table. Sleep, when it came, was fitful at best, too many bad dreams with knives and fists. The sunlight rousted me the next morning and the clock informed me it was past eleven. My head hurt. I slowly sat up and finished the water from the bottle. I wanted to go home. Every part of my body ached, and I had nothing to wear but the duds given me by the esteemed Mr. Jones. They were beginning to stink.

I got up and made my way to the bathroom. I looked terrible. I hadn't looked at myself since this nasty little party began. The left side of my face was a blackened-purple-bluish mess. My hair was a dirty pile going this way and that, and I needed a shave. A rivulet of dried blood traveled from the left nostril across my cheek. I grabbed the white washcloth and ran it under the faucet. The water caressed my sorry face, wonderfully soothing the bruised skin.

There was a soft knock on the door.

"Are you alright, Monk?"

"Depends on who you ask." A smile came to me.

"Sounds like someone is feeling a little better. Would you like something to eat?"

"I would, but I'd like to take a shower first."

There was a pause, no doubt concern I might fall and crack what was left of my skull.

"Do you think you can take care of that by yourself?"

"I think so."

"Well, call out if you need any help."

"I will."

With the powers vested in me, I prevailed, though not without a few anxious moments: when I had to sit on the edge of the tub, finding the inner shower curtain wedged in my ass, suspect balance, and my one good eye blurred by the cascading water. Turns out I did not actually wish to crack my skull. The water stung as it struck the wounds, but I cursed under my breath and continued. Once I finished and had very carefully dried myself, I realized I had nothing clean to wear. Sitting on the toilet, I pondered my options. There weren't any. I combed my hair, wrapped the towel around the waist, and called to Coretta.

"Yes, Monk?"

"I don't have anything to wear."

"Oh." Awkward silence. "I have a robe, I'll get that."

While I sat in the terry-clothed robe, Coretta rummaged through closets and drawers looking for something appropriate for me to wear. All she could find was an old tracksuit Marcus used to wear for school. Kismet being what it is and given that Marcus was approximately my height, the tracksuit fit as well as was possible. I had no underwear or socks, but I was, once again, modest before the Lord. Coretta was kind enough to make me a sandwich for lunch. We sat in the kitchen waiting for Orville. Something was on her mind, but she seemed uneasy, unwilling to just blurt it out. Or so I thought.

"If you don't mind my asking, did you know the men who attacked you?"

"No. I don't know who they were. At first, when I noticed the door was open, I thought it might be a man I knew years ago, he had come by earlier, but I was wrong. Everything happened so quick it was all I could do to protect myself. If Joanie hadn't been around I don't know what I would have done."

She let that hang in the air for a moment.

"Do you think they might target Orville?"

I had to think. "I don't know? I don't think so. Orville's a big man after all, and seeing how he's in the security business, he's better at defending himself. Now that I think about it, and I believe this has to do with the woman we're looking for, it was more about what I might know than what Orville might know."

"What do you mean the woman you're looking for?" Uh oh.

"You haven't discussed this with your husband?"

"Orville can be a little tight-lipped when it comes to his business dealings. I don't like it. I worry about him, but he just brushes it off, saying it's no big deal. Looking at you, I'm thinking it's a bigger deal that he'll admit to. So who's this woman you two are looking for?"

I had to think. I had nothing.

I tried to be careful with what I said. "Her name is Desiree Marshan. She killed a man and took some money." Maybe that wasn't the best thing to say. I had no idea how Coretta would react, and after my talk with Mallory I had no good explanation for why we were looking for her. That made me wonder; why *were* we looking for Desiree Marshan? I hadn't had a chance to fully work through what might be going on. We didn't even think to go to her current address. My head continued to pummel me.

"Why aren't the police looking for her if she killed a man? Why would you be looking for her?"

"I don't know now. I talked with the police about that. They consider it self-defense and have no reason to pursue it further. As for the money, the police, apparently, weren't told about that. I don't know."

"How much money?"

"Twenty-five thousand."

"That's a lot of money."

"I suppose it is."

Coretta watched as I somewhat nervously tugged at the tracksuit. I was feeling hemmed in by the nature of our little escapade. I wanted to have good answers for what we were doing and why, but there was nothing to offer. I didn't know what we were doing to begin with, just going with the flow, but that was a copout and I knew it. Whatever we had gotten ourselves into was a lot more problematic and involved than finding some thief. Every twitch and every movement reminded me that this was darker and meaner than I'd been led to believe or had given any thought to. It was time to stop being a sap.

The front door opened. We could see it from the kitchen. Our man Orville was back. He saw the two of us at the table and paused just long enough to get caught.

"Orville Riley, we need to talk!"

Orville Riley, aka Mr. Jones, played dumb. I sat in rapt fascination as our man rope-a-doped his wife as to the possible nature of our improbable affair. There were misunderstandings, we were simply a means of communication between interested parties, it was easy money. I know what I'm doing; I'm not a dumbass like Buttman! For each punch she threw, he ducked and weaved. Her exasperation was evident; his denial manifest, yet they continued to press their position. I kept my mouth shut having done enough damage already. Orville meant to wear her down, and wear her down he did. The questions and evasions continued. After a period of tense silence, she relented.

"You worry me, Orville Riley; you worry me and I'm tired of it!"

She shook her head as she left Orville and me to the quiet of the kitchen. Mr. Jones turned to me with his own look of exasperation.

"What?"

"You're not helping matters, Buttman."

"And what matters would those be, Mr. Jones, or should I say Orville Riley?"

Orville held his tongue certain his wife was within listening distance. It was obvious he had words for me, but was not prepared at this time to share. That was ok by me.

I had a plan.

"I'm ready to go home. We can discuss this on the way over."

Mr. Jones feigned interest in my well being. "Are you sure you can take care of yourself?"

"I'll manage. Besides, I need to put on some of my own clothes. Speaking of which, what happened to my stuff from the hospital? You know, wallet, keys, stuff like that?"

"It's in the bag in your room. No one took your thirty dollars."

"Well good, I might need that thirty dollars."

"Yeah, you just might."

We spread the news of my imminent departure to the family. The kids, having no interest and more important things to do, shrugged. Coretta voiced her reservations that I was pushing my luck. I should stay a day or two longer. I needed the rest. She was right, and I said so, but I had things to do, and I promised to rest when I got home. Orville said next to nothing, content to collect my meager possessions and deposit them in the car outside. I thanked Coretta for her kindness and gingerly hugged her. She seemed genuinely concerned, which caused me a pang of regret at my not staying, but I had a plan, and a plan requires action. I sounded like the old man as he ushered Astral, Rebekah, and me out of the state all those years ago. I got in the car and waved. Mr. Jones hit the gas and we were off.

The freeway was its usual sundrenched kiss of fits and starts, packed with all the other lamentable souls forced upon this accursed asphalt and concrete. I felt the urge to puke come and go, welling in the back of my throat. Orville was back to the more comforting visage of the cool calculating Mr. Jones: back in black, ready for whatever came our way. I was longing for the cool of my bungalow and the comfort of my own bed. Maybe Joanie was back.

Joanie.

I had to let go of her.

I tried to think of something else. I thought of Agnes. Sweet wonderful Agnes! I found myself conflicted over whether it was a good idea to call or whether it was better to wait. One part of me worried about moving too quickly, another part wanted to see her, to lay my sorry head against her breasts. I could feel the erection growing in my loose fitting running pants. Evidently I was getting better. I needed to get back to the plan before the focus of my thoughts became obvious. I pushed away Agnes only to have Judith take her place. Judith, standing there in all her naked glory, smiling as I pictured her let loosening the drawstrings on the track pants. The erection started to ache. Whether he noticed or not, Jones interrupted my sexual reverie.

"I don't appreciate you getting my wife all worked up over this."

"You don't?"

"No."

"Then maybe we should have conferenced prior to you taking me to your house on what should or shouldn't be discussed."

"I don't need the bullshit, Buttman."

"And I don't need to get the shit kicked out of me, but here we are so enough of the supposed outrage. You haven't exactly been honest in why you're involved in this, and don't tell it's about the twenty-five thousand because I know that was a ruse."

"Agnes tell you that?" For the first time Orville fused with Mr. Jones.

"No, Agnes didn't tell me, you did. I'm not a complete idiot!" I let that sink in for a minute. "So why are you in this anyway? I asked this before, remember? You may know security, but that's not finding people and neither of us was bright enough to think of going to her house unless, of course, you already knew she wasn't there or assumed she'd split. And if it was only about the money, Dulcimer has guys who have no problem taking care of those kinds of things, remember?"

"So, what's your point?"

"I don't have a point. I'm saying this whole thing is bullshit and unless you can explain why we're doing this, I'm done, or I'm on my own, or something!"

Mr. Jones pondered his options.

Neither of us had been particularly open with the other. There were things I knew that I hadn't shared. Like being asked to be circumspect by one of the most powerful lawyers in the city, a man who could have gotten the best in the investigative business, but instead gave it to me, a complete nobody. Why would he do that? We didn't even discuss what I would be paid. I was simply going with the flow, nice and easy. Never mind it being the quickest way to end up in the canal face down and dead. Maybe that *was* the plan. And who would know or care?

It didn't make any sense.

It didn't add up to any number I recognized. Still, I walked into this mess. It was up to me to try and walk my way out.

Really, that was my story?

What choice did I have? I decided not to answer that.

Mr. Jones pulled off the freeway and stopped alongside a small community park. Evidently, he had something to say.

"I'm here to keep an eye on you, Buttman, that's my gig."

"Why?"

"Because they believe you know more than you let on."

"Who?"

"You know who."

"About what?"

"I don't know. It has something to do with this Marshan woman, but I wasn't given a lot of details. I was asked to do a job, to do a favor. I'll be honest; this isn't my thing. Personally, I'm trying to branch out into entertainment. I've always wanted to be a promoter, and after all these years of seeing how it works and what people do, I know it's something I can do, but you need connections and you need money. Dulcimer has that. With the violence associated with some of my clients, Coretta wants me to find something safer, and you telling her about a killing didn't help. So, in return for *assisting* you, Dulcimer promised to grease the wheels. He also intimated that there was money to be had if we found her, a lot more money than the twenty-five."

More money. I wondered if Jones had any idea how much.

"I don't understand. If they want to talk to her why don't they just do that? Why do they need us? What's the point? The cops didn't have any trouble finding her?" I thought about that. That wasn't right. "No, Mallory said she came to them. Once they bought her story she took off. I still don't understand. Why us?"

"I don't understand either, but there must be something otherwise why rough you up?"

"Yeah…" Images were floating across the inside of my eyes. Places, words on documents, faces. "And that Dahlia woman, as you say, she was roughed up too, right?"

"Black eye and bruises; as far as I know she still wants to see you."

"Yeah, I wonder…" The sun was beginning to outstay its welcome. The urge to vomit was roiling in the back of my throat once more. I could feel my legs shaking. We needed to go. "I have a few ideas, and I know a guy I think can help, but I need to rest, my head is killing me."

"Alright, I'll get you home."

I told Jones I'd see the woman Dahlia in a few days. He would set up the time and place. Meanwhile, I would take the car in for a checkup, talk to Bernie. He knew people who could help me. Fortunately, we were close to the bungalow. Jones helped me in. Someone, probably Joanie, had cleaned up the mess. I sat in my chair as Jones stood in the doorway. The light haloed around him obscuring his face.

"Thanks for your help. It was kind of you."

"Sure. One more thing before I go."

"Yeah?"

"Keep your phone charged; charger's in the bag."

"Do I have to?"

It's possible he smiled, but I couldn't tell in the light. I took the phone and the charger and went to the bedroom. I plugged it in, went to the bathroom to wash down another pill, and carefully laid down on the bed. It was soft and inviting. I closed my eyes. The light faded into darkness.

I was home.

The phone started ringing.

It was the next day.

17

"Mr. Buttman?"

It was my attorney, Ms. Lagenfelder.

That triggered the answer.

Money.

The Lawyer's voice brought the words I remembered reading suddenly into focus. Money, they say, is the means by which all men are corrupted. I could hear the old man preaching it to me as a kid. It made me think of Judith in her magnificent house. Judith, captive as anyone to her wealth, veiled it in languid ennui, and Martin, sullen obsessed Martin, stuck with a woman he loathed, pined after one who sulked and stewed.

The papers he's so angrily tossed about the living room were instruments of transfer. I sat there reading them as I waited for Bartholome. At the time I thought it might be a tax dodge. The wealthy always rail about the taxes they have to pay. If that were so, why would Dulcimer, or the people Benitez represented, care? I could see how Durant would be involved, even Boyer and his killer, but what of the others? They had been in contact with Martin. Or so Benitez said. Had they? Why?

Money.

A lot of money, overseas, had been hidden away. Now somebody wanted that money. No, many people wanted that money and I was a pawn in their game.

"Yes, this is Monk Buttman."

"I'm calling to see if there's a time we can meet to discuss your recent troubles. We were made aware of your assault recently, and Mr. Durant is concerned for your well-being." My well-being? How thoughtful, and she emphasized the word, troubles. Touching.

"I'm home now. I'm still pretty beat up. If you'd like you can meet me here."

"Would this afternoon be convenient, say two o'clock?"

"This afternoon at two would be fine."

"I'll see you then, Mr. Buttman. Goodbye."

"Goodbye."

Company. I should get myself together.

I was still wearing the tracksuit Coretta had given me. The bungalow was quiet. I surveyed the room, more as a sense of belonging than as an exercise in whether it was presentable to guests. It appeared to be as it had always been. In the bedroom a twin bed, dresser, and nightstand. A good-sized window provided light and a small closet kept all my meager possessions requiring a hanger. On the wall were two rather delightful prints I bought at the second-hand store while shopping for clothes. Both colorful abstracts added just the right amount of panache to the room. The bathroom was a white tiled throwback to a time of clean lines and utilitarianism. To break up the whiteness, the walls were painted a soft blue. The lines of the sink and tub belied their art deco origins and I marveled that they still looked so good after so many decades.

The mirror reflected my sad face as I washed it. I discarded the tracksuit for underwear, clean slacks, and a cotton shirt. My stomach was grumbling. Unfortunately, there was little in the kitchen to eat. My trip to the store had been interrupted by two thugs with their own agenda. Fortunately, there was enough bread for toast, and I had enough tea for a pot. I watched as the filaments charred the bread, the knife in my hand ready to spread the butter and jam. The teapot was whistling on the stove. My meal prepared, I sat in the sunlit glow of the kitchen examining the small table with its two chairs, another second-hand find. Other than the underwear, everything I owned was someone's castoff or throwaway. And yet it was all such wonderful stuff. Forlornly passed off to the thrift stores, hoping for a man of my stature to rescue them, and bring them here to my little patch of second-hand heaven.

The phone was ringing.

I retrieved it from the bedroom. "Yes?"

"Monk?" It was Agnes.

"Yes, it's me." The night's rest had softened my anxieties. It was nice to hear her voice.

"I thought I'd call and pester you. I was worried and what could be better than me annoying you on your new phone."

"I'm not annoyed."

"Are you still at Mr. Jones's house?"

I almost laughed, Mr. Jones; the name never came up in the Riley home. "No, I'm back at my place. Eating some toast, having a cup of tea."

I could hear Agnes' mind whirring through the tinny speaker. I had awoken something in her and she was adamant in going after it.

"If you're up for it, maybe I could come over there, or if you wanted, you could come to my place. It'd be good to see you. It's been kinda quiet around here and I kinda miss you, so what do you think?"

"Well, I don't look very good right now, and with my left eye still swollen, it's probably not a good idea for me to drive, especially at night. You're welcome to come over here, but I have to warn you I'm out of food, so you'd have to bring something or be seen in public with me which may or may not be a good thing. But other than that, I don't think it would be such a bad thing to get together."

"So long as it's not bad," she laughed.

"No, I don't think it would be bad at all."

"Alright, I can be there around seven if that works."

"Seven works."

"Ok then." I was certain I heard a big sigh of relief but it could have been my imagination. I gave her my address and told her anything for dinner, other than liver, was fine. I turned off the phone and smiled. Yeah, Agnes was going to be trouble, yet I was already looking forward to seeing her.

I cleaned up the kitchen and made sure the living room was in respectable shape for my many lady callers of the day. I searched for the cards given to me by the police, Benitez, Ms. Lagenfelder, Agnes on behalf of Dulcimer, and of course, Mr. Jones. I put them in a pile and then duly added the info to the contact list on the phone. Next it was time to psych myself for the task at hand.

No more being a sap!

If I was indeed being played as a patsy, I was going to go out my way and if there were people out to harm me, like any good detective, I was going to strike first. That way I wouldn't have any excuses the next time I got the shit kicked out of me. Yeah, time for Monk Buttman, hard-boiled private dick, to kick some ass!

After I finished laughing, I returned to the matter at hand.

I had a couple of hours before Ms. Lagenfelder was to arrive. It was time to flesh out the plan. I'd head over to Bernie's tomorrow. He could help with finding the two guys who jumped me. I had an image of their faces and the Rosarita remark made me think of the riders. Bernie knew a guy, good with computers and the Internet, who might be able to find out who the riders were and where I could find them. I already knew Martin was one. I'd deal with him through Judith and maybe Ms. Lagenfelder. It was what to do with the people behind Benitez. I assumed they were big hitters and I'd have to be very, very careful in what I said or did as far as they were concerned. If the money I thought was in play involved the drug cartels, I could end up in a thousand pieces out in the desert.

I didn't want that.

For the first time, in a long time, farming didn't seem so bad. I'd always hated it, yet I worked at it for years with no definable purpose. It was where I was. It was what I did. I could claim to be progressive, that I was part of the farm to table movement; that what we grew was organic, although technically it was all-organic, to me it was still digging in the dirt. After Astral left me, I couldn't get away fast enough. For the last few years, life had been a free-form existence. I'd created my own little cocoon. Just enough stuff and just enough money to survive the way I wanted. No real responsibilities, no real ties to anyone. Nothing new, nothing fancy, just a quiet invisible life. The only real fly in the ointment had been Joanie, and that was more me than her. I could see her smiling at me, calling to me...

"Buttman!"

I opened my eyes, the right more than the left, to see her beautiful face looking down at me. I must have dozed off.

"Joanie?"

"No, it's Mildred. Why are you home?"

"Because I live here?" I didn't understand the question.

"No, I mean why aren't you with the big black guy, Jones?"

"Because I live here and I didn't have anything to wear. Besides, I'm all right, chilling, hanging loose. How are you?"

She was trying hard to be mad at me, but I could tell the fury was contrived. I found it deeply comforting.

"I'm fine, and you, you look terrible."

"Thanks, it was the look I was going for."

Yes, very funny. Do you have anything to eat around here? Can you drive? Can you take care of yourself?"

"Jeez! I'm not an invalid! I can probably drive, and while there's not much to eat around here, I was planning a trip to the store. Of course if you're worried, I wouldn't object to your helping me with that, but I know you're busy so I won't impose."

"Uh-huh." She stood there with her arms crossed.

"But we have to be back by two, so I can see my lawyer. She's coming by to see me."

"Uh-huh."

As a further affront to my ability to organize my own affairs, Joanie methodically inventoried my pantry, which included a number of unnecessary comments about its contents before gathering me up for our trip to the grocery store. "You know, for a guy who knows how to cook, you have very little in the art of cooking, spices, herbs, anything."

"Well, after you broke my heart there was no reason to care about such things."

"Oh brother, I don't buy that for a minute."

"No?"

"No."

"Such is my lot in life, I suppose."

"Alright, sad sack, let's go. I wouldn't want you to be late for your appointment with your lawyer."

"Thanks, but I think that sad sack remark was rather hurtful."

"I'm sure you do."

And to think I wanted to marry this woman.

At the market I was the main attraction, or distraction, to those plodding through the drudgery of buying groceries. Everyone looked at the guy with the puffy, disfigured face, no doubt admiring the many shades of putrescent color on display. Kids stared while the older folks utilized their well-honed ability to look without being obvious about it.

The store was one of those remodeled affairs, light and airy, bustling and intimate; meant to recreate the feel of the old time mom and pop store that no one our age could ever remember. I followed Joanie and dutifully answered her questions about what I wanted and what I could legitimately eat with my stiff sore jaw. Apparently, tough and chewy would not be on the menu. The checkout lines were full, filled with exasperated old people, tired moms with their unruly children, and a few sunglass-clad hipsters clutching their organic produce.

"So, how was San Fran?" I needed something to take my mind off the bug-eyed kid in the cart in front of us. He was transfixed by the contours of my face.

"It was a very nice couple of days."

"Yeah?"

She smiled a little. "Yeah. The gig went really well. They want me to perform regularly which would be a good mix with the gig at Ballinger's. Add a little more money to the Joanie needs a retirement fund. Plus, out of nowhere, Mikal showed up. It was so good to see him. Had a chance to talk through some stuff. You know, have a little together time. Boy, did I need that. So yeah, it was a nice couple of days."

"Well good." It was important for me to be supportive even if I didn't want her to be with the guy.

"It was, but it went by so quickly. Now he's off to Asia for a month. Apparently, they'll be doing some session work along with the shows while they're there. He says it'll go fast. Then we can get back to normal. I sometimes wonder if that'll ever happen, normal. I guess we'll see. I'm hopeful."

"I'm sure it will, for all of us."

Our turn at the register finally came and we dutifully paid for our items. The drive back was quiet. I helped, as much as I could, with putting the groceries away and we had sandwiches for lunch. The kitchen was filled with light and we sat there lost in our thoughts. I assumed hers concerned Mikal. Mine wandered from door to door looking for whatever was there. I let my eyes drift on towards Joanie. I watched as she absent-mindedly brushed the hair out of her face. I almost said something when I heard a knock on the front door.

It was one-thirty.

Ms. Lagenfelder was early.

18

There in all her glory stood Judith Delashay. Her hair, soft and luxurious, was pulled back exposing her exquisite neck. A tasteful gold chain accentuated that beautiful neck. As usual, the dress she wore artfully defined her figure without being too revealing. I had a crazy impulse to kiss and run my hands along that figure, to make mad passionate love to her. Judith, alluring exotic Judith! Loving her might also cause me to end up in a thousand pieces in the desert. I realized I was smiling, perhaps overly so. She, on the other hand, had the oddest expression, as she looked me over.

"Oh my, Monk, you must have had quite an experience lately."

That made me laugh. Experience! "It was a moment to treasure."

Joanie silently moved next to me, amazed I think to find such an elegant woman at my door. I don't think she was smiling.

"Joanie, this is Judith. Judith, this is Joanie, my neighbor. She's been kind enough to make sure I'm not falling into disrepair." Joanie shook her head.

"It's nice to meet you, Judith."

"As it is for me to meet you, Joanie. Have you known Monk for long?"

"Sadly, I have."

I thought of a few pithy remarks, but decided to keep them to myself. The three of us stood there.

"Please come in, Judith. I'm surprised to see you here."

"I don't know why, I often venture out on my own these days." She passed us, took stock of my home, such as it was, and turned to Joanie. "Joanie, I realize I'm intruding, but I'd like to speak to Monk in private. Would you be so kind as to give us a few moments? I promise not to keep him too long."

"Not at all, I have my own errands to run and Monk here is expecting his lawyer. It was nice to meet you, Judith. I'll talk to you later, Monk."

Joanie shook her head again and closed the door behind her. Judith came close, her perfume inviting me to move towards her, confusing my neural pathways as I tried to figure out why she was here. She carefully placed her hand on my injured face, letting her fingers trace the contours of my swollen cheek and jaw. She leaned in and with the lightest touch kissed me. It was like an electric jolt. I wanted so badly to put her lips to mine, but she pulled back and sat down.

"This is a delightful little place, Monk. I like the pieces you've found." She looked around, motioned for me to sit as well, and disappeared into the recesses of her mind. "It's very peaceful here. I can see why you like it. I lived in a house like this once."

Her eyes wandered the room.

"What brings you to my peaceful little home? I'd like to think it's because you miss me, but I'm notorious for self-delusion." Which was true.

"Don't be too dismissive of your charms, Monk. I'm not. However, I came over because of something Martin said to me."

"Did he come home?"

"Good lord no, but he did call." She drifted off again. I wondered if I was going to have to pry the information out of her if she didn't stay focused on why she was here. "He told me to be mindful of what I say, that something important was happening, and if I wasn't careful I might end up like, as he put it, that little boy-toy of yours. I didn't know what that meant so came to see you. Apparently, I better watch out or I might be assaulted as you were."

"I certainly hope not, but why would you be assaulted? I don't know how what happened to me would be something that might happen to you?"

"Why is anyone ever assaulted? Money? Power? Anger? Domination? It's possible, certainly with Martin, that they are all in play."

Judith got up and wandered into the kitchen. I followed. She seemed transported by the modest trappings of the bungalow. I imagined her reminiscing about her time as a poor soul, even if I couldn't picture her as anything but rich and elegant. Her hands found each piece of hardware, touching cabinet doors, counters, the old style fridge and stove. I watched as she moved from place to place within the kitchen. The small Formica dining table was the last stop. A sweet smile crossed her face as she sat on one of the matching nylon chairs.

"We had a table like this when I was a child. It was where we were allowed to draw and play. My sisters and I. Feels like another life."

"I never had anything like this growing up," I countered. "My youth was all rustic handmade furniture. This is all second hand, which explains my attachment to it, like my yearning for a slice of Americana that was scorned in my youth. I associate a kind of normalcy to it, even if, intellectually, I know it to be illusory. I still find comfort in its kitsch."

"Comfort is a good word."

I sat down across from her. I figured while she was here, maybe I could get some answers out of her. After all, it wasn't like we spent a lot of time together; who knew when I'd see her again.

"Do you know where Martin is?"

That shook her out of her reverie, her features tightened.

"No, but I believe he's found a little hideaway on the beach somewhere. He's probably there with his whore. Is it important where he is?"

"It is. I need to find his whore. And as you say, she's probably with him."

"Why would you need to find her?" The curiosity was evident in her voice.

"You know why, my beautiful Judith Delashay." The desire was evident in mine.

"I do? And what would that be?"

"Money, lots and lots of money."

Her eyes lit up. I knew we were both on the same page.

It was two o'clock. I heard a knock on the door.

"That would be my next female caller, the delightful Taylor Lagenfelder, from A and A."

"I'm familiar with Ms. Lagenfelder." We got up and went to the door. "Can you come see me tomorrow, say in the early afternoon? I'm not an early riser, so mornings don't suit me. We can see if Martin's left a trail to his love nest."

"I can do that."

"I look forward to it." With that she kissed me softly before opening the door. Taylor Lagenfelder, the surprise writ large upon her face, pondered the sight before her.

"Mrs. Delashay?"

"It's lovely to see you, Taylor; please give my regards to Mr. Durant.

Goodbye, Monk, try not to injure yourself further."

"I'll try not to. Goodbye."

Ms. Lagenfelder and I watched the rich elegant woman head towards her car. I allowed myself a small sigh before turning to my erstwhile attorney.

"So what brings you to my humble abode, Ms. Lagenfelder?"

"Your health, Mr. Buttman. Mr. Durant was concerned after hearing of your assault. He wanted me to assure you that we would cover your medical expenses, and to ask if there is anything we can do to help your recovery."

"I appreciate the concern and am thankful for the support."

"Mr. Durant will be pleased to hear that. All I need is your signature on this consent form, allowing us to represent you when we negotiate with your healthcare providers." The dear Ms. Lagenfelder gave me the perfunctory smile crafted, I assumed, from her many interactions such as this. Another day. Another client. I signed the paper. "Is there anything else I can do for you?"

"There is, if you don't mind." It was time for my perfunctory smile.

"What would that be?"

"Information. Namely, I need to know if Martin Delashay has a second house or property on the beach somewhere, one he's kept from his wife. I'd also like your opinion on certain aspects of this job I'm on for Mr. Durant."

Taylor Lagenfelder pondered my request. The pleasant façade gave way to her more curious face, one I found infinitely more interesting. She was letting the wheels spin, working over how she would respond. I knew she was bright and a part of me was hoping she had some questions of her own about this little affair, enough questions that she'd be willing to help me find some answers.

"I'm listening. I don't know that I can ethically look into a client's file, as a matter-of-fact I can't, certainly not without their permission, and I doubt Martin Delashay would allow it."

"What if his wife allowed it? Isn't he technically missing?"

"I'd have to think about that. It might be permissible, why?"

"I'm looking, or helping to look, for Desiree Marshan, right?"

"Right." The wheels continued to spin.

"She was involved with Todd Boyer and she's involved with Martin Delashay. It's quite possible they're together as we speak. Neither is at their established residence. Judith Delashay believes Martin has a love shack somewhere along the coast. Boyer was handling Martin affairs, or was at least his contact within your firm. I think they were up to something, along with Desiree, that had to do with a lot of money overseas. Obviously, whatever they were up to took an ugly turn when Desiree killed Boyer, but I don't think Boyer's death has derailed their plans or everyone's interest, including Mr. Durant's, in it."

"Ok, so maybe Martin Delashay has a house on the beach his wife doesn't know about and you think we would have information on that?"

"I know you would because all his affairs are handled by A and A, taxes included. Someone has to pay the property tax."

"And you know this how?" It was time to show some of my cards.

"The papers I took to Martin's house on the direction of Boyer were instruments of transfer for overseas accounts..."

"You read his confidential correspondence?"

"I did after he threw them at me and stalked out of the room. I had to pick them up and naturally I took a look. Apparently, they weren't what Martin had agreed to, and it's possible Martin told this to Desiree as I was bringing them back. Maybe that's why she killed him, he was double crossing Martin."

"My understanding was that she killed him in self-defense during a sexual assault." Ms. Lagenfelder's tone betrayed her own disbelief.

"I was there and saw all of it. She may not have been thrilled with having to fuck Boyer, but it wasn't rape or sexual assault. I talked with Mallory about it and when she left the office she didn't have any signs of assault, like the cuts and bruises she had when she turned herself in, and she badly wanted the documents I had."

"Did you give them to her?"

"No. I let her take the money, but not the documents. Maybe that's why they had me beaten up."

Taylor Lagenfelder took a moment to take this all in. I had no idea what kind of player she was down at A and A. It might work in my favor. It might not.

"You said you also wanted my opinion on this little job of yours, correct?"

"Correct. Specifically, I was curious what you thought of Boyer; what was the word on him at the office, what did people think after he was killed in so gruesome a fashion?"

"I don't know that I'm comfortable discussing what goes on at the office, Mr. Buttman." she turned towards the door.

"It's important. I wouldn't ask if it wasn't."

The wheels continued to spin; I just didn't know which way.

"I'll consider it and get back to you. I think for now that's the best I can do."

"That's all I can ask for."

"Goodbye, Mr. Buttman."

"Goodbye."

Maybe I overplayed my hand.

I spied Joanie as Ms. Lagenfelder made her exit. I knew she was intrigued by my ongoing affairs. Three women through my door in one day with one more to follow; maybe this detective stuff was indeed a seductive pheromone to women. It certainly wasn't hurting my love life. I met her outside my door.

"It's been quite a parade through your place today, eh?" I noted the smirk.

"Perhaps a little out of the ordinary, baby, but when you're a hard-boiled private dick, it's the way the ball bounces." I tried to sound tough.

"Seriously?" She was unimpressed.

"It's my new thing; what can I say?"

The incredulity on her face was hard to ignore. She didn't see the benefit of my newfound career path. "Getting beat up is your new thing?"

"Some things go with the territory, baby. I'm not happy about it, but it is what it is. But, I got a plan and the plan's in play and the play's the thing."

"You sound like an idiot, you know that, right? I mean most people see the light after a beating and run the other way."

"Yeah, some do, but not Monk Buttman, hard-boiled private dick."

"Please stop saying that, it's moronic. A better thing to say it is Monk Buttman, hard-headed dumbass!"

"Maybe, but unfortunately, running isn't a viable option right now. So I have to do something, corny though it may be."

I went back into the bungalow with Joanie not far behind. We sat at the table in the kitchen after grabbing two bottles of water from of the fridge. The water was cool and clean, unlike the dreck coming out of the faucet. She was watching me, the purple-faced moron. I understood the concern, was even gratified by it. I didn't want her to worry, but other than kicking her out, something I would never do, I had to accept her criticism, especially since she was right. She was tapping on the table with her hand.

"So what did the rich woman want?" Questions. Questions. Questions.

"She was concerned for my well-being."

"Really?"

"Yeah, really."

"And you believed that?"

"For now, sure."

Joanie shook her head. "Monk Buttman, hard-headed dumbass!"

"Why do you say that?"

"Why on Earth would a woman like that be interested in you, and I'm not saying that to be cruel, but come-on, think about it; something isn't right here. Maybe you can't see it, but I do. People like that don't travel in our circles unless they want something, and that something isn't some altruistic concern for your well-being."

"I like to believe it's my tremendous love-making ability." The minute it came out of my mouth I regretted it.

"Good lord, you're sleeping with that woman?"

"Maybe."

"Jesus Christ, Monk, and the lawyer? Are you fucking her too? I thought Agnes was your new infatuation? How many women are you fucking?"

Yeah, I shoulda kept my mouth shut. It was too late to blame the drugs.

"It was only one time, and I met her before Agnes, and I haven't slept with her since, although sleeping wasn't actually involved now that I think of it…"

"Focus, Monk!"

"Sorry, and I'm not fucking the lawyer, I swear. It just happened. You saw her, would you say no?"

Joanie reached over and lightly slapped the non-purple side of my head. Exasperated, she flopped back onto the chair.

"Probably not, but that's a poor excuse."

"It'd been a long time and she put my hand on her ass, and…"

"And I don't want to hear anymore, ok?"

"Fine."

We sat there fuming for different reasons while the birds outside, indifferent to our melodrama, chirped to one another. I waited for the next question because no matter how mad or exasperated she might be, her curiosity always won out. She tapped on the table as I watched her, and she knew I was watching...

And waiting...

"So, what did the lawyer want, if not your tremendous love-making abilities?"

"I don't remember you complaining... "

"Monk!"

"Well, it's true, but anyway, Ms. Lagenfelder was here to say that the law firm would pay my medical bills, that's all."

"That's probably a good thing considering what an ER visit costs these days. I was wondering how you were going to pay for it."

"Hey, I do have some money. I'm not completely indigent!"

"Sorry."

For reasons best left to psychiatrists and the people who get paid to study human behavior, Joanie reached out and took my hand. She smiled and shook her head. I couldn't do anything other than squeeze her hand. Truth be told, the only people the two of us had was one another. We loved and cared for each other. That and we weren't terribly judgmental of each other's occasional stupidities. Her eyes were wet, and a tear rolled down her cheek.

"I don't want to find you beaten to a pulp again, you dumbass! You were so lucky to come out of this as good as you did. You could have really been fucked up! God only knows what would have happened if I hadn't screamed. And I don't want you getting killed for some rich woman, you understand!"

"I understand."

Apparently, she wasn't finished.

"And stop screwing around, that's not good either."

"Hey, if I want to screw around I will. No one's asked me to be exclusive, and it's not like I'm married..."

"Isn't *Judith* married?"

"Yes, but I'm not and her husband has run off with someone else, so it's not like I'm busting up the family, and since *we're* not married, you could be a little more understanding, and a little less condescending, yes?"

"Maybe."

"Besides, you've had your adventures in this part of town too, you know."

"I said maybe."

"Yes, you did." She was still holding my hand, "Of course, if you'd married me this wouldn't have come up, so you're kinda to blame too."

"Oh brother." The tears had dried and I got a laugh out of her. I figured that was pretty good for now. "So what's the plan, Monk Buttman, hard-boiled private dick?"

"Well, for one, I've got to stop being a sap, and two, I have to determine the best way out of this mess and go in that direction. I have a few ideas and some people to see. And while that includes Judith, I'm not going there for the purposes of fornication, just information."

"Uh-huh, and what if she puts your hand on her ass again?"

"I'll cross that bridge when I get there." I said this while fantasizing about Judith's fine ass.

"I'm sure you will. In the meantime, I do have some errands to run before I head off to the club tonight. Are you going to be all right by yourself?"

"Well, if you must know, Agnes is coming over later."

Joanie burst out laughing, releasing my hand, and nearly falling out of her chair.

"You get around, Monk Buttman, you get around."

And with that she left to run her errands.

19

It was with some personal interest that I noted the looks on people's faces when they first set eyes on me after the beating. Joanie freaked out, but that was while I was being beaten. Later she was just worried. Jones and the cops were terribly nonchalant about it. Judith was, I assumed, surprised that Martin hadn't lied to her, and while she was oddly alarmed by my appearance, she was still kind enough to kiss me where it hurt.

Agnes was just plain shocked.

"Oh my God, Monk, what did they do to you? Are you going to be ok?"

I had gotten used to the puffy black and blue face in the mirror. I figured it would take Agnes a while to adapt to my present condition, so I tried to keep my more attractive side to her. It didn't work very well. The shocked look was still there.

"I'm ok. It's getting better and it's not as painful as it was yesterday, so I'm making progress. I still look pretty bad, but it's mostly skin deep; sore muscles, bruises; that sort of thing, no broken bones. I hope you don't find me too repellant."

She frowned at that and very carefully put her hand on my cheek.

"No, I don't find you too repellant. I guess I didn't expect you to be so hurt. I'm glad you're feeling better. I just wish there was something I could do. Maybe I should go and let you rest."

I could tell she didn't want to go. "I'd like you to stay. You look wonderful and you went to the trouble of getting dinner. I say we do what we can to enjoy the evening. Besides, I need the company, ok?"

"Ok." It was good to see her smile.

Relationships are such awkward things. Our first date was as casual as could be. The second started out a little stiff, but quickly warmed up. I didn't know about tonight. For some reason, I thought of Judith and how laid-back she was towards me. The differences between Agnes and Judith were obvious, not only in looks, but in approach. The other difference was expectation. Here there were possibilities that didn't exist with Judith. Agnes and I were both open and amenable to the idea of being with someone on a more permanent basis. I could see it in her eyes. It wouldn't surprise me if she could see the same thing in mine, at least the one good one.

Those eyes.

That was also part of it, that inexplicable attraction; the curve of her face, the joy in her smile, the light in her eyes. I didn't get the tan thing. I assumed it was something California women of a certain age did; gotta have a tan. But it was alluring all the same. And she was easy to get along with, always a good sign. Maybe that was the problem, the idea I didn't want to entertain, the good thing. I wanted more and it bothered me, more than I wanted to admit. I was both attracted and repelled by the idea of love.

I dearly loved Astral, and while I only said it a few times, I loved Joanie. Neither woman worked out. Neither woman would ever be with me again. My heart sank at the thought of it. Love, that baleful cosmic kick in the nuts that everybody sings about; I was certain I could do without it. Joanie had cured me of such foolishness. Yet here I was, staring at this woman and a part of me longed to hold her, love her, all that silly romantic crap.

I was smiling.

"What did you decide on for dinner?" Time to put aside the dopey teenager. I headed for the kitchen with Agnes close behind.

"I hope you like Chinese."

"I do."

"Good, cuz for a moment it occurred to me that you may not like Chinese, but I couldn't fathom anyone not liking Chinese, but you never know, so I'm glad you do, otherwise what would we eat?" She was rambling.

"I agree completely. Where did you go?"

"Johnny said Fong's, which is right over there," Agnes stuck her arm out pointing to the left, "was really good, so I went there. Have you been there?"

"I have, and Johnny is right, it's very good. What did you get?" It smelled quite good as I pulled out the chair for her. She placed the three cartons, napkins, and chopsticks on the table. I grabbed two plates and two forks as a backup to the chopsticks. We sat down to our takeout delights.

"I'm not very adventurous with new places, so I went with the tried and true, sweet and sour pork, General Tao's chicken, and fried rice. I hope that's ok."

"Sounds and smells wonderful." I realized we had nothing to drink. "Would you like some tea?"

"That would be nice. I thought about bringing some wine, but it might not be good to mix alcohol with your pain medications, but then I completely forgot about something to drink."

"Not a problem, and sadly, I should abstain from booze for a while."

I got the tea going and listened as Agnes began to talk. I asked about her kids, which I knew would keep her going for a while. I was curious about them and disinterested in talking about myself. Seemed like a good way to go. She started with Barron. He was mulling whether to re-up or get out. He liked what he was doing in the Army, but wasn't sure he wanted to keep moving around, and he was wary of the deployments even if he wasn't a frontline guy. Military life was hard. Agnes worried about him, she wanted him to come home.

Her daughter, Anna, was speaking to her again and she was thinking of going to see her. The problem was having to face Simon and Eric, something she was loath to do. It wasn't the relationship thing, she insisted, she had come to terms with that; nor the sex thing, though she preferred not to think about it. No, it was the lost time, the lies, the part of life she couldn't reclaim.

She gave me a mischievous grin.

"I don't suppose you'd be interested in going with me? I'd prefer to drive, but it's a long way to go by yourself. I guess I could fly, but then someone has to get you and haul you around and if the situation goes to hell you're stuck killing time till your flight leaves. Other than Anna and Simon, I don't know anybody there, plus I'm not a big fan of flying to begin with. It gives me headaches and I think about not being able to breathe and crashing. Of course, if I had someone to go with me, like you, then it wouldn't be so problematic. Maybe I could make it worth your while." This was accompanied by a wink and her hand on my upper thigh.

"I don't doubt that at all. MaryAnn doesn't want to go with you?"

I was toying with her.

"No, she has other things to do besides hold my hand while I work through my personal problems."

So you decided to ask me to help you through your personal problems? Maybe that made sense, as I was one of them.

"Tell you what, let me think about it. If I do go, then, as a nod to my personal problems, you have to go with me a little further north to see the old man. I've been putting it off for years with no good reason other than I don't want to. But, like you, if I can con someone into going with me, I might be willing to make the trip."

"I might be interested in that." She continued to run her hand along my thigh. I found it hard to concentrate. "I don't mind being conned every once in a while."

"Well good."

"When did you want to go? I just need to give Johnny a head's up so he knows I'll be gone." For a moment the smile morphed into doubt then a wide-open look. "Am I rushing things? MaryAnn told me to not rush things. Am I?"

"Probably." The wide-open look took a bit of a turn as a corner of her mouth rose into a half-smile. She removed her hand and focused on her dinner. I did the same. The quiet wasn't ominous, as if I'd killed the mood, but a seriousness took over. It occurred to me that this was as good a time to ask the big question as any. "Speaking of relationship problems, should we make it worse by talking about what we're up to? As a purely mental exercise..."

"Maybe..." The big eyes were back...

"First though, I have a question?"

"What?" ...Focused intently on me.

"When we first met, I got the impression you were a kind of tough, no-nonsense gal, certainly when you yelled at the two goons, and even when you asked me to have drinks, but I don't get that sense now. How come?"

"I do that to keep the goons and some of the riff-raff that come around out of my hair. Johnny recommended that I toughen up around the place for my own good. It would be a better way to do business. It's an act. Keeps people in line. Plus, it seems to be attractive to certain types of men. And, to be honest, I have been with a few men since Jordan, but they weren't anything, really, and I found it easy to get through it acting tough, like a broad."

"I see, and what about me?"

Sweet beautiful Agnes looked me in the eye with all the seriousness she could muster.

"You're different. I want to be with you. I like you and I believe we could be good together. Even after two dates I think that's true. I know how that sounds, but I don't care. There's just something about you that tells me this is right. You're not stupid, or full of yourself. You seem like a decent guy, and I like the way you look, the way you dress. I assume you're not broke. I know you have a job, and I don't mind that you live a kind of Spartan life. I don't have a whole lot either. We're not twenty-five anymore."

Agnes looked down at her hands before looking back at me. "I know this isn't the thing to say. MaryAnn told me men don't like pushy women, or the ones who want to play house too soon. She said I should take it slow, but I don't see the point. I'm tired of waiting. You asked, so I'm saying. Maybe that's best. If you're really not that interested, then it's better to say so now rather than later after I've convinced myself we got something good going on here. I just don't know that I want to be an occasional good time with you, even though you treat me nice and I'm tired of being lonely."

Agnes reached out and traced the contours of my hand. I could see the longing in her face. "What do you want, Monk?"

"I don't know what I want. I know I like you, but it's been a long time since I was with anyone for any length of time. Part of me is open to diving right in, but another part wants to stay back, although for what, I don't know. Maybe it's because I pushed too hard when I wanted to be with Joanie and it went nowhere, but you're right, we're not twenty-five anymore. I think you're a fun sexy woman and I like being with you. Whether or not we're right for each other, I think, is what we make of it. I don't think I'm ready to move in just yet, but I'm willing to move in that direction, see how it goes."

"Are you seeing anyone else right now?"

"No, my dear, you're it."

"What if Joanie changes her mind? Wants you back?"

"That's not going to happen. If she was going to do that, she would have long ago, and right now it's Mikal that she wants. Besides, I know that once I tell her that you and I are together she would never come between us. That's our rule; we don't interfere in each other's love life. We might tell each other they're fools, but we let life happen. So don't worry about Joanie. If anything, she'd be thrilled I have someone to be with." I held her hand to my lips and kissed it. Corny, but it was that kind of day. "Tell you what, if you're up to it, we can head out this weekend, nothing like a road trip to see how quickly we can get on each other nerves."

"It'll give us time to talk about the wedding."

I leaned over and kissed her. "No it won't."

The rest of the meal was blissfully free of angst, worry, and longing. That was our dating pattern. We would wonder what's up and then find there was nothing to wonder about and get down to the business of enjoying each other's company, what we really wanted. We sat at the table talking, mostly about kids, MaryAnn's disappointment in her son's boyfriend, and what we would tell people when they inevitably asked how I got hurt. I proffered some choices from I fell off my bike, not that I actually owned one, to duking it out with a biker gang.

She said she would make the hotel arrangements, and I said we'd take my car. It would be a good excuse to take it over to Bernie's tomorrow. We cleaned up the table and I let her wander around the bungalow. She told me she found it charming and I allowed myself to buy into that. The bed was too small! She hinted that maybe I should consider getting a larger one. I promised to give it some thought. We moved to the living room and sat down on the couch. I put my arm around her and we listened to the sounds of world outside the door. It was rather pleasant. I wanted a drink, but we settled for more tea. Agnes stirred a bit before putting her head on my shoulder.

"I asked Johnny if he had anything to do with what happened to you. He said no. He says he doesn't like violence as an everyday tool. Says it's too expensive and it leads to hard feelings, but I know he uses it when he has to. Do you think he had anything to do with it?"

"I don't think so. I think it does have to do with what I'm working on, and he's a part of that, but if those had been his guys I'm pretty sure I'd still be in the hospital. So no, I don't think Johnny had a hand in this."

"Good." The hipsters had the jazz playing on their retro stereo. That soft mellow mid-fifties sound: muted horns, brushes on the drums and the bass walking us down that long lonely street. "Would you like me to stay tonight?"

"Well, the bed's not very big and it'll be a crumby drive tomorrow morning with rush hour traffic, but if you'd like to stay, I don't mind."

"I don't mind either, and it's ok if I'm a little late."

It had been an interesting day all things considered.

20

The night, however, didn't go quite as I had imagined. It started out fine with a little foreplay. After all I was sore, not dead, and we both found ourselves aroused, but with the size of the bed and the fact that I could only rest on my back or right side; sleep didn't come easy. Agnes, as I was finding out, liked to cuddle nice and tight, occasionally flopping her arm along my tender arm and leg. I found her a safe spot around my waist, which worked for about an hour, but I couldn't stay still for longer than that, and then, as if I weren't uncomfortable enough, my head started to ache. Finally, I loosened myself from her grasp, took a pain pill and fell asleep on the living room couch.

The past opened its arms.

I started dreaming about farming. I was in the field, but couldn't find the seeds or remember the crop rotation. I kept tilling the same small area over and over. Judah showed up and followed me no matter how hard I tried to get away, continually offering unwanted advice. Astral was off in the distance with Rebekah. I waved and waved, but they didn't see me. I started towards them as they went into a cabin set along a rise at the edge of the field. By the time I got there it had changed into a large home overlooking the ocean. I thought of Judith and wondered if it was her home? I looked throughout the house, but no one was there. I walked to the end of the yard, watching the ocean churn in the distance. I turned to go back in the house, but it was gone. I wandered along the bluff kicking the grass beneath my feet. I lay down, watching the clouds drifting by. The dream drifted into darkness.

"Monk?" A soft voice was calling my name.

"What?" The room was still dark. Agnes was bent down alongside the chair. "Is it morning?"

"No, I heard you from the other room. You were talking in your sleep. Are you ok?"

"I had a headache and couldn't sleep, so I came out here. I guess I nodded off."

"Why don't you come back to bed?"

"Is it morning?"

"Come to bed."

I must have made it back because the next time I opened my eyes it was morning and I was in bed. Agnes was already up and dressed. She leaned down and kissed me.

"I have to get going. Are you going to be ok by yourself?"

Am I going to be ok? Good question.

"I'll be ok. I have some things to do today. I should get up."

"You should rest. Take it easy, whatever you have to do can wait."

Agnes looked really good. I reached for her hand and tried to pull her towards me. Evidently, she got my drift. She stood there smiling.

"There'll be time for that later. Get some rest. I made coffee if you want some. Call me, ok?"

"I will. It's possible I might be up in your neck of the woods this evening."

"Alright, but seriously, take it easy. Bye, Monk."

Another kiss.

"Bye beautiful."

I watched her leave with that big smile on her face, waited for the front door to close and her footsteps to recede. When I was sure it was safe, I got out of bed and made for the shower. It was just what I needed. For the first time since those guys jumped me, I felt the urge to move and get going. I dressed and had a cup of coffee. I found my phone. It was flashing, telling me I had a message. After a few minutes of fumbling with the keys, I figured out how to play the message. It was Jones, telling me Dahlia wanted to talk, today if convenient, and left her number. I punched the number into the phone.

"Yes?"

"It's Monk Buttman; you want to talk to me?"

"Yes." Short and sweet.

"I have some time at noon. Do you still have my address?" She did. "There's a diner a block down from here called Pearl's. I'll meet you there."

"Alright, I should be able to get there by noon."

Next I dialed Bernie's number after rummaging through the drawer in the kitchen for his business card.

"This is Bernie."

"Bernie, Monk Buttman."

"Monk Buttman calling me on the phone? Interesting. What's up?" I could hear his chuckles even though it sounded like he was trying to stifle them. One of our many talks had focused on the cellular phone and the ability of the phone companies and the government to track and spy on an unsuspecting public. I had sworn never to get one, and technically, I hadn't. It was a gift.

"I'm taking a road trip this weekend and was hoping you'd have some time to make sure the Falcon can go the distance."

"Sure, how about five tonight; I got some time then."

"Great. Also, I was wondering if you could get me in touch with Llewellyn. I remember you said he was good if I needed to find some information."

"You're in luck. He happens to be in town this week. I'll let him know, anything else, Monk?"

"No, that should do it. Thanks, Bernie."

"See you then."

It was ten-thirty, time to get serious. Hidden under the dresser in the bedroom was a locked metal box. In it I kept a gun and a sap. The gun I'd had since the old man gave it to me just before I left for Virginia. He had always condemned our obsession with firearms so I was surprised when he gave it to me. It was an old 1911 Navy 45-caliber automatic, a big heavy hunk of metal.

Along with the gun, he gave me a box of shells and a manual for keeping it clean. In all those years I'd only fired it once. A collector in Virginia had stopped by to look at it when I considered selling it. He wanted to know how accurate it was, so we went to a field and fired the thing. It made a lot of noise and kicked more than I thought it would, but it was accurate. For reasons I can't explain I decided not to sell. Now, the gun rested in my hand. It felt hard and mean. I loaded the magazine and set it aside. The sap I'd found at a second-hand store. The woman there didn't know what it was, but an old dude told me it's what they used in the old days to take a guy out. A quick strike at the back of the head or neck was all it took. I thought it was cute.

Now it was in my pocket.

The gun was destined for my other pocket. I slid in the magazine, made sure the chamber was empty and the safety was on. The thing gave me the willies. With the implements of destruction safely deployed upon my person, it was time to check out the car. The sun was bright and angry, beating down upon me and the dry tired ground. What little clouds there were drifted thin and high above the haze below. It hurt my eyes, but I'd left my sunglasses in the car days before.

Out in front of the bungalows a number of landscape workers were trimming up the hedges, pruning the plants, and cleaning the weeds out of the beds. I couldn't remember there ever being anyone to take care of the yard. It was a sad patch of earth, overgrown, unloved, and forgotten. Now there were guys cleaning it up. They were finally fixing up the place. Perhaps it was a good thing Agnes came along; I might need a new place to live.

The car hadn't moved and appeared to be unchanged. A coat of dust obscured the light blue paint and dulled the white soft-top. There was nothing in it to steal, not even the old AM radio held enough value for a would-be thief. I opened the trunk, noting the smudges near the bottom of the rear bumper, and placed the 45 in a small handbag that held a few emergency tools. The trunks of old cars had a smell all their own and the Falcon was no different. It was like an old friend, a combination of decaying fabrics, rubber, with a little oil thrown in for effect. Other than the spare tire and the small bag, the trunk was empty.

The driver's door had a few dings in it. I couldn't tell if they were new or not. I rolled down the window, hopped in, and released the latches so I could lower the soft-top. That released the pent-up heat and allowed the breeze to take away the fifty-year-old musk that collected when the car stayed closed for too long. I put the key in and turned it over. The motor roared to life, and I sat there enjoying that beautiful sound. I loved old cars and this was mine. I popped the hood and made sure there were no missing connections, leaks, or odd noises. I knew the car well enough to tell if something wasn't right. I closed the hood, took the sunglasses off the dash, and headed down to the gas station. I filled the tank and cleaned the windows. It was then I noticed the envelope under the front seat. I put it in my pocket. The landscapers were still caring for the yard when I returned.

I decided to walk to the diner. Nobody was on the street and I could use the exercise. There were twenty minutes to kill till Dahlia was supposed to meet me. The same shops lined the street: a place for hair and nails, a computer repair store, and a tattoo parlor that now had a full-time person for body piercings. The diner was next to the parlor. A plump middle-aged woman with blue hair directed me to a booth and handed me a menu.

"What happen to you, hon?"

"I fell off my bike."

A knowing smirk plastered her plump face. "Don't we all."

The diner's specialty was sandwiches; big fresh monstrosities made with only the best meats and cheeses. Here in the middle of our old, disheveled neighborhood was this great rib-sticking food. The aroma in the diner was filled with its glorious bouquet of lunches to be. I ordered a Rueben, onion rings, and a Guinness. It was noon and I was both hungry and thirsty for something thick and tasty. The meal arrived as Dahlia haltingly entered the place. I waved her over. Other than the sunglasses, she looked exactly as she had the last time we'd met.

"Hungry?" I inquired.

"I don't eat meat."

"They have a great avocado club. No meat. Try that."

"Alright."

Dahlia was processing my multi-colored face. Her eyes were hidden by the big dark sunglasses she had on. Her nose was puffy, and the same purple hue I saw in my mirror was there just outside the lens covering her right eye. I ate as she took the tour of my new look. The onion rings were perfect, crisp and sweet. The Rueben, too, was just the way I liked it with the corned beef and sauerkraut complimenting the Swiss cheese and the rye. A swig of Guinness and it was time for business.

"What's on your mind? What don't you want to say in front of my partner?"

"I wanted to tell you to be careful, but that doesn't matter now." She was still hiding behind the glasses.

"Yeah, I guess after you told them where I lived, that kind of became secondary."

"I'm sorry about that. I thought I could call before they got there, but I couldn't find your number. I didn't think they were going to hurt you that much."

"These things happen, part of the game." I decided to lay on the detective shtick.

"I wouldn't know."

"I think you would, but we'll save that for later. What do you really want? Spare me the concern for my health and well-being and get to the point."

Dahlia removed the sunglasses revealing the shiner the goons delivered. It didn't look that bad, more for effect, same with the glasses. She had a nice face. Maybe a little plain without the makeup, but it went with the rest of her, lean and smooth. I wondered what she used to look like, before she decided she was a woman. What was the sex like? It was an idle thought. I didn't really care, but it was what got her together with Desiree, whether for business, pleasure, or both.

"I want to know why you're looking for Desiree, and what you know about what happened where she worked."

"What did she tell you?"

"She didn't say other than it was taken care of. No more cops, no more lawyers."

"You said you didn't care what happened to Desiree, or that you'd talked to her; only that she was a horrible bitch who stole and lied and fucked you over. Yet now you want me to be open and honest with what the fuck I'm up to as concerns our dear, dear friend, Desiree Marshan. This after you had two goons work me over."

"I didn't have anything to do with that."

"Did you know who they were?"

Dahlia's puffy nose crinkled as she thought up a reply. "No, but they might be those creepy rider guys."

"And just who are these creepy rider guys?"

"They started out as fans who had a thing for Desiree. They were jerk-off buddies or something like that. Anyway, one of them contacted her to see if she'd be interested in some personal services work and over time she and this group of creeps got together so they could take turns fucking her while the others watched and jerked off. It made me sick. She didn't care. For her it was easy money, no worse than what she had to do on film. They were very protective of her and their little gang." She picked up the menu, then put it down.

"I'm pretty sure one of them is the guy who got her the job with the lawyers," she continued, "but now that I think of it that was bullshit too. We were on the outs by then, but we'd talk from time to time. She always had a number of dinks in play. The guy who helped her; the guy she killed, and those rider creeps. I don't know why she killed him, but she knows that you know, and she wants you to leave her alone. That's what I wanted to tell you. I know she's up to something and she doesn't want you to mess it up."

"That's what she told you."

"Yes. She also told me I should mind my own business otherwise I might get another visit from her friends."

"Well, no one wants that."

"I don't need your bullshit, Buttman. I'm just trying to help."

"My apologies. So you have no interest in the money, just our health." Her expression didn't change. "She probably didn't mention there was a lot of money involved, did she?"

"She said there was some, but it belonged to her man."

"Do you know where she is?" I watched her eyes twitch.

"I know she left her apartment. She wouldn't tell me where she is."

"But she's with her new man. Do you know his name?"

"She didn't say, but I think she is. I don't know his name." Her lips were trembling.

"How about her phone number?"

"She had it changed. To anticipate your next question, she called me."

"Anything else?" I noticed her eyes tearing up.

"No. Maybe this was a bad idea. I should go. I just wanted you to know I didn't mean to get you beaten up. I didn't think it would be like this when I met her, but I don't want to be assaulted again, and I don't want to be a part of some crazy money scheme or whatever she's got going on. I just want to be left alone, alright?"

"If I see her, I'll let her know."

Dahlia, of the trembling lips, donned her sunglasses and left me where she found me. I watched her exit the diner and head down the street. I finished my lunch and prepared for the next little challenge of the day.

Judith.

I thought about what she might be wearing.

21

The beautiful homes and gardens along the way were resplendent as always. If nothing else, money buys a kind of visual beauty. I pulled into the drive and hit the intercom to let her know I was here. The buzzer sounded and the gate opened. Judith, dressed in a thin gauzy blouse and a pair of silver slacks, stood at the door, a drink in her hand and a smile on her face.

She handed me the drink.

"You're looking better today, Monk, I'm glad you could make it. Come in."

"You look as delightful as ever, Judith, I'd be a fool not to stop by."

She came close and kissed me softly at first and then with more pressure. "I don't care for Judith so much, please call me Judy."

"Whatever you like, Judy."

The kissing continued as she closed the door.

I don't have a good reason to explain my lack of fortitude in resisting the embrace of Judith Delashay. After spending time in the desert, a thirsty man will drink all the water he can, knowing it may be gone tomorrow. I didn't blithely ignore my comments to Agnes concerning other entanglements; a lovely buzzword, and I had no good excuse for lying other than I didn't consider myself in a relationship with Judith. It was a temporary partnership that had a sexual component. That was my answer. Hypocritical? Absolutely, but should I ever have to explain myself to Agnes or Joanie or whomever, it was business, simple as that. I wasn't stupid enough to believe it would fly two feet, but it allowed me to take advantage of Judith's favors, and as I told myself, once she had what she wanted my butt would be kicked to the curb. I could live with that. What it might do to my evolving relationship with Agnes depended on variables not yet in play, so as a matter of conscience, I left them alone. I would bravely face that mess when and if it blew up in my face. Till then I was happy to delude myself and accept all the favors Judy was willing to offer.

I had, if I was honest, expected that maybe sex would be a part of our afternoon together. I was not disappointed. One thing I've learned as I've aged into manhood is that any relationship either grows or stunts depending on all those little things we like or dislike in the person we're with. For now, we were in our growth phase. What we started the last time branched out this time. Judith was more playful and more giving in responding to my desires and I was happy to do whatever she asked. The pleasure more than made up for the pain. Today we ended up in her bedroom with its spectacular view in all our erotic glory. If I was indeed destined to end up neck deep in trouble, I felt it was worth it. The breeze through the window kept the temperature in the room comfortable, and took away the heat from our exhausted bodies. We lay in the shade of the room waiting for the other one to break the spell.

"Mind if I ask you something?" I was feeling mischievous.

"Not at all."

"Where do you see this going, you and me?"

"Into the kitchen for something to eat."

"Meaning you don't see this as anything beyond the here and now."

"Meaning I'm hungry. We can discuss as we cook."

We moved to the kitchen to indulge in our William S. Burroughs moment. Having never eaten naked, nor prepared meals sans clothes, it was a new experience with the obligatory fear of spilling hot oil all over my exposed genitalia. Sensing my anxiety, Judith handed me an apron, furnished with a knowing grin.

"It's for the inevitable splatters, they can sting." She found one for herself.

"Yes, they can. What are we making?"

"Garlic shrimp over angel hair pasta. I assume you cook, Mr. Buttman?"

"On occasion. What would you like me to do?"

"I'll let you clean and devein the shrimp."

I gathered my thoughts along with the shrimp and the knife and got down to business. Judith rummaged through the cabinets for what she needed to cook the pasta. We were an efficient team; by the time I had the shrimp ready, the pasta was cooking, and the olive oil, garlic, butter, and parsley were waiting for me.

"You cook," she said this while fondling my exposed butt, "that way I can properly focus on the nature and future of our budding romance."

"Excellent." I put the oil in the pan and began sautéing the shrimp.

"If I may anticipate your questions, you want to know if this is serious, if I'm using you, can this be love, what's next, and what about Martin?" She was standing right behind me. "Is that about it?"

"It's a start." I gave her the raised eyebrows treatment. "I just want to know if we're on the same page, so that neither of us is surprised later by whatever happens."

Judith, in kind, raised hers. "If you must know, I don't have any illusions about what we're doing or where we're going. I'm not looking for someone to replace Martin, I'm not looking for love or romance; although if I'm honest, I wouldn't say no to a little romance. I've met a lot of men over the years, slept with a number of them and learned some hard lessons in the process. To me love is simply a collection of emotions rolled into one: desire, longing, affection, and hope. Martin did his best to beat those out of me."

"I'm sorry to hear that. Was it the kinky sex or other women? I ask because I found his tablet the other day and saw what was on it. Some of it was pretty wild."

"No, it wasn't that. I'm no innocent. I've tried a lot of things over the years, the kinky and the wild. It wasn't the acts so much as the attitude that went with them, the objectification, the pornographic nature of the encounters. I didn't want to be some whore he was fucking. Martin lost his ability to make love to me, to care about the meaning of intimacy. In some ways, I suppose, he's no different than all the other men driven by fortune and fame. It's all about them. And in a town filled with beautiful women, and men, more than willing to tell them what they want to hear, I grew tired of it. At one time I wanted to be loved, but that was long ago. Now I just want to be made love to, even if there's no depth behind it. I don't expect or want you to love me, Monk. If there are moments of intimacy and desire, even affection, then I'll have what I want." Judith returned to the pasta. "And you, Monk, what do you want from this?"

"Are you sure you don't want some handsome young stud? This town's full of those too, you know."

She laughed.

"Why would I want that? To pretend that I'm younger than I am? I already hear enough about how my looks are fading, that I need to lift my face, enhance my breasts, tuck my tummy, tighten my clit, and bleach my ass. On top of that I should parade around some kid who doesn't know a thing about love or romance and who most likely is only interested in my money or has no greater ambition than to be the companion of an older woman? How is that better than you? You're a nice cheap date, Mr. Buttman. The kind of date I prefer at this point in my life. And you? You didn't answer my question?"

"To be honest, I'm simply living in the moment. I have no idea where this will go, when or how it will end, whether it has to be anything. I don't generally find myself in these types of situations. I suppose when you tire of me that'll be it. I don't know that I want anything beyond what I'm getting now. It's not every day a man like me finds himself in the arms of a beautiful woman. I think that would be enough for any man."

"You would think, wouldn't you? I would like to say that I'm no dragon lady, quick to dispose of her lovers." She smiled at that.

The shrimp were ready. I scooped them out and ladled them over the pasta Judith had placed on two plates. We sat at the table and ate. She seemed lost in time.

"What do you think Martin is planning with Desiree?" I didn't really want to talk about Martin, but at some point we had to.

Judith started to speak and then paused. "I believe you mentioned money yesterday as the motive in their ongoing affair."

"Do you believe that?"

"And if I do? Do you?" Judith very seductively wrapped her lips around a piece of shrimp and pasta; making sure to slowly suck the angel hair into her mouth.

"It wouldn't surprise me. From what I know of the woman, and I'll admit I only know so much, money is a big motivating factor in her decision process."

"That's a rather deliberate way of phrasing it." Another bite of lunch passed through her soft smooth lips.

"Yes, but I'm having a hard time concentrating on our conversation when you eat like that."

"Like what?"

"Like that!" Like the languid strand of pasta drawn up in the circle she made with her mouth.

"I can't help it if this is the way I eat, Monk. You should know that by now."

"I probably should." It was a good thing I had an apron on as I rose to pick up the dishes. I wasn't embarrassed so much as concerned that some things should not be flopping around on the table. If nothing else, I knew lunch was over. I motioned Mrs. Delashay to come my way. She came around the table and pulled herself in close, her arms tight around my waist.

"I thought we were going to see if Martin left any information here as to his present whereabouts," I said

"Were we? From my vantage point that's not what's on your mind at all."

"Maybe not, but I still think we should find out."

"Find out what?" She traced the curve in the apron.

"What's in Martin's office? It'll let the food settle before we go out by the pool." Her hands were untying the apron.

"You must be getting more comfortable in your skin?"

"I must."

Busy hands.

Martin's office, like his bedroom, was in the north end of the house. Judith's bedroom was on the south end; the blessings of a big house, each to their own side once they found the other repugnant. It was, like the rest of the house, beautifully decorated; although to my eyes it seemed unused and out of the way. There was no computer to break the sightlines from the desk to the view of the ocean. It was a mahogany desk with a deep-set leather chair, the soft beautiful expensive kind. It was a luxurious white, as was the couch, with a comfort that made it hard to get up once you found yourself in it. My naked butt found it most inviting.

I went through the desk drawers and the filing cabinet built into the bookshelf lining the far wall. Whatever Martin did with his time, business didn't seem to play much of a part. There were a few documents or papers referencing a company called Sphere, but they were from the late Eighties, early Nineties. I asked Judith, who had returned from Martin's bedroom carrying the tablet I had found in the bathroom days before.

"What's Sphere?"

"That's the company Martin started with Jeremy back when they were in college." A smile crossed her face. "It was very exciting in those days. Jeremy was an incredibly smart man. The company barely survived in those first years, then they hit it big when Jeremy's security program took off. They sold it for all the money in the world; that's what paid for this place. Later it was pushed to the side by the company that bought it."

"What happened then?"

Judith was preoccupied with the tablet. "Nothing really, Martin, for all intents and purposes, retired, although he had a seat on the board. He left that a few years ago. Jeremy went to Europe to work on setting up some new kind of company and then disappeared. I don't even know if he's still alive. There were rumors he had died but I think they were just that. Of course, I haven't seen him, so maybe it's true." She waved me over. On the tablet a video was playing, Rosarita and a black man; her bored, him pounding away. "Is this the one?"

"That's her doing her thing."

"It also answers a lot of questions."

"Should I ask?"

A scowl covered her face. "No."

I sat next to her and watched some more. It was monotonous and repetitive, a joyless gangbang featuring a bored "star". I carefully took it from her, turned off the porn and looked at what else might be on it. There were three icons on the screen: one for the porn, and two I couldn't open. Both required passwords.

"Do you mind if I take this? I'm meeting a guy who is good with computers. Maybe he can unlock these other two icons, see what's there."

Her face tightened. "Maybe you just want it for the porn?"

"No, I don't find it erotic at all."

"No? You've never wanted to do that?"

I didn't quite know what she was driving at, but this mood killer needed to be nipped in the bud. "Not if it's like that!"

She took my hand. "Why don't we go out by the pool? This room depresses me."

We snuggled up together on the chaise lounge under the umbrella. The light and the quiet carried us away to that place where we were unburdened by images of Rosarita, thoughts of Martin, Agnes, or adultery. Judith fell asleep in my arms, breathing softly, the breeze playing with her hair.

I closed my eyes, caring for nothing more than the sound and rhythm of her breathing. It was one of those moments where you marvel at where life takes you, the places and people you meet. Ten years ago I was in a field worrying about whether my crops would provide a sufficient yield to support my unhappy wife and distant daughter. I was tired and bored, wondering how I ended up in that field to begin with. Astral was moody and uninterested in sex, Rebekah uncommunicative, and I was resentful and angry. Now it seems inevitable that the three of us ended up where we did. I assumed Astral and Rebekah were happy with their straight-laced husbands. I was drifting, but if that landed me in the arms of Judith and Agnes I wasn't going to complain. There were worse ways to end up. The birds were singing and I was drifting off again.

"Monk."

"Yes?"

"Something's buzzing in the house." Judith, warm and naked, was roused by the timer in the kitchen. I set it before we went into Martin's office. It was time to head up to Bernie's. I was regretting setting the damn thing.

"I have to go."

"You do?" She was awake now, running her hand along my chest. We both noticed I was aroused by this. "Why don't you stay a little longer?"

"I have to get cleaned up too…"

"Martin has a big steamy shower. You can violate me there while we clean ourselves. That would really make him angry."

"You talked me into it."

"Imagine that."

The shower was large enough for ten people with showerheads everywhere. There was even a steam feature, perfect for the dual-purpose action of sex and cleansing. Such are the lives of the wealthy. A teak bench allowed us to maneuver, as we desired, with the additional benefit of giving us a place to sit after the sex. I was as cleaned and probed as I would ever be. We took advantage of Martin's vast supply of towels to dry each other, and once again I helped myself to his aftershave and cologne. I retrieved the tablet, kissed Judith goodbye, and opened the front door. She put her arm around my waist.

"Don't be a stranger, Mr. Buttman."

"You've got my number, baby, use it if you need it." I said this with my best tough guy impression.

"I'll keep that in mind, lover." We were both laughing at our attempt to be cute.

Now it was back to work.

WHERE FOOLS DARE TO TREAD

22

The sun was fading along the Pacific horizon as I inched north along with the other million or so drivers that packed the interstate highway system. As a diversion from the snail's pace, I noted certain driver's frantic and futile efforts to beat the system by jumping from lane to lane. It was pointless, but I suppose it kept them from any real reflection that might cause them to question why they were on this road in the first place. Maybe they had and were desperate to get off. I also tried to count the number of people on their phones. I stopped after fifty. The radio beckoned and I spent the remainder of the drive listening to Mariachi music. I didn't understand a word of it, which I found relaxing. A woman to the right of me, in a minivan, was screaming at her kids, while the one to the left, in a truck, was texting.

I continued to marvel at how many people lived here. All the houses, businesses, and cars crammed onto a desert plain. All these people trapped in their cars.

How was I any better?

Bernie's was nestled in a small commercial park in Glendale. Like Johnny D's bar and the pornographer's office, it was nothing to stand and shout about. To me they all looked the same, boring and non-descript. I assume that was for a reason, out of sight, out of mind. The shop had a quaint neon sign above the garage door and a pair of topiaries bracketing the main entrance. Bernie sat at the front desk watching as I came in.

"Monk Buttman, long time no see."

He was a small wiry guy with a thick head of blondish red hair, a thin nose, and black-rimmed glasses. He specialized in older cars. There was also talk it was a front for something far more interesting, or problematic, but what that might actually consist of I didn't know. I knew he was older than he looked and at one time his business was far more covert, before the cars, before the garage. Beyond that, all I knew was that he could keep my heap running. Well, that and his overriding suspicion that the government was watching us all, all the time. He got up and we shook hands.

"Bernie, you look good."

"Living the dream. Whereas you look like so much tenderized beef. So what's this about your ride needing some work?"

"Yeah, I fell off my bike. Anyway, I'm heading up the coast this weekend, and it might not be a bad idea to make sure it's up for the trip, plus, I have the sneaking suspicion I may have picked up an uninvited guest."

"Really?" Uninvited guest was Bernie's term for tracking devices, bugs. One of his less advertised specialties was sweeping vehicles for these uninvited guests. "I'm surprised, I thought you were doing plain old grunt work these days."

"I was until I witnessed a woman kill her boss. Now I'm trying to find the woman for some very interested parties. And yes, I'm way out of my league on this."

"I see. Is that where the bruises came from?"

"I assume so. There wasn't a lot of discussion while they were kicking my ass."

"Anybody I know?"

"The guys who beat me or the interested parties?"

"Either." Bernie had a habit of throwing out questions one after another.

"Where to start? The woman's name is Desiree Marshan. She used to be an adult film star. Later she got a job at the law offices where I do my grunt work. The interested parties include Marsyas Durant, John Dulcimer and an enforcer named Benitez working for an unnamed business group. I believe she's run off with a man named Martin Delashay after killing a guy named Todd Boyer. My partner in this mess is a man named Orville Riley aka Mr. Jones. Know any of those people?"

"Interesting group. I know of Marsyas Durant, he's a well-connected lawyer, someone to be mindful of. Johnny D is a very careful, very savvy moneyman. If he's involved I would suspect there's a lot of money in play. I've heard of Martin Delashay, but Llewellyn would know more about him. I don't care for porn, so I wouldn't know the woman, and the other two don't ring a bell, but I like the nom de guerre for Mr. Riley."

"He's no more a detective than I am."

"Then why are you doing it?" A young man of middle-eastern heritage came in the room, "This is Llewellyn."

He didn't look like a Llewellyn.

"How do you do?" I asked.

He had piercing black eyes and a strong jawline. His hair was combed straight back, and he wore a black tee and black jeans with just the right amount of attitude. "That depends on who's asking, but Bernie assures me you're an ok guy. The answer then is I'm doing reasonably well all things considered." He was very professional in his mannerisms, which he served with a sly smile. "I hear you have some work for me."

"I do." I removed the tablet from my jacket. "It involves two parts, maybe three now that I think of it. One is can you unlock the two icons on this tablet. The second is can you find out the names of the people in a group called Rosarita's riders, and third, what can you tell me about Martin Delashay and Sphere. I know that's a lot, but any help you can provide would be greatly appreciated."

Llewellyn pulled out a small notebook and jotted down what I had said.

"That shouldn't be a problem, although it may take some time to find the passcodes for the tablet. What do you know about this group?"

"They're a bunch of guys that shared files on a porn star named Rosarita, which, as I understand it, morphed into some kind of sex group. I'm almost certain two from this group were the guys who jumped me. I believe they're in contact with the woman I'm looking for, who happens to be the former porn star. I also believe that Martin Delashay may be a part of the group."

"Should I ask what she's known for in the business?"

"Interracial stuff."

Llewellyn took the tablet and played with it for a moment or two. "Should I expect porn on this? Is that what you're looking for?"

"I wouldn't be surprised if there is more porn, but I'm hoping there's information that details any non-sexual ventures Martin Delashay may have with Desiree Marshan."

"Desiree Marshan?"

"Desiree is Rosarita."

Llewellyn put the tablet on the table. "Can I ask how you came into possession of Martin Delashay's tablet?"

"His wife gave it to me."

"Judith Delashay?"

"Yes. You know her?"

Llewellyn's broke from his business façade and cracked a wide smile. "Not personally, I know her reputation and that she's quite a woman for what that's worth."

"What reputation is that?" He must have noted the somewhat defensive tone in my voice. The smile faded.

"It's part of the answer to your question about Martin Delashay and Sphere. I didn't mean to impugn the woman's honor."

"My apologies, I only recently met her so whatever her reputation might be, I haven't a clue, however any information you have will help."

Bernie, who was listening intently, spoke up.

"Why don't we take this into the lounge, it's more comfortable and more private. Give me your keys, Monk, and I'll have Javier take care of the Falcon."

I gave Bernie the keys and we followed him out into the garage. He gave them to Javier after a quick word. From there he led us through a door at the far end of the garage. Inside was a pair of rather nice couches, a small kitchen, a good sized TV, and some tables and chairs. They were lined up against the wall across from the kitchen. On each table was a computer. Whatever Bernie was into, it happened here.

Llewellyn sat at one computer and signaled that I should sit next to him. Bernie pulled up a chair behind us. Llewellyn's eyes grew bright.

"Let's see what's out there, shall we?"

All I could think of was Judith's reputation.

23

"What would you like to start with, Mr. Buttman?"

Since Judith was on my mind, I figured it was time to face whatever it was I didn't know. An obvious downside to becoming emotionally involved with a woman no matter the rational.

"I'd like to know about Sphere, the Delashay's, and a Guy named Jeremy."

"That would be Jeremy Tophanovich. He and Martin Delashay started Sphere in the late Eighties. It was a software design company. Their breakthrough was a security program that, at the time, was quite progressive and very effective. The program had a quiet little feature that allowed companies to shield certain transactions and activities. This, ostensibly, allowed them to protect their most important work from would be industrial spies and thieves. However, it was also used by certain companies to quietly move monies and information internationally without detection. Some of it, obviously, was a means to launder money, but a lot of companies used it to hide profits in order in avoid taxes. This, naturally, created problems for the Feds, and in the end Sphere was forced to adjust the program to allow for oversight and investigation. They did good business, were later acquired, as all small profitable tech companies inevitably are, and have largely faded from view. That's the official story."

I had to ask, "And the unofficial one?"

Llewellyn turned to me with a knowing little smirk.

"Nobody I know in the computer software business believes any of it."

"Why's that?"

Llewellyn leaned back in his chair. "Oh, the bones of the story are probably true, since the company existed for years before doing anything notable, but Sphere was a too good to be a true story. While Jeremy

Tophanovich was a smart tech guy, Martin Delashay...was not. A number of people I know met him and came away believing he didn't know a thing about software other than buzzwords. They were convinced he was a fraud. Then stories started circulating about Tophanovich and a man named Fyodor Denesova. The word going around was that Denesova was either the actual creator of the security program, or that he had stolen it from someone else. Later, the word was that Tophanovich and Denesova were one and the same, and once Tophanovich disappeared in Eastern Europe, so did Denesova. The story now is that all of it was a front, that it started as a money laundering scheme that, inadvertently, turned out to have some very good security features, or those were added later as a way to fend off any federal investigations into money laundering."

"Laundering money for whom?" Like I didn't know.

"I assume the usual, drugs, weapons, and sex trafficking."

"And the reputation of Judith Delashay?"

I wanted to know; Llewellyn hesitated.

"Now this is what I've heard. I can't say it's true, but the story is that Mrs. Delashay was screwing around with Tophanovich and that it caused quite a rift within Sphere. I assume between Tophanovich and Delashay. Apparently, it produced a lot of gossip in the tech community as well. It was shortly after that that Tophanovich left for Europe. Evidently, Judith Delashay was quite a party girl. There were a number of rather salacious stories going around about her for some time. Like I said, I can't personally say that they're true. I don't know her so I can only tell you what I've heard." He moved a little in my direction, the curiosity compelling him. "You've met her?"

"Yes, I've met her. She's a very interesting woman."

Llewellyn seemed at a loss for words. "I heard she's a very beautiful woman, that's she's active in the art's scene now."

"I heard that too," straight from the woman herself.

Bernie, who hadn't uttered a word, chimed in.

"Can I ask what you're looking for informationally, Monk? Why the interest in this particular ménage a trois?"

I thought about it. "I don't know at this point. I do think a lot of money may be involved, and it's possible it has to do with Sphere and the Delashay's. I don't know what my part in it is other than trying to find Martin and

Desiree. That's why I'm trying to gather as much information as I can, so maybe it'll become clear to me what's going on."

Bernie turned to Llewellyn. "What do you think?"

"Could be anything. Why don't you let me take this tablet for a few days and I'll see what I can do with it, and I'll look into this group of yours, maybe see if I can dig a little deeper into the Sphere story. I know a person who's more knowledgeable about that time."

"Thanks. Llewellyn, we'll be talking soon." Bernie put his hand on Llewellyn's shoulder.

"No problem."

I said goodbye to Llewellyn as Bernie and I headed into the garage. Javier waved us over. He conferred with Bernie, who then turned to me. He was smiling like the Cheshire cat.

"The car is fine. Changed the oil, checked the brakes, didn't find anything obviously wrong, but..." He let the "but" hang in the air. "It turns out you do have an uninvited guest behind your back fender."

"Really?"

"And a far more sophisticated one on the inner frame."

"So what should we do?"

"That, my friend, is up to you. I like to think it gives you a head's up. You can remove them, but given the way one's attached, it'll alert whoever's tracking you that you're on to them, or you can leave it and use that knowledge for your own benefit."

"What kind of devices are they?"

"One is a fairly simple locator; which means it's tracked locally so whoever is watching you can't let you too far out of sight. The other can be tracked by any number of mobile devices all the way up to a satellite. We didn't find any listening devices, though, for what that's worth."

"I see..."

Bernie noted my agitation. "Why don't we step into my office for a moment while Javier takes the car down from the lift."

I dutifully followed him back through the garage to his front office. I looked at my watch. It was six-thirty. I sat down, as did Bernie.

"Life's an interesting journey isn't it, Monk?"

"It's certainly going in that direction." Too bad I didn't know which direction.

"Care for a drink?"

I thought about Agnes. "Mind if I make a quick call first?"

"Not at all."

I found my phone and pressed the magic numbers. I could hear her voice in my head. It didn't match the one that answered.

"Yes?"

"Agnes?" My chest started to tighten.

"Yes..."

"Are you alright? I thought I might come over for a little while..."

"I don't think so, Monk. I don't feel very good. I think I'll just go home and go to bed."

"I'm sorry to hear that." Tighter and tighter. "Get some rest and I'll talk to you later, ok?"

"Ok." That was that. The tightness migrated to my stomach. I put the phone away.

"I'll take that drink now."

"Matters of the heart?"

"Yeah."

Bernie poured two drinks and we sat in silence nursing our bourbon. The last of the evening light was barely visible through the front door. Ethereal was a good word to describe its effect on the room, too bad it wasn't working for me. Normally, I found such sights soothing and relaxing. Instead I was worried and tense. Something was wrong with Agnes and I was being followed. I guess it makes it easy to jump a guy if you know where he is all the time. The room was growing dark. Only the desk lamp shone. It occurred to me that Bernie might have a life outside of this garage. Javier came in with the keys and I thanked him.

"I think it's time for me to work my way back home. Thanks for the help on such short notice, Bernie. What do I owe you?"

"Three should do it." I reached in my pocket for the bills. "Monk..."

"Yeah?"

"I've learned over the years that sometimes where you're going isn't where you end up."

"Is this about the job?"

"No, as far as the job goes, please watch your ass, it's about matters of the heart."

"Thanks."

I handed him the money and was on my way to my safe little bungalow. Traffic was no better going than coming.

Once home, I parked the car in my usual spot. It was along the street just beyond the entrance to our group of bungalows. There was very little activity in the neighborhood. No kids running around. No dogs pursuing their freedom at the end of a leash. I had to wonder if I was such a dog. Someone was watching me, tethered to me. And the leashes were many, keeping me contained like an invisible fence. There was that sense of travel and time, but no real movement.

I had nothing to do.

Foolishly, I thought I'd be with Agnes tonight. Not so fast, cowboy. Maybe her feet were getting cold now that she had time to think about it. She wouldn't be the first woman I'd known to get them. That's life. All this unexpected sex was going to my head. I was almost ready to tell myself I had a good thing going. But I was just running in circles, chasing this noise and that, never really having any idea where I was going.

The phone was ringing. I thought about throwing it out the window.

"Buttman?"

"That's me."

It was Jones. I'd almost forgotten about him. I got out of the car.

"What's going on? Did you talk to Dahlia?"

"Yeah, I talked to her. Turned out she was concerned about me after she gave the goons my address. In other news, she implied that Desiree was worried about what I know about her killing Boyer and whether I know what she and Martin Delashay are up to. She did tell me more about Desiree's kinky fan club, but beyond that it was fairly pointless. She left in a huff after I told her I appreciated her deep, deep interest in my welfare. I'm sure she's involved one way or another."

"What good does that do us?" I got the impression Mr. Jones was getting bored with our little enterprise.

"It means we need to keep looking for Desiree. I did talk to Delashay's wife and she believes they might be at a place out along the beach somewhere.

I think that's the next step, finding this place."

I took the gun out of the trunk and was walking towards the bungalows.

"And how do you think we should do that?" He was definitely bored.

As we were talking I noticed the front of the complex. It was amazing how much better the place looked. "I know a guy who is good with the Internet. He's looking for info on this rider group. I think Delashay's a part of it, so maybe there's something there..."

The landscapers had laid a thick layer of compost under the plants. It was well groomed except for a spot by two tall bushes where there were footprints. At the bottom of the bush was a shoe. I reached into my pocket for the sap.

"...That we can..." I saw the shoe start to move.

They were back.

24

The first one threw a haymaker, but I ducked before he hit me. I swung the sap and smacked him in the back of the neck, sending him to the ground. The other guy rushed in, knocking the phone out of my hand as I struck the first guy. With balletic cat-like agility I tripped over the first guy with the second falling on me, right on my left side. I'm pretty sure I screamed. I wildly swung the sap at the second guy hitting him in the chin. It was his turn to cry out. As he reached for his jaw, I hit him in the balls. He screeched as he rolled over into the fetal position. I got up and kicked the two of them in the stomach, one after the other. I was in a blind rage, kicking and screaming. Both were moaning in agony, flopping around. The first on rolled onto his back. I got down on top of him with my knee on his throat.

"Who the fuck are you?"

He just stared at me with uncomprehending eyes. Stupid bastard! I got the impression this wasn't their normal line of work, yet here he was stuck under my knee. I pressed down harder on his neck. I thought how easy it would be to kill him right now.

"Who sent you, motherfucker, who?" I continued to press down on his neck.

In a pinched little voice he said, "Derek, it was Derek."

I got up and stomped on his gut. He started puking, just as the idiot next to him had. I kicked him again. He flopped over on his side. I could see the outline of the wallets in their back pockets. I pulled them out and looked at their licenses. Gordon and Arthur. Gordy was from Pasadena, Artie from Manhattan Beach.

I heard sirens. The cops were coming.

I put the wallets back, then kicked them both in the ass.

"The cops are almost here you stupid pieces of shit! Are you ready for that?"

Whatever strength they had got them up and moving. For good measure, I gave them both another boot to help them on their way. I put the sap back in my pocket. I'd forgotten I had the gun. They needed to go. I quickly hid the gun and sap behind a planter by my door then went back to where the fight happened. It was a good thing I'd forgotten about the gun. I would have shot the both of them. Then what? My face was wet, more blood. Another jacket, shirt, and pants to clean, but this time I made out ok. I wondered where the phone was. I was looking for it when the cops arrived. I sat down and put my hands up. I figured they were in no mood for antics and I had no interest in being shot. It was then that I realized how badly my hands were shaking.

The neighbors came out to bear witness to my time of duress. That, or gawk at me and the fuzz. I gave the cops my statement, which, minus mention of the sap, followed the grisly details of the fight as best I could remember. I described the two. The first guy was older, maybe fifty, heavier too, wearing jeans, a tee shirt, and a dark jacket. The other guy was younger, maybe forty, thinner, wearing nearly the same outfit as the older one. I said I didn't know them, but believed they were the two who had jumped me the week before. I lied about not knowing their names. The aid car was called because of the blood, and everyone had on latex gloves. Surprisingly, both Mallory and Jones showed up at almost the same time. I persuaded the medics that I was ok and didn't need a return engagement at the ER. The nosebleed was staunched, and after all was said and done the cops and the medics departed, leaving me sitting on the curb with my erstwhile partner and the suspicious detective.

"I'm touched that you both came to help at this most precipitous moment," I said this with the delightful nasal buzz that goes with having absorbent stuffed up your nose.

"Every time I see you, Buttman, you look better and better," Jones snorted.

"Nice. Good to see you too. What brings you around, detective? You must have better things to do than follow up on local assaults?"

"You'd think, but no. I was in the neighborhood, and when I heard the address over the radio I thought of you. Apparently, I thought right. Same guys?"

"Same guys. Fortunately, this time I saw them first." I tried to stand, but couldn't get up. What energy I had left was swiftly leaving me, "Maybe we should take this inside."

"Yeah, you don't look so good."

They helped me inside. I sat in the chair as Jones moved to the couch. Mallory continued to stand.

"Any idea why they came back for more?"

"Because I hadn't gotten the message: stay away from Desiree Marshan. I got it, I just wasn't listening."

Jones chimed in, "You think that Dahlia woman sent them?"

"Could be, the two times I was to meet her, or did, the goons show up. Can't be a simple coincidence, can it?"

"Who's this Dahlia woman?" Mallory asked, but I think he already knew.

"A woman who used to be one of Desiree's film partners, used to be a man. She told us she and Desiree were on the outs, that she didn't care what Desiree was up to, that she was a conniving bitch and so on. Now she works at an LGBT clinic in West Hollywood. Someone roughed her up the last time I was. Well, before this."

My head was aching. Maybe I didn't do as well as I thought with Artie and Gordy.

"You don't believe what she told you?"

"No, I think it's a scam."

"It must be important to them, why else would they target you again?" Jones added his two cents.

"Must be." Mallory looked at his watch. He wanted to go. "Whatever it is, you two need to be careful. And remember, unlawful acts or actions require a call to the proper authorities, that's me! I don't recommend you play cops and bad guys. It's a good way to get killed. You have my number. Goodnight gentlemen."

Jones and I eyed the detective as he left. I turned to Jones.

"How's the promotion business going?"

He wasn't expecting that. "It's going. As a matter of fact, I was calling from a show when all this went down. I should get back; make sure we get paid. Speaking of which, I have to spend the next couple of days with my security people, we have some important clients ramping up their details, setting schedules, all of that. I don't know how much time I'll have to waste on this for the next week or so... "

I couldn't tell if he was trying to bag out or not. Didn't matter, it was time for a break anyway, time for other problems, personal problems.

"Actually, I think that'll work in our favor. I'm planning on heading up north for a week or so. It'll give Marshan and her group of goons the idea that we're giving up. Plus, it'll give Llewellyn time to find out where our lovebirds are hiding."

"Who's Llewellyn?"

"He's the computer guy. He's looking for the members of Desiree's fan club. Since it started out as a file-sharing group, more than likely it's still out there in one form or another. My guess is they still use it to communicate, if so, maybe we can find out where she is."

Jones, too, was ready to go. "Alright, give me a call when you get back."

It was then that I remembered my phone got lost in the fight.

"I need to find my phone, it's outside somewhere."

Jones shook his head. "I know a trick. Let's go."

We went out where the two attacked me. Jones dialed my number and a faint beeping came from over in the grass. I retrieved the phone.

"Neat trick."

"Goodnight, Buttman." The weary promoter left for his more promising endeavors. I made for the planter and my weapons of destruction.

They were gone.

A soft voice spoke.

"You should be more careful with these, especially this." There was Benitez holding the gun. I nearly collapsed; my heart was pounding into my throat.

He was smiling.

I tried to hide the look of terror in my eyes. "Yeah, I should." My legs were shaking so badly I was certain I would fall down.

"Easy, Amigo, let's go inside."

"Yeah."

We went in and I fell into the chair. I didn't have the energy for this. Benitez settled onto the couch where Jones had been a moment before. My heart continued to race. I couldn't breathe; I was going to have a heart attack. Right here, right now! Benitez put the weapons on the table and went into the kitchen returning with two glasses and the bottle of whiskey. He calmly poured the liquor, handed me a glass, and sat down. He took a drink and placed the bottle next to the gun. I reciprocated, the glass rattling in my hand. The whiskey tasted harsh against my throat as I forced it down. I could tell blood was mixing with it by the aftertaste of iron. Slowly the heartbeats began to ease as I finished the whiskey.

"Now that you've nearly frightened me to death, what brings you back to my door?"

"My apologies, it was not my intention to frighten you. I was merely waiting for the right time to announce myself."

"I see. So how long have you been here?"

He sipped the whiskey. "I waited till you left your car. For a moment I thought I might need to assist you, but you handled it well..."

"Yes, my Kung Fu skills came in nicely."

"...Enough. After that I thought it better to remain hidden 'til you were finished with the police and Mr. Jones."

"Ok, that answers that. So, why are you here?"

"Mainly to keep in touch."

"Did you put the bug in my car?"

The dispassionate Miguel Benitez smiled. "I have no connection with that. I'm here to help, if I can. In consultation with my associates, we've decided that it might be beneficial to your investigation if I shared a little more information from the people I'm working with, those interested in Desiree Marshan."

Finally, something other than guessing. "I'm all ears."

Benitez drank the last of his whiskey. "I'm going to tell you a story. You can believe about it what you like." He paused for effect. "Some time ago, back during the height of the US drug war, with all the violence in Columbia and some of the other countries involved in the trade, a patriarch of one of the families financing the business decided to begin moving his assets out of the country. He worried that the violence was destroying his family and his country. He did this very quietly, with the help of a few trusted associates, so as not to alert the people watching him. His legitimate assets were no problem; others were leaving as well, but his profits from the business were handled in great secrecy. This went on for many years. Finally, after he had moved the last of his wealth, he made plans to leave the country and the business. Unfortunately, he and a number of his family were killed by a car-bomb just days before they were scheduled to leave. Ironically, he had been so careful that no one knew where the money had gone because the two men who had helped him were killed too. It was as if it had all just disappeared. Not surprisingly, many have tried to find the money over the years, but they were unsuccessful, and the money became nothing more than an interesting story, a kind of myth."

"But we know better."

"Do we?"

"Then why the interest? What would be the point? Desiree would be nothing more than an angry ex-porn star cavorting with a has-been tech guy. No one in the business would care."

"You're assuming the business does care."

"If it didn't then why are you here? Chasing down an old myth? Seems unlikely."

"Perhaps, but as I said, you can believe the story or not, just as others might. Motivation isn't always the product of clear thinking or based on known facts. Sometimes, it's based on hopes and dreams, wishes and desires."

"Ok, now you've lost me, and maybe that's because I'm tired, sore, and developing a terrible headache."

Benitez got up and collected the whiskey glasses. "Then I should go and let you get some rest."

I got up too, "That's not a bad idea. Who knows who'll be trying to beat my ass tomorrow?"

We went into the kitchen. He handed me the glasses and I put them in the sink.

"It's not as easy as it looks, is it?" He laughed.

"No."

"Moses asks about you. Why don't you go see him? He misses you."

Why hadn't I thought of that! Odd that he would bring it up just as I was planning to see the old man. "Maybe I will. Take a break from the hullabaloo of chasing people down."

Benitez put his hand on my shoulder. "Tell him I said hello if you see him."

"I'll do that."

"You might also ask him about Marsyas Durant. Your father, at one time, stood at the crossroads of this business."

"What does that mean?"

Miguel put his arm around me. "That's what you need to find out." He released me and headed for the door. "Be careful with those." He pointed to the table.

"I will."

"I'll keep in touch, my friend."

He closed the door. I took the gun and sap from the table. My head ached, and it was hard to stand. I went to the bathroom and surveyed the damage. Other than the plugs in my nose, I didn't look any worse than I did before. I carefully removed the plugs, took a pain pill, and washed my face. That would be enough for now. I needed to lie down. The bed was soft and inviting. I found myself dreaming of three small boys running through the fields of my childhood.

The sun, omnipotent and persistent, drove me from my fitful slumber and my comfy bed. I saw no reason to get up. I covered my eyes with the pillow in a vain attempt to circumvent its authority, but I failed. As I lay there in my dirty clothes, I noticed that dried blood was everywhere. My nose bled while I was sleeping, staining the sheets. I had to get up if for no other reason than to clean my sheets, my clothes, and myself. The dreary labors of domesticity awaited. Some things you can't get out of. Stiff and sore, I forced myself up, removed the dirty clothes, and showered.

After a cup of coffee, I gathered the offending apparel and set out for the laundry. It was in a small room at the end of the courtyard shared by the bungalows. I dutifully plied the machine with quarters and watched listlessly as the clothes made their seemingly endless circular journey in the washer. I wandered back to my place for another cup of coffee, offering polite hellos to the ancient couples seated outside in the cool of the morning. Afternoons were too hot and evenings were too tiring, leaving mornings as their time to gather in the sun's rays and commiserate about life's shortcomings. One of which was my waking them from their slumbers by fighting with Artie and Gordy. Joanie caught me as I headed back to the laundry room.

"I hear you had another run in last night, might be time for a new line of work, Mr. Private Dick."

"Might be."

She gave me the once-over, checking the fine lines of my features. "You don't look so bad, certainly better than the last time. I guess that's a plus."

"I guess."

"You think it was the same guys as last time?"

"I think so."

"So now what?"

"Exactly."

She followed me to the laundry room where we planted ourselves in two of the plastic chairs facing the washers and dryers. We sat there watching the clothes spin. Joanie looked over at me with an expression of both relief and alarm. I didn't quite know how to respond.

"How was the gig?"

"It was good, nice crowd. How's it going with all the women? Did you fuck the rich one?"

"Does it matter?" I wasn't interested in arguing about Judith.

"Sorry, that was probably unkind."

"Probably."

I got up and put the laundry in the dryer.

"So did you fuck her or not?" Curiosity beat out decorum.

"I didn't go there for sex, Joanie."

"Uh-huh. Really, Buttman, you know this can't end well?"

"Yes, yes, I'm aware of that."

"I'm just looking out for your best interests, you know. I don't want you to get hurt."

"How thoughtful."

"Well, we both know that." She leaned over and kissed me. "I'd just hate to see you crash and burn, but you'll go wherever your private dick takes you. See you later."

"Adios."

Me and my private dick.

The dryer hummed along, monotony defined.

I sat there mulling over the events of the last day. It was, if nothing else, eventful. I tried to piece together the information I'd picked up from Dahlia, Judith, Bernie, Llewellyn, and Benitez. Could it really be about a hidden treasure laundered through a tech company? And if it was, how did that work? And if it did work, how would you get the money back? Were they all in on it? Or better yet, where did they fit in? I was thinking specifically of Durant, Dulcimer, and Benitez, or whomever he represented. They were the more important players, or were they? From what Llewellyn said, Martin, and maybe Judith, were merely beards fronting the scam, living out the charade. I assumed Desiree was in with whoever could deliver the goods. Where Dahlia was involved depended on the real nature of her relationship with Desiree. It was possible they were scamming Martin. Whatever Desiree and Martin were planning, I couldn't see how they could get it past Judith or Durant, since it would require both hers and A and A's participation. Did killing Boyer screw that up? I had no idea how Johnny D fit in, other than money was a part of it, and money was his stock in trade. I assumed Benitez either represented the last of the family, or a group that felt entitled to, as he put it, the profits from the business. It was quite a group. Then there was Benitez's admonition that it may be nothing like what I think or believe. That didn't help.

The clothes were dry.

I gathered up the warm scented sheets and returned to the bungalow. The phone was ringing as I walked in.

"Yes?"

"Monk, Johnny D."

"Mr. Dulcimer, what's up?"

"Nobody calls me that, Johnny D is fine. I'm calling about Agnes. She's not at work, and when I checked my phone she left a cryptic message about being an embarrassment to me, and a failure in life. Rey said she had a bad night at the bar and that he had to take her home. You didn't hear from her did you, Monk?"

"No. I talked to her about seven last night, asked if she wanted to get together, but she said she was tired and wanted to go to bed."

"That's not good, not good. I worry about her, Monk. I want you to do me a favor."

"Sure."

"Go see if she's ok."

"I can do that." Should I do that?

"Good."

"No problem."

"And Monk..."

"Yes, Johnny?"

"She's a good woman, maybe a little emotional sometimes. Know what I'm saying?"

I got it. "I do, Johnny, thanks."

I put the clothes away and made the bed. I called Agnes, but got no reply. Not even her voicemail. The weapons were where I had left them, by the bed. They went back into my pockets. I'd worry about the implications of that later. On the way to the car I noticed the blood and vomit had been washed from the courtyard. No suspicious characters could be seen as I left. The car appeared to be untouched, so I unlocked the door and lowered the top. I turned it over and hit the road. The ride was pleasant and uneventful, even the traffic seemed lighter than usual. I pulled in front of her house, took a deep breath, and got out. The knot in my chest that started as I drew closer tightened. Tempting, as it was to run, I knew that wasn't an option. I knocked on the door and waited. Agnes opened the door.

She looked terrible. My heart sank.

25

"Why are *you* here?"

Her eyes were bloodshot, rimmed by streaked mascara. A sad disconsolate expression was all she had to offer. Her hair was a mess, and she was still in what I assumed was the blouse she had on the night before, same for the skirt which was twisted and bunched around her waist. Those bloodshot eyes were wet with tears as she looked at me.

Stunned doesn't do justice to how I felt seeing her.

"Johnny D asked me to check in on you. He's worried, said you had a bad night last night."

"You could say that." We stood there in the bright sunshine. It was oddly out of place given our emotions.

"May I come in?"

She opened her mouth, then stopped. She turned and went in. "I guess if you want."

I followed her in, closing the door behind me.

The house was a mess. Evidently, she acted out after Rey brought her home, and some of the furniture paid the price. Agnes sat on the couch. Out of habit I started putting the room back in order.

"Did you come here to clean?" She was still clearly angry.

"For a start, yes. Have you eaten anything today?"

"I'm not hungry."

"That wasn't the question, have you eaten anything today."

"No, I didn't eat anything, ok!" I finished putting the lamp and table back and held out my hand. "What?"

"You need to eat something. Let's go."

"Why are you here?" Tears were running down her face.

"I told you why."

"Then why didn't Johnny come?"

"We both know why, please, Agnes."

Reluctantly, she took my hand and I led her into the kitchen. She sat at the table while I looked in the pantry and refrigerator for something to eat. As I expected, the pickings were lean. I had meant to go to the store with her the night before. Fortunately, there was coffee, so I brewed a pot, and made do with some toast and jam. It was becoming the usual. We sat, eating in silence. I watched her as she stared off into space.

"What's got you so worked up?"

"What do you care?"

"Agnes."

"I'm tired of being an idiot and a fool, that's what's got me worked up."

"I don't think you're either." She just stared at me. "Then how about some specifics as to why you are."

She reached for her phone, which was on the counter. After playing with it, she handed it to me. It was a text message from her ex-husband. Simon wasn't happy with her wanting to come up. They were busy and he didn't want her upsetting Anna with any new boyfriends or comments about him and Eric, maybe another time, when they had more time. Agnes shot back that he was being unfair, controlling. Simon said that's because she was out of control. It went on, back and forth.

"I'm sorry."

"Oh, it gets better. Push the next arrow."

Next was a text from Anna parroting what her father had said; she was busy, maybe some other time. I looked over at her. She was crying.

"Keep going."

The next message was the garrote to the tightening knot in my chest. There, in living color, was a picture of me leaving Judith's house. The word *proof* was below it.

"Proof of what?"

"That you're fucking his wife." Agnes was staring intently at me.

I didn't see any more messages, "Martin called you?"

"He didn't say his name."

"What did he say? That I was fucking his wife?"

Her face softened a little. "Not exactly…"

"Then what exactly did he say?"

Agnes wiped her face and looked off in the distance. "He said, tell your fucking boyfriend to stay away from my wife, and when I said I didn't believe him he sent the picture."

"So, you assumed I was fooling around with her?"

"Yes. What would you think?"

I took this in. I wondered how they knew about Agnes, but then if they were following me… Either way, I had to be careful.

"When did you get this message?"

"Yesterday around five, right after my fun little text war with Simon." I handed her the phone. "You were there weren't you?" I couldn't say no.

"Yes, I was there."

"So he was right." Tears were falling down on her hands clutching the phone.

"Yes and no."

"What does that mean?"

"I was there to talk to her about where I could find her husband and his girlfriend. I didn't go there for sex." Joanie didn't buy it, but maybe Agnes would. I didn't see how a confession would help.

"Then why would he say that?"

"For the same reason they had the goons try to jump me again last night, to scare me off, to stop me from looking for them."

"They attacked you again?" Her head rose to look at me.

"Yeah, but this time I saw them first. Who knows what would have happened if I hadn't. Fortunately, I didn't get the shit kicked out of me this time."

"So your night was as good as mine." Agnes slumped back into her chair.

I put away the cups and the plates and looked through the kitchen window, peering out onto her little backyard. There was a set of outdoor furniture and a kettle BBQ. A large tree from the neighbor shaded the yard. It was a nice quiet place, much like the persimmon grove I had back in Virginia. I sat back down. Agnes looked at me with a mixture of hope and fear. What a mess. How did I turn into this woman's savior? I could barely save myself. I reached for her hand and she pulled me towards her. I caught her and I held her as she cried herself out. It was becoming clear to me how badly broken she had become after Simon left her. A deep terrible sorrow poured out of her. What else to do but let it out? I held her as best I could, something I often struggled to do all those years ago with Astral and Rebekah, funny how time changes you. After a while it slowed, then stopped. I brushed the hair out of her face.

"Better?"

"A little."

"That's something. Why don't we get you cleaned up and I'll treat you to lunch."

A soft yes came out of her, but she held on tight for a while longer before letting go and heading for the bathroom. I called Johnny D to tell him she was all right and that I'd bring her over after lunch. That was good he said.

He also wanted to talk.

Lunch was a somber affair. Agnes did her best to put on a brave face given everything that had happened. I did my best to be sympathetic. Besides, whatever had happened last night, and she seemed reticent to talk about it, I couldn't cast stones. I'd had my share of blowups and public scenes as well as embarrassing family moments. Everyone has an occasional emotional meltdown, and it's always after the pressure's spent that you have to figure out how to unscrew what you've screwed up.

We stopped at a sandwich shop not far from where she worked. I hadn't eaten much in last twenty-four hours and was hungry, ordering a large club. Agnes was not and picked at her salad, her eyes hidden behind a pair of large sunglasses, and her head down. The silence was unbearable. I was trying to not feel responsible, but that wasn't working. We sat there wallowing in uncertainty. Maybe this was it. Agnes was sad and unhappy, and I had no idea how to make it better.

"What do you want to do, Agnes?"

"I don't know, I feel so stupid. I've made a complete ass of myself in front of everyone I know."

"It can't be that bad…"

"Really? I yelled at my daughter, lied to you, drank too much, stupidly thought I'd get back at you with some guy I met at the bar only to freak-out in his car, and finished off the night acting so crazy Rey had to take me home."

"When did you yell at your daughter?"

"After I got her text." Agnes slumped in her chair.

"Alright, so you had your moments yesterday. We all have them; it's not the end of the world. Besides, it's not as bad as you think. Johnny's more concerned than upset, I understand why you said what you said, and I don't care what happened with the guy at the bar. You can call your daughter and explain. You never know. Tell her you love her, you're sorry, and that you'd still like to see her even if she only has a little bit of time. Then I'll take you to hippy-land to meet my freaky extended family and that should make you feel better."

"You still want to go?" She seemed surprised.

"Might as well, the car's ready and we could use the break."

"I'm a fuck-up, Monk!"

"Aren't we all? Look, I'm not expecting you to be the perfect woman, ok? If I'm honest, I like being around you because you make me feel good and you seem to like me. What else is there, really? We all have bad days; that's life. As for the trip, why not go? We might have a good time. What do you say?" I sensed a lift in her spirits. She did her best to smile. "It's unlikely to be as bad as last night was for you or for me. It'll be good to get away for a few days. The weather should be nice and I can be reasonable company most of the time."

"Fine. If you've got your heart set on my ruining your weekend, who am I to say no."

"That's what I like to hear, beautiful."

Now she was smiling.

"I like it when you call me that. It's nicer than Agnes."

"You don't like Agnes?"

"No."

"Ok, I'll call you beautiful from now on, unless you piss me off. How's that?"

I got a laugh and she was eating.

"I can live with that," she admitted.

The remainder of our lunch felt lighter and our trip more promising. Johnny D was in the office when we got there. He assured Agnes that he understood. They talked a bit about business, the things he needed before we took off. He then waved me over and I promised to be right back. We headed through the bar towards his back office. I said hello to Rey who was prepping the bar. Rey nodded and went back to work. Johnny sat down and motioned for me to do the same.

"I want to thank you for taking care of Agnes, Monk."

"No problem. I think we got everything worked out."

"That's good, that's good." I didn't quite know what to make of Johnny D. You can't be a softy in his line of work, and from what I'd heard, he wasn't. But this thing with Agnes... I didn't get it. "How goes the search for Desiree Marshan?"

"It goes. I'm certain she's shacked up with Martin Delashay. His wife believes they're hiding somewhere along the coast."

"Judith Delashay, the woman Agnes thinks you're fooling around with?"

"Yeah, she's the one, and I'm not fooling around with her."

Johnny D. was having none of it. "She's a beautiful woman, Mrs. Delashay, and no doubt interested in her husband's arrangement with the Marshan woman. I'm not going to judge what happens between you and her, Monk, you're your own man. Sometimes you have to make choices in what you do. Just don't kid yourself as to the motive behind those choices."

"I have no illusions when it comes to Mrs. Delashay. Nor do I have any illusions about what's motivating her. It's not me, and it's not whatever sexual thing Martin has for Desiree. It's money, and a lot of it. The question is why so many others are interested in it, how they fit in. You, for instance, where does Johnny D fit in?"

Johnny D leaned in, putting his hands on the desk. "My interest is in the money, I won't deny that, but not in the way you believe. I have all the wealth I need, Monk. My interest, for now, is in those involved, their motives. Times are changing. Attitudes are changing. Opportunities are possible that were not possible just a few years ago. That's what interests me. I like the action. I hear the whispers, the possibilities, that's why I'm interested. Just as I'm interested in whether you can get this done."

"Would you put money on it?"

He laughed. "Maybe, if I like the odds."

"I'd put them at even."

Johnny sat back. "Good enough. So, what's next?"

"Whatever Martin and Desiree are up to, they're concerned enough to go after me twice and to push Agnes over it. They're afraid of something. I believe I know what that is, but I'll keep that close till I have some more proof. For now, I plan to lay low. Agnes wants to go see her daughter, and I should go see my old man. That may lead them to think I'm backing off. It'll give my computer guy time to find what he can."

"And Mr. Jones?"

The lovable Orville Riley. "I don't know. I think my getting jumped spooked his wife. He might not be as interested as before. I thought maybe he could check down at the hall of records for property in the name of Delashay, Sphere, Tophanovich, or Denesova. Or he could keep an eye on Dahlia Leonard."

I was out of ideas.

"I see. Well, keep me informed, Monk."

"I will." I stood up. "And while I know my relationship with Mrs. Delashay might be suspect, I want you to know that I care about Agnes and I would never knowingly hurt her."

Johnny D walked me to the door. "I believe you, but you can't fool me, Monk. And I know Agnes. I know how she grows on you. Minus the foolish edges, she has a generous heart and she will take hold of yours. Are you prepared for that?"

"There are worse things that being loved or cared for. I know; I've been there. Thanks for the talk."

"Anytime."

I still didn't get Johnny's angle on any of this.

26

I went over to the bar and asked Rey for a whiskey and water. Rey served it up with his usual faux smile. It tasted good. The bar was growing on me. Sure, it was quiet, gloomy, with only a small amount of natural light making its way past the fixed shutters, but I didn't feel like a stranger here. Unlike so many other parts of this huge sprawling megalopolis, I didn't feel invisible. It was a good place to think. Johnny's words were ringing in my ears; she will take hold of you. I was trying to adjust to that thought, trying to decide if that was good or bad. Was today a harbinger of things to come or was it a temporary storm?

I took a drink.

Agnes came from the office and sat beside me.

"Can I have a tonic with lime, Rey?" Rey nodded.

"Back to normal?" Sometimes it's important to ask.

"I guess." Rey set down the tonic and put his hand on hers and nodded again. "Thanks, Rey, for everything."

"Anytime, Agnes, you know that." Rey winked and went back to the other side of the bar. I looked over at Agnes; she was stirring the tonic with her finger.

"I'm sorry about this morning." She was speaking so softly I could barely hear her.

"Why?"

"Cuz I don't want you to think I'm some crazy out of control woman."

"I don't think that." Well, maybe a little.

"It's just that the day started out so well, and then it went from bad to worse to terrible. I haven't seen Anna in months, and I miss her, and I'm trying really hard to be understanding about Simon and Eric, and then that guy called about you. It was just too much."

"It's ok." I put my arm around her.

"Monk..."

"What?" She looked me in the eye and ran her hand along the still bruised left side of my face.

"It's nothing. Would you like to do something together tonight? I thought if we're leaving tomorrow, maybe it would be easier if you stayed with me, then we could take off from there."

I thought about it. It made sense, but oddly, *I* was having cold feet. I didn't know if I really wanted to go up north.

"I suppose we could, I..."

The goddamned phone was ringing again. I let go of Agnes.

"Yes?"

"Mr. Buttman, this is Taylor Lagenfelder. Mr. Durant is asking to see you, this afternoon if possible." Like I would blow off Marsyas Durant.

"I can be there in an hour if that's convenient?"

"That would fine, Mr. Buttman. We'll see you then. Goodbye."

Agnes had a quizzical look on her face. "Anyone I should worry about?"

"I don't know what you mean." I was lying. "However, I have to go down to Aeschylus and Associates and talk to the boss." She was holding my arm.

"Will you be back?" The cold feet were warming.

"I'll be back. This'll give me a chance to go home and grab a few things today instead of tomorrow morning. When I get back we can hit the store, get some food and snacks for the trip. Do you have a cooler or picnic basket?"

"No. Simon took them."

"Then I bring mine. You'll like them, hip, old school. Sound good?"

"Sounds good," I gently pulled away.

"I'll see you in a few hours." I gave her a long soft kiss.

Leave 'em smiling.

Taylor Lagenfelder met me in the lobby. I tried to discern whether she had considered my earlier proposal or not. For a young woman, she was no fool, careful not to say too much or overplay her hand.

"It's good to see you, Mr. Buttman. Your appearance is improving."

"Small favors, Ms. Lagenfelder, small favors." I waited until we were safely ensconced in the elevator to pop the question. "Have you thought about my request from the other day?"

"I have. Unfortunately, I've been very busy and haven't had the time to look into it. I won't access any information on Martin Delashay unless I'm directed to by someone with the authority to do so. As for Mr. Boyer..." Ms. Lagenfelder hesitated. Hesitation is good, right? "...He did not have a sterling reputation among the staff."

"Meaning?"

"Meaning that he made a number of the women working here uncomfortable by indulging in inappropriate comments and suggestions. I haven't inquired into his relationship with Ms. Marshan, but I do know that several individuals heard rumors that it went beyond the bounds of our corporate policies regarding personal relationships. Anyway, Mr. Durant has discouraged the staff from talking about Mr. Boyer, Desiree Marshan, and the incident between them."

"I see." We had reached Mr. Durant's suite. I entered while Ms. Lagenfelder stayed in the elevator. Mr. Durant was at his desk.

"Come in, Monk. Have a seat."

I took the seat across from the desk and waited as he worked through the papers on his desk. He spoke without looking up.

"I was told you were attacked again last night."

"Yeah, same two guys, only this time I came out of it in better shape."

"Good for you. Do you know why they were targeting you?" He looked up.

"Because of Desiree Marshan, but it could also be about Judith Delashay. Either way, they want me to stop looking for Martin and Desiree."

Mr. Durant sat back in his chair and rubbed his hands together as if they were dirty or cold. "What did Judith have to say?"

I wonder how he knew I'd been seeing Judith. Was he behind the tail? Had she spoken to him? "She believes Martin has run off with Desiree, that they're holed up somewhere along the coast."

"Did she say why she believes that?"

"She says he's run off before, but didn't elaborate as to why she thought he was at a beach house. I assume she would have said something if they owned one. Do you know if he owns one that his wife might not know about?"

"I couldn't say. Not that I'm being diffuse, but I don't know all the particulars of the many people we represent. Would you like us to look?"

"I would." Marsyas Durant had a quiet face. It didn't shift or fuss, no ticks to alert those watching him to what was on his mind. His expressions were muted. I imagined it worked well for him.

"What else have you uncovered, Monk?"

"Mostly stories and possibilities, but no clear-cut reason for why this is what's going on. It might involve a lot of money, maybe not. It might have to do with Sphere, Martin's old company, or his partner, Jeremy Tophanovich, then again maybe not. I found evidence that Martin knew of Desiree's adult film work, that he had copies of her films. It's possible he was part of a group that availed itself of her services. It may involve drug money, but then again, maybe not."

"Who told you that?"

"Ever heard of a man named Miguel Benitez?"

Durant raised his eyebrows just a touch. "I do know Mr. Benitez. How do you know him?"

"We grew up together. After I left, I heard he became an enforcer. He looked me up after this started. I don't know how he knew I was involved, but he said he represented people who were interested in Desiree Marshan too."

"Interesting. Let me ask you this, how you see these possibilities coming together, Monk?"

He was tapping the fingers of his hands together.

"As an assumption, one might conclude that money from drug profits in the late Eighties and early Nineties were laundered through Sphere using a security program as a cover; that the people who originally moved the money were killed, so that the money remained quietly hidden in foreign accounts. It's possible that because the Delashay's were principle owners in Sphere, their participation would be required in order to repatriate the money. I don't know how someone like Desiree Marshan would know about this, but maybe our wildcard did, and he started the ball rolling."

"Our wildcard being the deceased, Mr. Boyer..."

"Yes."

Mr. Marsyas Durant smiled. He rose out of his chair and came to the front of his desk. It was a little intimidating.

"That's quite a convoluted tale. Do you believe it?"

"Yes and no. Benitez inferred that it could be true; but that it could also be nothing more than something certain people choose to believe. I think it's possible, but I wouldn't put money on it."

"So what's your next step?"

I hesitated to say. Still. "I'm going to go north. Both as a feign to the people after me so they will think I'm backing off, and to see the old man..." I paused, collecting my thoughts. "Benitez said I should ask him about you and the early days. I don't exactly know what he meant by that. Meanwhile I have a guy doing some computer research about Desiree's fan club to see if we can find anything there."

Durant walked over to the wall of windows facing west.

"Yes, a talk with Moses might be beneficial. I'd be interested in what he remembers of those days." He turned towards me. "Is there anything else I can do for you?"

"We never discussed compensation. I'm going to need some money to continue."

"I imagine so. How much do you believe you will require?"

"Five grand for now, and at the end?" It couldn't hurt to ask.

Durant smiled, "Not to worry, Monk, if this turns out as I think it will you should be well compensated. I'll have the money transferred to your account. Anything else?"

"What about Boyer?"

"Our wildcard." Durant motioned me to follow him to the elevator. "We'll discuss Mr. Boyer when you return from your forays to the north. Goodbye Monk. Good luck."

"Goodbye, Mr. Durant."

27

The next stop was the credit union, but I needed to call my erstwhile partner. I knew his interest was flagging. Maybe some cash would bring him around. I instinctually reached for the object in my pocket.

I had to laugh. I'd forgotten there was more than one.

These damn phones were too easy. I hadn't had the thing a week and it was already a part of my hand. I punched in Jones's number.

"Jones."

"It's Buttman, I'm calling back."

"And?"

Such love and affection!

"And, I think it would be a good idea to keep an eye on Dahlia, see if she likes the beach. I'm heading up north for a week, so I need you to take care of this."

"I have my own priorities, Buttman, I don't have time to waste watching some transvestite."

"She's transsexual, man! So if you don't have the time, maybe you know someone who does and needs the money."

"What money?"

"I got us some pocket money for our little adventure."

I noticed the inflection in his voice pick up. "How much?"

"Twenty-five hundred."

"I might know someone willing to work for us." Money eases all concerns.

"Good. Meet me at my place in an hour and I'll get you the bread, man."

I could hear him smirking through the phone. "Goodbye, Buttman."

I had an account at a small credit union not far from my place. Checking and savings with a safety deposit box. I normally didn't do the online thing, so my interactions were in person. A woman named Tanesha patiently provided me with the information I requested on my balances and on the withdrawal I was making, Jones's pocket money. I was surprised that the money Durant had promised was already pending, always a good sign. After pocketing the cash, I asked to see my box. I had the absurdist fear that it might be tampered with, so as is common for those of us with this affliction, I made a point of periodically checking its contents. I hadn't come round since the day this affair started, it was time.

In the box were a few documents, some money I held mostly for sentimental reasons, and a passbook. I looked through it and made an annotation on the page with the last entry. It was a quaint exercise that I habituated even though I no longer needed to. Mostly it was for the tactile quality of the book itself, a talisman for a virtual sum of money, but more so for a point in time, a time I couldn't forget. After reassuring myself that what was there was what I expected to be there, I pulled the envelope from my pocket. It was a document with signatures. Something told me to hold on to it. I could always retrieve it if needed.

I closed the box and left the credit union. From there I made a quick run to the library and its many computer terminals. I had a separate account from my time in Virginia that I had held onto. It wasn't with the credit union. That virtual sum of money was connected to the passbook. I would periodically transfer money to keep the account active, like today. It was the only time I used a computer, and the library was anonymous enough to salve my fears of predatory surveillance. The account was my little secret so no one knew about it. In it were the receipts of payments and deposits best forgotten or rued, like the blood money Judah paid me for my plot of land after he stole Astral from me. Even then he believed he deserved a church discount.

I didn't give it to him.

It was my black day's fund, held tight, just in case, because a small part of me was still deathly afraid of the past.

I went home. The landscapers were back. I couldn't imagine what else they had to work on, but it wasn't my money so I kept moving. There were no suspicious footprints, nor were any persons milling about our little enclave so I felt reasonably safe. I went in and looked around. It appeared as it had when I'd left earlier in the day. With a kind of zeal, I found the picnic basket and cooler situated below the jackets in the hall closet and the small suitcase I owned in the bedroom closet. I packed what I thought I would need, including toiletries, and placed them all by the door. That being accomplished, I sat in my chair and wondered what the hell I was doing. It occurred to me that I was spending an inordinate amount of time going round and round over the same subject.

That can't be good.

It was time to get back to the nice and easy, roll with it; go with the flow. I wasn't stupid enough to buy that as an actual philosophical principle or as SoCal existentialism, no matter what some beach bum or aging hippie might tell me, but I needed something less frantic, something less fraught with peril or poor personal choices. I needed that laid-back vibe, man, bullshit or no bullshit. I was willing to wade if necessary. I found this very soothing for reasons I couldn't adequately explain. Maybe that was the point. The room was oddly serene, so I put my feet up and closed my eyes, determined to believe it would be alright if I just didn't think about what I was doing too deeply. I could hear the birds singing.

"Buttman!"

I didn't care for this particular bird.

"Mr. Jones, how good to see you. I assume you're here for the money?"

An exasperated Jones stood there as he normally did; arms crossed, arrayed in black, stern in visage.

"This ain't a personal visit, Buttman." He accented the name with a certain brio.

"How disappointing." I reached into my pocket, retrieving the twenty-five bills. Jones came closer as I raised my hand.

"I'm sure it is, but that's life."

"It sure is. You know when we began this partnership it was my understanding that you were adept at finding people, yet I'm the guy leading this clusterfuck, how come?"

"You got me."

"They said you were good at this sort of thing."

"They lied, get used to it." Jones took the money and deposited it in the pocket of his jacket. "So we keep an eye on the woman, and I use that term loosely, to see if she leads us to Desiree, correct?"

"Correct." I sat there contemplating the reserved black man, a man whose race had been systemically persecuted for generations, yet he had no compassion for a man whose gender he felt trapped by, or so I assumed, but what did I know? "Why are you so worked up by that woman Dahlia?"

"Cuz she's a dude, man. That's the way God made her, him. You may think it's ok, Buttman, but it's bullshit to me. Why don't I just run around calling myself a fucking white dude because it makes me feel better to do so, huh? You are what you are. Live with it. Why can't people be who they are? It doesn't make any sense to me, that's why."

"Alright, I was just curious. So, yes, have your man, or woman, keep an eye on Dahlia to see if she slips off to the beach. I mean a beach house. I don't care if she goes to the beach. You know what I mean."

Our uncomfortable conversation had hit the skids.

"I know what you mean." He stood there looking off at the walls. "Will there be compensation as we pursue this?"

"Yeah, I don't think money will be a problem so long as we're reasonable with our requests." I assumed that to be true.

"Then I'll keep in touch."

Mr. Jones left as he entered. Me, I just watched. It was that kind of day, and yet it wasn't over. I would need to head back to Agnes's house. I was ready, I just wasn't moving. The breeze was traversing the room, carrying me away from Jones and Agnes, from Judith and Durant. I closed my eyes.

Nice and easy.

Joanie had quietly come into the room and was sitting on the couch, watching me. I opened my good eye.

"You know it's kinda creepy when you sneak in like that. Especially given what's happened here lately."

"Kinda. I saw your door open and came in to make sure you weren't curled up on the floor in a pool of blood. Those things are kind of traumatic. But, you seem to be in decent shape, for now." She looked over at the pile by the door. "Plans?"

"As a matter of fact, yes. Since you were unwilling to go to the farm with me, I talked Agnes into it. Well, that and we're going to see her daughter in San Francisco, she kinda talked me into that."

"It might not be a bad idea for you to get away for a while. San Francisco is nice."

"Yeah…" I didn't like the way she was being so agreeable. "It'll be good to get out on the road."

"Plus, it'll keep you away from the rich woman, *Judith*."

"You don't like Judith, do you?" Joanie actually seemed jealous.

"Not particularly. I don't think she has your best interests at heart."

"As if I have hers in mine?"

"You know what I mean." I did, but I'd seen Judith's softer side, and I wasn't willing to see her as overly calculating where I was concerned. I was the delivery boy, for Christ's sake, nobody important. Sex will blind you like that. "Well, it looks like you're ready to go. I stopped by to make sure everything was all right. I guess you are."

What an odd comment.

"I guess so. You have plans?"

She smiled. "I have my new gig in San Francisco. Maybe you should bring Agnes to the club. It'll be fun."

"Maybe… What's the name of the club?"

"The Mind's Eye, it's a nice place." Agnes would love that. She was already worried about Judith. Why don't we throw Joanie in the mix? It'll be fun.

"I'm sure it is." I got up from the chair and straightened myself out. "I haven't heard you sing in a while, maybe we'll do that." I picked up the cooler and basket.

"Need a hand?"

"Maybe."

Joanie picked up the suitcase, and we walked to the car after I locked the door. I loaded up the trunk as she watched. It was awkward and I didn't quite know why, like I was leaving the family, or our little support group. Maybe that was it. For years we've always had each other to cling to because our love lives were either non-existent or a mess. Now with Mikal and Agnes gumming up the works, our future companionship was uncertain. No matter what anyone says, it's hard to be friends with the opposite sex when you're in a committed relationship.

Committed relationship.

I had to let that swirl around my head.

Committed relationship.

Me and Agnes, Mikal and Joanie; theirs seemed more real, mine more illusory. I guess that's what this trip was for.

Joanie was staring at me. I had to stop thinking.

"What?" It was all I had.

"I was about to ask you the same thing."

"If you must know, I was thinking about the two of us, whether our newfound romances would change us and our relationship."

"Yeah." She gave me a kiss, followed by a face I didn't recognize. "It's kinda scary isn't it?"

"I suppose." I didn't want to think about it. I looked around for a different topic. "The yard looks nice. I was surprised to see them fixing it up after so many years."

"I know. I asked Ardis about it. She said it was a promotional gift. You know to advertise their services to the neighborhood. They certainly do nice work, don't you think?"

"Yeah, they do." Free services, why? I was leery of the advertising gimmick. Maybe they were fishing for more maintenance services later. Old people were more susceptible to that kind of trick. It was like these phones, a hook to keep you on the line for more and more money. I opened the car door and got in. "It's time for me to go. Maybe we'll see you at the club?"

"I'd like that." Joanie stepped back. "See you, Monk."

Why did I feel like I'd never see her again? "See you."

Joanie walked back to her bungalow as I struggled to remember where I was going. Agnes, I was going to see Agnes. I looked up. The sky was falling, taking the sun with it. I called Agnes, asking where I should meet her.

She told me to come home.

Those two words started rolling around in my head again.

I pulled into the driveway, and took out the luggage, basket, and cooler. I put up the top as Agnes came out. It was then that I realized her tan was fading. Why hadn't I noticed that before? She picked up the basket and led me through the front door. After I put the cooler and the luggage down I went out to lock the car, but mostly it was to check the gun and the sap. I considered leaving them back at the bungalow, but I changed my mind, they were still in the trunk. Now I had to decide whether to leave them in the car or bring them in the house. I hesitated to ask Agnes what she thought. After a few minutes I waved her over.

"I need to ask you something."

Agnes moved closer as I put the key in the trunk lock. "There's not a body in it, is there?"

I had to laugh. "Sorry, no body, but there are weapons, a gun and a blackjack, a sap. Should I bring them in? Are you comfortable with that or do you want me to leave them here? Since this is your house, I wanted to ask."

"I don't know. I don't like guns, but do you think we'll need it?"

"I hope not, but I don't know."

We stood there contemplating our options. On the one hand, I worried that Artie and Gordy might grab a couple more knuckleheads from the gangbang and go for a third try, in which case a gun would come in handy. On the other hand, I was no professional, quick and able with a gun. I was more likely to shot myself, Agnes, or the both of us. Neither was particularly appealing. I looked around the street.

"Beautiful, do you see any cars you don't recognize around here?"

Agnes, responding to her new name, put her arms around me and surveyed the street.

"I don't think so. Why?" A puzzled expression joined the hug.

"I have an idea."

"Yeah?"

"Yeah. We'll leave these here for now. Later I'll show you what I have in mind."

Agnes ran her hand along the front of my shirt. "Is it that thing you like to do?"

"Focus woman!"

"I am," She was licking my ear.

"Save that for later, we need to go to the store."

"If you insist." Reluctantly, she let go, locked the house, and we got in the car.

The store was six blocks away. I methodically inventoried the vehicles we passed on the way. I had Agnes do the same. She found this exciting, like a Bond girl she said. If nothing else, I told her, she had the boobs for it. Ha, ha, but I knew she didn't mind. Between the two of us I hoped we would notice anything odd or out of place. I realized neither of us was trained or conditioned by experience to be good at something like this, but it made for an interesting drive. Agnes noted two homeless couples panhandling, and I couldn't stop focusing on the poor condition of the road, as I seemed to hit every pothole.

The store was its own adventure. Turns out Agnes has a yen for junk food, whereas I'm more the fruits and nuts type; partly due to my time farming, and the fact that I didn't often eat junk food. I didn't have a taste for chips and cookies. Agnes, on the other hand, did, so we brokered a compromise, after considerable debate, and ended up spending more than I would have liked. It was obvious that Agnes ate junk when she was anxious, and anxiety was on the menu. I decided being the "you should eat healthy" nag would not pay dividends, so I let it go.

Dinner, however, was a different matter, so I ruled out a pizza. Chicken and mushrooms over rice with a side salad. I told her if she didn't like it, she could cook.

"You don't like pizza?" The shock on her face made the whole argument worth it.

"I like pizza just fine, but not the awful frozen kind. There's a great pizza place in San Francisco. We'll have pizza there."

Agnes scrunched her face. "I can see you're a lot more judgmental than I thought!"

I scrunched back. "You got that right. Do we have everything?"

"How would I know?" she pouted.

"Exactly."

Having gone through her pantry I knew what she had and what she didn't and what we'd need that wouldn't spoil while we were gone. Agnes groused about soda, followed by my grousing as well. All in all it was an outing befitting two people on the cusp of the dreaded two-word description of two people who can't get enough of each other. On the way back we eagle-eyed the road for possible bad guys. I didn't notice any, and neither did Agnes.

After I parked and we put the groceries away, I snuck back out and found the bug on the rear bumper. It was a small round magnetic thing. It seemed terribly old school; I mean how many people drive cars these days with metal bumpers? I carefully removed it and placed it in the wheel well of Agnes's car. I looked around to see if anyone was watching. I then snuck back into the house.

Agnes sat at the kitchen table and watched as I cooked. I found it unsettling, but I could tell this would be a common occurrence should our attempt at a committed relationship survive. I decided to make small talk.

"Did you call your daughter?"

"Yes." She said this like a child who had been forced to do something she didn't want to.

"And?"

"And, I decided to take your advice."

"And?" It was like pulling teeth.

"And she agreed to meet us."

"So why the face?"

"Because she wants us to come to the restaurant tomorrow night around nine, that way she'll have more time because it slows down by then." Seemed reasonable.

"And you don't like that because..."

"Because it means Simon will be there, hovering, interfering."

Simon. I was growing tired of someone I hadn't even met.

"It'll be alright. Plus, it'll give you a chance to show me off."

"I suppose." Agnes was tapping on the table with her fingers. "Is it ok if we go up on highway 1 instead of I-5? I like that better. We can see the ocean and feel the breeze."

"We can do that."

Dinner was a chance to slow down and chill out. I found some outdoor candles and we ate on the patio in the backyard. We went easy on the wine. I was tired, and she needed to pack. The air was cool and, for this part of town, remarkably clear. We listened to the sounds of the birds comingling with the gurgling and rustling of the noises from the surrounding houses. It appeared, outwardly, to be a nice little neighborhood, a pocket of solace, like the bungalows, in this incessantly throbbing city. Agnes, as I suspected, was rapidly declining into repose. Not surprising given that she'd had too much to drink and too little sleep the night before. Throw in a decent amount of emotional turmoil, and I was amazed she'd lasted this long.

I gingerly roused her and got her into the bedroom where she slowly assembled what appeared to be enough clothes for a month. The suitcase was in the closet and she mashed it all in before falling on the bed. I grabbed a small case and once again roused her, onward and upward, to the bathroom, where she piled the wherewithal to maintain her beauty, reluctantly brushed her teeth, and relieved herself. She barely made it to bed before quickly falling asleep.

Ah, the joys of connubial bliss.

As I watched her sleep, it again amazed me how fast this had all come about. How long? Two weeks? Something like that. I thought of Astral, where I jumped all too quickly into a life I had given no thought to. I'd had no license with her either. You're supposed to learn from the past. Yet here I was, as Johnny D had warned me, caring for this woman I barely knew. I returned to the backyard to clean up and found myself back in the chair, where it was quiet, where the lights obscured the stars, where I could collect myself. I nursed the last of the wine and watched the moon, a waxing gibbous, break free of the neighbor's tree.

Who uses such language? I remembered a book on astronomy and cosmology I'd read years before back in Virginia. I had lots of time back then to read. The things you remember. I had a head full of them. They were swimming around, waiting to surface. The wine was finished and it was time to go inside. I cleaned and put away the dishes, then headed outside.

I had rethought the plan.

The street remained untouched. No new vehicle or person. I removed the bug from Agnes's car and put it back on mine. If they were going to follow me, so be it. I opened the trunk and took the 45 from the tool bag. Just in case.

It was still heavy.

28

The evening came and went, as did the night. Other than rolling Agnes onto her side, she snored when she slept on her back; sleep came easy. Maybe it was the loaded cannon under the bed, maybe it was the exhaustion from the day before, but unlike most mornings, I felt rested and was ready for the first light, ready for the day to begin.

Agnes? Not so much.

She remained deep in slumber as I got cleaned up and dressed. I loaded up the cooler and basket and put them in the trunk. I also put the gun back in the tool bag. I casually looked up and down the street. To my surprise, I noticed something different. At the end of the street, behind an old Honda Accord, was a blue sedan with two guys in it. I made a mental note and went back inside. I brought out the two suitcases, and looked to see if they were still there.

They were.

I took the gun back out and put it in my pocket. The car didn't move, nor the characters in it. I closed the trunk and returned to the house. I set out breakfast and went to the bedroom to wake Sleeping Beauty. I tried being gentle, but that got me nowhere. She finally relented after a few well-timed, well-placed gropes.

"I'm up, I'm up! Next time a 'mother may I' if you want a handful," she wailed.

"No, I'll have to come up with something else. Mother may I kinda weirds me out."

"Suit yourself."

Agnes wandered to the bathroom as I went to the kitchen to cook breakfast. Something simple, scrambled eggs with leftover mushrooms, peppers, and cheese, a muffin on the side, black coffee in the pot. I put out the plates, spooned the breakfast onto the plates, poured the coffee and buttered the muffins. After bellowing, I heard Agnes making her way to the kitchen. If nothing else, her disposition had perked up. She was still in her robe, but her face was on and her hair was done.

"How much time do I have?"

"Till what?" I knew what she meant.

"Till we go!"

"Fifteen minutes," I informed her.

"I'll need at least thirty, maybe more."

I looked at her with my most penetrating gaze. "Sorry, baby, but we're on a tight schedule, no can do."

She shook her head. "Tough! I don't do tight schedules."

I took a bite of my muffin and a sip of coffee. "Looks like we've hit an impasse."

She must have been hungry; she was wasting no time on breakfast. "Looks like."

Surprisingly, breakfast took another twenty minutes. Agnes finished off the last of the eggs and had a second muffin. After finishing the coffee, she let her robe slip open. I rose to pick up her dishes, and brushed up against her.

"Mother may I?"

She laughed. "Ok, that *is* a little creepy."

"You realize this will push back the schedule?"

She got up and planted a big one right on my lips. "I sure hope so."

The blue sedan was still there when we got in the car. I didn't say anything to Agnes as we pulled away. She was still reveling in the afterglow of glorious morning sex, but then so was I. Whatever problems we might potentially have, for now, sex wasn't going to be one of them. I wondered how common that was. If there were hesitations about this road trip, they were salved by our morning romp and we were on our way. I didn't look to see if the blue sedan had pulled out after we did. If it did, it did. I kept the top up, figuring there was plenty of time to be windblown later. It also obscured the view through the rear window. There was time and we had a ways to go. It was a pleasant day, minus the traffic, and before long we were off the interstate.

Agnes said little preferring to look out the window. Occasionally she would remark on the wonders of Mother Nature and how she loved going this way, but I could sense her anxiety picking up. I held back in saying anything. I thought it better to keep quiet. We made a few stops along the way after heading off on Highway 1 out of San Luis Obispo. At the first stop I pulled the top down and Agnes put on a scarf to keep her hair from blowing all over her face.

We eased along the coast road enjoying the views of the ocean and the national forest before stopping in Carmel for lunch. We found a small park overlooking the cove. Agnes grabbed the basket, and I pulled a couple of drinks and fruit from the cooler. The wind kept us from using a placemat and we tucked our napkins under our drinks. More than once we went scrambling after we forgot about the napkins and the wind took them for a ride. I'd made sandwiches and we shared a bag of chips and the fruit. Once lunch was finished we put the basket away and wandered down along the ridge to the water. Agnes grabbed my hand and held onto my arm.

"It's so wonderful out here, isn't it?"

"It is."

"Maybe we should just stay here, forget about San Francisco."

"And Anna, should we forget about her? Is that what you really want to do?"

"No." She wrapped her arms around me as we walked the beach.

"Then we weather the storms for the sun."

"Ok." The woman held on tight. "Remember, you said we."

"Yes, I did."

We climbed our way back to the car, said a small prayer, and drove off. The blue sedan was waiting by a Subaru near the entrance to the park. The two goons were sitting there looking, but not looking, in our direction. If they thought I didn't see them, they were idiots. If they wanted me to see them it worked, we all had things to do. Whatever their plans or motives, they were small potatoes compared to the ones burrowing inside Agnes and me. We had a thousand years of sad memories and bad vibes to deal with. A couple of goofs in monkey suits were the least of our problems.

We headed north to sit in traffic

Traffic in the bay area, like LA, like all of California, is its own disease infecting us all. We took our medicine and prayed for salvation, hoping, yet all the while knowing we were doomed to lose years of our lives wasted inside our mechanized sanitariums. The sick were anxiously packed on roads headed for home, or perhaps to a place of comfort, only to be struck again and again. The fevered jumped and swerved, desperate to shave those precious seconds off their journey whether they succeeded or not. The rest of us, bored and listless, followed the lunatics in front of us.

At least the sun was out.

We snaked along the western edge of the world, to the Golden Gate Park, and through San Francisco towards the hotel and Simon's restaurant. All the while Agnes grew quiet and still, her head barely moving, her eyes looking out to a place I couldn't see. Finding the hotel was its own adventure. It took a few trips around the block before I figured out the entrance to the garage. The hotel was one of those small boutique kinds of places, built out of an old office building long since repurposed. It reminded me of the buildings in the noir films I used to watch when I had nothing better to do. Films populated by shadows, dread, and the fatal consequences of poor or thoughtless decisions. I wondered if it was trying to tell me something.

The lobby was neither light nor colorful, instead muted in grays and whites. The woman at the counter was affable and the journey to our room unremarkable. The room, like the lobby, was also a host of grays and whites. It was a small room, but there was only the two of us and our baggage. Agnes sat at the edge of the bed and watched as I made a place for our things. A small window looked out onto the alley below populated with trash and recycle bins. There were rays of sunlight here and there as the clouds passed unseen above us. Two photographs of the building's previous incarnations adorned the wall by the door. The bathroom was small but fashionably tiled and papered. I gave the scented soaps a sniff before returning to the quiet woman sitting on the bed.

I sat down next to her.

She reached for my hand. "I can't go, Monk."

"Why not?"

"Because..." She was clearly upset, her eyes were moist and her hands were trembling.

"Because why?"

Agnes started crying. "I know she's still mad at me."

"I'm missing something here, why are you crying? Why is she mad?" I tried to figure out what Agnes was talking about.

"I'm sorry, I shouldn't drag you into this."

"Into what?" There were tissues in her purse. I reached in and handed her one. "Agnes, what is it?"

She wiped her eyes and blew her nose in a sad fitful burst. I put my arm around her. The crying had subsided, but the shaking continued.

"Agnes!"

"I..."

"What?" I was finding this exasperating. Just talk!

She balled her hands into fists and buried her head into my chest.

"I'm a very angry person, Monk, and it's made me do some terrible things."

"Like what?"

She shook as she spoke. "I had a breakdown the last time I was here, right here in this very hotel, a year and a half ago. Anna had left to come up here and I wanted to talk to her, to talk to them, because I wanted her to come home, but I was mad and ugly and hateful. I said so many horrible things. I called them home-wreakers and faggots. I was screaming and yelling. They called the police and told me I had to leave. Anna was so angry she said she never wanted to speak to me again. I ended up screaming myself hoarse in my car. If I'd had a gun I'd have killed them. That's how crazy I was. That's how crazy I am. I'm not a good person, Monk. You'll see. I'm angry and spiteful and stupid. You'll see me for what I am and then you'll be done with me too!" She put her hands to her face and sobbed.

I didn't know what to say. It was possible she was an ugly hateful woman, but I had a hard time believing that. I got the angry part, I'd walked that road many times, but I felt she was more broken than ugly, more lost than hateful.

"I don't think you're a bad person. I can tell you're angry, but you haven't been hateful to me, so it's unlikely I'd up and leave."

"You say that, but you don't even know me, Monk, you'll see. I'll fuck it up somehow, I always do. You'll see. They'll tell you all the miserable crazy shit I've done, all the things I've said. I'm afraid of that too. Once you see them, once you hear them, you'll know better. You'll see what I am, a crazy stupid bitch, and that'll be that, and I'll be alone again."

I let go and turned to face her. I carefully framed her sad teary face with my hands and kissed her. I didn't like this side of her.

"Agnes, no one's going to tell me what to think." I could feel an old anger of my own welling up. "I don't like it when you assume that I'll take off just because you've had a hard time with your ex, or said some things that you're are ashamed of. I know what it's like, I had a hard time with my ex too, and I said some terrible things to her. I know it's hard to have your dreams and watch them fall apart. I know it's hard to love someone and have it fail. I know it's hard to look back at all the time you've wasted, but that's life. It's hard and it wears you down, but Goddammit, I'm not someone who runs at the first sign of trouble and I'm tired of you telling yourself, and me, that I will."

My own life was weaving in and out of hers. I'd been here before, being told how I felt and what I would do. And I did run, didn't I? My failures we'd deal with later.

"You need to understand something." I held her tighter." We're not here to get back at Simon, or Eric, or Anna, understand? We're not here to scream and yell, or make a scene. We're not here to find something we've lost or wallow in the past. We're not going to do that. We're here to move forward, to say we're sorry, and to make amends for our mistakes, understand? The anger and the pity has to go. The past is past. It's time to move on. You got that!"

"Yes," she said meekly.

"Yes what?" Her eyes widened as she pondered this side of me. I didn't like it, but the pity party was dragging me into a nasty pit of self-loathing. I wasn't going to go there, not again, whether Agnes wanted to or not. I'd already spent too many years there.

"I understand." Tears rolled down her face, pooling around my hands. I softened my voice.

"If you want me to stay, then you need to find a little faith, in yourself and in me. I spent more than twenty years waiting for a love that was never going to happen. I won't do it again. I won't wait for you to forgive the past, I won't! And I won't be a stand-in and I won't let you be one either."

I kissed her, then let her go. Agnes tried to smile, but it didn't work. She put her arms back around me and I wiped away the tears. She wasn't the only crazy person in the room. I looked over at the window. There was still a hint of daylight. I didn't like this anger welling up again. I needed to get out of this room, get out of this corner.

"Why don't we go for a walk? We have some time before we have to be there; some fresh air will do us good. We can check out the neighborhood. What do you say?"

"Ok."

We sat up and wiped our faces. How old do you have to be before you get your shit together? I turned to her.

"I do have one question, though."

"What?" Those big eyes!

"If this place brings back such sad memories, why are we staying here?"

"Johnny D knows the owner, so I get a really good rate. Normally it costs like two-fifty a night to stay here. We're only paying a third of that."

I couldn't help laughing.

Money trumps everything!

29

While Agnes washed her face, I grabbed my wallet and pulled out an old sticky note. I took the phone out of my pocket and dialed the number. I'd put this off for too long. A woman answered on the other end of the line.

"Hello?"

"Is Moses there?"

"I think so, who may I say is calling?" Odd that she'd be suspicious.

"Tell him it's the prodigal son."

"I don't understand."

"Don't worry, he will." Agnes was standing by the bathroom door listening.

His voice filled the phone. It was still the same, only quieter.

"The prodigal son?"

"Yes, it's me."

"Then should I be expecting a return?" I considered hanging up even though there was no reason to. I wasn't angry with Moses, just me.

"I'm in San Francisco and I thought I come up for a few days."

"You know you're always welcome. Will it be just you?"

"No, I'm bringing a woman, a friend with me." I looked up at Agnes as I said this.

"She's welcome too. When should we expect you?"

"In a couple days, I think we should talk." I blurted this out.

"I think so too." A pause. "It'll be good to see you."

"I hope so."

"Are you still using that silly name?"

"Maybe." He laughed at that.

"Goodbye, Monk."

I said goodbye and put away the phone. Agnes came and sat with me. She'd redone her makeup and spritzed a little more perfume. I put my arm around her. She tried to smile.

"Shall we?"

I kissed her. "No time like the present."

The lobby was small, fitting the size of the hotel and nothing like the large open spaces found in grand hotels. Consequently, it was inhospitable to mugs on the tail of a crazy woman and a runaway. As I looked around the lobby I figured they'd have to be outside or in an establishment within view of the hotel entrance. I couldn't identify them exactly, but it gave me something to dwell on other than why Agnes was so sure I'd drop her once I heard the truth about whatever happened between her and Anna.

The hotel was on a busy street filled with those addicted to an active lifestyle. Agnes and I weren't exactly a part of that crowd, but we made the most of it by watching the people around us hustle by when we weren't window-shopping. Most of the stores were closed or closing, but there were bars and restaurants up and down the street to peer into. Our walk, as expected, was a quiet affair with neither of us eager to return to our worries and fears. That was just as well, I was tired and longing for a drink. Most of the bars were of the look at me type rather than those where you could hide in a booth. I wasn't interested in fancy new martinis or cosmopolitans; I just wanted a glass of whiskey.

It was while looking up the street that I noticed the clowns. They looked more out of place than we did. They reminded me of Gordy and Artie, same general build, same attire; must be their gang colors. I laughed at that causing Agnes, who was off in her own little world, to look at me.

"What?"

"It's nothing. How far is the restaurant? I was thinking of getting a drink."

"It's on the next block. I think there's a bar. We'd be early." I think she said that to put me off, but I wanted a drink and it was less than a half-hour before we were officially meant to drop by.

"It'll be ok, I promise not to make a scene."

"You're a jerk, Buttman!"

I laughed, "That's right, baby!"

"Funny guy." Hey, at least she smiled.

Anna Barron's was the name they'd given the place. I guess that made sense. It was a mid-sized space with high ceilings, wood beams and glass light fixtures that gave it a bigger feel. It was, in truth, a high-end shotgun shack, about thirty feet wide and maybe a hundred feet deep. I couldn't tell for sure how much of that was kitchen. It was obvious they'd put some money into it, but having checked out the other places along the street, that was the norm. The bar was to the left. A cute young woman manned the front desk. I was about to mouth off that we knew the owners when a thin gregarious man saw us, or I should say, saw Agnes and waved.

This was Eric. He was of medium height, had light brown hair, was well groomed, and appeared easy going with a flair for the theatrical. He was dapper in the same odd way I was, with a penchant for an older style of clothes that fit him well. He had a deep laugh and a grace that made him the perfect host for the restaurant. If he disliked Agnes it wasn't evident in his greeting.

"Agnes, I'm so glad you're here. You look wonderful. And who's this dashing young man with you?"

"Hello, Eric. You look wonderful too. The old guy is Monk." She took his hand when he offered it. I considered that a good sign. I didn't care for the old guy remark, though.

"It's nice to meet you, Monk. I see you've had some misfortune."

"Yeah, I fell off my bike." Agnes grimaced at that, something Eric noticed.

"Well let's hope the rides go better in the future. Can I get you a table? I'll let Simon and Anna know you're here."

"That'd be great," I answered.

Agnes looked around before asking Eric for the location of the restrooms. He gestured to the doors down by the kitchen entrance. She thanked him and we watched as she slowly walked through the tables.

"How's she doing, Monk?"

I was surprised by the question and his evident concern.

"Tight as a drum. For some reason she's certain I'll dump her the minute I meet you."

"That's too bad, but I'm not surprised. The last time she came up it didn't go well." He raised his eyebrows and tilted his head as he said this.

"She mentioned that. If I had to say, I think she's still deeply conflicted about a lot of things. Some of that's because she hasn't accepted what's happened to her and is ashamed that she continues to be resentful. She wants to move on, it's whether she has the will to do it. I say that having no actual credentials to back it up."

Eric gave me a knowing glance.

"I hear you. Simon is, in some ways, no better. I think he still feels he should have a say in how Agnes behaves. She's the only person he does that to. I think it goes back to their early years together when they were teens. It doesn't help, certainly not now. He should have been honest with her a long time ago, but he kept going back and forth; stringing her along just made it worse at the end."

He led me to a large table in the back. We sat down.

"Monk, I don't know what you're in the mood for, but I think the two of us need to make sure the party stays light-hearted."

"I with you there. I'm done with all the crying and bad humor. A drink and a few laughs are what I need."

"Amen." We both smiled at that.

I could tell Eric and I would get along just fine.

Agnes saw us as she exited the restroom. Eric stood up and left to meet and greet, as well as inform Simon and Anna that their cross to bear was here. That was probably unkind. I guess I'd find out how unkind, and whether this family gathering was a combustible stew. A sweet young woman named Daphne brought us something to drink. The alcohol went down easy. I realized I'd have to be careful with how much I drank. It was the kind of night to drink heavily.

Simon and Anna came out of the kitchen, both in their chef's smocks. Anna was the female version of her father, lean and tall. She had her mother's hair and eyes, which, like Simon's, were tight and focused on Agnes. Apparently neither thought it was party time. We rose to greet them. Agnes introduced us all. Eric came over to make sure the peace was maintained. A young man with a white hat brought out a series of plates. Simon explained he thought it would be interesting if we were able to sample a number of their dishes. It sounded good to me. I ate and Eric watched while the nuclear family nibbled here and there. Maybe Simon and Anna would eat later, and I expected Agnes to have no appetite. I didn't hesitate; lunch had been a long six hours before. And the food was good...

...Really good! Whatever Simon's faults might be, cooking was not one of them.

After I finished stuffing my face, during which they made small talk about the successes the restaurant was finally achieving; Barron and his plans, work and Johnny D, their attentions turned to me, the new guy. Anna spoke for the group.

"So, what is it you do, Monk? I'm sorry; I don't think my mother told us your last name."

"I know she didn't, it's Buttman, Monk Buttman, and I'm an odds and ends man. I do a number of things from information services to investigative work for a big law firm in LA. I like it. I'm not trapped at a desk and I get to do different things rather than the same thing over and over."

Anna mulled this over. "That's quite a name..."

"Yeah, I should have given it more thought..."

"You weren't born with that name?"

"No, I acquired years ago, and for good or bad, it's kind of stuck."

Anna turned her attention to her mother. "How long have you known each other?"

"About two weeks. It's been something of a whirlwind romance," Agnes announced.

They all looked at me. I didn't think it sounded very good either.

"It's true, we're still in the process of getting to know one another, our quirks, family histories; that kind of thing. We decided it had potential and now we're on the road seeing family and friends. You know..." I was just sputtering hoping Daphne would return soon.

Eric popped the next question.

"You have family up here?"

"Up north near Ukiah."

Simon, who had been mostly silent, went next. I don't think he approved of me.

"What are your plans while you're here?"

Agnes started to say something, but Simon interrupted, "Aggie, let the man talk."

Aggie?

I cracked a big grin and started to chuckle. Agnes pinched my leg. When I looked at her I knew I was to never call her that. Simon, Eric, and Anna watched this with an odd kind of fascination. I didn't know if they had met Jordan or any of her other boyfriends, but I wondered what they thought of the two of us.

"Our hope is to spend some time with Anna, but we know you're busy. I thought it would be fun to tour the city, hit the parks, wander across the Golden Gate, touristy stuff."

"Do you think you'd have some time, Anna?" Agnes was pleading.

Anna looked at Simon and Eric. Simon turned to Aggie, but didn't say anything. Eric motioned with his head toward her mother.

"I have some time tomorrow. I guess we can get together for a while." Her reluctance was writ large.

"You'll behave, right Aggie?" Simon added.

Agnes did a slow burn, so I pinched her leg. She jumped and nodded. It was terribly condescending, but it didn't warrant an argument. Instead, she apologized.

"I want you to know that I'm sorry for what I said before. I didn't come up here to argue or fight. I just want to have some time with Anna. I miss you, and I love you, and..."

I took her hand, and handed her a tissue hoping to nip any possible crying jag in the bud.

"Mom, please don't cry." Anna was more annoyed than sympathetic.

"You're right, no more crying." Agnes paused long enough to excuse herself. Simon, who seemed embarrassed, said he had to check the kitchen and Eric left to schmooze the last remaining customers, it was closing time. That put me square in the sights of her daughter.

"Can I ask how you met my mother?"

"Sure, I met her at work. I had a meeting with Johnny D and she asked me if I wanted to have a drink later. I did, and we've been seeing each other ever since."

I could see the wheels turning in Anna's head.

"She told me you were different. Not like some of the other men."

I could see the Agnes in her eyes.

"I like to think I am. I like your mother and we enjoy each other's company."

Anna pondered this. As she did, I gazed out towards the front windows. One of the clowns was walking by, looking in. I looked back. He turned away and sped off. I was half tempted to take out the gun, find the clown, and get some answers, but that only worked on TV. In real life you get arrested for felony assault and possession of an unregistered firearm. That wasn't the way any of us wanted the evening to end. Agnes came back, trying to be brave, trying to smile.

"I think maybe we should head back, Monk. They have work to do."

"True, you're tired and it's been a long day. We'll get some rest, and start out fresh tomorrow."

Agnes gave Anna a big hug and kissed her. We said goodbye to Eric, who in turn gave us a big hug. Simon came out to say goodbye, but kept his distance. Anna said she'd be at the hotel around noon. They watched as we left and headed down the street.

"Aggie, huh?" I had to say it.

"Don't ever call me that, Buttman!" She smacked me in the arm.

"Jeez, what a temper..."

"Live and learn."

We laughed while the clown followed a block behind.

30

An idle thought occurred to me as we approached the hotel. Agnes was fading, worn out by a second straight emotionally wrought day. I, on the other hand, still had some energy and a bizarre desire for confrontation. My hand had been fondling the 45 in my pocket and I had the urge to turn the tables on our erstwhile tails. I looked as we entered the lobby door to see if the guy was still there. He was, though partially hidden by a doorway. I told Agnes to go up, that I wanted something from the car.

After I made sure she was in the elevator, I found a corner by the window where I was obscured by the drapes. I watched as the tail slowly passed in front of the hotel, stopping momentarily to survey the interior. He then moved on. Once he passed the windows, I quietly went to the door and noticed him standing on the corner. He took out his phone. I knew from my trips around the block that there was a doorway from the parking garage to the backside of that corner. I left the lobby for the garage. No one was there, nor did I see any cameras. I walked through and carefully opened the door to the alley. The mug was still standing there, watching.

I pulled the gun out of my pocket and checked it. I had to be smart about this. I drew back the slide to chamber a round and checked the safety. I put it back in my pocket. My heart was pounding. I'd spent my entire life running and avoiding just these kinds of confrontations, but I was tired of being followed. The clown was preoccupied with a group of young women coming out of a bar across the street. It was perfect. I came up from behind and got close with my hand on the gun.

"Hey buddy, got a light?"

"What? No..."

As he turned he realized who I was. He eyes focused after he saw the bulge in the coat pocket where the gun was. It was pure movie cheese, but he bought it because, like me, he didn't have any idea what he was doing.

"Nice night out, huh?" I played it thick.

"I guess."

"I'd be careful, buddy, if I were you. You never know who you might meet."

We slowly circled so that I was by the street and the clown was in the alley.

"Yeah…" That was all he said.

I took my hand off the gun and headed for the hotel door. When I got there the clown was still watching.

"Tell your boyfriend the same thing."

I returned to our room.

Agnes was sitting on the bed when I opened the door. At first I thought she was crying again; her eyes had that look, but then she smiled and came over and gave me a hug.

"Thanks, Monk."

"For what?"

"For being here."

"No problem. Feeling any better?"

"I don't know. It still bothers me to be around Simon, but I didn't want to hurt him like I did before. I should be happy for him and Eric, and I'm trying, I am."

"I know how it goes. I don't like to see my ex with her new man, but the truth is she's better off with him than she was with me. It took me a long time to accept that. Simon is what he is, and he wants to be with Eric. Since he's gay, it's probably better that way. You'd never be happy together."

"I know, but it still hurts."

The evening was over. We cleaned up and went to bed. I couldn't help thinking of Astral and all the mistakes I'd made. It'd been more than six years since she threw me out and married Judah. I laid there in the dark listening to Agnes breathe. I never really understood Astral. She was quiet, distant, but then I wasn't much better. I thought it would just happen between us, the understanding, the love, the forgiveness… it never did. At the end we barely spoke. Yet here I was with a woman I'd just met and I felt I knew her far better than I ever knew Astral. Maybe it was the six years; too long to be alone, too long to not have someone to care for. I put my arm around her and she drew herself to me. I kissed her shoulder and drifted off to sleep.

The light woke me up. I'd forgotten to draw the shades. I tried to roll away from it, but that did no good. I looked at the clock. It was already eight-thirty. Agnes had the covers over her head to block the light. I was half tempted to get out of bed, and half tempted to do as Agnes had and pull up the covers. I did neither. I just lay there. After a half hour I roused Agnes and got up. She mumbled something about ten more minutes. I washed my face and got dressed. I sat in the chair and watched as she fitfully tried to get up. The covers were off her face and she was sitting up.

"Well, you're almost there."

"What time is it?" I told her the time. "Really, I have at least another hour before I have to get up."

"Not given how long it takes you to get ready. You're on the clock, beautiful. I'm going to go scope out places to eat. I'm hungry."

"You always seem hungry. How do you stay slim and eat so much?"

"That's the key, I don't. Up and at 'em."

"I think I made a mistake with you, Buttman."

"That's what makes love so special."

She smiled and threw a pillow at me.

I didn't see either of the clowns as I exited the hotel. I wondered where they were. I was beginning to enjoy our game of cat and mouse. The street wasn't nearly so busy in the morning. It was quiet with just a few stragglers like me. Off to the left was a sign for a café. I headed that way and came upon two guys just inside the alley where I'd met the clown the night before. They were looking down the alley. At first I didn't see it, but there it was. The blue sedan was parked behind the dumpsters. The two guys looked at me with mild concern. I didn't see the problem.

"What's up?"

The older one pointed down the alley. "Roddy here thinks something's going on with that car."

Roddy was a pint-sized guy who couldn't have weighed more than a hundred and twenty pounds. He had a blast of black hair and a splotchy beard.

"I went to dump the trash and I saw the car. It didn't look right, so I grabbed Mr. Buzzkirk to come look."

Buzzkirk wasn't much taller, but weighed twice as much, reminding me of a human bowling ball. Neither wanted to approach the car, but I was feeling brave after my encounter the previous night. Fools rush in.

"I'll go check," I offered.

The two nodded. I walked towards the car with the two of them following at a distance. The car was as far as it could get to the side of the building. I wondered if they were sleeping. As I got closer I could see why Roddy was concerned. The passenger window was down. I thought it might be cute to startle them; arouse them from their slumber, but as I approached I could see that wasn't an option.

The two were dead, both shot in the head.

It wasn't so cute anymore.

The passenger took it in the forehead, the driver in the right temple. I don't think he saw it coming. The passenger, the guy I spooked, looked out in wonder, eyes wide, mouth open. I thought there'd be more blood than the small streams coming out of the bullet holes. Instead, the blood was on the back seat and the window. I stepped away and turned to Buzzkirk. My stomach started to knot.

"You have a phone?"

"Yeah?" He hesitated to answer.

"Call 911. These guys are dead."

Roddy and Buzzkirk carefully approached the car for a look. They didn't stay long. I was headed for the entrance to the alley, certain I was going to throw up. I was regretting my willingness to be brave. I told the two we needed to wait for the cops. Both were as white as I assumed I was. Buzzkirk mumbled he had to check the café, but would be right back. Roddy and I tried made small talk about the weird stuff that happens around dumpsters. I thought he was stammering too much, but I wasn't listening. This wasn't a good thing. Small potatoes following other small potatoes shouldn't end up dead in an alley.

It didn't take long for the cops to arrive. Buzzkirk came back out and we told our story plain as it was. I was getting nervous about the gun in my pocket. I had forgotten about it until I heard the sirens and I realized I had no explanation for it or a permit. Fortunately the cops weren't focusing on us as potential suspects, we were just the poor slobs who stumbled onto the bodies. Buzzkirk worried it was a drug deal gone bad. Roddy wondered why they were in the alley in the first place. A pair of detectives showed up and asked the same questions the officers had. I didn't know anything, just wanted some breakfast. I gave my name and the number of A and A if they needed to talk to me. After an hour or so they let us go. I went back to the hotel.

I wasn't hungry anymore.

Agnes and Anna were waiting in the lobby.

"Where have you been all this time?" Aggie asked. "We came down when we heard the sirens."

I hesitated to say anything. "Two men were killed in the alley. That's what the commotion is about."

Agnes was shocked "That's terrible. Did you see it?"

"I'm the one who found them."

Both of them looked at me like I was nuts. We sat down and I told them of seeing Roddy and Buzzkirk, and of my grisly discovery. Agnes reiterated how terrible and Anna sat there wondering what to say. What do you say? I suggested we get going. They agreed. Anna volunteered to drive. That was ok with me. While they went to her car I made a beeline for the Falcon. I put the 45 away and waited as Anna brought her car around. She had a small sky blue Toyota. I sat in the back so Agnes could more easily converse with her daughter.

Not a whole lot was said.

First we headed towards Golden Gate Park. Anna knew of a good place for lunch. It was a warm day with high clouds. I tried not to think of the dead men by watching the people on the streets and in their cars. The tension from the night before was gone, or at least I didn't sense it. Anna parked the car and we got out. The restaurant was tucked into what used to be a big old house. We found a booth by a window and sat down. Both mother and daughter looked beautiful, both had their hair pulled back. They were wearing nearly the same outfit. Anna wore a cream-colored shirt, while Agnes' was dark blue. Anna's was more demure owing to the fact that she did not inherit her mother's bosom. Both had on stretchy jeans. We ordered lunch and waited for someone to say something other than how nice we all looked.

I went first. "What would you two like to do today? I don't know how much time Anna has before she has to go back, so maybe we should make some plans?"

"I have the day off. Dad wanted me to come back at five, but Eric told him I should have the whole day off, so we can do whatever you like." Anna didn't seem thrilled.

"Great," I enthused, perhaps too much. "Yeah, I like Eric. We had a good time last night."

Agnes chimed in, "That's because he like boys, you know."

"And he knows I like girls, so it works out."

Anna was annoyed. "Ok, we can do whatever you like, but there are two things we won't talk about, me coming back to LA and dad's sexuality, Ok?"

We both glared at Agnes. She relented. "Alright, I'll be good."

I reiterated my desire to hit the parks and the bridge. I also asked if they wanted to go hear Joanie sing. Anna thought that would be fun. Agnes was less enthusiastic, but didn't say no. I asked Anna how she liked work, which got her talking about how much it took to run a restaurant and all the things she had to learn. Simon had her doing different things, whether it was prep, or line work, or assisting the chefs. She said she enjoyed it, that the nights went fast. Agnes asked about boyfriends, but Anna demurred, blaming work and being too busy to have time for romance. We ate our lunch as the two women talked about Barron and his future. Agnes talked about work and being by herself. It was her way of skirting around the please come back to mamma and LA restriction.

Inevitably the talk turned to Agnes and me.

I didn't mind talking about what Agnes and I were up to, but I had to resist the impulse to be glib or cavalier. All I wanted was a kindred spirit with a reasonable sex drive and no more goofy idiosyncrasies than I had. I believed that was why we were drawn to each other. We'd done a lot worse and this wasn't so bad.

I expected Anna to be more critical, perhaps more demanding, but I soon began to understand the complications in their relationship. Anna wanted to know if this meant her mother had changed, gave more thought to what she was doing, thereby avoiding the damage she inflicted on herself and her children. Agnes was defensive and just wanted Anna to be more understanding about how difficult it was to suddenly be on your own, to have the person you thought you'd be with forever tell you it was all a fraud. Anna countered that she understood that, that it had been difficult for all of them, not just her mother.

Though his name didn't come up, I felt that Jordan and whatever had happened between them still afflicted this mother and daughter. For the most part I kept my mouth shut and answered the questions directed at me, but the tension I sensed last night was beginning to simmer and I had no interest in watching it boil.

"Maybe we should take a break, see the sights."

"What do you think about this?" Anna was looking at me.

So was Agnes.

"Well…" What did I think? "I think there are issues that the two of you are still struggling with, and I have no idea whether there's been any talk about what each of you expects that the other is willing to accept. I know a little about some of your history, about your father, and about Jordan." I took stock of their response to that name. Anna's eyes darkened while Agnes turned away. "Obviously, I don't know you very well, and while I feel I know your mother reasonably well, there are going to be things I'm unaware of, but having said that, I believe your mother is a good person who did what a lot of us do in times of stress, which is to fuck everything up, and when we do, it can be a monumental challenge to convince the people we've hurt that we're worthy of their trust and understanding. I know, I've been there, and I'm still mending fences," I rambled.

Agnes reached out for Anna's hand. "You see what I mean?"

Anna arched her left eyebrow. "Yeah, he's a little different."

I assumed that was a good thing, like a carnival prize.

Agnes excused herself to go to the bathroom. At least she wasn't crying. I watched Anna watch her mother. She turned to me.

"What did she tell you about Jordan?"

"That he was younger, a rebound, that he fooled around on her, and hit on you which is why you left."

The darkness in Anna's eyes deepened. "No, he was much worse than that! He was fucking abusive, physically and emotionally. He beat her, and I know he sexually assaulted her, but she wouldn't leave. He tried to rape me while she was waiting outside, and when she came in, he hit her and hit her until we were both screaming, but she wouldn't call the police, and she wouldn't let me call the police. She went back to him, time and time again!"

Anna's face was red with anger; her hands were knotted around the napkin, tearing at it.

"Good Lord!" It was all I could think of to say. The knot in my stomach was back, nice and tight.

"I wish!" she sounded like Moses when he cursed God. The tears were slowly forming around her eyes, but I could tell she refused to cry.

"What stopped it?"

"Johnny stopped it. I told him about the assault. I didn't know what else to do. You know I didn't believe the stories about him, because he never seemed to get mad, but that day he did. He'd already told my mother that he'd throw her out if she saw him again; loud enough that everyone there heard it. It's the only time I ever heard him raise his voice."

"And Jordan?"

"Johnny had two of his men find him and they beat him to a pulp. I heard they drove him to the Nevada border and told him if he ever stepped back into California, he'd never walk again. Now do you understand?"

"Yeah, I'd have left too."

Anna was glaring at me.

"Goddamned right! It still pisses me off. I go to therapy and I try to understand, but it's hard. It's really fucking hard."

"Yeah..." It was all that came out.

Agnes was standing by the door.

It was Anna's turn to use the restroom. She didn't look at her mother as she passed her. Agnes very gingerly came back to the table. She sat down but wouldn't look at me.

"She told you, didn't she?"

"Yes." I didn't want to say anything. I just sat there. Agnes stared off in the distance as we waited for Anna to return. "Is it true?"

In a sad dead voice, a quiet "yes" came out. "I told you this would..."

"I don't want to hear that!" I needed a few moments of silence.

Anna came back and sat down. Both were taciturn. No tears, no nothing. They were waiting; waiting for something to make the horror and the hatred fade away, to take away the stupidity and the mistakes, to let them move on.

"What do we do now?" Somebody spoke.

"We go to the park," I said.

31

The good graces of a warm wind and a bright sky made a difference, if only for me. It felt good to be outside, to be moving. The park was filled with people out having a good time. I asked if they still wanted to go to the club to hear Joanie sing. I didn't hear no. Anna said it was a good place to eat, but not very big. Reservations might be tough. I called Joanie to see if she could reserve us a table. She sounded thrilled that we were going to show up. It was good to hear her voice.

I was trying very hard not to judge Agnes over what Anna had said, but my mind kept playing back sordid images of Agnes with Jordan and the idea that she would allow that to happen, that she would let it continue. I watched her as we wandered around the park. I was both appalled and sorry. She kept her distance from Anna and me, although they were talking, even if it was all superficialities about pretty flowers, happy children, and cute dogs. She would look at me from time to time, as if checking to see if I was still here.

We headed to the Presidio; following the same pattern we had at Golden Gate Park. Agnes and Anna continued to converse, and I would join in every once in a while, but there was no life to it. They were dutifully keeping to the script, waiting for it to be over. We stayed mostly on the north side of the park near the bridge. We stopped at the Palace of Fine Arts before heading to the Golden Gate Promenade. Agnes and Anna walked ahead of me. We found a bench and sat to watch the people walking by and the tides slapping against the rocks.

Joanie called to say we had a table at eight, about the time she started her show, the first of two. I thanked her and checked my watch; it was nearly six. I relayed this to my companions. Anna wanted to stop at the house she shared with her father and Eric.

"Mom, I want to talk to Monk for a moment."

Agnes's face fell, but she didn't object. She stayed on the bench while Anna and I walked towards the water.

"I want you to know that I still love my mother. I do, but I don't like her anymore, and I don't know if I ever want to see her again. I know that sounds harsh, but it's taken me a long time to get to the point where I feel safe and happy with where I am. Seeing her is painful and I still feel a lot of anger towards her and I don't like feeling this way. You seem like a decent person, but so did some of her other boyfriends and look what happened. So you'll have to understand if I keep my distance. I don't want to chase you away, but don't let her fool you."

We both looked over at Agnes who was staring at the bridge.

"I don't know what to say. Obviously, there's a lot I don't know or understand, and it's not my place to tell you what to do or what to think, but forever is a long time. Maybe it's best to simply enjoy today and let tomorrow take care of itself."

Anna just looked at me. Her crooked smile followed me to the bench. We gathered our thoughts and returned to the car. The ride to her house made me wonder if this trip was a mistake. This half wasn't going well and there was still my half, which I didn't think would be any more promising. No one had an interest in making small talk, which left us in the throes of our disquiet. There was a phrase for you. I laughed. Mother and daughter both said *what* at the same time, which made me laugh even more. Anna pulled the car into the driveway shaking her head. Agnes stayed in the car.

"You're not coming in?"

"No, maybe some other time." As if other opportunities would be ever forthcoming.

I shrugged and went with Anna into the house. Eric was there. He appeared ready to hit the town in a silver suit with a black shirt and a red tie.

I whistled. "Man, you look sharp tonight. Plans?"

"I'm meeting friends. You?"

"The same. A friend of mine is in town. We're going to listen to her sing."

"Excellent. Where's she singing?"

"The Mind's Eye, ever heard of it?"

"Oh, yeah. I've sung there many times. It's a great little place." Eric came closer. "How's the day been?"

I couldn't hide the fact that I knew more than I wanted to. Eric lost his smile.

"Not so good. I didn't realize the depth of the problem 'til now."

"So, now you know?" he asked as if hoping I didn't.

"Yeah, Anna spilled the beans. If nothing else it answered a lot of questions. I just don't quite know where we go from here." Eric put his arm on my shoulder.

"It was a terrible time, a terrible time. Everyone was so angry, screaming and yelling. Anna couldn't function; Agnes had a breakdown, which Simon made worse by saying some horrible things to Agnes, who then said some horrible things to me. It was the only time I threatened to leave him. I mean I'm not defending what Agnes did, but there was no reason to say those things and I think a lot of what Agnes said was in reaction to that. Anna's only now coming back to something like what she was before, but I worry about her relationship with Agnes. I know I shouldn't have any sympathy for Agnes, she has, after all, said some really nasty things to me, but I know what it's like to be estranged from your family."

"They didn't understand your lifestyle choice?"

He smiled.

"You could say that. I guess my point is I hope you don't give up on Agnes. I can tell she likes you, and she hasn't had much luck with men. I think she has a good heart; it's just that sometimes it doesn't show. She's been lost long enough. She could use the love."

Love?

"You're the second person to tell me that. There must be something about her, but I already knew that. The problem is reconciling that to what she did."

Eric straightened the lapels on my jacket. "It's easy to stand on the sidelines and judge, Monk. He treated her very badly, knocked her around; raped her. I don't think any of us really understood how bad it was. Think about what it must have been like for her? The shame, the degradation, feeling trapped; believing this was all she deserved? Maybe she took it because she suffered a lot of self-loathing after Simon left? Maybe she felt she didn't deserve to be loved, I don't know. And I'm not saying that to excuse what happened, but it matters. I watched my father beat my mother when he drank and she stayed for years."

Anna was ready. I hadn't noticed her as I was talking to Eric.

"Thanks, Eric, I enjoyed meeting you. I hope we have another opportunity some time."

"Me too. You're leaving?"

"Yeah, I think we'll head north tomorrow, drive through Napa. Thanks for letting Anna spend the day with us."

"Don't thank me, I just backed her up with Simon. She wanted to know about you."

"Great, more pressure."

"It builds character," he said with a big smile

"Just what I need."

We said goodbye. Agnes was out of the car, leaning against the trunk. I told her we were going. We got in the car. I sat in the front this time. Anna was curious about Joanie, so I gave her the short version of our relationship. I wondered why we were even going given what she had said to me earlier, but here we were, on our way.

Anna wanted to know about me. So we talked about my past. She seemed interested in Rebekah and our relationship. I had to confess that I needed to do better. I had a bad habit of thinking I should stay on the sidelines rather than get involved. Anna suggested that only made the distance worse. I had to agree. I had plans to see her; I just had to follow through on them. Then Anna said a remarkable thing.

"I think you should take my mother with you. I don't think she's been to Virginia."

Agnes who hadn't said a word spoke up, "I'd like to go with you."

"We'll work something out. Rebekah has also talked of coming here."

Agnes smiled. It drew some of the darkness out of me.

The Mind's Eye was a supper club, or had been in its day. It wasn't very big, but it wasn't packed together and the stage, which had been part of the original design, hadn't changed so it wasn't mashed into a corner of the bar or by the doors in and out of the kitchen. I told the maître d' we were guests of the entertainment and he showed us to our table. It was a happy bubbly place, which we were sorely in need of.

We ordered drinks and listened as Joanie began her set. We'd made it just in time. She sang with the house trio, drums, piano, and a standup bass. I hadn't been to one of Joanie's shows in a while and I'd forgotten how wonderful her voice was. Anna seemed to enjoy it and I took Agnes's hand, which buoyed her spirits. She moved closer to me. It felt good. Maybe the past was shit, but for now, things were good.

We ordered dinner after the first set. Joanie came over. I introduced her to Agnes and Anna.

"Monk, you didn't tell me your guests were this beautiful."

Anna complimented Joanie on her singing. "Monk tells me the two of you had a torrid affair?"

"Monk has a vivid imagination."

"I can remember it however I like, truth be damned."

"Uh-huh. It nice to meet you Agnes, Monk's been a little coy about you, but I'm glad you and Anna decided to come listen. It's always appreciated."

Agnes, ever vigilant, chimed back, "You have a lovely voice. I hear your boyfriend is a musician?" I raised my eyebrows, something Anna and Joanie picked up on.

"Yes, Mikal is a musician. Right now he's finishing up a tour in Asia, but he also produces and arranges. He'll be back in a couple of weeks."

"Mikal Thorvaldsen?" asked Anna.

"Yes, you know him?"

"Eric does. I met him once at a party. Mikal played while Eric sang. He was very good. We had a great time."

"Wow. Small world, huh, Monk?" Joanie was surprised.

"Small world." So was I.

We had our dinner and stayed for Joanie's second set. It was quieter with more ballads and love songs. Agnes took my hand and held on for dear life. Anna was more talkative, telling me of her love of music and her hope that one day she might have a place like this with both food and music. I told her that sounded wonderful and Agnes added that Anna used to play the piano and flute when she was younger. They asked if I played an instrument or was even musically inclined. I confessed that I knew how to play the guitar and thought I had an ok voice, but I left that in Virginia. Both encouraged me to take it back up.

Once Joanie was finished, we said our goodbyes and Anna took us back to the hotel. She hugged her mother and allowed that it was nice to get to know me. I told her I felt the same, and that I looked forward to seeing her again. She didn't say no. I figured that was as good as it would get. We watched as she pulled away and went inside. I didn't bother to see if anyone was watching us.

Agnes put her hand in mine on the way to the room and seemed determined not to let go. It wasn't until I had to use the bathroom that she relented. I promised I'd be back. It was there I tried to quiet the voices in my head going back and forth. Eric was right; I had no right to judge, but I was tormented by the revelation that she was willing to return to someone who tried to rape her daughter and who had done the same to her.

The phone rang.

It was Llewellyn.

"Monk, I have some news for you. I got into the tablet."

"Really?"

"Yeah. One of the icons is just more sex, though it appears to be homemade, but the other is the group file."

"Whose in it?"

He gave me the names. As I suspected Martin was in the group, as was Boyer. He listed my attackers, Artie and Gordy, and two other names, Brent Holly and Wilmer Fordham. I wondered if they were our two dead guys in the alley. Boyer was the last to join. Recently. There was one other thing.

"A name came up I didn't expect."

"What name?"

"Denesova."

"Really? Thanks Llewellyn."

He said he'd call if he found anything else. I said I'd pick up the tablet when I returned to LA. I put the phone away and found Agnes sitting on the bed. I sat next to her.

"Who was on the phone?"

"Just a guy."

I put my arm around her and focused on her face. I hadn't looked closely before. She had beautiful eyes and a sweet mouth with a smallish nose. I noticed it was a little off, and there were marks, scars, on her nose and around her temples. Her eyes were wet and her face was warm. I kissed her.

"I'm sorry, Monk."

"Why?" I kept up the kissing.

"For not telling you the truth."

I put my hand on her cheek. "You don't owe me an apology or an explanation."

"I don't..."

I put my finger to her lips. "Agnes?"

"Yes?"

"We're ok."

The tears started falling but I didn't care. We fell back on the bed tugging at our clothes; tugging at the covers. Her tears were salty and I wanted her so badly I couldn't stop. She moaned and cried and pushed against me as hard as I pushed against her. I couldn't remember the last time I'd had such a violent orgasm. Agnes didn't want to stop or let go. I went as long as I could until I was out of breath. I pulled the covers over us and held her tight. I was fading fast.

"Thank you for being here with me," she whispered.

"Get some sleep."

Tomorrow's another day.

32

We slept till ten, something I didn't normally do, but the day before had been long and more than a little stressful. Between two dead guys, the truth about Jordan, and all the pent-up emotions, I was exhausted. So was Agnes. By the time we were up and ready, the continental breakfast was over and it was time to check out. I dutifully hauled our bags to the car, and quickly made sure the 45 was safe. On the way out of town we stopped for donuts and coffee, crossed the bridge and ate our healthy breakfast on the other side of the bay looking back at the city in the late morning light. Agnes wanted to stick to the coast. I wanted to go through Napa, so we split the deck, up along the coast and back through wine country. She didn't care that we'd have to backtrack and I wasn't in a big hurry to get to the farm. I called Moses to say we'd be there eventually.

It was another warm and sunny California day.

Agnes didn't say much but her mood was better. I assumed it was from many things, good sex, sleep, and distance. I smiled at her and she smiled back. We stopped whenever the mood struck us so we could look at the edge of the world. In the afternoon we had lunch at Redwoods State Park, down by the Navarro River. We listened as it made its way to the ocean.

"I wish I could live out here, Monk. A long way from everything."

"Wouldn't you get lonely or bored?"

"No, I'd have you come live with me."

"Really?"

"Oh, yeah."

"You got this all worked out then?" She looked at me and grabbed my hand.

"I do. I decided you're not going anywhere."

"No?"

"No. You're the first decent man I've ever known."

"I can't believe that. What about your father?"

Agnes frowned. "My father never really cared for me. He didn't care for the girly stuff, and as you can imagine, I was a girly girl. He liked Simon a lot more than me because Simon was an athlete. After Simon left, he all but accused me of turning him gay."

"You know, you don't have to tell me this."

Agnes smiled at me and squeezed my hand. "I know, but I want you to know and that includes all the bad stuff and all the mistakes. I want you to know so you'll understand why I want you to be with me. I want you to know why you're so important to me. I don't care if it's only been a couple of weeks or whatever; I don't care if you don't believe me. For the first time in my life I'm sure of something and no one, not even you, Monk Buttman, is going to change my mind about it."

"Really?"

"Really!" Agnes wasn't upset or teary. In fact, it was almost as if we were discussing our favorite food rather than her recent troubles.

There was a trail nearby. She spoke as we walked.

"Believe it or not, Simon was the only man I knew till I was thirty-five. I didn't sleep with anyone else, I didn't know any better. We got married when we were eighteen, and I was pregnant at nineteen. After Anna was born, Simon became less and less interested in me. I spent most of my twenties and thirties alone. It's not a nice thing to say, but I spent a lot of nights masturbating to foolish fantasies."

"No one knew he was gay?"

"I'm sure people knew, but no one said anything to me. The closest was a girl I went to school with who said Simon liked boys, but I didn't know what she was talking about. I just thought he was shy or didn't know what to do. I suggested we try different things, but he wasn't interested. Of course, that's because he was in love with Eric."

"Why would he marry you if he was gay? I mean it's not like you got married in the fifties?"

Agnes sighed. "He told me, later, it was because he wanted a family. So he put up with me long enough to father two kids. I also know he was terrified of AIDS. A lot of his friends got sick and quite a few of them died. I guess I should be grateful he was careful. And to be honest, he was nice in the beginning. Later he just avoided me and complained about the house or this and that. He was probably as miserable as I was. Then there was the fiasco with his coming out but not leaving, then leaving. I remember him saying he was sorry but he couldn't love me anymore, and I wondered if he ever really did. I was heartbroken and lashed out. I started running around with men I had no business being with. That's how I ended up with Jordan."

We sat on a bench made from an old tree trunk. Agnes began making circles in the dirt with her shoes. She took my arm and put it on her shoulder.

"You don't have to talk about Jordan?"

"I know, but I need to say it out loud, to get it out. Jordan was a lie from the start. All that stuff I told you was a lie. It's what I wanted to believe because the truth was so ugly. I was a mess and he took advantage of that, but it's not like I didn't know what was going on. I was angry. I hated myself and hated my life. He was the perfect piece of shit to go with my perfect piece of shit life. I didn't deserve to be loved and I took a kind of perverse pleasure in the misery he inflicted on me. I lied and told people he meant to treat me better, that it was the alcohol, but deep down I knew better. And he hit me from the start. I don't know what I was thinking. I know it continued to get worse, and I know that everyone kept telling me to leave, but I was defiantly going to let my life kill me no matter what anyone said."

Agnes pulled away from me and stood up.

"After he broke my nose the second time, MaryAnn called the police, and that really got him worked up. He told me if it happened again he'd kill me. And for the first time, I realized he probably would. By then I was working for Johnny, and he had taken an interest in the kids and me. He tried to get me to leave, but I wouldn't listen. Jordan didn't want me to work there, but I needed the money. That's when he started acting up with Anna.

"When I told him he couldn't do that, he broke my arm. I told everyone I fell down the stairs. Barron couldn't stand it and enlisted. Anna spent more and more time with her father. Jordan would come over and ask where Anna was and would get mad when I said he couldn't see her. He called me an ugly worthless bitch, told me nobody loved me and nobody ever would. And yet I stayed, even though he beat me. Even though he fucked me whether I wanted to or not, and he would laugh and tell me how worthless I was."

She bent down and picked up a pinecone and handed it to me.

"It came to a head when I found out he was stalking Anna. She came to see me to say she wouldn't come over anymore until I left him and called the police. I told her ok, but I lied. He came over and he told me to get out and…"

"You don't have to say anymore, I don't need to know…" I didn't want to know.

Agnes smiled at me. "Yes, you do, you need to know."

She was rubbing her hands as if trying to remove the stain. "I left ,Monk; I left her with him. I was in my car, crying, waiting for it to be over. I don't remember getting out, I don't remember going back in. I didn't want to, I was so afraid. Maybe that's my only saving grace, I did go back in. He hit me and hit me and hit me. Anna was screaming and screaming. After what seemed like forever Jordan left. Anna kept screaming and it finally dawned on me that she was screaming at me. She ran out and I tried to chase her but I couldn't get up.

"I was completely numb. It was then that I realized how terrible a person I had become. I just lay there. I couldn't even cry. The next day I made it to the living room. He was waiting. He knocked me down, tore off my clothes and…and then, he beat the living daylights out of me. I don't remember much else."

Agnes sat down and put her hand on my face, on the side that was still discolored. What did I know about pain? My life was a veritable joyride.

"Who found you, the police?"

"No, Johnny did. He covered me up and took me to the hospital. I was in bad shape, but I deserved it. I had gotten what I'd asked for. I considered myself worthless, and that's how I was treated. After what I did to Anna, I didn't care if he killed me; I wasn't worth saving." She sat there staring at the ground. "Johnny took care of me, paid for everything, even fixing my face. See?" she pointed to it.

"You have a beautiful face."

"I guess," she said in a self-deprecating way. "The doctors did a good job. They had to fix my nose and cheek. My arm broke again and I had a fractured skull. I was in the hospital for a long time. When I got out I had nowhere to go. I don't know why he cared, but Johnny helped me move and I spent the next two years hiding in the bar. All my relationships were ruined. Even MaryAnn was mad at me. I wish I could say I learned my lesson with men, and in some ways maybe I did, but mostly I still picked up guys in the bar after drinking too much and fucked them in their cars. I tried not to, but I'd get lonely. I drank and I said yes, so I was popular with a certain crowd. I wish I was a decent woman, that I had a nicer story to tell, but I don't. I am what I am."

Her eyes were staring in at mine. I found it disconcerting.

It was hard to square what she said to the woman I thought I knew. It certainly didn't paint a flattering picture, and it made me wonder about the choices she'd made. How was I going to change who she was? Her savior? That was all pie in the sky bullshit; people don't change.

"It's not a very pretty story," I said, mostly to myself.

"No, it's an awful story, but I don't want you to have any illusions about me."

"I still don't think you're a bad person or a lost cause, Agnes."

She shook her head and smiled at me.

"I'm not going to let you go. You know that, right?"

"And when did you decide this?"

"Last night. I spent the whole day believing you'd hear the truth and be so disgusted that, that it would be over, but then you said we were ok and it was as if everything changed. I thought maybe we really did have a chance, you and me, Monk and Agnes. I told myself that I was going to do everything I could to hold on to you, no matter what. For the first time since I've known you, I didn't feel afraid. I want to be strong with you. You know Johnny told me he liked you, that you would be good for me. He's never said that about anyone else I've known. I didn't listen to him before, but maybe this time I will."

"Yeah?"

"Yeah." She was serious.

"Alright, but there are a few things we need to get straight."

"What?"

"You're right, after what you told me, you don't exactly smell like a rose. I might be a fool, but I'm not stupid. I can't wave a magic wand and make everything better. I can't make you into somebody else." She nodded, which didn't help. "And I don't want to hear anymore talk about hoe you're terrible or worthless or any of that, I don't like it. It's a waste of energy, a waste of time, and it makes you look pathetic. And no more jealousy, I don't like that either."

Agnes wrapped her arms around me. "I love you, Monk Buttman!"

"Then you're the fool."

"I don't care."

Agnes squeezed as hard as she could. I did what I could to coax her to the car. If we were going to get to the farm before everyone was in bed, we had to get moving.

I called Moses once we got close enough to a town where my phone worked. I told him we were running late and apologized for being an inconvenience. He laughed and told me I was never going to change. We arrived with the moon illuminating the valley. I recognized the road and the hills, but the rest of it was foreign. Where I remembered pastures there were vineyards. There were more houses. The gate was different as were the lights on the houses built around the courtyard. Everything was what I expected, but I didn't remember any of it. The name above the gate, Our Home, was new or so I assumed.

I didn't remember it.

I was a stranger, an exile repatriated. I drove to the second house on the left. There on the porch stood Moses and Meredith, his wife. I parked the car.

"You're still driving this old thing? Well, good for you."

"Yeah, Bernie keeps it running." Agnes came around. "Moses, this is Agnes; Agnes, this is Moses, my father."

"Welcome, Agnes. It's good to know my boy has a woman in his life. We worry about him." Moses wrapped his arms around Agnes, hugging her and kissing her on the cheek. She looked at me for guidance.

"He a hugger, I should have mentioned that."

The old man laughed. "You got that right. Human contact is the glue that binds us." Moses then wasted no time giving me the same treatment. I put my arms around him and closed my eyes. He still felt strong. He put his hand to the bruises on my face and shook his head. "Should I ask?"

"I fell off my bike."

"And I thought I taught you how to ride..." His smile wasn't convincing.

We said hello to Meredith and more hugs ensued. Meredith looked the same as I remembered, though there were more wrinkles and her hair was now white. The billowy field dress was gone, replaced with jeans and a blue cambric shirt. Moses still had that great mane of hair, but it too was white and shorn of its ponytail. The beard was groomed, no longer cascading down his chest. He remained trim, but the overalls were gone, he wore what Meredith wore. His shirt was tan.

"Come in, you must be tired from your day on the road."

Meredith took Agnes' hand while Moses and I brought in the luggage. We were given the guest room to the right side of the living room. I took it all in. It was a big room with a kitchenette, a small table and two couches. They were new to me. When I was a kid, the room only had chairs; couches were kept out front facing the courtyard where the families gathered. Moses wanted a communal place where the families could come together and share. I wondered if that still occurred or if it had gone along the wayside as times changed.

Moses and Meredith slept in the bedroom on the other side of the house. We sat down for a few minutes during which we were informed that breakfast was at seven and, if Agnes was interested, Moses would be delighted to show her around the farm. Agnes seemed unusually enthusiastic. I just smiled and said we could do whatever she wanted.

It was time for bed.

"Are the toilets still outside?" I was curious.

Moses rolled his eyes. "You should come more often, we've had indoor plumbing for twenty years. There's a bathroom right off your room. Get some sleep, we rise early around here; that part hasn't changed."

Agnes and I went into our room.

"Figures they'd put in toilets after I left. I spent my youth going to an outhouse."

Agnes patted my ass and told me to "get over it". We unpacked and got into the smallish bed.

"Was this your room?"

"No, we kids had our own little bunkhouse. You'll see it tomorrow. It was very communal in those days. When my stepbrothers were born, things changed; they added the other rooms. Us older kids stayed in the bunkhouse until we left."

She snuggled up close to me. "You'll have to show me all your secret places."

"There are no secret places, just a sad one, and it's not on the farm. Maybe we'll go there tomorrow or the next day. In the meantime get some sleep. Moses wasn't kidding about rising early."

"I have to get up at seven?"

"No, beautiful, you have to get up at five-thirty to be ready for breakfast at seven. We're expected to help."

"Oh..." Who's enthusiastic now!

"You'll have to learn to cook, whether you like it or not!" I couldn't suppress my delight.

"You're a jerk, Buttman."

"Yes, I am."

33

Agnes did not like getting up early. Nor was she prepared for communal life and the idea that we all had our part to play. I, on the other hand, fell right in line as if I'd never left. I found that rather disturbing. In the old days, I was responsible for the animals. As a visiting relative, I went where I was directed and tried to stay out of the way of those with work to do.

The point, as I remembered it, was to be as self-sufficient as we could and to forgo that which we could not produce ourselves. I saw it as deprivation while my father saw it as the noble existence of an honest man. He didn't object to commerce; he objected to the belief that labor's value should be subsumed to profit. He saw no benefit in the accumulation of wealth. Wealth was a disease that made men greedy and maleficent. He didn't believe in individualism as a code or philosophy. Community was his thing, the belief that our time was best spent in the service of each other. These thoughts all came flooding back as I wandered through the barn and helped where I could.

I had to continually remind myself I once lived here.

Agnes was in the communal kitchen. It was a big place on the north side of the courtyard around which the houses were built. I had furtively pulled Meredith aside before Agnes finally swore her way out of bed to ask her to have mercy on Agnes as she was, by her own admission, not much of a homemaker. Meredith gave me a hug and told me not to worry. So it was quite surprising to see the self-avowed non-cook merrily helping the other members of the day's cooking crew. She was baking. Her hair had been hastily pulled back, and there was flour on her hands and clothes. She saw me and with a big smile raised her sticky fingers. I gave her a thumb's up.

Moses was at the other end of the square by the shed where the equipment was stored. Much as he tried to integrate the sexes, whether in the kitchen or fields, a certain amount of self-segregation occurred. Few of the women had any interest in fieldwork. Maybe that had changed and I was just ignorant of the facts. I guess I'd find out.

Moses flagged me over, introduced me to the people I didn't know; and there were many, then went over the day's schedule. I listened and shook my head like I knew what was going on. It wasn't technically any different from what I used to do in Virginia, other than there I was working my own land. Here it belonged to the collective. Once the workday and its particulars were discussed, it was time for breakfast. Moses put his arm around me and kissed the side of my head. I flinched, more out unfamiliarity than dislike. It'd been a long, long time since we'd spent any time together.

"I hope that doesn't bother you?"

I smiled at him. "No, it doesn't bother me, it's just been too long."

He turned to face me and put his hand on the fading bruises. "We were always here."

We were always here. One of the few things I always understood, but I couldn't accept that *I* should be here.

"I know. It wasn't you that kept me away."

"You say that, but..."

"But what?" I didn't want to talk about it.

The bell chimed. Moses led me towards the dining hall.

"There was so much you missed, so much. It's been years since you've slept here. For a while, there was hope you might come to the gathering we had a few years back. We planned it for months. Rebekah told us you knew of it; that she asked you to come. She said you were coming. Everyone was so excited. Old friends from the early days came. Your mother was here as was Lilith and her husband. All the children; we had a marvelous turnout, a wonderful time. The only one missing was our Sunshine."

"Please don't call me that."

He sighed. "It's a beautiful name, what's not to like?"

"It's no name for a grown man."

He laughed. "And *Monk Butt*man is?"

"Ok, maybe in hindsight it wasn't the best choice, but I'm the one who's had to live with it, not you."

"It does matter to us."

"Us who? How often do you even think of my mother?"

He stopped just as we reached the door to the dining hall. That old serious face I ran away from was glaring at me.

"I talk with your mother more than you think, far more than you do. She loves you and worries about you. She longs to see you and your response is to hide in that hellhole of Los Angeles. When was the last time you spoke with her? When was the last time you laid eyes on her? We won't last forever. If it's not us, then what's your excuse, Mr. Buttman?"

I had no answer.

Moses reached down and picked up a handful of dirt. He placed it in my hands.

"This is your home, this is your land. I told you this before; you belong here. Will you spend the rest of your life cut off from your family and your land?"

The others were watching, listening. I'd forgotten we'd opened the door to the dining room. I could feel them pressed in around me. It was a replay of six years before, only then Moses was yelling at me in that booming baritone. I stormed out then; I wanted to now. Agnes could find her way home.

I carefully put the dirt back on the ground.

"We're keeping everyone from breakfast."

Moses looked at them. "So we are."

I found my seat beside Agnes. She, like the others, had been watching.

"Are you alright?"

"I'm fine," I lied.

We joined hands and said grace, something we didn't do when I was a kid. There were about thirty people at the table. It was a long heavy wooden structure we'd built years ago. I remember being part of the crew; it was my first big project. I assisted Arturo in building the legs and gluing and binding the top. The food was passed around. Agnes noticed I wasn't taking anything and put food on my plate.

"You need to eat." When I started to object, she shushed me. "If you can say it, so can I!" Damn!

On top of the eggs, pork, and potatoes, rested two biscuits. She motioned for me to try one. I put a small amount of butter on one and took a bite.

"Well?" she asked. I noted the light in her eyes.

"Well what?"

"How does it taste?"

I leaned over as if to kiss her. "It's very good. You made them?"

Agnes smiled broadly, "I did! Of course, Meredith showed me how, and it's her recipe, but I was so excited that they turned out ok, and I wanted you to like them."

"I do. See, I told you cooking's not so hard."

"I don't remember that at all, Buttman."

It didn't occur to me that people might be watching. I don't know why I thought that. I was the long lost son of the founder of the commune. Once word spread that I'd be there, and I knew the word would; why would I be surprised by their curiosity? I know I'd been talked about and here I was, back after all those years. The name Buttman resounded throughout the room.

A young girl across from us named Emily pointedly asked Agnes, "Why do you call him Buttman?"

I looked at Agnes. *Please* don't say anything!

Agnes retorted, "Because that's his name."

Emily looked at me. "My mom told me your name was Sunshine, not Buttman. Isn't your name Sunshine?"

A deep odious groan percolated through me. Agnes was all smiles. They all knew.

"Yes, Emily, my name was once Sunshine, but I don't use that name anymore. I'm called Monk now."

"I like Sunshine better, Buttman sounds nasty." More than a few people laughed. Agnes couldn't contain her glee.

"Oh, my beautiful Sunshine!" That was followed by a big sloppy kiss on the cheek and the roar of everyone at the table.

This was why I didn't come back. Years of hard work down the drain. I was back to being Sunshine, fucking Sunshine!

With that the floodgates opened. Where have you been? What do you do? Where did you two meet? I think you should get married, that from the irrepressible Emily. You could get married here. Groan. Questions for Agnes, who did not say no to questions concerning weddings, and naturally, there was the big white elephant in the room, why did you leave and why haven't you come back? I answered the ones I wanted to and demurred on those I found too painful. I tried to rope-a-dope as Orville had done and hoped to run out the clock.

Didn't these people have work to do?

I made vague promises to talk about it later once the day's work was over, maybe at supper. I turned the tables and made them talk about themselves. There were seven families; many were multigenerational. For a number of them, that's why they were here, to live and work together as people had done for generations before industrialization and modernization. They wanted to care for the Earth, to be a greater part of it.

Since I didn't actually have any work to do, I helped clean up after breakfast. I did the dishes and put them away. Agnes stood with me, merrily drying the dishes and humming to herself. The sad fearful woman from the day before was nowhere in sight. Instead, here was this almost bubbly woman happily drying dishes and rubbing up against me. Every time I looked at her she would smile and make a kissy face. I would shake my head and she would laugh. The others helping thought we were just so delightful together. When we were finished, Moses and Meredith, as promised, showed us around.

We took the road that led out from the courtyard. They had added some land, but for me it was much the same. The change was in the vineyards. They were everywhere. "This was wine country," Moses said, and they decided to expand into that. He thought it advantageous to grow varietals that were less well known to carve out a niche within a very robust market; this from an avowed anti-capitalist. When I called him on it, he shrugged and told me times change. He was too old to storm the parapets; better to organize with like minds and make the best of the world you're in.

"And the angry man, the one I can still hear bellowing in my head, what happened to him?"

The old man chuckled. "He's still there, and I haven't changed my mind when it come to the conditions working people face, but, yes, I've mellowed, much as I dislike that word."

We stayed along the road. Agnes kept up with Moses as Meredith and I fell back. She and Moses formalized their relationship when she got pregnant. I was ten. Since I lived in the bunkhouse, our lives didn't intersect like they would have had we lived under the same roof. During those seven years she made no effort to be my mother, which both vexed and pleased me.

What I did remember was an understanding and empathy that allowed people to speak more openly to her than they otherwise would to someone else.

"What do you think of Agnes?" I noticed Meri watching her.

"I think she's a bit of a lost soul. I felt a terrible kind of sadness around her. From what she told me, her life's been a series of disappointments and bad choices. We had a chance to talk this morning and I was struck by how quick she was to disparage herself. I had to ask her to stop apologizing for her perceived shortcomings. As if every woman knows her way around a kitchen. I know she loves you. She expressed it many times. I was a little surprised when she told me that you've only known each other a short while, but she didn't care. She said that for the first time in her life she felt she had a chance to be happy, that you were the first man she'd known who accepted her. Apparently, her other relationships didn't go well."

"Did she talk about them?"

"Only in passing. She said they didn't matter anymore. She wants to put her energy into what she has now. And you, what do you think of Agnes?"

"I don't know. I've always disliked the idea that two people are made for each other, that seems so fairytale-ish to me, but I find myself surprised by how well we get along. I mean I like her, the way she is, and she feels the same about me. At least that's what she tells me. She annoys me in the best way and has no problem giving me grief if. I think about her when we're apart. Other than that, I don't think there's much there."

Meredith smiled. "And the sex?"

"Oh that. I can't complain. I could say it's been very good, but that might be too much information."

"For some."

Agnes and Moses were waiting for us up the road.

"How's Moses doing?" I figured it was better to ask her. "Not that I'm complaining, but he seems a lot less intense, almost easy-going if that's possible."

Meredith took my arm, surprising me.

"He's less ornery to be sure. Some of that is time passing. The other is that life deals you challenges and Moses has had his share. I'd say there were three that changed him. The first was the revolt about a decade ago. You know your father can be very headstrong; how else do you explain that this community is still thriving? But he can rub you raw at times and there was quite a blow-up between him and the Mackinaws; all over what kind of grapes to plant, but really it was your father being overly demanding for too long and the brothers had had enough."

Franco and Brewster Mackinaw were there from the beginning, back in the freewheeling Sixties. The three of them decided to go off the grid, although in those days, as I recall, it was getting back to working the soil with your hands They were the patriarchs of the farm, the three heads of the family.

"They always argued," I said.

"True, but divisions build up. The brothers decided to leave after that and there was a lot of worry that the farm wouldn't survive once they were gone, but fate made that a secondary concern." Meredith held on to me as she spoke.

"Why, what happened?"

"Your father's heart began failing. He had to have surgery to fix it. It removed him from the day-to-day operations for the first time in his life. He didn't even want to go. If life kills me so be it, he bellowed, but I'd had enough as well. He was going to have it fixed whether he wanted to or not. He was not going to drop dead. I convinced the brothers to stay and put them in charge. Moses had to step back while he recovered, and lo and behold, the world did not end. As a matter of fact, our little community prospered. Your father had to admit that there were other paths to take, other voices to hear. He still groused, but there was no going back."

Meredith paused. Her head turned to the man ahead of us. She started to say something before turning to me.

"What?"

"What? It's his sons and you in particular. A father believes in his sons, you know, believes they see the value of his life. Yet all of you left. Sterling is our liaison to the wineries. He learned the business here and we had hoped he would stay, but he prefers to live in Napa these days. Isaac fell in love and followed Allison, his wife, on her missions. They work in Africa helping the poor. And Jacob, he surprised us all and became a Marine."

"Really?"

Jacob the youngest of my half-brothers was supposed to be the second coming of Moses. He was the favorite. At least that's the way I remember it. In truth, I remember very little of them. They were just kids when I left, Sterling, the oldest, was seven.

"Yes, after 9/11, he decided he needed to do his part. We were shocked to say the least. Moses, surprisingly, had little to say when he told us. We see him when we can. I can't tell you how worried I've been every time they send him over for another tour. It terrifies me."

"Agnes' son, Barron, is in the Army." It was all I could think of to say. I was still trying to process the idea that one of us would end up in uniform. It wasn't encouraged, particularly by Moses, who viewed it as giving up your life for people who never see you as anything more than a statistic. It never occurred to me to join. It apparently occurred to Jacob.

"Yes, she told me. Odd, isn't it, where you find a kindred soul?"

"It is..." I looked at Moses. "And then there's Sunshine..."

"And then there's Sunshine, lost for so long. He'd never say it, but he was heartbroken when you missed the gathering. After it was over, he did a lot of rationalizing, but I think he believed you would never return. He retreated to the vineyards. In some ways I think that's best. Your father's not a young man and it's important that the younger members have their say."

"I don't have a good reason for staying away. I wish I did, but..."

"But you're here now. That's all we can ask. I've learned over the years that nothing is easy or uncomplicated, no matter how hard you try to burrow back to a time where it all made sense. Your father loves you. I can't tell you how much it means to him to have you here, what it means to all of us."

I had no idea what to say to that. I had no idea what to do except to keep walking. Meredith let go of my arm. I gave her a hug and she smiled back at me.

"Welcome home, our dear Sunshine, welcome home."

"Thanks." I tried to keep my eyes focused on the road.

Agnes and Moses were waiting.

So was James.

34

It was an access road, crushed rock and dirt, one of many crisscrossing the fields. I stood in the same spot I had on that afternoon when I was seventeen. I remember my legs shook so badly that I could barely stand. I shit myself as the man with the gun laughed at me. I didn't want to die. I wanted to be back with my girlfriend and our baby. Miguel and James were crying too. The three of us crying as the Pronto brothers taunted us. I could see them as clearly now as I had then. We were just boys stupidly thinking we could deal with gangsters. We were wrong. The sun, high above, burned as we waited to be murdered. I didn't understand any of it. James was confident it was an easy score. Miguel was not. He literally begged us not to go, but James told him not to worry.

It was in the bag.

Agnes was with me as I stood there.

After the vineyards, Moses and Meredith took us to the orchards, the fields and the herb gardens, then to the barns and the pens to see the livestock. Agnes was charmed by this rural life. To me, it was just the past. We had lunch with the others, but my thoughts were elsewhere. The road was calling me. James was calling me. The three of us were as tight as boys could be. All those years raising hell, getting into trouble, dreaming; the black kid, the migrant, and Sunshine. Outcasts we were, but we didn't care. We had each other. Agnes listened as I thought out loud, there on that lonely road.

"I was the idiot. I didn't pay attention and I didn't care. I thought it was something to do to pass the time, something to do in a place where not much happened, but for Miguel and James it was serious business. James was the believer; he had big plans. Miguel was the strategist, the one to get us there. I was the third wheel, but they needed me because I was the white kid. I could do what they couldn't. People watched them. They don't trust black kids and migrants, but a white kid? I had a free pass just about everywhere."

The memory stretched out. Too wide for me to compress, but I had to get it out, out of my head and out into the atmosphere. There the wind would carry it away, far far away. That day had buried me for too long. I had to get it out. Just as Agnes needed me to hear about her time with Jordan, I needed her to hear about mine with James. Someone had to know what I had done here.

"We were just kids, doing a little dealing. I considered it harmless fun. I remember being asked if I could score some bud for a guy. I guess since I was a hippie kid everyone thought the farm was filled with potheads. I knew the old man and the Mackinaws smoked, but they didn't do in front of us kids and they were very discreet around other adults. I told Miguel about it and he said he could get some from his cousins. So we got into the business, but we were small timers.

"Every once in a while I'd go south on a run for the old man to pick up supplies and I would sneak into Mexico to pick up some bud for Miguel's cousins. It was easy money. I'd take Astral and then Rebekah along. We never got stopped. I was an all American white guy with his all American girlfriend and his all American baby. Neither Miguel or James would've made it past the border, but I was just another white kid living it up in Mexico for a day or two. They all cooed over Rebekah and it never occurred to me that if we'd been caught I'd probably still be in jail. That's how I was then, a thoughtless idiot."

I reached down for a handful of dirt. It was red with James' blood. I flung it out towards the field. My hands were still bloody. They had been for twenty-six years.

"We came out here to meet the Pronto brothers, Frankie and Gene. They were the local thugs. I didn't know anything about territories or any of that. Like I said I was just riding the wave, acting as if it was no different than surfing at Laguna. They heard about our dealing and didn't like our horning in on their turf. Miguel wanted us to work with his cousins to broker a deal, but James said he had it taken care of. He'd run a deal for them. I didn't know what his deal was, but he told me to play dumb; there was a lot of money at stake. It didn't dawn on me that we were in big trouble till we were on this road. Miguel told me to turn around. James told me it was all right. Back and forth they argued. I believed him right until they stopped us. Before I knew it, the guns were out and we were on our knees."

I picked up another handful of bloody dirt.

"They grabbed James and pushed him up against their truck. They wanted the money. He said he gave them everything that was given to him. No, they said there was a lot more; that we were holding out on them. Then they started to beat us. They were going to kill us here in this field. I couldn't breathe. They had broken three of my ribs. There was blood running out of my mouth and nose. They held James up against the truck and dragged Miguel and me over to him. They put a knife in our hands and told us we had a choice. We either killed James or they would kill us all. I was blubbering and whining, but Miguel didn't say a word. His face was like a stone. He looked at me and I said I couldn't do it. I dropped the knife, but he picked it up and put it back in my hand. James just stared at us. He didn't say anything even though his lips were moving. The brothers were screaming at us to kill the fucking nig...to do it. They hit us with their guns and pressed them against our heads. Miguel took my hand and we..."

I was on my knees, my hands on the ground. Agnes had her arms around me. She was crying.

"We killed him. We killed our friend. We killed James, because we were afraid, because we didn't want to die. They told us we had two days to get the money or they'd do the same to us. They said they'd kill my stupid bitch girlfriend and that fucking kid of mine. James was tied to the rear bumper. I can still see him staring at us, holding his stomach as he bled to death. They were laughing as they drove off."

"I'm sorry, Monk; I'm so sorry."

"Why?" I wanted to be whole again, but that part was gone. "I can still see him" There he was, standing in front of me, that uncomprehending look on his face.

"What do you want me to do?"

I looked at Agnes. "I can't leave him here."

"He's not here. We buried him with his father."

We turned to find Moses behind us. I hadn't heard him drive up. He put his hand on my shoulder.

"It's time to forgive yourself. Please son, come home."

35

I sat in the car as Moses drove. Agnes followed in the old man's truck. She didn't know how to drive a stick, never mind a column shifter. I stared at the fields. I didn't feel any better. If anything I felt worse. All the land did was remind me of my failures and my cowardice. I was back where I started.

After they left us on the road, Miguel said we had to tell Moses; there was no other way. He was all we had left. What else could we do?

He was so angry, but he never raised his voice. That didn't prevent him from telling us how badly we'd fucked up. What was he going to tell Esmeralda, James's mother? How was he going to explain how we'd gotten him killed? We had no answers, nothing. We were in bad shape as it was. He took Miguel to his cousins. He packed me, Astral, and Rebekah into the Falcon, gave us enough money to get going and sent us to Virginia. I hurt like hell. He patched me up, told me it was of my own making and I'd have to live with it. I'd heal. I told myself I'd never come back...

"Where did you find him?"

"In the field off Lorry Road," he said.

I couldn't ask what was left of him.

"Marsyas Durant said I should ask you about the early days. He said he knew you?" I was tired of the road noise. I wanted something to think about other than James.

"Marsyas Durant? Where'd that come from?"

"I work for his firm now. I met him on a road in Santa Barbara after his car broke down."

Moses smiled. "Marsyas Durant came to us a long time ago when word got out about the quality of our weed. He said he knew a group that was interested in buying some of our plants. He told us there was big money to be made, but I said we weren't interested. Brew and Franc were and we argued and argued. Of course, in those days we grew it for ourselves and a few friends. We had an agreement with sheriff Bob that we'd keep it low key, no hanky-panky. I had no interest in the money, but after what happened with James and then the Pronto brothers, Bob laid down the law. He wasn't going to have the Feds or the Staters rooting around his county! There would be no more drug-related killings, so we sold our stock and seeds to Durant's people. I haven't grown any since."

"Is that all?"

Moses looked at me. It was the face he saved for those times when I'd say something stupid. I laughed and told him of my more recent adventures, of Boyer and Desiree, Martin and Judith. I told him about seeing Miguel again and the story he told me. I wanted to know why Marsyas Durant, one of the most powerful men in LA, would have me ask an aging hippie about his recreational pot.

Moses wasn't having it.

"I couldn't tell you why he had you ask about the old days, other than as a cautionary tale. We like to think it was all peace and love back then, but there were always angry violent forces in play. Look at Manson and his little family; the assassinations and bombings. I have no illusions about my youth or that time. Neither should you."

"I had those beaten out of me."

Moses let out a deep sigh. We were back at the farm. He pulled to the side and waved Agnes around. She waved as she passed us. We followed her in and parked. Meredith was by the door. Agnes stood with her as we approached.

"Meri, would you and Agnes excuse us for a while. Monk and I have some things to talk about." Meredith gave me a hug. I knew my eyes were red and I was sure I didn't appear overly festive.

"So long as you don't miss supper, we have a big celebration planned for tonight remember?"

"I'd be a fool to forget." He kissed her, and then said something to Agnes. She smiled and the two of them went into the house. Moses and I stood on the porch surveying the valley. The sun had settled into a nest of clouds, playing peek-a-boo.

"It's always been peaceful here. No endless blasts of noise or the harsh lights that never seem to go out. It's quiet here. Don't you miss it?"

I thought about it. "Sometimes, but I had that in Virginia. It too was peaceful and quiet. It was also lonely and isolating. I spent my time feeling angry and lost. I was mean to Astral and absent to my daughter. I spent years doing work I detested."

"I think you exaggerate. I asked Lilith about that. You know she doesn't like to be called Astral anymore. She told me you were, in fact, quite successful. She said your yields were always strong. Something Judah could never quite replicate."

"It was my penance. I had nothing else to do, so I put my efforts into that."

I don't think he cared for the penance crack. "And all of this was because of what happened with James?"

"Yes."

Moses stepped down off the porch.

"We all struggled with what happened. It was a terrible thing to have to deal with. Esmeralda was devastated. She loved you boys, and in an instant, you were all lost to her. Miguel took care of her, but only from a distance. You left, and James was dead. She asked about you, many times. Like me, she had hoped you'd be at the gathering, but... She died two years ago of cervical cancer. We buried her with James and his father."

"I'm sorry to hear that." Esmeralda was a black woman from Jamaica. Her family moved to New York when she was a child. James' father, Franklin, grew up in this valley. He met Esmeralda in Washington, D.C., where she was going to school. Franklin had been in the Army and was working for the government. They moved here when Franklin was sent to Vietnam, but he was killed in the last year of the war. Moses asked her if she would teach us kids. That's when I first met them. Miguel ended up with us after being booted out of public school. His mother pleaded with Moses to let him go to Esmeralda's class. He was too smart not to be educated. Both he and James did well. I did what I had to in order to avoid her grave disappointment when I did less than stellar work. That seemed to be the story of my life. "What did Miguel do? I thought he had to get out too?"

Moses sat down on the porch step. "Miguel supported Esmeralda by setting up an account for her. There was no pension after Franklin died, and we could only pay so much. After James was killed she withdrew for a while. She needed time to heal, so Miguel, with the help of his cousins, made sure she had enough money to support herself."

"And the Pronto brothers? Miguel told me they were dead. I thought for years they would find me, come after me."

Moses shook his head.

"No, they made the mistake of underestimating Miguel cousins. They were connected to people in Mexico who were a lot more powerful than the Pronto brothers could ever be and they were angry about what happened. They wanted revenge. Miguel told the brothers he had what they wanted and set up a time to meet them out on that same road. I think the Pronto brothers thought they'd do exactly what they had done before, but the cousins were waiting. They took the men who were with them and left the Pronto brothers tied to their truck. They were found with their guts opened up."

"Miguel did it?"

"That surprises you?" Moses' face was dark.

"No." I remembered Miguel's face, how angry he was.

"After that, Bob got everyone together and basically told us it was over. He didn't care if it was just us and for our own use. He was way ahead of his time in that regard, but when people are being killed it changes everything. We were on our own, no more looking the other way. The state came up to investigate. Esmeralda hated that her son was considered a drug dealer, but that perception never changed, and you three *were* dealing. Since there were no witnesses or weapons, no one was arrested. Those of us who knew kept quiet. It wouldn't bring anyone back. The Pronto brother's family, shit that they are, thought they had it made after a hundred grand was found at their place, but the Feds took it, deeming it drug money. That was that. There are still drug problems around here, but they're no different from anywhere else. I don't mean to downplay what happened or how it affected you, but you can't let it bury you; life goes on."

Life goes on.

I was tired. I wanted this to be cathartic, an end to so many years of grief. It was out there, but it didn't change anything. I took the old man's hand and thanked him. For the first time in my life I saw tears well up in his eyes. He put his arms around me and kissed my cheeks. I kissed him back. We went to find Meredith and Agnes. It was time for supper.

Meredith wasn't kidding. There were balloons and flowers, and above us all, tacked across the entrance, were the words any grown man would love to see:

Welcome home, Sunshine.

I'm pretty sure my parents were high when they named me.

Emily came and stood by me as I took in the decorations. She put her hand in mine. This surprised me, as did her smile when I looked down at her. I'd forgotten how safe this place felt as a child. I smiled at her and asked if she helped with the decorations. Yes, she stated emphatically, those were her letters above the door. She personally directed the other kids to help bring closure to a man named Sunshine, although I doubt she thought of it in those terms.

"They're very beautiful. I want to thank you for your hard work." I don't know why I said it that way.

"You're very welcome. You can sit by me."

So I did.

Agnes helped bring out the food from the kitchen. She was wearing an apron that gave every sign that once again she was elbow deep in the preparation of the celebratory meal. As with the other meals, we held hands and said grace. As the guest of honor, it fell on me to give the invocation. I stammered through it trying very hard not to sound like an idiot. Moses rose to speak. Everyone at the table looked at him and then at me. I found it exceedingly uncomfortable being the center of attention. I didn't see myself as worthy.

"I'm so glad you were all able to be with us today." He was looking at me. "It's not often that my oldest has come home to see us. My hope, naturally, is that he will come to see us more…" He was choking up. Brewster, with fork in hand, cleared his throat. "Yes, yes, yes, I see you're hungry. All right then; to a very good day, I commend this supper."

We raised our glasses and dug in. I, as the center of attention sat at the end of the table. Moses, at the head of the table was to my left and Emily to my right. Meredith sat across from me with Agnes next to her. On the other side of Emily was her mother. She was a small intense woman named Calista. Calista and Emily came from Philadelphia. Emily informed me they had been here for almost four years and that she was learning a lot. Like most children, the animals, especially the babies, were her favorite, but she also found gardening interesting. Her mother, she pointed out, was in charge of the herb garden and she helped her organize it this year.

Emily reminded me of Rebekah, energetic, smart, and opinionated. I told her I had a daughter. Calista chimed in saying they met her when she came back for the gathering. I hadn't seen Rebekah in more than a year when she had come to LA. She needed a break and wanted to see me. I don't know why. I was a poor father. Emily brought that into stark relief. I longed for a do-over, to have Rebekah when she was…

"How old are you, Emily?"

"I'm ten, almost eleven."

"It's a great age, ten, so much to look forward to."

"I guess."

I didn't expect her to understand, but Moses, Meredith, and especially Agnes understood. They were caught up in my talk with Emily and Calista. They'd never seen me with a child before. Rebekah was just a baby when we left. I'd never come out with her, and they never traveled to Virginia; too many nevers. Emily wanted to show me her part of the garden. She had twenty different plants, you know! I told her if there was time, we'd go look after supper; if not we'd do it in the morning before school.

"Thanks, Mr. Sunshine."

"Call me Monk."

She turned up her nose. "I like Sunshine better!"

The audience applauded.

Supper concluded after dessert of homemade apple pie and ice cream. This had been touted as one of my favorites, which, I had to admit, it was. Again, I felt overpowered by a sense of personal fraud, but I kept my mouth shut. Feigning surprise didn't fit the bill. We cleared our dishes, and Emily grabbed my hand to take me to her garden. Agnes asked if she could come along. Emily said no, but Calista overruled her. The three of us ventured out with Emily in the lead, me right behind, and Agnes carefully keeping her distance. We listened and made pleasant noises as Emily detailed the various herbs she had planted. There was basil, cilantro, and dill, fennel, lavender, and parsley. Agnes and I marveled at the plants she had and her knowledge of them. Emily warmed to Agnes as we went along the garden, showing both of us rather than simply favoring me. We wandered the garden until the light began to fade, at which point we took Emily back to her mother.

Agnes sat with me at the edge of the courtyard. The rest of the folks had turned in leaving the two of us to the twilight and the quiet. It was a warm evening. I was half tempted to gather some wood for the fire pit; something I hadn't done in years. Agnes liked it here. It freed her from the worry that buried her when she was with her family. Mine was a fine substitute she said. I was feeling better. Emily did more for me than the trip to that goddamned stretch of dirt. I still grieved for James and the part of me that died with him. Miguel had made his peace. I needed to make mine.

The next morning I gathered up some flowers and went to the place where they were buried. The graveyard, set just off the road, was quiet and still, save for the faint rustle of the trees that were spread about the cemetery. I followed the hand-drawn map Moses made for me and found them by a stately Wilderness Oak. Three small markers. I bent down and ran my fingers along the ridges of the stone. I said a prayer and asked James to forgive me. I was better with prayer. Even if I wasn't a good Christian anymore, I remembered enough to say what I meant, and I believed enough of it to keep myself from being a complete hypocrite. I sat with them for a while. It was a beautiful day. I wondered if it was monotonous to continue thinking that. I decided it wasn't. Before I left I asked both Franklin and, especially, Esmeralda to forgive me. I wiped my eyes and said goodbye.

We stayed another two days, most of which Agnes spent either with me wandering around or with Meredith in the kitchen. The woman who refused to learn to cook! I got to know most of the people there and we promised to come back as often as we could. Minus the fact there was no guarantee Agnes and I would stay together, it wasn't a completely idle promise. As we had planned, the trip home went through Napa where, on Meredith's urging, we got together with Sterling. He showed us around and took us to dinner. Agnes, emboldened by her successes in my part of the world, called Anna and asked if she would like to meet for a few minutes. It took a number of pleases, but Anna relented.

We found a place to stay not far from Simon and Eric's house, made our way to say hello, and for the most part had a nice time. Eric, as usual, was charming, Anna reserved but more receptive to her mother's entreaties, and Simon put out but careful not to say anything to piss off either Eric or Anna. Before we left, Agnes took her daughter aside for what I assumed were promises to do what she could to make things right between them. I promised we'd come back in the future, and there were hugs and kisses that intimated that while everything was not forgiven, at least, for now, there was a sense of it being possible one day.

After Eric hugged and kissed me, on the cheek, I casually mentioned he was a lot like my father. Agnes started laughing and nearly spilled the beans on my terrible secret.

"You should hear what they call him..."

"Aggie!" I shouted.

That stopped them. They were fascinated and shocked that I used Simon's nickname for her. Agnes saw them staring at us and noted my grave disapproval. This was not the time! She sheepishly smiled.

"I'll be good."

We got in the car and waved goodbye. Simon, Anna, and Eric watched us, wondering what that was all about. Agnes tried to make nice.

"It is a wonderful name, you know."

"Uh-huh."

"Say what you will, but I like it." She paused and put her hand on mine. "And I'm being serious here..."

I hesitated to say anything. "Yes?"

"You will always be my Sunshine."

She burst out laughing.

Good grief.

36

"Monk, do you know your phone is blinking?"

I was standing by the window watching the cars go by. "It is?"

"Yes!" She said this with a great deal of exasperation. "You have four messages. Don't you ever check it?" It was in her hand.

"It has messages?"

Agnes shook her head and handed me the phone. "We really need to get you up to date on this stuff. What if one of those messages was from me?"

"But you're right here?" I did my best to look like the hayseed she took me for.

"Oh, brother! It's a good thing you're decent in the sack."

I put my arm around her waist and started kissing her neck. I tossed the phone onto the chair, "You know why?"

"Why?"

My hands were undoing the buttons on her blouse. Her hands found my slacks and made their interest more explicit.

"Because I'll always be your Sunshine..."

"Yes you will." We maneuvered to our delightful motel bed.

The phone would have to wait.

Turns out the rest of the world, ignorant of our need for cathartic or near cathartic epiphanies, continued to churn on. There were three messages from Mr. Jones and one from Taylor Lagenfelder. Only the first message from the esteemed Mr. Jones had any relevance to the work we were engaged in. The remaining two echoed Agnes's lament of my cluelessness concerning modern telecommunications. It's too bad I didn't care. Toying with the phone, I replayed the first message. They were watching Dahlia. I had almost forgotten about that. Other than the short synopsis I gave to Moses, it hadn't crossed my mind. They followed her to South Laguna. There were three to five other people there. CALL! Reluctantly, I pressed the button for Jones's phone.

"Buttman?" Mr. Jones sounded remarkably happy to hear from me.

"The one and only. So what's the good word?"

"I think we may have found our girl!" Girl? I couldn't picture Desiree Marshan as a girl. I know she must have been one once, but now she was a tattooed killer with a rich married boyfriend.

"Yeah?"

"Yeah. My girl Martisse has been keeping an eye on her and yesterday she finally did something out of the ordinary, she went down to a beach house in Laguna. She said there were at least three people in the house and two guys hanging out in front. One of them was a woman who matches the description I gave her of Marshan. When are you going to be back? You want me to let Dulcimer know?"

I was trying to process all of this. The last few days had eclipsed any interest I had in the goings on of these people or what, in the end, they were after. Now it was right back on my plate, flopping around, waiting to be cooked.

"No, let's wait to say anything till we're sure. I'll be back tomorrow. We'll get together then and head down to see for ourselves. How's that?"

"Alright, I'll keep Martisse watching the house."

"Works for me."

I hung up. The next call was to my attorney. Her message was to please call at my earliest convenience. That was now. She answered and I told her who it was.

"I have some information for you. We have no record of Martin Delashay owning any beach property. The records of properties owned by Mr. Delashay are also in his wife's name. They have two, the house in Beverly Hills, and a property in Michigan." That made sense. Judith once lived there.

"Thanks."

"One more thing,"

"Yes?" I had the bizarre impression that Taylor Lagenfelder was playing with me.

"While Martin Delashay does not own any beach property, Todd Boyer did."

"Down in South Laguna?"

A delightful moment of silence, "That's correct. I was going to give you the address, but seems like you know it already. Can I ask how you came by this information?"

"Tricks of the trade..." I then explained my answer and asked for the address. After all, there could be more than one beach house. She passed it on and I thanked her for getting me the good word. I also asked her to thank Durant. I hung up and sat in the chair by the window. Moonlight broke the edges of the shade. Agnes was on the bed. Neither of us had any clothes on. I went over and got on the bed with her. I was tired. We pulled up the sheets. Agnes wrapped herself around me. I found it comforting.

"Monk?"

"Yes, beautiful?"

"You know, I don't really know what it is you do?"

"Then it works out because neither do I."

The lingering question, at least to the woman in my car, on our return to the greater Los Angeles area, concerned our living arrangements. The success of our trip, the fact that we were still on speaking terms, lent itself to the notion that we should consider living together. I wasn't necessarily against the idea, merely that, despite our newfound understanding of each other's personal flaws and emotional baggage, which had led to a deeper awareness and connection between us; it might be too soon.

"So you don't want to live with me?"

"I didn't say that."

"Then what did you say?"

I marveled at her annoyance.

"That it doesn't have to happen this minute. Besides it's not like we're not going to see one another for a while or anything like that. You know, there's no rush..."

"Uh-huh. It's this other woman, isn't it? Now that we're back in town, you want to go back to your a la Carte menu." I couldn't quite tell if she was joking or not.

"You mean the rich woman?" Maybe I was.

"So, she has money too. Figures. Let's just go then."

There are times when I should keep my mouth shut, like now. "We're already going."

"Not funny, Buttman."

"Alright, but remember I'm tidy, you tend not to be..." Looking for excuses...

"I'll let you clean."

"Very generous. There's no room in your closet..."

"Seriously?" I got the pout.

"Seriously! Ok, maybe that's a bit of a stretch, but you'd have to put up with me and my stuff, and my habits. I'd have to put up with yours, all the time. Are you ready for that?" I was out of ideas. In truth, there weren't a lot of reasons I couldn't live with Agnes, I just didn't think I was ready.

"Anything else, Sunshine?"

"No, I've said enough." She crossed her arms and slumped into the seat.

The last of the trip to her house was a little uncomfortable, but I had an ace up my sleeve. I parked in front of the house and brought in the bags. We stood there at the door, eyeing one another. I tried to be serious, but I couldn't do it. I kissed her and said I had to go.

"When am I going to see you next?"

"I don't know. I'll call, assuming I remember how to work the phone."

"You're a jerk, Buttman."

"Yeah, but I'm your jerk."

"That's not very comforting."

"I didn't say it to be comforting. See you later, beautiful."

She just stood there. If I wasn't planning on returning later, I'd probably feel bad, but I was, so I didn't. I called Jones, told him I'd meet him at his place just to change things up. First though, I had to drop off my stuff at the bungalow.

I made it past the front door before I realized something was wrong. I had the 45 in my pocket, but it was broad daylight; what could happen? The place didn't look too bad, but I'd had visitors in the last little while. My junk was in the right place, but not the right spot. I pulled out the gun and checked the rooms for surprises. Fortunately, I was alone. I methodically went through every room which, considering it was a one bedroom, one bathroom with a small living room and kitchen, didn't take long. I couldn't find anything

WHERE FOOLS DARE TO TREAD

missing; there was nothing valuable to steal, but I didn't think they were after my junk. What they wanted wasn't here. I put the basket and cooler away and grabbed a few things to keep at Agnes's. If I were going to basically live there I'd need more clothes.

I was fairly certain I'd lost my mind.

I took a second look at the lock on the door. It wasn't broken, so I locked it and headed out, on my way to Orville's. Joanie was standing by the Falcon, a smile on her face.

"Well, how'd it go?" She smirked as she noticed the clothes over my arm and the suitcase in my hand. If I was going back to Agnes's, I might as well do the laundry there.

"All things considered, I think it went well."

"Considering what?"

"Considering that neither one of us had the guts to go alone and that we're still on speaking terms." Joanie took the clothes from my arm as I opened the trunk.

"It also appears that you're on your way to the dry cleaners or that your living situation is changing, yes?"

"I suppose it could be construed from simple observation that that might be the case. However, to anticipate your next question, I'm not going the dry cleaners." I put the suitcase in the trunk, and retrieved the clothes from my ex-lover and put those on top of the suitcase. I also, surreptitiously, took the 45 out of my pocket and placed in the trunk. I don't know if Joanie noticed or not, but she didn't say anything about the gun.

"Sounds like this thing with Agnes is getting serious."

"Serious is a good word. I like the woman; she likes me. She wants to spend more time with me, and I don't really have a good reason not to want to spend time with her. So, what the hell."

"Wow, that quite a declaration of having nothing better to do. I'm sure Agnes is quite taken with it. Not exactly I can't live without you, or you are the love of my life, but I guess it's better than nothing. Not much, but better."

"Exactly." I didn't particularly care for her moralizing tone, but she had a point.

"Do you love Agnes, Monk Buttman?"

"That's the hundred thousand dollar question. And since I have places to go, it might be smarter to save that topic for another day. Are you busy tomorrow afternoon? We could do lunch; go over to the diner. I've had good luck with women there." I was thinking of Dahlia.

"If you like. How about one or so?"

"Till then." For a moment, as I looked at Joanie, she almost seemed wistful. I didn't quite know what to make of that. Another thought occurred to me, "Have you noticed anyone hanging around here lately? Around my place?"

"No, the only strangers have been the landscaping guys. Why?"

"Just curious. See you tomorrow."

"See you, Monk."

I watched her in my rear view mirror as long as I could.

Coretta was at the door. She smiled and gave me a hug. I gave her one. She took stock of my face. "Your bruises have faded nicely. You look so much better."

"Thanks, no doubt the benefit of curling into the fetal position and covering my face. My forearms are still a little sore. Is the man in black here? I'm supposed to meet him." The minute it came out of my mouth, I wondered if the black reference was insensitive.

"Yes, he's donning his costume now. I don't know why he needs to wear dark clothes all the time, especially in this heat? Have a seat. Would you like something to drink, Monk?"

"No, I'm good, but thank you for asking. How are the kids?"

"They're fine, off to this and that. I worry about them, but I can only do so much. I try to lead by example and pray the good Lord watches over them. These days that can be hard to do. There are so many distractions."

I nodded in agreement. "It's all a little overwhelming. I know kids think it's no big deal, but they don't know any different. Maybe it's different for us. I just got back from the farm I grew up on. I'd forgotten how tranquil the place was. Even with the work, and there's plenty of that, it doesn't seem so chaotic, but that could just be me."

Coretta smiled.

"I remember going to my grandfather's farm. He had a patch of land that he worked all his life. It was his grandfather's land they got after the civil war. It was hard work; it was, but that was a different time."

Orville Riley, aka Mr. Jones, entered the room.

"Time to go. Sorry to interrupt the conversation, but I got a show tonight, so we need to get down there and back before eight." Orville kissed his wife. "I'll try to get back sooner, but if not, don't wait up."

"Alright, but remember, tomorrow, you belong to me."

"I remember." He was grinning.

I said goodbye and we were out the door.

37

"Date night?" I was curious.

"What?"

"With Coretta? Your wife?"

"Yes, I know who she is, and yes, if you must know, we have date nights. Between security details and the gigs, I sometimes don't get home much in the evenings, so, a few years ago we started having date nights."

"Just curious." For once, Mr. Jones was driving. This gave me license to rubberneck on the way to South Laguna. I'd driven all around LA when I first got here, marveling at its size and breadth. Some of it was more interesting than others, the mountains to the east and north, the ocean to the west corralling the mass of us banging up against one another. So much of it was the same, a commonality of structure and space, of roads filling and backing up; disgorging its refuse like a gigantic sewer system; its fluids always in motion. Jones interrupted my thoughts and inquired about my love life.

"How are you and Agnes doing?"

Why is everyone so interested in me and Agnes?

"We're doing. Had a nice trip, can't complain. I'm a little surprised at how quickly it's all happening. She wants me to move in with her. I don't know if that's good or bad."

"You don't know? Come on, Buttman, how old are you?"

"I'm only twenty-nine!" That wasn't exactly true. However, as I had no birth certificate, having been brought into this world on a commune free from government intrusion, the exact day and year were less official and more oral history.

Mr. Jones was laughing at me. "You're so full of shit, Buttman."

"It's possible. And Coretta? How soon did you know?"

"Coretta and I met at a church dance not long after I got out of the Army. I'd seen her there a bunch of times and at the dance I got up the nerve to talk to her. We've been talking ever since. I knew right away, Buttman. I wasn't a kid anymore. I'd seen guys do all kinds of stupid shit around women, and I had no interest in that. I wanted a serious woman of faith who wanted that kind of man. I wanted a family and a life. Plus, she's a damn fine looking woman."

"Yeah, can't deny that."

Mr. Jones turned to me as we stopped at a light. "You could do a lot worse than Agnes, Buttman. I know she's had her ups and downs; I've heard the talk, but I trust Coretta when it comes to people, and she knows Agnes. She says she just needs a good man. And a man needs a good woman! Maybe that's just talk, but if you didn't like the woman, you wouldn't be running around with her; that's human nature, and you ain't rich enough or important enough to have women hanging off you." He looked over the top of his sunglasses to emphasize the point. "Besides, you ain't no kid either. No one says settling down has to take forever. Neither does love."

"I'll take that into consideration."

Jones shook his head. "Do you like the woman?"

"Yeah. Maybe."

More head shaking. "Just admit you like the woman and move on."

I thought about it. Like it's that easy. Maybe this was a conspiracy? All the people who knew Agnes before me were after me to be the guy. Dulcimer. Jones. Eric. Come to think of it, I didn't even know Eric's last name. Even Joanie had her radar up on this. Why? I'm not that special of a guy to be *the* guy. I must be missing something, or over thinking it.

"You know I get to decide this. I don't quite get everyone's interest in my relationship with Agnes, but if and when I'm ready to notify the world of my devotion and love for the woman, I will."

I got a big grin from the cool dude. "You don't think people see it, but we do; that's how we know. If you want to deny it, I don't care, but you don't fool me."

How comforting.

Fortunately, we weren't far from our destination.

It was a quiet place. Other than the breeze and the ocean, there was little sound in the air. Jones was looking for Martisse. She was a small light-skinned black woman. We found her near her car a few blocks south of the house she was watching. After parking, we walked up alongside the road; not a car went by. I wondered if Jones and Martisse would stick out in this little burg? I put that thought away. The number on the house matched the one given to me by Taylor Lagenfelder. It was Boyer's beach house. There wasn't much space between the house and the road; a few bushes were growing through an old picket fence. Then again, there wasn't a whole lot butted up against it. The houses had enough space separating them that, as we found out, a perch could be found that allowed for a fair amount of observation without being detected. Martisse's spot was across the road on the lot of an empty house. We sat back and watched. She said there were usually two people there, but two older guys would come by periodically. They would park in front, and Dahlia was sometimes with them. That's how she found this place. She was watching Dahlia at the center in West Hollywood when the two guys picked her up.

"What'd they look like?" I inquired.

"A couple of middle-aged white dudes."

"Anything odd about them? Bruises, odd markings, tattoos?"

"I didn't notice much other than they dressed the same. I didn't get close enough to see if they had bruises or any of that other stuff. I just followed them here. I was worried they might notice me so I took a chance and turned off down the road. I used the GPS to look through the neighborhood after a little while. They were parked in front of the house so I went back, parked the car, and worked my way to where we are now."

I had to ask. "The two people in the house, a man and woman?"

"Yeah."

"These two?" I showed her pictures of Martin and Desiree.

"Yeah, that's them," she said.

Jones who had been silent till now leaned in, "Once we ID them, then what? Are we done? Are we supposed to confront them? What?"

What do we do? I didn't actually know. Maybe because I wasn't sure we'd ever find them. "I'll make a call and find out."

Taylor Lagenfelder was in court. Did I want to leave a message? No. I decided to take a chance. I'd like to speak to Mr. Durant. I gave the woman on the end of the line, Tiffany, my name. I was asked to wait. Muzak. Wouldn't it be funny...

"Monk, what do you have for me?"

... If he took my call?

"Mr. Durant, I've located Mr. Delashay and Ms. Marshan. What would you like me to do? They're here in South Laguna at Todd Boyer's beach house."

For a moment, he didn't say anything. I wondered if something had happened, things do.

"Please ask them to come see me. If they value their lives, as soon as they can."

"I'll pass that along." The wind had picked up.

"I appreciate your taking care of this, Monk."

"Glad to do it."

I hung up and gave the word to Jones and Martisse. I stepped back towards the vacant house. I wanted to talk to Miguel on my own. He answered on the second ring.

"Amigo."

"I've found them." I told him about Durant's message.

"Finish up and leave, all of you. I'll talk to you soon."

"Ok." My stomach started bothering me. Suddenly, I didn't want to be here anymore. I'd grab Jones, deliver the message, and head to Agnes's. Our part of the play was over.

The car arrived just as I got back to where Jones and Martisse were hiding. It pulled into the driveway of the beach house. We watched Dahlia, Artie, Gordy, and a man I didn't recognize, get out. Dahlia started pounding on the door. Martin answered the door telling her to keep her voice down. She told him to fuck off. Where was Desiree?

The wind was blowing their conversation our way.

Desiree came out. Where were Wilmer and Brent? Nobody knew. It's been a week? That's not my problem. This whole fucking mess is your problem, both of you. You said this would be a piece of cake, is it? Where's all this fucking money you've been promising. It's coming. Bullshit! The only thing coming is our being killed. I told you this was bullshit. Get out of here before somebody sees you. Fuck you. Fuck both of you. Dahlia stormed back to the car, followed by the two goons. They drove off. The stranger remained. I had a hunch.

"You have one of those phones where you can look stuff up like pictures?"

Jones gave me the same look Agnes had earlier. "Yeah."

"See if you can get a picture of Jeremy Tophanovich."

"Who?" Exactly!

"I think it's the guy who just went in the house," I spelled the last name and a number of images came up. It was him. The long lost Jeremy was hanging out with his old partner. I looked at the two of them, Jones and Martisse. "I've been asked to give the two lovebirds a message. After that we're done with this." I suddenly remembered I didn't have the 45. "Are either of you armed?"

"I have my weapon. Should we expect trouble?" Jones had his serious face on.

"I don't think so."

"I got a gun." Jones and I turned to Martisse. "I'm not sitting here by myself without some protection."

Jones took control. "Alright, Buttman and I'll deliver the message. Martisse, you stand back by the car. Have your phone ready just in case we need the police."

Martisse nodded.

We gathered our courage, or at least I did, and approached the door. I knocked. We could hear the murmurs on the other side of the door.

"Who is it?" The voice called from the other side. It was Martin.

"Monk Buttman, I've got a message for you."

"Who?"

"Open the door, Mr. Delashay." More murmuring. The door cracked open. Peering from the other side was Martin Delashay. Desiree was behind him.

"What the fuck do you want?"

"I'm here to give you a message from Marsyas Durant."

Martin's demeanor softened. "I'm listening."

I gave him the message.

"Anything else?" The snarl was back.

"Yeah, I enjoyed fucking your wife. Have a good day."

He slammed the door. I could hear him swearing as we left. I wondered why he even cared. Then again, it'll give him and Jeremy something to reminisce about. Jones didn't say anything. We collected Martisse and got to our cars. I thanked her for helping and we followed her out of the neighborhood and onto the freeway. It was only after we were enjoying the always rapturous highway crawl that Jones chose to speak.

"You really fucking that man's wife?"

"Yeah, but it was before Agnes if that's what you're driving at."

"Good looking woman?"

"Yeah, revenge sex, and I was the lucky recipient. Sometimes it pays to be a nobody."

"Damn!"

Yeah, they all say damn!

Agnes was more than a little surprised to see me stride through the front door of JD Financial. I sat in the chair by the window.

"I'm gonna need a key and what are we doing for dinner?"

38

We decided to celebrate at the bar. While not getting into specifics, we admitted to both Johnny and Rey that things between us were good and we were happy together. They both seemed genuinely pleased. We had steak sandwiches, some wine, and danced the night away. The only odd moment came when I pulled Johnny aside to tell him we'd found Desiree. His face darkened for a second before he thanked me for taking care of it. He didn't ask where she was. It was as if he didn't care, but before I could ask, Agnes grabbed me and we were back to dancing.

The next morning followed our usual pattern. I rose first while Agnes hid under the sheets. I took stock of the house. If I was going to be spending more time here, I'd have to find places for my stuff. On the plus side, Agnes wasn't a slob, but wasn't organized either. To my surprise, there was quite a bit of storage in the house. As I wandered around I found the house filled with this and that. In truth, it just needed to be culled and organized. That would be the price of having me live here.

I rousted her out of bed once I had breakfast cooking. She tried to get me back into bed. It was tempting.

Mockingly, I asked her if she ever got enough.

"That's a joke, right?" She mocked back.

"Come on, beautiful, we got work to do."

"Work?" She seemed surprised.

"You heard me. It can't be all loving and dancing. If I'm going to live here, we need to make some room. So get your cute butt out of bed."

The following hour was a romp through closets, cupboards, shelves; anyplace where knick-knacks and the dross of a lifetime accumulate. She grumbled about having to get to work. I told her that was wonderful, but she wasn't getting out of it. Our plans for the weekend were set. She grumbled some more before leaving. I shook my head and went back in the house. It felt odd to be here without Agnes. I did what I could to ignore the feeling and carved out a small space in the bedroom closet. I made a list of things I would need and congratulated myself for not freaking out and running for the hills. I attached her key to mine and locked the door. I had a few stops to make before meeting Joanie for lunch.

The first stop was Bernie's. Bernie wasn't there, but Javier called him and retrieved the tablet from his office. I wondered if Javier had any advice. The next stop was the store for toiletries and the like. For a while I'd need two of everything, just in case. Finally, I was back at the bungalow. I kept an eye out for the unfamiliar. I knocked on Joanie's door. I was early. She opened the door groggy-eyed and admonished me for waking her up early.

"We're burning daylight," I told her. "I'll see you in an hour."

She said something nasty under her breath and closed the door. I had to smile. Every woman I've ever known did not like to get up early, except my mother and Meredith. Astral had to be conditioned by the other women when we first got to Virginia. Joanie wouldn't have it. We'd see about Agnes. I unlocked the door and took the gun out of my pocket.

You never know.

I was alone. I moved through the rooms, resetting the items my recent visitors had fondled. Once I had everything in its place, I checked the fridge for any funky smells and took out a bottle of water. I returned to the living room and my modest chair. I put the water on the table next to the chair and pulled the 45 out of my pocket. I knew I wasn't finished with Martin and Desiree. There was more, I just didn't know when or where. I removed the magazine and counted the rounds. Next, I disassembled the piece and inspected it. Having it with me made me feel better. It didn't matter that I'd never fired it in anger. It didn't matter that if I did I would most likely shoot myself. For the moment, it was a nice heavy pacifier. I cleaned it, put it back together, and set it on the table. Joanie came in just as I set it down.

"What's that for?"

"It makes me feel like a real man."

She laughed. "That doesn't surprise me. However for my own peace of mind would you please put it away?"

"Sure," I tucked it into my pocket, "Are you ready to go?"

"Yeah, do we walk or drive?"

"We need the exercise." I got up and gestured towards the door. "Shall we?"

"What the hell."

It was a pleasant enough walk. I commented on the shops while Joanie continued her questions about the gun in my pocket. Why? Why now? Aren't you worried you might hurt yourself? Please don't shot me, ha, ha. In order to change the subject, I brought up Mikal and her problems. She could talk about that for a while. Not much new though which, of course, turned the tables on me.

"So?"

"So what?" I preferred to play dumb.

"Oh, for Chrissakes, Monk, it's like pulling teeth."

We had reached the diner. The same happy woman from before seated us. I ordered a club and Joanie a hoagie. I decided to confess.

"I'm sorta moving in with Agnes. Sadly, that means you'll have to do without my exquisite company, but if, as you say, you and Mikal are on the same road, it's all for the best."

"The best. Are you happy about this? Think about it; we've been such loners for so long, it seems a little scary." Yeah.

"I 'spose. If I'm honest, I really don't mind. Agnes doesn't grate on my nerves. She's fun, the sex is good, and she's a fuckup like me. I don't care for the word happy; kids are happy, but I enjoy being with her. And living with her is fun, oddly enough. In some ways, it weirds me out because we haven't known each other very long, maybe a month, but nothing comes up to make me think I'm making a serious mistake. As Mr. Jones said to me, it doesn't have to take a long time. I'll hold on to the bungalow just in case, but a part of me hopes it works out. I'm tired of being by myself."

Joanie smiled, but as before it struck me as wistful. I was always around if she needed me. Now, I was bailing. That guy Mikal had better not fuck this up.

"It's nice to hear you've found someone you like. When I met Agnes and her daughter, she seemed a little out of sorts."

"She was. It was an interesting day to say the least. Agnes and Anna have struggled lately and the fence mending was so-so. That and she gets a bit insecure around my previous conquests." I knew that would get a rise out of her.

Joanie frowned. "I refuse to be known as one of your conquests or a torrid affair."

"Jeez, what a killjoy…"

"You got that right!" I was going to miss this.

The food arrived and we ate in relative silence. The diner was half full, the conversations ebbing and flowing. Joanie talked a little more about Mikal. She also worried about whether something was up with the bungalows. She didn't want to contemplate moving before she was ready. I told her not to worry about that. You're already out the door, she countered. I laughed. We have a spare room at Agnes's house. She could stay with us. She threw a piece of lettuce at me. I retaliated with a fry. I asked about the old folks, I needed Joanie to keep me informed; never mind that I was leaving. We shared a piece of apple pie, I paid the bill and we walked back home.

"You know, there won't be much of this anymore."

She had to bring that up.

"True, but that's what happens when you chose not to marry me."

"It's always on me isn't it, Buttman?"

"It is, it really is." We both laughed. I was going to miss Joanie.

She invited me into her place, and we shared a glass of iced tea. I asked her to sing a little something. I closed my eyes as she sang *Embraceable You*, the old Nat King Cole standard. I could hear a buzzing in my head, on and off. It was messing up the song.

It was the phone.

If only I had turned off that fucking phone or ignored it, but no, I had to answer. Maybe I could have avoided it all. Maybe, but the little voice in my head said no.

I could barely hear her.

"Mr. Buttman?" It was Dahlia, something was wrong.

"Yes?"

"Desiree wants to talk to you. Could you come out?"

"Why, so your goons can work me over again?"

"No, no, I promise, nothing will happen. Please, Mr. Buttman. It's important." I sat there. "Please."

I should say no. I should! But I knew I had to go.

"Alright, I'll be there."

Joanie was watching me, noting the change in my expression. All the joy was gone. I called Jones. I would need him. He didn't want to go either, but I whined and cried and cajoled him into it. I'd be by to pick him up. I said goodbye to Joanie, thanking her for the beautiful song. I was hoping I'd get to see her again, Agnes too. The ride was too easy, too quick. Where was all the traffic when I needed it? Jones was waiting outside his house, armed. We both were. There was nothing to say. Before long we were back in South Laguna on the quiet street in front of Todd Boyer's beach house. A car was in the driveway. Dahlia was nowhere to be found. We got out and approached the car. We pulled out our guns. I felt completely out of place.

Artie and Gordy were dead, just like Wilmer and Brent up in San Fran, shot through the head. Neither saw it coming, just like Wilmer and Brent. Two pairs with a thing for a tattooed woman they'd found on the Internet. Jones looked at me. He wasn't happy. Neither was I. Scared shitless described it better. I gestured towards the front door.

"Let's check out the house. We'll call the cops after that. "

"I don't like this, Buttman!" Like I did. Jones reached in his pocket and took out two pairs of black latex gloves, "Put these on."

"Where'd you get these?"

"Part of the job, just do it!" he ordered.

I did as I was told.

Only three days ago, I was up north with a little girl, helping her in the herb garden. It was a million miles from here. Now I was standing at the door of a house with two guys dead outside and possibly more inside. All I could hear was the ocean off to my right. The front door was partially open. I looked in, nothing. I slowly opened it the rest of the way. The house was an old beach bungalow, biding its time before swallowing us whole.

We looked around.

The living room and kitchen were empty. The bedrooms were down a short hallway. We looked in the first bedroom. The blood was splattered against the wall on the other side of the room. Lunch wanted to come up. It started barking when we came upon the dinks in the car. It was howling now.

I put my left sleeve in my mouth. Jones had no color in his face either.

Desiree and the man next to her on the floor were dead. The blood, congealed and darkening, was at the height you'd expect if they'd been standing when they were killed. At first, I thought the man was Martin. He and Jeremy had similar builds, but the dead man was not Martin. Jeremy had a small hole in his forehead atop the anguished expression on his face. I wondered how many shooters had been here, certainly more than one.

Desiree was on her back. She, too, had a small hole in her forehead. Her blouse had been cut open and her breast was exposed. That climbing tattoo was there for all the world to see. There didn't appear to be any signs of sexual violence; the rest of her clothes were undisturbed. Evidently, the killers wanted to make sure she was the one. How many other women could possibly have that tattoo? I looked at Jones. He bent down to look a little closer. He just shook his head. We checked the other rooms expecting to find Dahlia, but the house was empty. There was no reason to stay. The only question was whether to call the cops. Neither of us had any appetite for spending the rest of the day answering questions along with a possible trip to the police station.

"There's a phone in town. We'll call from there," I said.

"Yeah, let's get the hell out of here."

We tiptoed out of the house and headed back to the car, straining our necks this way and that to see if anyone had seen us. I said a small prayer and assumed Jones had as well. Once in the car, we drove away as normally as we could. It was hard to breathe. For once, being on the highway sounded really fucking good to me.

Jones shouted.

Dahlia had jumped out of the bushes and was wildly waving her arms. I nearly hit her. Jones had to brace himself against the dashboard as I slammed on the brakes. Bizarrely, I congratulated myself on having Bernie replace the old drums with disc brakes. Dahlia came running towards us. She was in terrible shape. Tears, snot, and based on how she smelled, shit were all over her.

"Please get me out of here. Please."

She could barely stand up. It was bringing up a lot of bad memories.

"You set us up. You knew she was dead, Desiree, and the rest," I shouted.

"I didn't know, I didn't know, I was outside, I heard something and saw them shooting ... I just ran. I'm so scared. Please, please, I'm sorry, I'm so sorry. Please get me out of here."

"This is your mess, honey-bunch. They're probably looking for you right fucking now. I don't want to be killed like those in the house..." She was hanging on the door, having lost her strength. "Or the two in San Francisco."

She was sobbing, shaking on the side of the car; crying please, please over and over again. Fuck, why me? I opened the door and let her crawl in the back. She did stink. I considered opening the top, but thought better of it.

"I expect some fucking answers!" I couldn't stop shouting.

She made some kind of noise between sobs. Jones was not happy.

"You're gonna get us killed over this stupid bitch, you know that, right?"

"Yeah, yeah, roll down your window." I knew.

With nothing further to say, we taxied down the road with the wind in our hair and the sobs of the hysterical woman in our ears.

39

The convenience store was at the end of the street. Gas pumps outside, a phone booth just off the entrance, and restrooms in the back. I went in and gave the kid behind the counter twenty bucks for gas and got the restroom key. I told Dahlia she had five minutes to get cleaned up, otherwise she could walk home. I checked to make sure the phone worked and called 911. I gave them the address and told them to get the cops over there now. There were four dead. I hung up before they could ask me anything more. I gassed up the car. Jones had gotten out and was leaning against the right front fender.

"What now?"

"We find a place to talk."

"Talk?" Mr. Jones did not want to talk.

There was a park nearby. Dahlia finally came out of the restroom. She still looked terrible, but was now a better class of terrible. She returned the key and got in the car. We drove over to the park. I found a place to park. Dahlia looked around.

"Why are we here?" She started shouting, "Are you going to kill me? Why are we here?"

"Oh, for the love of God," I snapped, "we're gonna talk. If we were going to kill you we'd have just shot you by the side of the fucking road. Get out of the car."

"I'm afraid," she continued whining.

"We all are. Get out of the fucking car."

A short distance away was a picnic bench. Close enough to watch for unsavory characters, but far enough from the others to speak in private. Dahlia was shaking and Jones and I wanted to be doing anything other than this.

"Alright, time to talk. No bullshit, no attitude, just talk. What the fuck were you guys up to? Was Desiree even alive when you called?"

"Yes." She looked at the two of us. "She was! She said you could help her."

"How?"

"I don't know, something."

"Then tell me what you do know. How did it start?"

It took her a few minutes to get going. She tried making eye contact, looking for sympathy, but Jones and I had none.

"Desiree owed me money, about ten grand. She kept putting me off, to the point where I didn't want to have anything to do with her anymore. Then about a month or so ago, she said she'd have the money, but she needed my help. I told her to fuck off. She'd done that before. She said this time was different. She made me a proposition: two thousand now, a hundred grand later. A hundred thousand dollars! I let it get into my head. I met her and she had the two grand. I was supposed to help her deal with Boyer. She said he was getting in the way with her and Martin. She was tired of fucking him. Then it all blew up when she killed him. So we had to deal with you. She said you had something she wanted, and wanted me to help frighten you so you'd give it to her."

"Did she tell you what it was she wanted?"

"She said it was some documents."

"You sent the goons, Artie and Gordy?"

She lowered her head, the dirty hair falling onto her face. "Yes."

"You made a big show of how much you disliked Rosarita's riders, what gives?" For a moment I had a strong urge to hit her.

"They were the only creeps I knew. Believe it or not, this isn't what I normally do. Desiree made a deal with them. That's how they got involved."

"Look what it got them, beat up and killed."

"None of that was supposed to happen. I just wanted my money back. I didn't expect any of this." She was crying.

I wanted to be pissed off; I wanted to be righteous in my anger. I wanted to smack the hell out of her, but I couldn't do it. I'd worn those shoes too. I got pulled into my own harebrained scheme and nearly got killed because of it. A part of me pitied this woman. We were all a confederacy of fuckups.

"What about Jeremy Tophanovich?" She looked at me shaking her head.

"The guy in the car, yesterday, with you and the two goons," I said.

"I don't know who he is. He was with Arthur when they picked me up. He stayed behind after I left."

"Yeah, he's dead too. Was Martin there when the killers showed up?"

"He was in the house."

"He's not there now."

The woman Dahlia brushed the hair out of her face. "I don't understand?" She seemed genuinely surprised.

"That's why you're in this mess." We could hear the kids at the other end of the park running and shouting. "Where was all this money supposed to come from?"

"I don't know. It was supposed to be Martin's or something like that. They were trying to keep it away from his wife," she whimpered.

I looked Dahlia in the eye. "No. It's drug money, lots and lots of laundered drug money, wanted by the kinds of people who wouldn't think twice about killing a little girl like you."

Jones couldn't contain himself. "She's a fucking dude, man. Not some little girl."

"I'm not gonna argue about that now! If we make it through this fucking mess we can argue about it then, but it doesn't mean shit now."

He slammed his fist on the table. "I don't want to fucking hear that, man, it ain't right! It ain't fucking right!"

I realized we were shouting. I lowered my voice. "It's not important." Dahlia just sat there. "You have anybody you can stay with? You can't go home and there's no guarantee work is safe either. You might need to be sick for a few days."

"I have a friend by the clinic."

"I'll drop you off there."

Now that we were all pissed off we could head back. I didn't notice anything or anyone who looked out of place in the park. I didn't see anyone hanging out in their car as we got to mine. I couldn't tell if anyone was following us, and once we got on the freeway, there was too much going on. I did what I could. Nobody talked. Jones was the first to go. I told him to be careful after we stopped in front of his house. He just shook his head. Dahlia got in the front and directed me to her friend's house. Traffic was heavy and the going slow. She kept tugging at herself. It's never fun to be filthy and dejected. The friend's apartment was tucked in around a strip mall. Dahlia didn't seem to want to get out.

"Why are you doing this? Helping me?"

Why? "Because enough people have died over this. If you don't hear from me in a couple of days, get the hell out of LA."

"Where would I go?"

"I hear Virginia is nice," I offered.

She started to cry. "I don't want to go to Virginia."

"Neither did I. Goodbye."

I watched her knock on the door. Someone answered it and she went in.

It was almost seven by the time I got back to Agnes. To give myself time to calm down and get my thoughts in order, I went to the grocery store; two birds. There was little to eat at the house. I stocked up on the fruits, vegetables, and dairy we would need. I also picked up some pork, beef, and chicken. Pasta and bread finished off the list. The cashier took my money. I knew what I had to do. I had a plan. There was nothing left to do but go home and wait.

Agnes met me at the door.

"I got some groceries."

"I was worried." That made me smile. I kissed her.

"Me too." She didn't get the comment. I wished I didn't. I was half-tempted to confide in her, but I wanted her to be safe. "Why don't you give me a hand?"

The self-described bad cook helped with dinner and we ate on the patio. It was an inviting place, peaceful with a nice breeze. We sat there holding hands and enjoying a glass of wine. I wasn't going to dwell on the fact that it might be my last night here. I chose to believe I'd be back here tomorrow night. When the light was gone, we cleaned up and I took her to the bedroom. Her lips brushed against mine as I removed her clothes. I meant to savor every inch of her. I didn't care how much time it took. Agnes didn't seem to mind. It was sweet and sweaty and I went as long as I could. When we were done, I held her as tight as she held me. Sleep came after a while. I don't remember any dreams.

I was sitting in the kitchen when Agnes got up. I was working on my list.

I had people to call, Durant, Miguel, Judith, and Mallory. I had the TV on. They mentioned four people found murdered in Laguna, but that was about it. Maybe the cops were keeping a lid on it. I'd ask Mallory. Agnes sat down at the table with me.

"Are you alright? You look worried."

"I am. I have to be something I'm not very good at."

She waited for me to say what. I didn't oblige. "Anything I can do?"

"Yeah, I want you to stay at work till you hear from me," I told her.

"Why?"

I wanted to say more, but stopped. "Just do it for me, ok?"

"Ok. Does Johnny know? Maybe he can help?"

"He does, but he can't help. This is something I have to do. Speaking of Johnny, don't be surprised if he's a little on edge."

"Why?"

"I'll tell you later. Don't say anything to Johnny, it won't help."

Agnes didn't know how to respond to all this cryptic talk. I saw her off to work, all the while looking for anything out of the ordinary.

Nothing.

I had my list, the weapons, and a charged phone.

It was time to go.

40

The first call was to Mallory. Leave a message. It was the same with Durant. I got the sneaking suspicion no one wanted to talk to me. After leaving the house, I stopped at a playground down the road next to an elementary school. It was still mid-morning and few people were there. I counted three mothers and seven children, all preschoolers. I took stock of my bullshit and its limits. It worked great if no one cared and you weren't broke, but once you found yourself in the turning gears there was little to stop the movement or the profound fear that you were doomed to be crushed by mechanisms beyond your control. I danced around this. What could happen, I'm a nobody? My willingness to look for the woman Desiree, something I now regretted, had me cornered. I remember thinking this wasn't a good idea. Maybe I should have listened.

The phone beeped once.

There was a message, eight letters and numbers in a jumbled sequence from an unknown phone number. Judith. Who else would send an access code? It was back to the car.

I came to the keypad and punched in the code. The house showed no hint of trouble. I hadn't actually spoken to Judith. I just assumed she sent the code. It could be Martin or those responsible for the killings. The 45 was in my hand. I pulled back the slide. A light breeze floated through the car; there was always a breeze here. My hands were shaking. Virginia was sounding really good right now. I still had family there and I had promised to visit. There was time. Start the car and go. They wouldn't kill Agnes. She had Johnny D. If I disappeared, so what? I'd done it before. A man needed strength in these situations. I wasn't that man. My hand was on the key, ready to turn it.

I removed the key and got out of the car.

It was a beautiful day to die.

I'm an idiot!

The front door was unlocked. I looked up at the camera and smiled. I keep forgetting these places are always monitored, always on the lookout for some unwashed goof like me. I went in. It looked the same, sun-drenched and languid, the colors playing off the light. Judith was on the couch facing the patio and the pool. I didn't see anyone else. For a second I thought she might be dead, but she turned her head towards me. I put the gun away and placed the tablet on the bar. She pointed.

"Do me a favor and bring my drink to me?"

A glass, filled with ice and a dark red liquid, was on top of the liquor cabinet. I took another glass, poured in a little whiskey, and grabbed a bottle of water. Judith reached out as I came towards her. She took the glass from me and watched as I sat in the chair across from her.

"I don't want you all the way over there, please come sit with me."

I did as she asked. She was wearing yellow capris and a soft white blouse with no sleeves. Her hair was pulled back, exposing that exquisite neck. I leaned in hoping for a kiss. She moved towards me. Our lips grazed each other before meeting in the middle, the taste of pomegranate and vodka mixing with the textures of her lips and tongue, soft and sweet.

"I missed you, Monk."

I kissed her long beautiful neck. "I can't imagine why."

"You're a terrible liar." She smiled as she put her hand on my face.

"Well, I can't be good at everything."

"Isn't that always the way it is?" The kisses lingered a while longer.

"I'm afraid so." I wanted to do more, but I wasn't here for love and affection. I had that at home. It was as I looked at her that I noticed how tired she looked. "Are you ok?"

"You know I'm not. I haven't slept in days."

"Martin?"

She laughed. "Martin's dead, or soon will be." She turned away. "He or they expect me to save him. Imagine that." Despite the tough talk I knew she was terribly frightened.

"You've seen him?"

"No. He called the other night, begging me to give him the papers. I told him I didn't have them. He was crying, to me of all people, asking that I save him from his stupid mistakes. I told him there was nothing I could do. I didn't have his stupid papers."

"And Jeremy?"

A sad half-smile crossed her face. "Jeremy was here that morning. How did you know about him?"

"He was at the beach house. That's where I found Martin and Desiree. He was there with them." I wanted to see what reaction that got, whether I should say more.

Her eyes grew wet as she looked at me. "They said he was dead. Is he?"

"Yes, along with Desiree Marshan and two others. Who are *they*?"

"I don't know. *They* gave me till today to turn over the papers. They still believe I have them."

"Or know who does." I wiped the tears away. The half-smile returned, mingling with the tears.

"You have them, don't you, Monk."

"Yes, I have them." I kissed her again, those soft electric lips.

"Why?"

"What did Jeremy want?" Judith took my arm and put it around her shoulder, tucking herself in beneath it.

"He came to warn me. If I had the papers, I had to give them up. If I didn't, I had to get out. We were all in real trouble. He told me to leave and go as far away as I could. I thought he was being overly theatrical. Why would they kill me over some stupid papers?"

"The money," I answered.

"The money?" she snorted. "What money? I asked him that. He said it was time to be honest. It was all a fraud. The company, he said, was a front for money laundering and now they wanted it back. I said that didn't make any sense. We had years of earnings reports, years of corporate statements. What were we paying all those taxes on if it wasn't our money? He didn't have an answer. Jeremy was a real charmer, but he was also an inveterate liar. You could never trust a word he said. That's why he ran away to Europe; too many lies to too many people, people like me. I loved him once. Between him and Martin, I've had my fill of love. Periodically he'd sneak back into town looking for this or that and would come around thinking I'd forgiven him. He just wanted another Judith special."

Like I didn't want the Judith special.

"I still don't understand why you didn't just divorce Martin and move on?"

"The house is why."

"Just take the house in the settlement."

"It's not that simple. The house is owned by the corporation, in which we have shares. Division or liquidation of those shares would necessitate selling the house because Martin knows I love this house and he would do everything he could to keep it from me. I'm not giving up my home."

"I think a good lawyer could work that out?"

"Or I could wait for the miserable bastard to die." I was tempted to say that might just be what's happened. "What are we going to do, Monk?"

"Try to survive. The document are our wild card, so we have to be smart with them."

"Why did you take them?" She was looking at me, wondering.

I gave myself a few minutes to figure out how to explain it.

"That's the joke on them, or me I didn't technically take them. They fell out of the envelope in my car. I didn't find them till later. They're the transfer documents and I realized they were in fact signed and ready to be processed, I thought it'd be fun to return them to you so you could rub it in Martin's face."

"What changed your mind?"

"This whole thing with Desiree. Having a lot of very powerful people wanting me for this job. Me! It made no sense, unless, of course, I was nothing more than a patsy or a chump, and an easily expendable one at that. I'm well aware of what I can do and what I can't, and when I couldn't get any straight answers, or plausible explanations, I had to accept that I'd have to figure it out, so I decided to hold on to them just in case. And, as I found out more about what was going on, it only made me want to hold on to them more. Now, it's probably the one thing keeping us alive."

"I hope you're right."

"Me too."

Judith ran her fingers along the crease of my slacks and up along the front of my jacket.

"I heard through the grapevine that you're involved now. I kind of liked having you come around when I needed you."

"Yeah, it throws a bit of a wrench in that."

"Possibly, is it serious?"

"Yeah. I figured with you being married our long-term prospects were not good, so…"

"I see." Judith briefly smiled before looking at me. "Do you really think they'd kill us?"

"Before yesterday, I wouldn't have thought so, but after finding four people shot to death execution style, plus the two in San Francisco, I've changed my mind. Counting Boyer that's seven people. Seven people! That's not good. The only thing saving us right now is their belief that we have the documents they need. That's our bargaining chip. Unfortunately, I don't know if that's enough."

"That's not making me feel better, Monk."

"Sorry." It wasn't helping me either.

Her hand was back along my slacks. "I don't suppose you'd be open to one more go around the block? I need someone to hold me."

"Should I take this as a last request?"

"I sure hope not."

My conscience said no, but the rest of me wasn't listening. Judith was just too inviting. I knew Agnes would be angry if she found out, but I'm a dead man walking, and if I should get through this I promised I'd hate myself later…sort of… "Then yes, I'd like that."

"So would I."

"First, though, I think we should lock the doors."

Dead man sex was, I had to admit, incredible. Maybe it was the spectre of murder, or of having witnessed so much of it lately, but it certainly heightened the experience of intimacy, both with Agnes and Judith. I wanted it more than anything else. It changed my perspective, and it seemed to change Judith's as well. Before, our encounters were playful, certainly erotic, but there wasn't a lot of emotional connection. This time I felt Judith was more vulnerable, that she wanted more than just sex. It felt so much more personal. She held me tighter, called my name, looked at me. When we were finished she was reluctant to let go.

"Stay here, Monk, stay with me."

It's possible I would have stayed with Judith if Coretta hadn't called. She was frightened; even if Orville had assured her it would be ok. She knew better. Orville had never done anything like this before, and she could tell, no matter how hard he tried to hide it, that it was very bad.

"What did he say?"

"He said to tell you to wait for them at your place. He said you'd know what this is about. What's going on, Monk? Is Orville in danger? I know that man, and he didn't sound right. I'm worried, Monk."

"When did he call?"

"He just called. Monk, what's going on?"

"I have something these people want, and they're using Orville to make sure I give it to them."

"Are they going to hurt him?" I didn't want to think about that.

"Not if I can help it. It'll be ok, Coretta, I'll take care of it."

I waited for her to respond. "I expect you to keep your word. I want that man back!"

"So do I."

I did my best to assure her it would be all right. Judith sat with me as I talked to Coretta. I looked at the clock, it was already late in the afternoon; I couldn't dither. I kissed Judith. "I have to go. Is there someplace safe you can stay till this is over?"

"I'll be safe here. After there were some break-ins around here a few years ago, Martin decided we were vulnerable and had a safe room built. I can stay in there. I'm not leaving my home, Monk." She held on to my arm. "Do you have to go?"

"Yes"

I dressed and she followed me to the door. We kissed for what seemed like ages. It still amazed me this woman wanted anything to do with me.

"Lock the doors, arm the security system, and stay safe. Don't let anyone you don't know in, and maybe some you do, ok?"

"Ok."

I wasn't going to say goodbye, it sounded too final. I kissed her one more time and got into the car. I watched to make sure she closed the door. I took out my phone and called Joanie.

"You rang?" She sounded surprised.

"Yeah, where are you?"

"I'm at home, where else would I be?"

"I want you to leave, get out of there and go someplace safe. Stay with a friend, a hotel, anywhere but there. Do you understand?" I knew how that sounded.

"Is this some kind of joke? I can't just up and leave? I have a show to get ready for."

"Goddammit, I don't have time to argue with you. They already grabbed Jones, and they know about you. Take the stuff you need and get out of there. This isn't a fucking joke. They've already killed six people, Joanie! Just do it, please."

"Ok, ok, I'm going. You know this is really frightening, Buttman, you know that?"

"More than you know. Call me when you're out of there."

"It may be the last time you do hear from me," she fumed.

"As long as you're safe."

She hung up and I left the beautiful house in the hills.

41

I turned off the engine and sat there, just like they wanted. Waiting, like I was told. Thinking of Judith, wondering what I would do... if I survived.

I didn't see Joanie's car. I looked at the phone. She'd left a message: she was at her club. She was safe. She also called me a fuckhead.

I continued to replay the time with Judith in my head, convinced that her newfound affection was more a response to what was happening along with a lack of sleep. Once all of this was over she'd come to her senses. Alarmingly, I was becoming remarkably good at convincing myself my actions had workable solutions. Whether I could convince anyone else was, for now, beside the point. That I could defend them at all struck me as important. It was while daydreaming that the man with the gun tapped on the window.

He had a pleasant face and a nice smile. He and the two men with him had on the uniforms of the landscaping company. That answered that question. I rolled down the window.

"Time to go?" I asked stating the obvious.

He merely kept up the smile. He gestured to one of the men, who got in next to me.

"Please follow me. No funny business."

"Yeah, no one wants that."

The man next to me pulled out his gun. I got that part. I waited for the truck to pull out and eased the Falcon into first, following at a respectable distance. The guy next to me was checking out the car.

"This is nice."

"Thanks. It's a 1964 Falcon Futura Sport convertible, 260 V-8. You like old cars?"

"Yes."

With nothing better to do, the gunman and I chatted about vintage automobiles, early sixties in particular. He was into Impalas. They were ok, but I was more of a Ford man. He asked what I'd done to it. I told him I'd had the brakes redone; all discs, and that I'd had fuel injection put in. I was tired of dealing with carburetors. He talked about how hard it was to find an Impala for a good price. He had two that needed a lot of work. He was hoping to get one good car out of the two.

The truck wound its way to an industrial park, where the landscaping equipment was stored. I pulled into the spot the guy in the truck pointed to. While the gunman next to me looked at his compadres, I quietly took the 45 out of my pocket and set it down under my seat by the door. I got out and was led into the warehouse.

There was a large storage bay by the front door containing pallets of boxes. A set of stairs to the left led up to a long hall at the end of which were a series of offices overlooking the storage bay. In the first office was another gunman sitting at a desk. On the desk a computer monitor showed the entrances to the building. He motioned for us to go in the room behind him.

There in the room was another gunman, Jones, and Martin Delashay. Both were tied to their chairs. Jones looked ok minus a nasty welt on the left side of his head. Martin, on the other hand, was a bloody beaten mess. A third chair, next to Jones, was unoccupied. I sat down. Across from the chairs was a big desk, behind which sat a well-dressed man in his early forties.

"We have a problem to resolve, Mr. Buttman."

"That we do. What do you propose?"

"That you turn over what you stole." I admired his sense of ownership.

"And in return?"

"In return for what?" He wasn't particularly jovial.

"The papers, I have something you want, you have something I want. We make an equitable trade. Straight up, no funny business as your man said." I looked at the armed man standing next to him.

The man at the desk took a harder look at me. I don't know what he was expecting, but it wasn't what I was giving him. I played my part. Forget the roiling stomach, or how hard I was trying to keep my leg from shaking, I had to stick to the game plan, there was nothing else.

"And what do you expect me to give you, Mr. Buttman?"

"These two." I pointed to Jones and Delashay.

"Nothing more?" he asked.

"Nothing more."

The man smiled, but not the kind that made you feel good or happy. "And what makes you think I'd be willing to do that?"

"It's a fair trade, one that's eminently doable. I suppose you could work me over like you have Delashay, but that won't help because the papers are in a bank deposit box that requires my signature and my face not beaten to a pulp; people notice that kind of thing..." I gestured to the fading bruises on my face. "If you kill me like the others, then you'll never get it, and if you could get a replacement document you'd have done that already, but with Boyer dead and Delashay's wife unlikely to play ball, I don't think that's an option. I'm your best bet."

The man got up and came towards me. "Why should I believe you? You might not have anything, just a smart mouth. What's to say you won't demand more; money, as an example."

"I might not be very important in the grand scheme of things, but I'm not an idiot. I get that I don't have a lot of bargaining power, so I'm not inclined to ask for more than I can get. As for money, believe it or not, that's not terribly important to me. It might be to you, or to Delashay and his people, but I'm not interested in having you put a bullet in my head, or in the heads of these two. So no, I'm not demanding anything more. As to whether or not I have the documents, I have till tomorrow to prove that I do."

"You act as if you have me right where you want me? Do you think that's a wise thing to do?" He took a pistol off the desktop and held it in his hands.

"No, I'm merely stating my position. I'm well aware that you can do what you want, and there's little I can do to stop you."

The well-dressed man put the gun to my head. The sweat was rolling down my forehead and I was extremely thankful I hadn't eaten anything recently, but I kept my eyes on the man. He went over to Delashay and put the gun to his temple. Martin's was shaking, tears running down his face.

"Why are you so interested in this man? You're fucking his wife."

"Yeah, I'm fucking his wife, and, truth be told, I don't particularly care about him, but enough people have died already. I won't be party to another. If killing him is that important, you can hunt him down later, but not now."

"And if I kill him now?"

"How important is what I have? It's your decision, but you can't have both. If you kill him, then you might as well kill me."

He turned to Jones. I could see the ghost of James standing behind him. "And this man, this…"

"Because he matters to me and because I promised his wife, that's why."

The well-dressed man returned to me. The wheels were turning. "Alright, Mr. Buttman, we have our terms. Tomorrow you get me the papers, and in return you get these two, nothing more. Until then you stay right here."

"Agreed. Oh, one more thing though."

"You said nothing more…"

For some reason that made me smile.

"I lied. If we have to stay here then we need food and I want these two untied. We're not armed and we're not going anywhere, plus at some point they may need to use the bathroom. Martin already does."

Our captor laughed. "Alright, but you pay."

It was a good thing I went to the bank.

The food, for the most part, went uneaten. Much as I tried to get them to eat, Jones and Delashay weren't hungry. We were, in turns, taken to the bathroom. I found some medical supplies for Martin. He was slumped down in a corner. Jones, too, had found a corner, but on the other side of the room. I sat in a chair nursing a BLT.

"They're just going to kill us, you know." Jones, ever the optimist.

"Probably, but there's more going on here than meets the eye. The three of us are just pawns. You know, lures, bait." I looked over at Delashay. "Martin, who first suggested this to you? Boyer, Tophanovich, Desiree?"

"Why do you care?"

"Just answer the fucking question!" I still didn't like the guy.

"All of them. Jeremy needed money. He said there was a private account that had been set up years ago when Sphere was sold. We could use the money to solve our problems. Boyer would take care of the paperwork."

"That way you could run off with Desiree and not have to deal with Judith and the corporation."

"Yes."

Jones was listening. "I don't understand? Why would you kill Boyer if you needed him to do this?"

"She didn't mean to, she…" What a dope.

"Yes, she did," I interrupted. "She just killed him too soon. Maybe she was supposed to wait till after I gave her the papers, not before, but he pissed her off. Boyer liked to humiliate her, and when I walked in, he thought he'd have some fun at her expense. They may have been playing you for a sap, Martin, who knows. It doesn't matter, you were all dead the minute you agreed to this and by pulling in the rest of your motley crew you got them killed too."

Martin leaned up against the wall. "What do you mean?"

"To them, our hosts, this is about a lot of money, millions upon millions, and they're killing everyone who has any connection to it to cover their tracks, but there's no money. It's all a setup. A trap! People; people a lot more powerful than you and I, are using us to flush them out. And for our sakes, you better hope they're watching and waiting. Why else would someone like Marsyas Durant give a damn about us? It's about revenge, vendetta; all that crazy shit."

"Whose vendetta?" Jones was unconvinced.

"I don't know and I don't want to know. I'm just trying to get us out of this alive." Maybe they were right outside, Miguel and his people. I could only hope. I had a plan for the trip to the bank, but that depended on guts and a steady hand, something I didn't have. "I'm tired. We should try to get some sleep."

But sleep was hard to come by. I kept going over my plan until I nodded off. It didn't last. Between Martin moaning and Jones snoring, whatever passed for sleep had no effect. Maybe the man had coffee. I thought about Agnes and Judith, if for no other reason than I liked to think about them. Their curves, the feel of their skin, the way they tasted, all played back again and again. It was better than dwelling on a bullet to the brain. It must have worked, or exhaustion took over because the next thing I knew they were standing over me; the gunman, the well-dressed man, and an older gentleman I didn't recognize.

"When does the bank open?" the old man asked.

"9am."

I got up and looked at the others. The fear had returned. It was eight-thirty. I was taken to the front door where the car enthusiast was waiting.

"Get him there and back. Understand?"

We understood.

42

The car guy wasn't as talkative this trip, no doubt due to the fact that he might have to shoot me. I made sure the 45 was where I left it. Other than the gloom in the car, the weather was quite lovely, cooler than normal with a nice ocean breeze. That's why we live here. Traffic wasn't bad either. I turned on the radio and we listened to Mariachi music. The credit union was open for business. The car guy told me to park where he could see me. The windows were big enough that you could see most of the interior. Like I was going to run away. I did what he asked and found a nice spot right in front. I got out. The car guy thought about joining me but I told him no. It wouldn't take long. I'd be back.

I left him in the car.

The teller led me back to where the safe deposit boxes were. I pulled out the box and grabbed the papers. My phone went off. The number was unknown. I didn't like that the phone went off just as I was ready to leave.

"Buttman," I said, my heart pounding.

"How many are upstairs?" He asked.

It took me a minute to figure out what he wanted. Oh yeah...

"One in the first office at the top of the stairs, and three inside the second office with two captives, the desk is to your right. That's where the old guy and the guy in charge are. The guy with the shotgun is straight across from the door. The chairs, where the two captives are, are to your left. What about the guy with me?"

"Bring him back."

"What if he shoots me first?"

"He won't."

I didn't find that particularly reassuring.

That was it. The line, or whatever it was, went dead. It was on and I was going to pass out. With my heart racing and my head faint, I took a few deep breaths, closed the box, and locked it. I thanked the teller and went to the car. The car guy was still there. I was hoping he'd get cold feet and take off!

No such luck.

"Let me see the papers," he said as I got in. I handed them over. While he was checking them out, I grabbed the 45 and pointed at him.

"I'll take those back now," he saw the 45 with the hammer cocked back, "and your weapon." He put the papers down and took out his gun. I took the papers. "Take out the magazine and throw it in the back. Now the gun, throw it back there too." He did like I told him. "This is what we're going to do. You're going to drive, no funny business. Maybe you were told to shoot me, maybe not, but I like this arrangement much better. With any luck, it'll work out and we'll both get out of this alive. Got that?"

"Yeah, I got it."

I got out of the car, papers in hand, while he slid over to the driver's side.

"You know how to drive a stick?"

"Yeah." The car guy was not happy.

I didn't care. I put the papers in my jacket while keeping the 45 level. He turned the motor over, and we drove back to the warehouse. I felt more and more anxious as we got closer. What the fuck was I going to do? I didn't want to shoot the car guy any more than I wanted him to shoot me. And God only knows what was going to happen once we made it to the warehouse. I didn't think I could face Jones and Delashay shot to death, but what choice did I have? I had nowhere to go. That chance was gone. I was certain I was having a heart attack. Something terrible was happening and it was dragging me down with it. We pulled into the lot.

The car guy stared at me.

"Alright, let's go."

We got out and I kept the 45 by my side, as if I could hit the right side of a barn. The car guy opened the front door. Before I knew what happened we were both on the ground, the 45 out of my hand, surrounded by four men in black clothes and black masks; all well-armed. They quickly put a bag over the head of the car guy. He started whimpering.

"You Buttman?" It was the voice from the phone.

"Yeah..."

"Your friends are upstairs." I watched as they took the car guy to a van in the warehouse. The other four from upstairs, all with bags over their heads and their hands tied behind their backs, stood by the van.

"What do I do now?" The minute I said it I found it a patently absurd thing to say.

"Go home."

They packed up their cargo and left.

I sat a while before getting up to close the loading dock's rolling door. I have no idea why I did that. My legs were shaking and I felt incredibly tired. I picked up the 45 and put it in my pocket. As I went slowly up the stairs, it occurred to me that the man in the mask hadn't said whether the two upstairs were still alive. That's all I needed. I looked around, listening. The doors were open. Jones was at the desk. Delashay was still on the floor. He was in a terrible state, prostrate and weeping uncontrollably. Jones didn't seem to notice. We'd have to get him to the hospital. I looked again at Jones. He didn't look like he was all there either. We looked at each other.

"Are they gone?" he asked.

"Long gone," I said. "Anything interesting?" Jones was going through the drawers.

"I'm looking for my stuff: wallet, keys, phone... here they are. The other guy's things are here too."

"We need to get him out of here."

"Yeah..." Jones was playing with his phone. "Damn battery is dead."

"Come on, we need to go."

I took out my phone. The first call was to Coretta. Yes, he was ok. Yes, he's here. I gave him the phone and listened as she first cried and then yelled at him. He said all the right things and handed back the phone. He grimaced through most of it. We carefully moved Martin down the stairs. I was certain his ribs were broken as were his hands. They fucked him up pretty good. We gingerly put him in the back seat, after which I inexplicably went back and locked up the warehouse. Jones didn't get it either. I returned the 45 to its bag in the trunk.

"What do we tell the people at the hospital?" he asked. Did we need a story?

"We just say we found him and brought him in. Other than that, I'm keeping my mouth shut." Jones shook his head. I worried about the welt on his head. He said they hit him with something, a pipe maybe. He owned up that his head really hurt.

"How'd they even get you? I thought you were too hip to it to get taken down?"

He didn't like the question. "I was leaving the club, I had other things on my mind..."

"Just asking. We should get you looked at as well." Again he shook his head.

Once we arrived at the ER, I called Judith.

"Are you ok?" she asked. I was kind of surprised by that.

"Yeah, I'm ok, it's all over, but Martin's in bad shape. We have him here at the hospital. Do you want to come see him?"

"Martin? No!" I could hear her breathe. "I don't like this feeling, Monk."

"What feeling?"

"I don't know." I didn't believe that, it just wasn't the time to dig deeper.

"You're just tired, I know I am. Get some sleep, you'll feel better." I told her which hospital in case she changed her mind.

"Don't be a stranger."

"I won't." That wasn't going to be the problem.

They took Martin right away, asking a lot of questions we had no good answers for. I'd save that for Mallory when he finally came by. We waited for them to take a look at Jones. In the meantime I called Joanie and Dahlia to say it was over. Joanie spent the night with a bandmate. She said it was weird. I mentioned I'd be at the bungalow later if she wanted to talk.

"You're something else, Monk!" I liked that better than fuckhead.

Dahlia didn't say much. She was still freaked out. I know I was.

"You'd have thought she'd learned from her first go around with people like that." I was referring to how Desiree ended up in porn.

"None of that was true. It was something she made up, a good story she said." Dahlia was quiet for a moment. "I'm sorry, I really am." That was it.

For whatever reason, I saved Agnes for last. She acted like she'd won the lottery, thanking God I was still alive. I worried she was pinning too many hopes on me. I assured her I was ok, told her we were at the hospital, but for

Jones, not me. I promised I would see her soon and asked where she spent the night. Turns out she stayed at the bar. Johnny D had a safe room behind his office. She slept there.

"Did Johnny say anything about this to you?"

"He said something strange about blood money, but then told me not to worry, which only made me worry more. Come home, Monk."

"I will."

Jones finally went in. They were fairly certain he had a concussion and wanted to do an MRI. When they took him back to the machine, I called Coretta and she said she'd be right there. After he returned, I waited with him.

The phone rang. Fucking phone!

Taylor Lagenfelder. *Now* they had time to talk!

"Mr. Durant would like to see you, today, if possible."

I promised to come over as soon as Coretta got to the hospital.

It was noon and I was exhausted. I fell asleep in the chair. Coretta woke me and thanked me with another big hug. I told her she was welcome. She said there would be a dinner for me just as soon as possible, and I was to bring my woman, this from Jones, who until then had said nothing. I said I looked forward to it. I told them I had to see Durant and then I had to get some sleep.

"We better get paid, Buttman, and no lousy couple of grand," Jones grunted.

"I'll let 'em know. In the meantime, take it easy." It was time to move on. Mallory was waiting outside. I started laughing, what else was there to do?

"Good times, Buttman?" Even he was smiling. Moses was right; they're all fucking bastards.

"Like you don't know."

"Believe it or not, they don't tell me everything." It was his turn to laugh.

"Really, then what did they tell you?" I wasn't laughing anymore.

"That it wasn't our concern, straight from Goncalves." I tried to be angry, but I knew it wasn't Mallory's fault any more than it was mine. I just wanted to go home, but even that wasn't an option. "You don't look so good, Mr. Buttman. Maybe you should try another profession…"

"Excellent advice."

"Just trying to help. Get some sleep, we can talk later if you want."

"Thanks."

I said goodbye, leaving Mallory to his thoughts. I had to make it downtown. It took twenty minutes. I don't remember any of it. I also realized how hungry I was as I approached the building. Nearby was a sandwich shop. I went in for a bite to eat. Imagine my surprise, Taylor Lagenfelder was there. I shook my head; it was that kind of morning! She bought me lunch. We sat down at a small table in the back of the shop.

"Thanks for lunch," I said. "I don't suppose you'd be willing to let me in on how much you really knew about this little escapade, which I might add I barely survived!"

"What do you mean?" Right.

"I mean isn't it curious that the bad guys knew that the documents they wanted were not in the pile of papers I returned *after* their guy, Boyer, was already dead. They knew to key in on me, and Judith Delashay; knew about our rendezvous, knew where I lived. Kind of interesting, don't you think?"

For the first time since I met the woman her demeanor seemed unsure. "Perhaps. Are you suggesting I had something to do with it?"

"Wouldn't you?" I took a bite of my sandwich.

"I don't know how to answer that, Mr. Buttman, but I can assure you anything I may have been a party to was done with your best interests in mind." A sly smile came to the lawyer.

"Of that, I have little doubt."

The rest of our lunch was without comment. The food gave me the energy I needed to get through the afternoon. There wasn't any small talk to occupy us. What was there to say? After we finished, she escorted me to the grand office of Marsyas Durant, who, like Ms. Lagenfelder, thought highly of my best interests. I was offered a seat and gladly took it. As I sat there I reflected on the anger I felt the night before. There was the temptation to let loose on the man across from me, but time and tide had taught me there was no benefit to be gained from such a scene. I might need the man's help someday.

"I imagine you have some questions, Monk?"

I smiled at that.

"A few. I could ask why me, but the answer to that is simple, I became more important when the documents fell in my lap. Keeping them was a stupid thing to do, to be sure, but I felt they were important enough to give me a decent hand in the game, because you never know. A nobody has to protect himself. My only real questions are how long has this set up been in place? I mean the supposed *missing fortune* everyone wanted to get their hands on, and whether I should ask who the two men were, who were so surgically removed this morning?"

"The answer to the first question is many, many years. I assume you have a general understanding of the events that lead to the initial transfer of funds from Columbia. It was, contrary to popular lore, perfectly legal."

"It wasn't drug money?"

Durant smiled. "It may have, at one time, been that, but when currency is moved through institutions and countries it loses its original skin very quickly and becomes nothing more than a commodity like any other to be invested or traded. After the great man was murdered, there was a lot of talk about his money, his wealth, a lot of inaccurate talk. It was well known that the people who had him assassinated wanted that money, but were wary of being too overt in acquiring it. Memories are long, Monk. In order to draw out these individuals we used their greed and their willingness to believe in fictions to trap them. The account was set up long ago. Mr. Tophanovich learned of it through Sphere, where he also heard the story of its supposed origins. He conspired with Mr. Boyer to gain access to it, but Mr. Boyer was already engaged in that enterprise with Mr. Delashay and Ms. Marshan. When word of their actions reached me, I let it be known to certain parties."

"Seven people died because of it."

"Yes, but I have little sympathy in that regard. It wasn't theirs to take, and I did warn Mr. Boyer that the account was not to be tampered with, but they thought they knew better. Evidently, they didn't understand or appreciate the type of individuals they would be dealing with." He smiled at that.

"And the name of the great man and his assassins?" The cat was curious.

Durant sat back for a moment and then leaned towards me. "I think the less you know about that, the better. I can say that the bounty on the assassins was quite substantial and for your part you will be very well compensated, but beyond that I think it best to let the day pass."

"I see, and the compensation?"

"A half a million dollars. Johnny D will take care of Mr. Jones' compensation."

A half a million dollars! Who the fuck were we dealing with? "A half a million dollars? Good lord, what was the total bounty?"

"A fair amount. Are there any other concerns I can help you with?"

A half a million dollars?

"Don't you think you were taking a chance using us as bait, given that we were completely unqualified for the job, and why did you tell me to talk to Moses? It had nothing to do with this?"

Durant got up and gestured that I should too. "I didn't consider you bait, Monk. Yes, you weren't whom I would typically choose for this kind of job, but I had a feeling you'd be able to handle it. True professionals would have scared them off. As for Moses, word came to me that you needed to see your father, so I thought I'd give you a push. Anything else?"

"Only this." I handed him the documents. The ones I remembered reading on that bloody afternoon, the ones that somehow ended up in my car.

Marsyas Durant smiled. "Good. I imagine you must be exhausted from this ordeal, get some sleep, and take a break. Maybe take a vacation. I hear Virginia is nice."

"Thanks." Virginia, who told him about that?

Sleep did sound nice, though. Time for one more stop.

I found the door to my bungalow was open, again. I was too tired to care.

"Are you going to kill me now?"

Miguel laughed. "Why on Earth do you believe such a thing?"

"I don't know, something to say." He acted like this was normal behavior. Doesn't everyone just break in when they want to visit? "Do you have a key or something?"

"Something. I stopped by to make sure you were still in one piece."

"Other than being totally freaked out, and running on fumes; I couldn't be better."

"I'm glad to hear it." He was smiling. Everyone was smiling.

"Well, I'm glad that you're glad to hear it." He laughed.

"You're sense of humor appears to have returned."

"You'd think, but who knows." I sat down. "So now that it's over, assuming it's over, what's next?"

Joanie walked in, interrupting Miguel and I.

"Monk Buttman, I..." We were looking at her. Miguel was smiling. "I'm sorry; I didn't know you were with someone."

"It's quite alright, I have to get going," he said. "Monk, keep in touch. We have a lot to talk about."

"Yeah, I guess we do."

He said goodbye to Joanie and left. Once he was out of sight, Joanie smacked me in the head, "You had me really worried, Buttman! What the hell is going on?"

"It's a long story."

"And?" And I gave her the condensed version. She stood there with her mouth open.

"Wow! Maybe you *should* go back to farming?" Her arms were crossed again.

"Maybe." It was safer, but didn't pay as well.

"Well, I'm glad you're not dead." She gave me a hug and a kiss. "Monk?"

"Yeah?"

"Don't ever do that again!"

"Yeah."

She smiled. I watched her walk back to her place.

I found my chair and placed it on the patio. The neighbors raised a hand and said hello as I returned the favor; finally, a familiar moment. I stretched out and let the sun warm me. My eyes closed and I once again listened to the sounds of an ordinary life. The last few days seemed dreamlike. Had it really happened and to someone like me? It was all so implausible, but then all of my life had felt that way. I'd spent so much of in conflict. Yet even here in this sea of humanity, where I was just a small fry among millions, the wash had taken me in unexpected directions to unexpected places, one of which was now home. Home? I was too tired to think about it. I let the breeze take me away.

The phone was ringing.

Agnes.

Read on for a look at the next exciting installment
in the *Monk Buttman* series,

A TWINKLE IN THE EYES OF GOD

I was supposed to be at the beach.

Instead, I was in a small-dilapidated church in the middle of nowhere keeping Lucian, or what was left of him, company while Agnes and Rebekah went for the authorities.

Lucian was dead.

In the decaying gray house of the lord, the two of us sat. Well, I did. Lucian was leaned up against the front of the pulpit, his legs splayed out, his hands by his side. There under the cross of Calvary he'd been stabbed to death. Among the twelve rows of pews, the twelve windows, and the eyes of God, we waited. I didn't know how long he'd been dead, but it couldn't have been long. The process of decomposition had not yet distorted his features, though his corpse's odor was on the cusp of ripe.

Here, where the heat of the plains would find us, the late Lucian DeBerry, the man who would bring order and sanity, as well as a needed righteousness back upon the firmament God had so joyously given, would less resemble himself than a figure from a faded Mathew Brady daguerreotype; bloated, black, and a feast for maggots.

My stomach was barking.

A week ago the two of us had been arguing over the nature of God, of belief. He was, as these types were, charming, talkative, and thoroughly engaged in turning me to his way of thinking. I found the personal touches, the use of my name, the deep interest in my physical and spiritual well being, somewhat touching. I wasn't buying, but I enjoyed the spiel. I could see how those lost or looking would find comfort in his words, which naturally were the words of God Almighty.

He was, he told me, God's messenger.

Lucian looked smaller now that the light was gone from his eyes. The dark suit, caked with blood, clutched at his thin frame. I noticed his shoes were untied. Images of James and Boyer filled my head complimenting, if that's the right word, this vision of the dead preacher. All dead. All killed with knives. My stomach continued roiling with whatever bile it contained. I'd have to think of something else.

The beach, I should be at the beach.

I left the dead man.

On the decaying porch of the decaying church I found a box to sit on. Lucian was on his own. I didn't need any more flashbacks of bloody murder.

When would the girls be back?

I had to think of something else!

ABOUT THE AUTHOR

An engineer for 40 years, David William Pearce, following open heart surgery, decided to pursue his muse and write. After completing a debut novel, Pearce so enjoyed the experience that he began writing the *Monk Buttman series*. When not writing, Pearce is the accomplished recording artist, Mr. Primitive. He and his wife live in Kenmore, Washington.

Thank you so much for reading one of our **Crime Fiction** novels.
If you enjoyed our book, please check out our recommended title for your
next great read!

Bailey's Law by Meg Lelvis

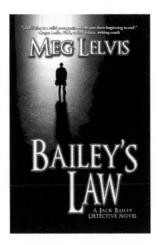

"An intelligent, immersive police procedural that will leave you pining for
another Jack Bailey novel." *—BEST THRILLERS*

CPSIA information can be obtained
at www.ICGtesting.com
Printed in the USA
BVHW081710140219
540173BV00001B/32/P

9 781684 332038